THE
CUTTING
ROOM

JILLIANE HOFFMAN began her professional career as an Assistant State Attorney prosecuting felonies in Florida, with special assignments to the Domestic Violence Unit and the Legal Extradition Unit. She has advised more than one hundred special agents on criminal and civil matters in complex investigations involving narcotics, homicide and organized crime.

Her previous novels are the bestselling *Retribution*, *Last Witness*, *Plea of Insanity* and *Pretty Little Things*. Originally from Long Island, New York, she presently resides in South Florida with her husband and two children.

www.jillianehoffman.com

Also by Jilliane Hoffman

THE
CUTTING
ROOM

JILLIANE HOFFMAN

HARPER

Harper
An imprint of HarperCollins*Publishers*
77–85 Fulham Palace Road,
Hammersmith, London W6 8JB

www.harpercollins.co.uk

This paperback edition 2013
3

First published in Great Britain by
HarperCollins*Publishers* 2012

Copyright © Jilliane P. Hoffman 2012

Jilliane P. Hoffman asserts the moral right to
be identified as the author of this work

A catalogue record for this book is
available from the British Library

ISBN: 978-0-00-748738-7

Set in Meridien by Palimpsest Book Production Limited,
Falkirk, Stirlingshire

Printed and bound in Great Britain by
Clays Ltd, St Ives plc

MIX
Paper from
responsible sources
FSC
www.fsc.org
FSC™ C007454

For the usual suspects – Rich, Monster, Amanda, mom, dad, and the writing buddies – who make everything seem possible.

And for Ed Sieban and Uncle Tommy McDermott, forever missed.

THE
CUTTING
ROOM

PART ONE

1

The pretty girl in the tight 'COED' T-shirt leaned all the way back against the bar, so that her chestnut hair lay strewn out behind her across the white epoxy bar top. Straddled directly over her, his Vans balanced precariously on two bar stools, stood a shirtless guy with the most cut chest Gabriella Vechio had ever seen, a shot glass clenched tightly in his flexed abs. While the crowd cheered him on, he rocked his body over the coed's, pouring the amber liquid into her open mouth. Southern Comfort splashed across her face and over her T-shirt, but the laughing girl definitely didn't care. And neither did the rambunctious crowd.

'Ho, man! Look at this guy work it!' mused the DJ as he amped up the music. 'Open your mouth wider, baby! Let's see how much you can take in!'

Gabby ran a finger along the sugared rim of her lemon-drop martini as she watched the scene play out across the restaurant. The thickening crowd was already three deep at the bar, and the indie-rock music that'd been playing when she and her friends had first sat down for appetizers was now a pulsating throb of Top 40. Beyoncé was singing/screaming so loud, the knives and forks still left on the table danced and tinked together. Even the waitress had changed – whether it was a different blonde or just a different outfit, this one was decked out in much higher heels and a much shorter skirt than the frazzled girl who'd served up quesadillas and Buffalo wings a couple of hours earlier.

'So how long you think you're gonna stay?' Gabby's friend Hannah asked with a frown as she stood from the table, gathering her purse. She cast a disapproving look in the direction of the circus that was still happening over at the bar.

'What?' Gabby answered, gesturing to her ear. It was getting impossible to hear. Friday-night happy hours at Jezebels always started out sort of mellow, but once food stopped being served alongside the Heinekens and cosmos, the crowd really built up. One of the reasons Gabby usually hated coming to Jezzie's was because after nine the place turned into nothing more than a noisy meat market. And two days shy of her twenty-ninth birthday, Gabby was already old meat. At least in here, where she'd actually heard females over twenty-five called 'cougars' by other girls.

'I said, so how long you gonna stay?' Hannah repeated. 'We don't want to leave you all alone here. Not with this crowd . . .'

Gabby shrugged and raised her half-empty martini at Hannah and her other friend, Daisy, who sat beside her, wide-eyed and still fixed on the ab man and the coed.

'Just till I finish this, I guess. Don't worry about me; I'm parked right across the street.'

'I don't know about you all, but I'm feeling mighty thirsty right now,' Daisy announced as she, too, slowly stood to leave.

'I wish I could stay, but I promised Brandon . . .' Hannah started, hesitantly slinging her laptop bag across her shoulder.

'Don't be silly. I was gonna head home early anyway. I got a ton of shit to do tomorrow,' Gabby lied. 'You go and have fun, Han. Think of me when you do,' she added with a wink.

'Don't you worry. Brandon won't be having any fun tonight. I'm exhausted.'

'Poor Brandon,' Gabby laughed. 'You're not even married yet and he's already not getting any on a Friday night.'

'I'm easing him into July; the boy can't say he wasn't warned,' Hannah returned. She looked uneasily around the restaurant again. 'But I really hate leaving you here all alone, Gab . . .'

Daisy's eyes caught on Gabby's. 'Maybe he'll come back,' she mused with a sly smile as she wrapped a lilac cashmere scarf around her throat.

Hannah smiled as if she'd just understood a dirty joke. Gabby felt the blood rush to her cheeks and she buried her face in her drink. All three of them knew who Daisy was talking about – the quirkily handsome recent MIT grad with the ginger hair who'd plopped down uninvited at the very same table last Friday night as happy hour was coming to a close. He'd charmed all three of them before the rest of his drunk entourage finally found him and pulled him away to hit another establishment down the block. He and Gabby hadn't talked for long, but for some reason she couldn't seem to get the guy out of her head. Jeff, his name was. And while she'd tried to convince herself that Mr Still Seeking Gainful Employment as an Electrical Engineer wasn't the sole reason she'd suggested Jezzie's to the crew for tonight's girls'-night-out, she couldn't deny he was a consideration. But she hadn't expected anyone else to know that. She rolled her eyes. 'Hope not. Please. I'm not waiting on him.'

'Okay . . . then can I?' Daisy replied with a laugh, unwrapping the scarf that went perfectly with her gorgeous trench coat and trendy Alice + Olivia booties. Everything about Daisy always went together perfectly. Her cute name, her size-two wardrobe, her beautiful, butt-length, espresso curls, her tanned Spanish complexion, her seductive chocolate eyes. 'He was freaking hot! A little young, but you can still teach them things at that age, you know.' She sighed. 'And they can go for ever. Three times a night, if you're lucky.'

'You're so bad,' Hannah scolded.

Gabby motioned to a seat next to her. 'Be my guest, chica.' But she didn't mean it. In fact, she secretly hoped Daisy would just go. And for thinking that, of course Gabby felt super-guilty. Hannah, Daisy and she had been instant friends since freshman year in college when fate had thrown them all together in the same cramped dorm at U Buff – the University of Buffalo. And they'd stayed close through ten years of boyfriends, break-ups, bad bosses, family bullshit, illnesses, therapy, cross-country moves, cross-country moves back, and the general drama and angst that accompanied all of the above. But it always seemed to be Daisy who enjoyed most of the boyfriends and break-ups, as well as most of the drama. Daisy's enduring popularity had never bothered her as much as it had this past year, though, when, for Gabby, just landing a stupid date had become about as challenging as picking all six lotto numbers in the same drawing.

Back in college when the three of them were cute and inseparable and the nicknames were being handed out, they were known around campus as 'Charlie's Angels'. Hannah had been branded the Smart One; Gabby was the Funny One, and Daisy, the Pretty One. Even now, almost seven years after the final note of 'Pomp and Circumstance' had ushered the Angels officially into adulthood, the labels had held fast, and being the Funny One was no longer the compliment it used to be. Gabby's hang-up, no doubt; Daisy was still the same great friend she used to be. But the fun, hard-partying *Sex and the City* lifestyle fantasy they'd all joked they were actually living was one day supposed to come to an end – with each of them landing high-powered husbands and popping out a couple of beautiful babies who would play together on the living-room floors of their fabulous homes while their mommies gossiped over lattes in the kitchen. Phase II, as Gabby called it in her head, was supposed to begin before the age of thirty. Or at least be in motion by then, which meant a serious boyfriend and hopefully a ring on her finger. Of course, life is what happens when you're busy making other plans, as Gabby's mom liked to remind her. The Smart One had broken the mold and surprisingly landed the first fiancé. The Pretty One was still fielding multiple propositions and proposals from multiple suitors and was in no rush or need to settle down anywhere. And the Funny One . . . well, she was 'still looking', as Mrs Vechio told all her friends with a soft sigh when they asked why little Gabriella hadn't yet found herself a man. Thirty was coming at her hard and fast and Mr Wonderful was nowhere in sight. Maybe a relationship with Jeff the Wannabe Engineer or a dirty dance with Mr Unbelievable Abs was totally in her head, but the truth was, no one was gonna want to talk up the Funny Accountant when the Pretty Fashion Magazine Publicist was seated a barstool away flashing a beautiful smile and sporting an amazing body.

'Oh, I would, trust me. If I didn't have to be at work at freaking five in the morning, I would,' Daisy replied. 'But we have to set up the shoot before the sun comes up. Gotta get that "first light" or it's all for nothing, and that means working Saturday.' She looked at her watch and added, 'Eech, I'm going home at ten. That's pathetic. You know, I should just stay up all night. Sleep? Who needs sleep? Remember those days, girls?'

Hannah winced. 'I'm still trying to forget those all-nighters, Daisy. The hangovers were the only thing that stopped me from becoming a raging alcoholic.'

'That and your Born Again mother would've killed you,' added Daisy as she finished her drink.

'True.'

'You gonna stay then?' Gabby asked Daisy anxiously, twisting her pin-straight honey-blonde hair around and around her index finger. The curl collapsed as soon as she pulled her finger away. Being around Daisy lately made her so self-conscious. It was like the girl never aged, or gained weight or had a bad hair day. At five foot four and 130 pounds, Gabby definitely wasn't fat; she just wasn't Daisy-thin. And her blonde hair and light eyes would normally attract some attention – until you sat next to a Spanish temptress who looked a lot like a young Sophia Loren. Gabriella hated herself for being so competitive, especially since Daisy obviously wasn't. She pushed aside the brewing jealousy and forced a smile. 'Should I get another round then?'

Daisy sighed. 'Nah. This is one of those moments when you have to do the right thing or pay later. I got a hot date tomorrow and I need to look fresh. He runs a hedge fund.' She fanned herself again and rubbed her fingers together. 'Lots of cash. We're talking big money, girls.'

'Which means lots of competition,' Hannah cautioned.

'Precisely. I need at least five hours or I get circles.'

'Circles probably look great on you,' Gabriella offered.

'Circles look good on zombies, Gab, but thanks for the compliment,' Daisy replied.

'All right then, guys,' Gabby said. 'I'll be heading home in a little bit myself.'

'Be good,' Hannah warned with a wag of her finger. 'No weirdos. And no circus freaks,' she said, motioning to the still shirtless Ab Wonder. 'Oh, and in case I don't see you, happy birthday!'

'Yes! Happy birthday!' Daisy said, blowing an air kiss at Gabby as she and Hannah slipped into the crowd. 'Call me Monday. Do anything I would do, including hot circus freaks. And text me if Ginger and his friends show up. Maybe I'll come back!'

Gabriella raised her martini in the direction of her two friends as they disappeared into the sea of writhing bodies. She saw Hannah wave and then the crowd swallowed them whole and they both were gone. The guilt pang disappeared as fast as it had come on, replaced by an exuberant feeling of freedom. Gabby wasn't a clubber, but here she was out in a club with a couple of drinks in her already to loosen her up and no competition to hold her back. She opened another button on her blouse and sipped her martini, moving to the music as the lights dimmed and the last of the tables in the center of the restaurant were cleared out, forming a makeshift dance floor that was quickly filling with bodies. It was getting crowded. Soon enough the bouncers would stop letting anyone in.

Although it was still early by club standards, hookups were already happening. Guys and girls. Girls and girls. The dirty dancing was definitely a lot sexier than Gabby remembered it being when she used to hit the clubs. And the clothes – or lack thereof – that the girls were wearing . . . damn! She could unbutton her blouse to her belly button and it would still be modest by some standards. Everyone was either here with their BFFs or they were busy making new ones. Gabby suddenly felt as if there was a spotlight shining down on her – the Old Maid All Alone With No One. And everyone looked so freaking young . . .

A herd of short skirts and stilettos pushed by, knocking into Gabby's chair and spilling her drink a little. She blew out a controlled breath. It probably was crazy of her to think he'd come back here tonight. Even crazier to think that, if he did, he'd be looking for her. Here she was, all by herself in a club, still dressed in her lame poly-blend suit from work, sitting by herself at a table for four, surrounded by people who didn't look close to worrying about turning thirty, or having babies, or meeting Mr Right. The exhilarating feeling of freedom was quickly sinking into a panicky depression that she didn't want to feel tonight. Gabby glanced at her watch and threw back the rest of her drink. That was it. She'd lasted a half-hour. It was time to go . . .

As she grabbed her purse and stood to leave, the waitress brought over a fresh lemon-drop martini. 'Compliments of the gentleman at the bar,' she said, motioning behind her with a toss of her blonde curls.

Gabby looked around for her ginger-haired engineer. *Had her instincts been right?* Her heart started to pound. If so, this would be one helluva story to tell the grandchildren . . .

But there were no tall, lean redheads to be found. She dipped her finger in her drink and swirled it around as her eyes canvassed the crowd.

That's when Gabby spotted the stranger with the dark, wavy hair and piercing eyes who was standing next to the bar across the dance floor, sipping a bottle of Bud and staring at her. He smiled softly and tipped his beer in her direction.

And so, with a coy smile and a quick wave, Gabriella Vechio welcomed over the stranger who would soon change her life for ever.

2

'Thanks for the drink,' Gabby began when he sat down beside her.

'How'd you know it was from me?'

'I . . . well, I just assumed,' she stuttered.

He grinned. 'You're welcome.'

'I'm Gabriella.'

'I'm Reid. Nice to meet you, Gabriella.'

'God, that sounds so formal. Only my mom and my boss call me Gabriella. My friends call me Gabby.'

'Gabby. Okay,' he replied, nodding. 'I like Gabriella, though. That's a beautiful name. So, are you from around here, Gabby?'

'I live in Forest Hills. I just came here after work.' She fidgeted with the collar of her blazer. 'In case you couldn't tell.'

'What do you do?'

'I'm out of high school, for starters,' Gabby answered with a short laugh.

'Yeah. This is a bit of a younger crowd, huh?' Reid said, looking around. 'But they have great wings.'

'Yup. And quesadillas. We – me and my friends – we've been here a couple of times before. They have a good happy hour. That crowd is a little more . . . let's say, mature. You know, with everyone getting off work and all.'

He nodded and looked around. 'Where are they? Your friends?'

'Oh. They're gone,' Gabby replied quickly. 'They left a half-hour or so ago. They had to get up in the morning. I decided to stay and finish my drink. I was gonna head out right before you sent this over.'

'Well I'm glad you stayed. And I have to say, I think I like the crowd in here.' He didn't look around when he said it – his dark chocolate brown eyes never left hers. Mesmerizing, bright flecks of amber and gold lit his pupils.

Gabriella blushed. He was handsome – Reid. Not in an obvious way, like Ab Man. He had a bit of a big chin, but a nice smile that took over his whole face when he flashed it, and that's what she really noticed. His teeth were straight and super white, like a toothpaste model's. No gums in sight. Some girls were attracted to abs or curly hair or eyes or big muscles, but Gabby went for the smile every time. She used to think she'd marry a dentist until she realized a lot of them actually had terrible teeth. What was that proverb? Physician heal thyself? Dentist fix thy overbite. As Gabby studied Reid's rugged, fair face, set against the backdrop of a raucous Spring Break-aged crowd, she thought perhaps his very best feature right now was the fact that he *wasn't* twenty-one. She guessed late twenties, but didn't want to ask, because she didn't want to be asked that very same question and then watch for the disappointment on his face. Demi Moore might've broken ground with Ashton Kutcher, but for most female earthlings who didn't have movie-star looks and a celebrity-sized bank book, it wasn't so easy to bridge even a small age gap with a handsome guy. And definitely not in a place like this. Most men heard 'twenty-eight', swore the woman said 'thirty', and pictured the thought-bubble above her smiling, anxious head that read, 'Looking for marriage, a house and a baby!' That's when they excused themselves to use the bathroom and you never saw them again. Maybe she was being silly and down on herself, but tonight she didn't want to take any risks with having fun. She just wanted to have it. 'I'm an accountant with Morgan and Tipley,' Gabby replied. 'It's a really small firm in Midtown. Lex and Forty-third. You've never heard of it, trust me. I've been there a couple of years now. I like it.'

'Accounting . . . ooh. Sooo not what I pegged you for and sooo not my strong suit. I'm good with my money – not so sure I'd be good handling other people's. I might get jealous.'

'You don't actually get to touch it, which takes away some of the temptation.' Gabby sipped her drink. 'Interesting. What did you peg me for?'

'Oh, I don't know . . . an astronaut? A rocket scientist? A nuclear physicist?'

'Do I look that smart? It's the suit, I tell ya.'

'Nah. I really thought that you might be a lawyer or a paralegal. Something with the law. Maybe an FBI agent

14

or a cop or maybe a spy. Just a wild guess. You look too fun to be an accountant.'

'Accountants can be a lively bunch. The life of the party. Especially on April sixteenth.'

'Really? Mine's named Sy, he works for H&R Block, and I don't think he's been to a party in a few decades. So tell me, what do you like about it, Gabby? Accounting?'

'Hmmm . . . good question. Let me think. Well, for starters it's not subjective, like a lot of careers are. My friend's a writer and I could never do what she does, because she never knows if it's good. I mean, there's always someone telling her what she wrote sucked, even if a hundred other people tell her she's the bomb. It makes no sense. She ends up banging her head against the wall. Same for my friend who's a publicist. Someone always second-guesses what she did. Claims they could have done it better. And that they would've had a better result: more people at a premiere, a better photo from a better model, whatever. But accounting, you know, is predictable. It always works out, if you do it right. And if you *really* do it right, you can make people very happy. Numbers don't lie and they don't care what other people think of them.'

'Interesting . . .'

Gabby had never had to explain why she liked accounting to a guy before. She wondered if she'd given the 'right' answer. No matter how you phrased it, accounting never sounded thrilling. 'What do you do, Reid?' she asked.

'I'm a filmmaker.'

Gabby's heartbeat sped up a bit. Filmmaker was up

there with surgeon in both the excitement and good-catch departments. 'That's really cool,' she said.

'Well, I'm working at it. It's not an easy profession to crack. Lots of competition. You have to be real original to stand out.'

'What kind of films do you make?'

'Okay, now don't get too excited, because you're not talking up the next James Cameron. I, well . . . I make documentaries.'

'I still think that's exciting.'

He smiled. 'I do, too. I think real life is much more interesting than make-believe, actually. Real people having real reactions, expressing real emotions. It's capturing those moments on film that can be difficult. But . . . well, it doesn't bring in much money, unless your name's Michael Moore.'

'I still think it's exciting. Money isn't everything, you know.'

'Hmmm . . . didn't you say you were an accountant?'

Gabby laughed. 'I've done taxes for a lot of people that make a lot of money, but their lives are still a mess and they're not happy. No, money isn't everything.'

'I agree. There's a lot more to life.'

Gabby gestured to her ear. It was getting really loud.

Reid leaned in closer, placed his hand firmly on her back and whispered in her ear. She felt his warm breath on her neck and it gave her a shiver, as his strong hand massaged her lower spine. 'So tell me more about yourself, Gabriella. I wanna know more about you.'

She smiled coquettishly. To think she had almost walked out and gone home all alone again to her cat and a bad movie on Lifetime. Her luck was definitely changing; she could feel it. And so over two lemon-drop martinis, as he stroked her back and played with the ends of her hair, she told him everything he wanted to know.

3

God, she liked the way he said her name. *Gabriella.* And she liked that after a few drinks, a lot of meaningless conversation and, perhaps most importantly, after a few more short-skirted, long-legged stiletto packs had wandered by en route to the Ladies' room, that he still remembered it.

Reid moved a strand of hair off her face and leaned in close. 'Listen,' he whispered, his mouth on her ear. 'I don't normally ask girls back to my place. I don't, but . . .'

She nodded. 'Yes.' The room was spinning.

'Yes?'

'Yes, I'd like to go home with you. You don't normally ask, and I don't normally say yes, but here we are. Yes.'

He smiled. 'Great. I don't live too far.'

'Great.' Gabby reached for her purse under the table and the world went belly-up. She put her hands on her head to get it to stop spinning. And she said a prayer that her stomach would settle back down. She definitely shouldn't have had that fourth martini. That was what put her over the edge. And that's why she was making such an impetuous, crazy-ass decision to go home with a total stranger. It was the alcohol; it had definitely made her horny and her overactive pheromones weren't helping the decision-making process. What was worse was that she was still sober enough to recognize what she was doing was stupid but she was gonna do it anyway. *Damn* . . . She was definitely missing sex, no doubt about it; it'd been almost a year since she'd been with anyone. And it had been three years since she'd had anyone serious in her life. It wasn't like she was thinking Reid was 'the one' or anything, or even that this relationship might go someplace past tonight – no, that would require lucid thinking. On the other hand, he did have a great smile and he made freaking movies for a living, which was a total turn-on. Plus, when his hand had traveled up her skirt underneath the table it had given her tingles in all the right places. Perhaps saying yes was a much easier decision than it should've been, but, as Daisy would say if she were here, 'You only live once . . .'

Thankfully, her legs worked when she stood up. Reid put his arm around her and led her protectively by the elbow past the tightly packed bodies that surrounded the dance floor and the bar and out of the club. On the sidewalk outside, a chattering line of minimally dressed people had formed and was wrapping around the side of the building. For them, the night was just beginning. It would end only when the sun came up.

The cold, damp, night air was refreshing. It sobered her up a bit and slowed down the spinning, which was good, but the quiet was almost deafening. Her head was still pulsing to Britney.

'You okay?' he asked as he opened the door to a car and slid her into the front seat.

'Oh sure,' she lied. 'I'm fine. How close is your place?'

'Not far,' he said as he got behind the wheel.

'Are you in Manhattan?'

'Who can afford Manhattan?' he replied with a laugh, pulling away from the curb.

'True. Tha's true. Iss so damn expensive. Everything is so s'pensive.' *Did she just slur expensive? Damn.* He reached over and touched her thigh, tracing it with his finger, moving up and under her skirt. She rubbed his hand, watching as the halos above the streetlights blurred together into long streaks of white as the car slipped under what looked like the Midtown Tunnel. She leaned her head back and closed her eyes. Then she drifted off to sleep.

'Okay, Sleepyhead, we're here.'

Gabby opened her eyes. The passenger door was open and Reid was leaning in. There were no bright lights, no skyscrapers, no double-parked cars or beeping taxis. They were in front of a two-story house on a quiet, deserted street. Gabby wasn't sure where she was, but it definitely wasn't any of the boroughs of New York. At the end of the block she saw a red light, only there were no cars stopped at it. In fact, there were no cars anywhere. Though the neighborhood didn't look completely residential, the couple of restaurants she did see were closed for the night. *What time was it?* She tried to check her watch, but couldn't make out the dial; it

20

was too dark and she was too drunk. She fumbled to find her heels on the floorboard, and with them in hand, stepped on to the sidewalk. The world was spinning again. It would be so embarrassing if she fell on her ass. *Where was she?* Then her stockinged feet stepped in an ice-cold, freaking puddle. Gabby looked down. The sidewalk glistened. 'Did it rain?' she asked.

'Did it rain?' he answered with a laugh. 'It poured. Cats and dogs. You slept through the whole thing. Even the traffic jam. You might want to put your shoes on – the walk can flood sometimes.'

'I definitely should not have had that lass' martini,' she said as she slipped on her pumps, holding on to his arm for support.

'Don't worry; I'll warm you up when we get inside.'

'Sounds fun . . .'

His arm around her waist, Reid led her along the side of the old Victorian with the cute front porch. A broken brick path twisted through a dead winter garden toward a cement staircase that led down below the house, like a crypt. But for a light coming from the basement on the opposite side of the yard, the old house was completely dark.

'Is this yours?' Gabby asked.

'Nah. I rent the apartment in the back.'

'Downstairs?'

'That's the one.'

'Iss a pretty house.'

'Yeah, well, I hope you don't spook easy. It's actually a funeral home.'

Gabby stopped walking. 'Wha?'

'Not where I live, obviously. The main house upstairs

is the business, you know, where people have wakes and stuff. I guess they do other funeral parlor things on the other side of the basement, but I've never heard or seen anything. Promise.'

'You mean there are dead people in there?'

'I don't know about right now. Listen, it took me a while to get used to it, but you do. My friends think it's kind of funny, actually. And I get a great rate on the rent. Come on,' he said, pulling her along by the hand, 'I'll make sure the ghouls don't get you.'

'A funeral home . . . Damn, tha's fucked up.' But she found herself following him anyway as he led her to the staircase. 'Where the hell are we?'

'Paradise,' he returned with a smile.

At the top of the staircase she hesitated. 'A funeral home . . . I dunno, Reid . . .' Every instinct in her body told her not to go down.

He rubbed her hand and moved to kiss her on the lips. 'I'll take care of you. Promise,' he whispered, his mouth moving over her ear. 'You trust me, right? If I was a real bad guy I never would have told you about the funeral parlor. Only a stand-up guy would be honest about something like that when he's taking a girl home and trying to seduce her.'

'Or a fool,' Gabby replied with a laugh.

'Or a fool,' he conceded with a shrug. He kissed her then, a long and wet and lingering kiss. His warm tongue probed the inside of her mouth. And his hands ran over her ass.

That was enough for Gabby.

Her hand in his, he led her down the steps and into the pure darkness.

'Is there a light? Jesus, I . . . I can't see a thing, Reid. These stupid heels . . . I'm gonna break my damn neck . . .' she whispered with a nervous giggle. She wondered why she was whispering.

'The light's broken. I keep meaning to fix it, but I always forget. Hold my hand and the railing; the stairs are real steep, Gabby. There we go. We're almost there.'

When they'd reached the bottom she heard the jingle of a key as she looked around. The moon was hidden behind thick clouds and there was no light. She wondered how he could see the lock, because she couldn't see a thing. It made her more than a little uneasy, enclosed in the darkness, encased in cement, a flight of stairs away from the rest of the world, right below a funeral home. Even putting the funeral parlor thing aside, she had never been a fan of basements. In the eighteen years she'd lived at home with her parents, she could count the number of times she'd ventured down into the root cellar. *Bad things live down there,* her sister would warn with a smug smile whenever their mom sent Gabby down to retrieve some jar of homemade pickles or canned fruit. *Bad things that don't like the living . . .*

'Careful,' he said as he led her inside. 'I'll get the lights.'

After a second or two he flicked on a light and she was relieved to see they were standing in a bright, white galley kitchen, which led into what appeared to be a small studio apartment. There were no metal gurneys with bodies on them, waiting their turn to be taken upstairs. No caskets pushed up against the walls. A loveseat, coffee table and television defined a living room. A breakfast table with two chairs made for a dining area.

And off in the corner, partially blocked from view by floor-to-ceiling black drapes, was the bedroom. One of the drapes was pulled back a few inches and Gabby spotted a queen-sized bed.

He was behind her again. He moved quick, like a vampire. It was a little unsettling, especially given where they were. She shook the cobwebs from her head. Of course, that was the alcohol thinking.

'Another drink?' he asked, sliding her coat off her shoulders and tossing it on the couch in the living room. Her suit jacket followed.

'Where are we? Long Island? Jersey?' Despite the drunken stupor, a slight panic was beginning to set in. She ran a hand through her hair. 'I thought you lived close to Jezzie's. How am I gonna get home?'

'Don't worry about that; I'll take you in the morning, or whenever you want to go. You shouldn't be driving, anyway. Have another drink and relax.' He put his hands on her shoulders and caressed them. His soft lips traced the back of her neck, sending shivers down her spine. 'You smell so good,' he murmured.

'Damn . . . You feel good,' she whispered. Pushed up against her, she felt him now, his hard penis pressing into her buttocks. His hands moved off her shoulders and down her arms, working their way over her hips. 'I really shouldn't have another; I've had a lot to drink.'

'It'll help you relax.'

She shrugged. 'Okay. Although I don't usually drink this much, you know.' Even while she said it, she couldn't help but think her excuse for being three sheets to the wind in a strange guy's house, a couple steps from his bed, was lame. 'I want you to know,' she started as he

24

went to the kitchen. 'Not that you'll believe me, but . . . well, I don't go home with guys I jus' met: In fact, well, besize this one guy in college who was not a stranger – I actually knew him from my Calc class – I, I don't do this. I don't.' She was slurring, wasn't she? She took a deep breath. 'I'm not a ho', is all I'm sayin'.'

Perhaps it was her imagination, but she thought the room had a funny odor. It smelled like one of the Glade plug-in air fresheners that she used in her apartment to cover up the smell of mildew that was growing underneath her kitchen sink from a dishwasher leak that had gone undetected for too long. But then there was an undertone of something else. Something else the air freshener was covering up. It had the faint hint of a . . . medicinal smell? Like a hospital or nursing home. Or funeral parlor, maybe? Whatever the hell that smelled like . . . She pushed the thought out of her head. The apartment was, for a guy's place, really neat. And with the dramatic black curtains surrounding the bedroom, kind of sexy. *God, what was she doing here?*

He came back over and handed her a vodka and OJ, watching while she sipped it. 'Well, I'm glad you made an exception. Let me be honest here, too – I'm not a player. I rarely take home girls, Gabby. And when I do, well, they're special. Different. Unique. Like you. I think you're special. You're not like those girls in the bar. Those girls – they don't know what they want, they don't know who they are. But you do, Gabriella. I think you know what you want, and you're not afraid to go for it. I may be crazy, but I felt this connection between us, even from across the bar.' He ran his hand through her hair, tracing her chin and then down her throat to where her blouse was buttoned. His eyes moved over her. 'And I can't wait to see more of you.'

Maybe it was all just words, but they were certainly the ones she wanted to hear. Reid grasped the back of her neck, pulling her body to his. She could feel his heartbeat through his dress shirt. He smelled clean, like soap and a crisp, citrusy cologne. Versace, perhaps? Aqua di Gio? But as she stretched her head up to finally kiss him he leaned away and with a teasing smile, reached behind him and pulled out a long, black silk scarf. He dangled it in front of her.

'Ooh,' Gabby said, sucking in a breath. 'Whass that for?'

'Let's find out,' he whispered, taking her by the hand and leading her past the open curtain and into the bedroom area. Gabby's heart began to race. Bondage with a stranger – Daisy would be so impressed. Gabby took a final long sip of her drink before he gently took it from her lips and placed it on the side table. Then, with one hand underneath her chin, he lifted her mouth to his and kissed her. His tongue was thick and warm and probing, reaching all the way to the back of her throat. Gabby could feel herself getting wet for him. It had been so long since she'd been with a man. So many thoughts tumbled through the thick fog in her brain. She wondered if he was a good lover, or if she would know what a good lover was, given the state she was in. She wondered if he would think *she* was a good lover. What does someone who is into bondage expect from a girl? What other tricks might he have hiding in his closet or behind those sleek black curtains? If the scarf was any indicator, Gabby figured he would probably take his time with her.

And that got her even more excited. She closed her eyes and tried to drive out the jitters and second thoughts. If she was going to be a cheap ho' and have a one-night stand, she could only hope it would involve Tantric sex with a guy who could go for hours, then wake her up and ask for more.

Reid must have read her mind. As he kissed her, he raised both of her arms above her head. She felt him wrap the smooth silk scarf around and around her wrists. It was very erotic. Then he slipped the ends through something that must have been hanging on the ceiling – a rod or ring or beam, Gabby wasn't quite sure – and he pulled tight, so that she was almost suspended from the ceiling, although her feet were still touching the floor. It hurt a little, but the loss of control over the moment was both frightening and unbelievably sexy. She wanted him more than ever.

'Oh,' she murmured, surprised.

He unbuttoned her blouse and opened it, exposing her lace see-through Victoria's Secrets bra. The lights were still on and all Gabby could think was thank God she had put on nice underwear this morning. He ran his warm palms over the lace. 'Do you like that?' he asked when her nipples got hard.

She sucked in a breath and nodded.

He pulled his own shirt over his head and tossed it on the bed. His chest was hairless and muscular. Not body-builder cut, but defined. Especially his pecs. Then he bent down and starting from her ankles, ran his hands over her legs and up her entire body, pulling her skirt up as he did, so that it rested on her hips, exposing her sheer panties. He slowly pulled down her pantyhose, leaving her panties on. 'I said, "Do you like that?"' he repeated, his voice sharper. 'I want to hear you say it, Gabriella. Tell me you like it. Tell me you want me to touch you.'

She nodded again. She couldn't believe she was doing this, but it felt so good. 'Yes,' she said aloud. 'Yes, I like that, Reid. I like it a lot. I want you to touch me.'

He kissed her again and then he pulled away. In one fast motion, he took the pantyhose and tied it around her mouth, knotting it in the back. Her tongue was trapped and she couldn't speak. Her heartbeat quickened. A feeling of fright pulsed through her body. 'That's all I wanted to hear,' he whispered.

He walked over to the wall of curtains and pulled back the first curtain. Behind it was a video camera set up on a tripod. Flanking the left side of the video camera were three computer monitors sitting on metal carts. He opened the other curtain, revealing another three monitors on the right – six computers in total. The carts looked like the audiovisual carts teachers used to wheel into classrooms in elementary school when they wanted the class to watch an educational movie. Behind the push carts and video camera was another wall of black curtains. The monitor screens were all on. On each monitor Gabby saw a different person.

'Hello, Gabby,' said a man on one of the screens, leaning into the camera.

'Good evening, pretty,' said another.

And another. 'Hey there, Gabriella. That's a real sexy name you have. I like your hair.'

The man on the first monitor laughed. 'He likes naturals.'

Gabby's eyes grew wide with fear. She tried to speak but the gag wouldn't let her. She pulled hard on the scarf above her, but it only tightened on her wrists, twisting her hands around and around in mid-air. She tried to kick out, but there was nothing to use for leverage. She spun uselessly, her feet barely touching the floor.

Reid turned his attention away from the screens and back to her. He'd put on a tight, black mask that covered his face. Besides an opening for his mouth, the only part visible was his eyes. The flecks of gold in them that Gabby had found so intriguing a few hours earlier danced excitedly.

Gabby tried to scream but couldn't. She just twisted helplessly around and around, her suspended body jerking about. She thought of her mom and dad and sister in Bloomfield, sleeping in their beds, dreaming nice dreams. She wondered how they would react when they found out she'd been raped by a strange man she'd willingly gone home with. Her mom would break down and cry and scream and probably blame everything on the evil city of New York till her Dad told her to stop. Her Dad, though, would secretly blame Gabby for being a slut and hooking up with someone she'd met in a bar. The tears streamed down Gabby's face. Then a cold fear stopped her heart as she looked at the excited faces on the computer monitors watching her. Gabby knew then that as sure as the sun would rise in the morning she would never again see it. And she would never see her family, or have to witness her mother scream out in pain, or feel her dad silently condemn her judgment over the next Thanksgiving dinner. Because at that moment she knew she was going to die. Off in the distance, behind the wall, she heard the whir of what sounded like a motor, but it wasn't a car engine. It was more like a blender. Or a buzz saw. Scenes from every horror movie she'd ever watched flashed through her head.

'Gabriella, baby,' Reid said, as he slowly approached her, flashing his model-perfect smile through the mask's black slit. One arm was outstretched, the other hidden behind his back. 'You're about to become so very famous. You're going to be a star, Gabby. A star. And now I'd like to introduce you to some of your biggest fans . . .'

PART TWO

4

Miami, May 2011

City of Miami homicide detective Manny Alvarez chomped on a greasy beef empanada and sifted through the awful pictures that covered his squad desk. The crumpled body of a young woman dressed in just a pair of black panties lay inside a dumpster, her long blonde hair tangled in the mound of garbage she'd been found buried in. Only her face was visible in the first series of photos, peeking through piles of rotting food, trash bags, discarded paint cans, and broken furniture, her terrified brown eyes open wide, staring up at what was, ironically enough, a perfect, blue Miami sky. What was left of her lips was twisted into the most grotesque smile Manny had ever seen. The fingers of her left hand, the nails painted pink, reached out from her fetid grave. When Manny had first arrived at the scene with the rest of the crime-scene crowd and the pack of technicians from the Medical Examiner's office, his first thought – standing on a ladder over that filthy dumpster, surrounded by blue uniforms and onlookers straining for a peek, sweating his *cojones* off in the ninety-degree heat – was that it seemed as if something or someone was beneath the poor girl, like in that horror flick, *Drag Me to Hell*. Pulling her back down into the garbage, back into hell, by her pretty blonde hair while she desperately reached out for someone – anyone – who could help her.

But no one had.

Her name was Holly Skole, her case number was F10-24367, and she was the thirty-fourth homicide of 2011 in the city. Her body had been found by Esteban 'Papi' Munoz, the owner of Papito's Cafeteria, who'd apparently discovered Holly while disposing of spoiled trays of last night's special. Clutching at his chest, the old man had staggered back through the parking lot towards his restaurant – and straight into the path of an SUV that was pulling into the lot. Fortunately, the two ribs he'd cracked on the fender of a Lexus hadn't killed him. Unfortunately, the heart attack that was most likely brought on by seeing a dead body in with his leftovers had. It was only after the ambulance had come and carted off the grandpa of sixteen to the hospital morgue, the reports had been written, the rubber-neckers had dispersed, and the tow truck had hauled the Lexus off to impound that someone finally thought to take a good look around and see what had gotten the old *abuelo* so freaked out. A rookie traffic cop with twenty minutes on the job was the one who'd ultimately lifted the dumpster lid – only to spend the rest of the morning throwing up his Cheerios.

Manny washed down the last chunk of his lunch with a slug of crappy coffee from the machine down the hall as he flipped through the pictures and reviewed his reports. Dumped bodies were never good. Not that he relished a gory domestic or a gang-banger shootout, but usually with dumpers by the time you found them they were in a progressed state of decomposition and they stank and looked terrible. The real crime scene was missing, along with vital evidence. Plus, there was something tragic about a victim who'd been used up, right down to their last ounce of dignity, then their remains tossed away like a piece of trash. It was especially disturbing when the body being thrown out was that of a pretty, nineteen-year-old college coed with her whole life in front of her.

Clipped to the top of a Coral Gables PD missing persons report was a photo of the vivacious University of Miami sophomore from Connellsville, Pennsylvania, with the creamy complexion, infectious grin and honey-blonde hair. A communications major on a partial dance scholarship, Holly had vanished without a trace from the hardcore nightclub Menace after celebrating a friend's twenty-first birthday back in April. Her body was found nine days later across town in the Design District – a gentrified part of the city that bordered the crime-ridden and infamous suburb of Overtown, the birthplace of Miami's 1982 race riots.

It hadn't taken long to get an ID. Holly's purse, along with her wallet full of cash and credit cards, had been thrown in the dumpster alongside her. Thanks to her distraught mom, who'd flown in from Pennsylvania after Holly was reported missing by her roommate, pictures of Holly had made the rounds on all the local news stations, and Manny had known right away who it was he was staring down at from atop that ladder. In a cardboard box under his desk now sat the stack of family photos that Cookie Skole had given to him after her daughter had been pulled from the garbage and the investigation had officially changed course from missing persons to homicide. He hadn't needed more than one picture, seeing as the girl was dead, but it was hard to tell a bawling parent, 'One photo of your murdered kid's enough,' so he'd taken the whole box. Inside were pictures that started with Holly's birth and ended with her opening presents next to the Christmas tree the last time she'd come home for winter-break. They didn't exactly match up with the micro-miniskirts and mesh tops he'd seen Holly sporting on her Facebook page.

Although she'd been found more than a week after disappearing, unfortunately, Holly hadn't been dead that long. In fact, her body had likely been in the dumpster only a matter of hours, and according to the Medical Examiner, rigor mortis – a condition of joint and muscle stiffening that a body goes through in the first seventy-two hours after death occurs – was still in effect. That meant Holly hadn't been dead very long at all when she was found. And *that* meant someone had kept her somewhere for a long while before finally putting her out of her misery . . .

She had chemical burns on her feet, hands, and face, bind marks on her wrists, and a strange burn wound on the nape of her neck. Toxicology reports indicated that she'd been injected with copious amounts of diphenhydramine and dextromethorphan – the active ingredients in Benadryl and Nyquil, respectively – both of which, Manny knew, induced hallucinations when given in high enough doses. She'd been raped and sexually abused with an object or objects. The cause of death was asphyxiation. The most disturbing injury for Manny was the smile. Or lack thereof. Her lips had been melted with sulfuric acid, exposing her teeth and gums, so that it looked, from a distance, like she was grinning. As Manny figured it, Holly's killer had actually *wanted* her to be found. He'd wanted everyone to see the Joker smile he'd put on her face before it could be blamed on hungry rats or decomposition had taken the rest of her flesh with it. No wonder poor Papi had dropped right after he opened that lid on the dumpster – he'd peered down into hell, only to find it grinning back up at him.

Twenty-three years as a cop in Miami – eighteen of them spent working homicides – and some things unfortunately still shocked even Manny Alvarez, on rare occasions leaving the usually unflappable, physically intimidating six-foot-five, 280-pound detective unnerved. Because the way he saw it, murder usually had a point. You got mad at someone and you lost your temper and you pulled the trigger, or lashed out with a knife, or hit the gas pedal. Or maybe you exacted revenge on someone who'd wronged you, or stole from you, or cheated on you, or failed to fork over all the dope you'd arranged to pick up. Or you needed money and the gun went off while you were trying to take it. Or you didn't want to leave witnesses. Even with gang shootings that were committed solely to intimidate others, or gain initiation into a gang – as perverted as those reasons might be, slayings committed in their name had a point. But every once in a rare while a case landed on Manny's desk that

37

defied reason. *Any* reason. A life taken by someone simply for the purpose of taking it. Perhaps to satisfy a morbid, primal curiosity, or worse – for sheer amusement. Manny stared at the final picture of the coed's abused body, taken on a steel gurney at the ME's office. The macabre smile, bind marks, burns, chemical injections – all were obvious signs of sadistic torture. And her killer had held her captive for several days, undoubtedly to play with her, experiment on her, terrify her, before finally strangling the life out of her.

The suspect in custody whose bond hearing he was preparing for was not a boyfriend or an ex-lover, or a co-worker or a frenemy of Holly. He was not related to her, or mad at her, from what Manny could tell. In fact, it appeared that Holly had only met her murderer that night, as fate would have it, while she was trying to have a good time. She was not robbed; her car was found in the parking lot of Menace, right where she'd left it. There was no withdrawal from her bank accounts, or unauthorized charges on her credit cards. There was no evidence of a drug deal, no gang involvement. The rape in and of itself did not explain the overt use of torture or the violent sexual abuse. In fact, the injuries inflicted on Holly were way outside the psychological confines of what was considered 'normal' behavior for a rapist. Even a murdering rapist. Without any further explanation from the perp, it was a murder that simply defied any reason, and the most terrifying rationale for Holly's death was that there was none; her murder had no point.

Manny glanced at his watch. *Shit.* It was already

almost 2:00. Time to head over to the courthouse. His hearing was with an uptight, well-heeled prosecutor who probably really meant 1:30 when she said it – though Manny knew there was no way the case would be heard before 3:00, since it was Slow Steyn on the bench today and the man never returned from lunch before 2:00 and his calendars were always the size of a Harry Potter novel.

As he finished the last of his coffee, Manny stuck the photos and reports into an accordion folder that was already tearing at the edges. It was time to move up to a box. Or boxes. After enough years in the trenches, you developed a feeling for which cases would be 'quickies' – plenty of evidence, cooperative witnesses, a damning confession – all leading to a fast-tracked plea bargain. Then there were the headaches – sloppy scene, no witnesses, circumstantial evidence, and a closed-mouthed, cocky, SOB defendant. Not to mention the years of BS appeals if you did get a conviction. The *State of Florida v. Talbot Lunders* unfortunately fell into the headache pile.

Crumpling up the remains of his empanada in the deli wrapper, Manny pitched it across the room and over the head of the only other detective currently in the squad bay and not out to lunch. It landed in the over-flowing wastebasket next to the copier, causing an avalanche of paper down one side. Mike Dickerson, an ornery fixture as old as the building itself, shot Manny a dark look over his black spectacles. 'Watch it, Bear,' he grumbled, shaking the sports section of the *Miami Herald* in Manny's direction. 'You ain't no Josh Johnson.'

Then he buried his head behind the paper and carried on gumming his sub.

'I coulda been, Pops,' Manny said with a heavy sigh, as he crumpled up the paper bag lunch had come in and chucked that, too, across the room. This time he hit the copier.

'Yeah, yeah. I don't know what you was throwing those ten minutes you spent in the minor leagues, boy, but I'll tell you, your aim is for shit now.'

'Took your piece off.'

Mike's hand shot to the top of his head.

'Don't have a heart attack, Pops. I'm just busting balls,' Manny said with a hearty laugh. 'It's still there.'

'Bald fucking Yeti.'

'You should go natural, Mikey. It beats the rug. The missus would love it, rubbing her hands all over your smooth, silky melon.'

Manny had shaved his head the day he joined the force and worn it that way ever since. But he did let hair grow everywhere else it naturally wanted to on his body, including his arms, hands, back and chest – thus earning him the nickname Bear. He wore a five o'clock shadow by noon and a thick, wiry, black mustache 24/7. The decision to go bald wasn't solely motivated by vanity, though. It kept him cool, for one thing. And as a hulking, over-sized, olive-skinned, bald Cubano with a thick mustache and dark, full eyebrows that were perpetually furrowed, he looked menacing. Most defendants thought twice before trying to fuck with him. And confessions came faster for him than they did for most of the other guys. Plus, the ladies seemed to like it. Considering he'd been married three times already and hadn't had a hair on his head when he met any of his exes, being bald certainly didn't hold him back.

Dickerson snorted and shook the paper again. 'Don't you have some murder to solve, *Manuelo*?'

'Heading to court right now,' Manny replied, pulling a sports jacket on.

'Where'd you dig up that thing?'

'What?'

'The coat.'

'The prosecutor asked me to get all fancy. You don't like?'

'Are those patches on the sleeves?'

'Very funny. Ain't no patches, Pops. This is a genuine . . .' Manny peered at the label on the inside of his jacket, '. . . Haggar. I bought it at the Aventura Mall.' Manny shrugged. 'I can't find my good suit. It must still be in the cleaners' from my last trial.'

'Nice tie.'

Manny wagged the tip of his teal tie that was speckled with tiny Miami Dolphins football helmets in the old detective's direction. 'Thanks.'

Dickerson rolled his eyes again. 'You in trial?'

'I got an Arthur.' Arthur was short for Arthur Hearing – another way of saying bond hearing.

Dickerson smiled coyly. 'I'm willing to bet your prosecutor has a nice set of gams and the initials 'Ms' in front of her name.'

'Who the hell says "gams"?'

'You wouldn't wear a jacket to your own momma's funeral.'

'Not if it was in Miami in June, I sure as fuck wouldn't. That's why Cubans invented guayabera shirts, Pops.

Dressy when you need to be, yet still cool and comfortable. You're right – she is a she. And she does have fine legs. Not that I noticed.'

'I knew it,' Dickerson replied with the same lecherous cackle.

'Fuck you, old man. You don't know shit.'

'What case you going on? Is that the dumpster girl?'

'Yup. Holly Skole's her name.'

'Saw the pictures on your desk.'

'Sorry.'

'Didn't realize you had a suspect. Is he good?'

'I'm not counting chickens; I always get burned when I do. You saw the pictures – the guy's an animal. He needs to pay for what he's done.'

'For once, young Jedi, we agree.'

Manny laughed. 'For once.' Then he picked up his file and headed out the homicide squad-room doors and into the controlled chaos of the rest of the City of Miami Police Department.

'Call me if you get lonely, Sonny Boy,' Dickerson called after him, as he returned to his paper. 'I've only got one hundred and eighty-three days left. You still got time to learn from the master . . .'

The old man's voice faded away as the hallway crowd got louder. Manny had learned early on to never boast about the strength of a case or predict a conviction. No case was airtight, and especially not this one. He would have to make his case as if he was building a house destined to be hit by a hurricane – slowly, carefully, with a strong foundation.

He slipped on his Oakley's and stepped into the scorching sunshine. It was barely June and the humidity was already 95 per cent. He could feel his armpits start to drain as he headed across the steamy asphalt parking lot.

Bienvenido a Miami.

5

By 1:30 on a Tuesday afternoon, the criminal courthouse in downtown Miami was relatively quiet. The frenzied morning calendars had finally been cleared and the defendants, victims, witnesses, family members, defense attorneys, prosecutors and cops were long gone – their cases arraigned, continued, pled-out or set-over for motions or trials on another day. The hallways that had been clogged a few hours earlier were now deserted. Most of the building's courtrooms were empty and locked, their judges either still at lunch or in recess till the following morning. The courtrooms that were open were either in trial or hearing motions.

Assistant State Attorney Daria DeBianchi pushed open the heavy doors of 4-10 and made her way into the one courtroom in the building that was still a beehive of activity. On the other side of the railing that partitioned the lawyers from the general audience, an invisible line separated prosecutors from defense attorneys, like a boy/girl middle school dance. Correction officers manned the exits and flanked the jury box, which was also filled with bodies, except they weren't jurors, they were defendants – all dressed in bright orange jumpsuits, chained together at the wrists and shackled at the ankles. Filling the pews on the 'state's side' of the gallery were detectives and cops. For the defense, it was friends and family. The judge hadn't yet taken the bench and the courtroom sounded like a playground at recess. Seated at a desk in front of the bench was the judge's judicial assistant, checking in a line of attorneys while simultaneously digging for gold inside her ear with a curved, glossy black fingernail. Daria took one look at the printed court calendar on top of the podium and sighed heavily. It was over two inches thick. She was gonna be here till friggin' Christmas . . .

Standing four-foot-eleven and three-quarters, and weighing 94 pounds, with wavy auburn hair, blue eyes and skin so fair she broke out in freckles when she was next to an oven, everyone liked to tell Daria that: #1 – she didn't look Italian, and #2 – she definitely didn't look like a prosecutor. The Italian thing was understandable, she supposed. Every one of her relatives, including her *nonna*, was tan, dark-eyed, and blanketed in coarse, black hair all over their stocky, thick bodies. Daria got called 'mick' more often than she did 'guinea'. As for the comments on her non-prosecutorial appearance, she wasn't sure if those were intended as compliments or condolences, but since she was still getting them five years into her career, she figured the job had neither aged nor hardened her. To compensate for the fact that she wasn't an Amazon who could arm wrestle an AK47 out of a defendant's hands before carrying him up the river, she made sure she always wore heels – the higher, the better. And red lipstick – the redder, the better. She'd read in *Vogue* once that red lipstick made people think you were in control. For the most part it worked. Most defendants weren't sure whether they should flirt with her or send over a death threat.

The majestically intimidating, wood-paneled court-room was standing-room only. In the afternoons 4-10 was reserved solely for Arthur Hearings – bond hearings for badass defendants charged with non-bondable, badass offenses like kidnapping, drug trafficking, and murder. On a good day with a good judge, they were no big deal – a ten or twenty-minute defense fishing expedition that usually ended like it started, with a dangerous defendant denied bond and remanded to the county jail pending trial. But on Tuesdays Arthurs were presided over by Judge Werner Steyn, a former public defender who leaned so far to the left he had trouble standing up straight. That made him the natural favorite of defense attorneys everywhere, who all pushed to have their Arthurs set before him. With Monday's Memorial Day holiday shortening the work-week, and Steyn depend-ably late taking the bench, Christmas might actually come and go before she returned to the mess that waited on her desk across the street at the State Attorney's Office.

She found her case buried on page 22 of the calendar. With two defendants per page, it wasn't hard to do the math. Unless she got moved up, there'd be no *Toddlers & Tiaras* tonight.

'Hi, Harmony,' she said sweetly when she'd finally made her way on the attorney line up to the clerk's desk. 'How are you? How's your hubby feeling? I heard half of Probation is down with the flu. And it's almost *June*. What's with that?'

Harmony, the clerk with the name befitting either a stripper or a Life Coach, stared blankly at Daria as if she were a total stranger, not a Division Chief who'd appeared in her courtroom dozens of times before. And with whom she'd had dozens of – obviously meaningless – conversations. Her bulging eyes, which were lined like a dead body at a TV crime scene with black liner, blinked twice. Finally it clicked – at least that she had a husband. 'Good, he's good, thank God! Wow! No, no flu. What page you on, hon?'

So much for charm and chit-chat. 'Twenty-two. Lunders. Talbot Lunders. Has the defense checked in yet?'

Harmony leafed through her master calendar. 'Oh yeah. A while ago. But I got a lot ahead of you now, State; I can't let you be cutting the line. So you're gonna be number thirteen, hon.' She frowned and wagged a black talon to stop the words she knew were coming. 'And yes, that is the best I can do, even though, I know, I know, it's an unlucky number, but somebody's gotta be it.' Harmony finished with a dismissive sigh, before turning her head to address the lawyer behind Daria. 'What page you on, hon?'

Next! It was like getting served slop on a school lunch line. Daria begrudgingly waded into the pack of prosecutors. Thirteen was better than forty-four, but it still meant a long afternoon, although, she thought, as she surveyed the courtroom, her detective didn't appear to be on time anyway. This was her first case with City of Miami Detective Manny Alvarez. Last week he'd been forty-five

47

minutes late for his pre-file without offering up so much as a lame excuse why. Although he had brought her a *café con leche* and some weird pastry that oozed pink goo, along with a stack of reports that he'd already actually written – something most cops didn't get around to doing before the third discovery demand, and only after you screamed at them – she was still ticked off. And she was going to be *really* mad if he pulled the same stunt today, even if he did wind up beating the judge to the bench.

She peered at the degenerates that filled the jury box to see if her defendant had been brought out yet. He hadn't. Based on the mug shot clipped to the top of her file, she could expect the ladies in the courtroom to collectively start panting when Corrections ushered him through the door. She wondered if he'd be as striking in person, having fermented in a jail cell for the past couple of weeks.

Standing up against the wall on the prosecutorial side of the courtroom was her friend Lizette, a Domestics prosecutor, who was waving her over as if she were hailing a cab in rush hour. 'So what happened to you yesterday, *mami*?' Lizette demanded when Daria squeezed in next to her.

'Don't start,' Daria replied. Most of the young, single prosecutors in the office had spent Monday's unofficial start to summer sipping mojitos and sangria by the pool at the Clevelander on South Beach. Judging by the comments she'd fielded all morning, she was the only one who'd missed it. 'I was at my brother's all weekend. Dang, you're tan. Did you fall asleep on a tanning bed or something, Liz? You look like Snooki.'

Lizette waved a hand in front of her face. 'I'm

Columbian. I got this on the walk across the parking lot,' she shot back with a Spanish accent that became more pronounced whenever she got flustered or was in front of a Hispanic judge. 'You missed a good time, girl.'

'Don't envy me. I spent the past three days babysitting triplets.'

Lizette curled her lip like she'd smelled two-day-old fish. 'Triplets?'

'*Three-year-old* triplets. My brother and his wife went on a cruise to the Bahamas. So while you were working on that tan you deny intentionally working on, I was cutting up hot dogs and watching Disney flicks. Oh, and potty training.'

The curl grew into a grimace.

'Of course they're boys, so that means none of 'em can aim for shit. We're talking the ceiling, the walls, the door – anywhere but the bowl. They're cute and I love them to pieces, but, man, do I feel *old*. I was stressed the whole time. Couldn't sleep. Always afraid one of 'em might slip out in the middle of the night, ride out of town like Paul Revere, naked on top of the Great Dane, waving a Pull-Up in his hand.'

'Great Dane?'

'Her name's Petunia. She's shy.'

'I won't even watch my sister's fish.'

'Oh, and an albino ferret that the kids like to lock in the dryer.'

'I've heard enough.'

'I think my whacked mother's plan backfired. Instead of rushing out to find myself a husband and jump-start a family, I might go celibate.' Daria sniffed at her arm. 'Do I smell like grape jelly to you? I don't know what they put in that shit, but it stays in your system. I'm sweating it out of my pores. That and peanut butter. And my shoes are sticking to everything.'

Lizette nodded. 'You're right. I would never advocate celibacy, but you're not the mommy type. Good thing you don't need a man to have fun.'

'That's not a real concern right now for me, anyway; it's easy to give up what you're not getting.' Daria frowned before adding, 'Thanks for the mommy comment. I can be warm and fuzzy, you know.'

Lizette shrugged. 'Whatever. So who're you here on?'

'On today's menu we have one Talbot Alastair Lunders.'

'What kind of name is that?'

'A family one, I suppose.'

'Obviously not a Miami family. I'm guessing that someone with not one, but two, obnoxious Anglo names must come from money.'

'You're right. Young Talbot is of the Palm Beach Lunders.'

'Who are the Palm Beach Lunders?'

'Daddy apparently owns some luxury soap company. Or so I've been warned.'

'What company is that?'

'Dial.'

Lizette's eyes went wide. 'No shit. Really?'

Daria laughed. 'No, not really. Some spa brand I never heard of.'

Lizette surveyed the jury box. 'All of the boys today look like they come from the projects, not Palm Beach.'

'Oh, Talbot's not out yet,' Daria replied, flashing Lizette the mug shot. The tan playboy with the highlighted, shaggy hairdo and mesmerizing hazel eyes looked more like a brooding Dolce & Gabbana model in his booking photo than a murderer. 'You'll probably start drooling when Corrections brings him in. Maybe even consider a career on the Dark Side.'

Lizette sucked in a breath. 'If you could guarantee all of my client's would look like that, I'd enter pleas on their behalf. What crime did poor-little-hot-rich boy commit?'

'Murder.'

Lizette shook her head. 'What a shame. My mother can overlook many things in the hunt to find me a husband, but murderer would be a tough sell. Who'd handsome get so mad at?'

'A pretty college kid out clubbing at Menace. She was found in a dumpster near the Design District.'

'Is that the girl who was missing on the news a few weeks ago?'

Daria nodded.

'The UM kid. Hmmm. I didn't realize they'd found her.'

'It didn't make much press,' Daria answered. That was no coincidence. The University of Miami was a prestigious private university that came with a hefty price tag. Parents who shelled out fifty thousand a year on tuition didn't like to hear on the nightly news that one of their own had been the random target of a brutal sex maniac while out clubbing underage. So the university brass had contacted all parties involved – including the City of Miami and the State Attorney – to make sure they didn't. The order was no press conferences, no perp walks when the arrest came. Everything was kept on the

51

down-low, which likely explained why there were no cameras in today's hearing.

'How'd she die?' Lizette asked.

The back door that led to the judge's chambers suddenly swung open. 'All rise!' Steyn's bailiff shouted. 'The Honorable Judge Werner Steyn presiding.'

'Good afternoon, all,' the judge said with the slight hint of a German accent as he took the bench, nodding in the direction of a few cronies from the good ol' days. 'Sorry to be running a bit late. Let's get started; we have a real big calendar today.'

'No cell phones, no cameras, no talking. Be seated and be quiet!' bellowed the bailiff.

Everyone in the audience quickly found a seat, while the lawyers pushed up against the walls on their respective sides of the courtroom and Harmony called the first case.

Daria anxiously scanned the room for any sign of her detective. The one thing she did know about Manny Alvarez was that he was hard to miss. Anywhere. There was no sign of his shiny bald head towering above the packed courtroom crowd.

Although he hadn't expressly said it, Daria knew that Vance Collier, the Chief Felony Assistant and right-hand to the State Attorney, had personally assigned her this case for a reason. The Chief of the Sexual Battery Unit was stepping down in September and Daria had let it be known to the powers that be that she was throwing her name in the ring for the job. Holly Skole had been brutally raped before she was murdered. The case was potentially high profile – with a good-looking defendant from a privileged family, a cute coed for a victim, and a heinous, gory murder that was sure to command headlines if not handled correctly. The evidence, while damning, was completely circumstantial, which definitely complicated things. And there were multiple parties within the community whose feathers needed to be stroked, not ruffled, including the powerful University of Miami, and the even more powerful South Florida press. *The State of Florida v. Talbot Lunders* would be the perfect test case to see if Daria DeBianchi could head up one of the busiest, most contentious, most emotionally draining units at the State Attorney's Office.

But no more than five minutes out of the start gate and the horse she was riding was faltering. And at this point in the race, a stumble could be as tragic as a broken leg. Because if Talbot Lunders got a bond – for whatever reason – *she* was the one who'd be held responsible. It was always easier to negotiate a plea with a defendant who was behind bars. Statistically, it was also easier to secure a conviction. The biggest concern if Lunders got out was that an accused killer would be running around the streets of Miami for months before his case finally made it to trial. Joe General Public would not be at all happy to hear that. Neither would those powers that be on the third floor of the SAO who were studying her résumé and deciding if she was good enough to move up a rung or two on the company ladder. She was beginning to realize that the heat from the spotlight she'd been placed under could not only set her apart from the crowd, it could burn her just as well.

The parties on Steyn's first case began opening

arguments. She nibbled on a cuticle while frantically texting with her other hand under the cover of her file.

Depending on how fast Steyn worked, number thirteen might not be as far off as she once thought it was going to be . . .

6

And she was right.

Forty-five minutes later, Steyn was listening to arguments on twelve. A large clock hung above the courtroom doors, ticking off minutes and hours with jumbo-sized precision. Every time the doors opened with a whoosh, Daria would look to see if it was Manny. Not only was she consistently disappointed, she was also reminded to the second how late he actually was. He wasn't answering his texts or picking up his phone, and neither she nor her witness coordinator could get through to anyone in command at Homicide to find out where the hell he was. While it was possible that he was on a case that had taken him beyond cell range, or was lying comatose somewhere in a hospital bed, Daria thought it much more likely her lead detective had either forgotten entirely about today's hearing, or he'd enjoyed a late lunch and was taking his sweet Cuban time to get to the courthouse, figuring he could milk another hour or so out of a Tuesday afternoon Arthur with Slow Steyn before anyone would start to miss him.

He figured wrong.

'Next up, State of Florida versus Talbot Alastair Lunders,' announced Harmony.

Two stone-faced, black-suited lawyers – an older, heavyset man and an attractive woman in her thirties – emerged from the crowd of defense attorneys and approached the podium. The criminal bar in Miami was small; everyone knew each other. The fact that Daria had never seen either of the two people standing before the judge made her more than a little uneasy.

'Joseph Varlack on behalf of the defendant, Talbot Lunders. Appearing with me today is Anne-Claire Simmons.'

Varlack. She knew the name from somewhere. 'Daria DeBianchi on behalf of the state. I thought the defendant was being represented by Les Pfeiffer,' she replied, leafing through her file for the Notice of Appearance from Pfeiffer that she'd tucked away somewhere.

Joe Varlack looked at her and smiled. 'Not anymore he's not. I filed a Substitution of Counsel this morning.' He handed her a piece of paper. 'My Notice of Appearance.'

That was when she spotted the shoes.

She couldn't touch them on her state salary, but Daria had a weakness for designer kicks. Her eyes fell on the unmistakably red sole of a pair of Christian Louboutin black patent pumps that Varlack's co-counsel was wearing. Then on his shiny, manicured fingernails, which perfectly complimented the snazzy Rolex he had strapped to his wrist. Her Bottega Venetta handbag. His Louis Vuitton briefcase. The impeccably tailored suits on both of them that Daria – the great-granddaughter of a legendary tailor from Spoleto, Italy – just knew had to be Italian. The Palm Beach Lunders must have up and hired Palm Beach attorneys. Expensive Palm Beach attorneys.

'Are we ready?' asked the judge.

'The defendant's on his way out, Judge,' offered Corrections. 'Two minutes.'

'The defense is ready to proceed,' Varlack responded.

Daria hesitated. 'Your Honor, I'm waiting on my detective. Perhaps we could pass this case?'

Varlack looked at his pretty watch, then pointed it at Steyn, just in case the judge couldn't make out the huge timepiece above the courtroom doors. 'Your Honor, Ms Simmons and I were here at one o'clock. I expected the state and their witnesses to be here and be ready by one-thirty, which is the time this matter was set down for. I have a pressing engagement back in Palm Beach, which is why I specifically requested that the clerk put us on the calendar early today, and which is why I made sure I was here on time and ready to proceed.'

'I understand, Mr Varlack,' Judge Steyn responded with a conciliatory nod. 'Your time is valuable. What do you want? A continuance, then?'

The light bulb went off. *Joe Varlack.* Varlack, Metzer, Shearson & A Thousand Other Peon Associates Whose Names No One Besides Their Own Mothers Ever Remembers. Attorneys to fallen movie stars, wayward athletes and corrupt Fortune 500 companies. Their retainers alone were more than what most people made in a year. Forget the name, Daria should've recognized Joe Varlack from his TV days, when he used to do a Channel Ten *Nightly News* 'Justice with Joe' segment.

That was a decade or so ago – before he represented his first rock star and his legal career took off. Other rock stars began to fill his appointment book, along with football players and basketball greats – apparently leaving Justice Joe no time to dispense legal advice at six and eleven anymore to all the regular Joes sitting at home in front of their TVs. It must've been all those fancy client dinners over the past ten years that helped him pack an extra hundred or so pounds on to an already hefty six-foot frame, which probably explained why she didn't recognize him right away from his glory days on Channel Ten. And it must've been one of those eccentric, fading rock stars from the seventies who'd convinced him that it would be a good idea to let his hair grow out, too. What was still left of it, anyway. Shiny bald on top with a set of jowls that were more befitting a Bull Mastiff, and a ponytail of yellowed white curls running down his back, the man definitely made an intimidating impression, no matter what he was saying, which, even in his TV heyday, always seemed to be at decibel level 10. *She was gonna kill Manny Alvarez. Of all the cases to screw with her on . . .*

'Your Honor, I'd like to be heard on bond,' Varlack bellowed. 'The state's not prepared, but I am. It would be unfair to reset this matter and let Talbot languish in jail all because the state doesn't have its act together. He's an upstanding young man with no criminal record. His family is very important and highly respected in the community, as you probably know. He's the managing director for the Southeast Division of Flower & Honey Bath Products. He has well-established roots; he's not some drifter that won't show up for court. He's not a danger by any stretch. Had the state been ready, you would've seen that the case against him is entirely circumstantial. In fact, as an attorney who's been practicing for forty years representing other high-profile clients, I'm frankly shocked Talbot was even arrested. The fact that he was lured down to Miami and arrested like common street scum, without being given the courtesy to surrender himself, is outrageous. His arrest was done for show and to usher in a quick end to this case for the City of Miami Police Department – damn the consequences. It's imperative Talbot be released so that he can aid in his defense of these very serious charges and attempt to regain his and his family's good name.'

Daria bit her cheek so hard she drew blood, trying to contain the stream of expletives that wanted to fly out of her mouth. Most defense attorneys gave you a break and agreed to a continuance before they bitched about you not being ready or got on a soapbox about client persecution. And most did not grandstand about their big-name clients. Especially socialites nobody'd ever heard of anyway. What a prick.

Unfortunately, Steyn looked impressed. 'What do you propose?'

'The Lunders family is willing to post one hundred and fifty thousand dollars in cash today as bond. If the court deems it necessary, Talbot is also willing to submit to an ankle bracelet. I believe that's more than adequate.'

An inmate in the box whooped. 'Someone be bringing home the Benjamins!'

'I have to agree that does sound reasonable,' Steyn replied, ignoring the outburst. 'State?'

'Your Honor, the defendant's been charged with

murder, not jaywalking,' Daria protested incredulously. 'The case goes before the grand jury tomorrow, where Mr Varlack knows his client will be indicted, which is why he set down this matter for *today* and is pressing for a bond *today*, because once his client is indicted for capital murder, he'll be hard-pressed to find any judge that will give him the time of day when it comes to seeking a bond and he knows it. That's because the evidence will show in this case that Talbot Lunders tortured, raped, and brutally murdered Holly Skole.'

Steyn was shaking his head. 'No it won't, Counsel, because you're not—'

A loud, boisterous hoot broke out from the hallway, causing heads to turn and Steyn to stop in mid-sentence. A split-second later the door opened and hearty laughter filled the room.

'—ready,' finished the judge.

It wasn't hard to place the laugh. It belonged on a big body.

'Actually, I believe I am ready,' Daria announced before even turning around to confirm that it was, in fact, Manny – accompanied by two other city detectives, who were also in stitches but not half as loud – who'd walked through the door. All three were completely oblivious to the fact that they'd momentarily shut down court.

Judge Steyn scowled. The defense team simultaneously rolled their eyes.

'Detective, nice of you to join us,' Steyn sniped.

'I was out in the hall, Judge. Dixon just came and told me you called my case?' Dixon was the correction officer manning the courtroom door, who nodded at the judge.

Steyn glared at Daria.

The jangle of chains and leg irons sounded from the jury deliberation room as the door opened and a new crop of unruly defendants shuffled into the courtroom and the old ones shuffled out. 'Take your seats and ya'all shut up, now!' the CO barked as he moved them into their seats. 'The defendant is present, Judge.'

'Thank you,' Steyn said, rubbing his temple. 'You don't need to tell them to shut up. Be quiet is fine.'

'They won't do that, neither, Judge,' replied the CO. 'They're a rowdy bunch today.'

Daria looked over at the box. Her defendant definitely stood out, and not just because he was the only white guy in the row. Apparently unaffected by the commotion around him, he stared into the gallery, a curious smile on his face, like he knew a joke that no one else was getting. Even in that hideous orange jumpsuit, dressed to the nines in shackles and leg irons, with stubble on his cheeks and his highlighted hair a bit greasy, he was still – dare she say it? – handsome. Really handsome. Like suck-in-your-breath, Brad-Pitt-in-*Thelma and Louise*-handsome. The thought made her brain cringe and she shook it right out of her head.

'Hello? State? Are you with us?' the judge was asking.

Daria looked back at Manny. 'Can I have a moment, Your Honor, to confer with my detective?'

'No,' Steyn replied, annoyed. 'The defendant is here, counsel is here, your detective is finally here, you said you're ready, so have at it.' He leaned back in his chair with a loud squeak and folded his arms across his chest. 'Don't bother with an opening; I've read the arrest form. Give me the meat and potatoes and get on with it.'

In a perfect world, Daria would've had at least a few minutes to run through the questions she was about to ask. But the world was far from perfect.

So without further delay, she opened her file and called City of Miami Detective Manny Alvarez to the stand.

marks on her wrists and ankles, indicating she'd been tied up for a period before she was murdered.'

Joe Varlack sprang to his feet. 'Objection! Speculation!'

'An autopsy was performed by Dr Gunther Trauss of the Miami-Dade ME's office,' Manny continued, basically ignoring Varlack.

'There's an objection pending,' barked the defense attorney. 'I guess the detective didn't hear me.'

'Your Honor,' Daria responded, 'Detective Alvarez has been investigating murders for eighteen years. We can assume that he knows rope burns on someone's wrists when he sees them. We're getting to the autopsy, which will confirm the detective's observations.'

Steyn nodded. 'Go on.'

She held up the autopsy report. 'What was Dr Trauss's determination as to the cause of death?'

'Manual asphyxiation. She was choked to death with bare hands. She had finger marks on her throat, bruising, and a crushed larynx.' Manny looked over at the defense table and smiled smugly. 'I observed *that*, too.'

'And the bind marks on her wrists?'

'Dr Trauss determined that she was tied up with rope and tortured prior to her death.'

'Objection,' interrupted Varlack again. 'Not only is this hearsay, but it calls for speculation, both on the part of the detective and the pathologist.'

Daria sighed heavily so that everyone in the courtroom could hear. Patience was not her strong suit. She was gonna hit stop-and-go traffic the whole way home. Either Varlack was trying to fluster her by making loud, dumb objections or he was an idiot. 'This is not trial, Counsel,' she shot back sharply. 'It's a *bond hearing* and

65

the last time I checked, hearsay is admissible. Judge, the ME's report extensively details Ms Skole's injuries – the victim was most definitely *tortured* before she was *murdered*. And as much as Counsel might not like that word or want to hear it, *torture* goes to show *premeditation*, which is an element of *first-degree murder*, which is the crime his client has been charged with. If Mr Varlack wants to second-guess the findings of the Medical Examiner, let him do so at his deposition or at trial or in a written motion, but once again, this is a *bond hearing*. Now, can I get on with my case, or are we gonna bicker all afternoon about how to conduct an Arthur Hearing way down here in the bowels of Miami? Because I thought Mr Varlack had a pressing appointment back home with one of his degenerate high-profile clients in Palm Beach.'

Justice Joe looked taken aback, followed by embarrassed and then, finally, really, really angry – all in a spate of thirty seconds. The shiny part of his head turned red. It was war. And just like that, Daria had eliminated yet another law firm to float out a résumé to in the event she ever did decide to go into private practice. She had to stop doing that. With a pile of law school loans to still pay back, a $44,000 career as a prosecutor wasn't supposed to last forever.

'You don't need to worry yourself about my schedule, Counsel,' Varlack hissed.

She shrugged. 'Take a look at the law on a subject before you start making objections, is all I'm saying. It will make this go faster for all of us.'

'Enough,' Steyn cautioned, obviously flustered. 'Both of you, take your corners. Continue, Ms DeBianchi.'

Daria turned her attention to Manny. 'If you would, please describe Holly Skole's injuries.'

'She had a traumatic burn mark on the back of her neck and severe chemical burns on the soles of her feet and on her face, most likely caused by sulfuric acid,' Manny answered.

Those who had actually been listening in the courtroom collectively gasped. And that made all the others who were still whisper-chatting amongst themselves or reading files or secretly checking and sending texts stop and listen. The courtroom went completely quiet.

'She'd been both vaginally and anally raped,' continued Manny. 'Toxicology reports indicate that she'd also been injected with, or force-fed, large amounts of diphenhydramine and dextromethorphan, the chemical compounds found in cough syrup and sleep aids that produce hallucinations in high enough doses. Her wrists were abraded where she'd been bound with rope, and she had cuts on her gums, indicating she'd been perhaps fitted with a bit, like a horse – all indications of sadomasochistic behavior.' Manny turned and gave the defense counsel a steely look before finishing with his next sentence: 'Yet another clue she'd been *tortured* before she was *murdered*.'

Varlack snorted loudly but said nothing. The spanking had worked.

Daria hid her smile and the ice began to thaw. 'What caused you to believe that Mr Lunders was responsible for Holly's death?'

'On Monday, April eighteenth, Holly's roommate, Jenny Demchar, reported Holly missing to Coral Gables police. Holly had gone out two nights earlier to the Miami nightclub Menace to celebrate a friend's birthday, but didn't come home. When she didn't show up for class, Ms Demchar and Holly's other friend, Esther Flicker – the girl whose birthday Holly'd been celebrating – went back to Menace and discovered Holly's locked car parked in a municipal lot under the 395 overpass. Ms Demchar called the police. A missing persons investigation was opened by Coral Gables and, pursuant to that investigation, surveillance video from the nightclub was pulled, which records Holly leaving Menace at 4:16 a.m. with an, at the time, unknown white male. Coral Gables Detective John Coffey obtained additional video footage from a nearby traffic cam, which shows Holly getting into the passenger side of a dark-colored, late-model Mercedes. Visible in the video is the last digit of the plate. It was "Z", as in Zulu.

'Holly was entered into NCIC – the National Crime Information Center – as a missing person. Her photo, along with a still photo of the vehicle from the traffic cam and a still photo of the individual seen leaving Menace with Holly were distributed in the community and broadcast on several local television news stations.'

Daria held up a poster. 'Are these the photographs you're referring to?'

'Yes. That's a Crime Stoppers reward poster. A thousand-dollar reward was set up requesting information on Holly's disappearance.'

She moved the poster into evidence and continued. 'After Holly was entered into NCIC, what happened?'

'Holly's body was subsequently discovered on April twenty-fifth and her death was classified a homicide. A couple of weeks later I was contacted by a Ms Marie Modic of Hallendale, Florida. She told me that she'd been in Menace on Saturday night, May seventh, and in the club's bathroom she'd seen the Crime Stoppers poster. She recognized the male in the surveillance photo and called me. I interviewed her at the nail salon where she works and she identified the man in the Crime Stoppers' photo as "T", a guy she'd talked to in Menace on the night of April sixteenth, which was the same night Holly Skole had been in the club and disappeared. "T" was the name he went by, but Ms Modic didn't know his full name. He flashed a lot of cash, was dressed real nice. Said he was, quote, "slumming it down in Miami", endquote. Said he came from the land of the Trumps and Kennedys, where the real money is.

'So this "T" bought Marie Modic a couple of drinks and then asked her if she wanted to come back to his suite at the Mandarin. She initially said yes, at which time he placed his keys on the bar to pay the bar tab and she saw a car key with the Mercedes logo. Attached to the key was a metal plate that said, 'Automotive Expert'. Ms Modic then excused herself to go to the bathroom, where she said she had second thoughts about going with "T". Something just didn't sit right with her about him and she was not feeling well physically, so she texted her girlfriend, who was also in the club, and asked her to get the car and meet her outside. She snuck out the back entrance. Stepping into the car is the last thing she remembers that night. She blanked out until the next morning, when she woke up in her apartment some seventeen hours later. Her girlfriend told her that as soon as she'd gotten into the car she'd pretty much passed out. She now believes she was drugged by the defendant.'

'Objection! How much leniency are you gonna give this prosecutor, Judge? Hearsay upon hearsay, and now we have a medical opinion being offered up from a nail tech who downed one too many free drinks,' barked Varlack. He threw his hands up in frustration.

'Sustained,' replied the judge. 'Move on, Ms DeBianchi.'

'How did you come to identify this "T" as being the defendant, Talbot Lunders?'

'I contacted a company called Automotive Experts, a high-end car dealership with offices in Palm Beach and Stuart. I spoke with the owner and had him pull records for late-model Mercedes sales within the past two years. Then I did a records check on all of the Mercedes sold by Automotive Experts for plates ending in "Z", and I found a black 2010 S-class registered to Abigail Charmaine Lunders, age forty-six. A background check on her revealed that she was the wife of Frederick Alastair Lunders, age sixty-seven. An insurance check on the vehicle listed Talbot Alastair Lunders, age twenty-eight, as an additional authorized driver of the vehicle. I pulled Mr Lunders's driver's license and identified him as the guy captured on the surveillance video leaving Menace with Holly Skole. Marie Modic also identified him through his DL – his driver's license photo. A search warrant for the Mercedes was obtained and executed on May thirteenth.'

'What did you find?'

'A lipstick compact was recovered under the front passenger seat of the car, along with three long blonde hairs that the lab subsequently confirmed matched the chemical composition of Ms Skole's hair dye. Fingerprints were also lifted from the lipstick case, which matched both the index and thumbprints on Ms Skole's right hand. DNA analysis of the lipstick is pending. Fingerprints matching Ms Skole's right thumb and right palm were also found on the inside door handle of the passenger side of the vehicle. So we know she was in that car.'

'Objection.'

'Overruled.'

'Was the defendant present when the Mercedes was seized?'

'Yes. It was seized from the parking lot of Flower & Honey Bath Products in Palm Beach, where Mr Lunders works. He appeared very agitated and upset, pacing the lot, threatening to call his attorney. His mother accompanied him. She wasn't very happy, either. At that time I asked him if he wanted to talk about the disappearance of Holly Skole. He declined.

'Three days later, while lab results were pending, I learned that the very afternoon the Benz was seized, Mr Lunders had gone and listed his 2008 Cigarette High-Performance Top Gun for sale through a broker in Coconut Grove, Miami. The racing boat was being offered for thirty percent less than other Cigarettes listed for sale of the same year and style. That raised my eyebrows way up. So I ran a system search of airline flights and learned that one T. Lunders was booked on a one-way JetBlue flight out of Palm Beach International to New York's JFK the following afternoon. And a T. Lunders and A. Lunders were also booked on a Lufthansa flight to Zurich the day after that. His mother's name is Abigail Lunders. Based on that, Mr Lunders was asked to come down to his boat broker to provide additional paperwork to facilitate the pending sale of his boat. When he arrived at the marina, I approached the defendant, identified myself once again, and told him his boat was being searched pursuant to a homicide investigation. Mr Lunders didn't like that; he again declined to talk to us.'

'Objection!' Varlack barked. 'The defendant has a right against self-incrimination! He doesn't have to talk to the police if he doesn't want to and that can't be used against him. That's Criminal Law 101!'

Steyn frowned. 'Was the defendant free to go at that time?'

'I had not yet taken him into custody,' Manny replied.

'That, I'm thinking, is going to be up for debate in a future motion,' the judge replied with a cocked eyebrow. 'Sustained.'

'The fingerprint analysis of both the lipstick and the prints left on the interior passenger door of the Mercedes confirmed Ms Skole had been in Abigail Lunders's vehicle,' Manny continued. 'Based on the prints and hair of the victim being found in his car, the video surveillance of her getting into the defendant's car, and then the quick sell-off of his worldly possessions and his impending flight from the jurisdiction to a country that doesn't have an extradition treaty with the US, a decision was made to arrest him for the murder of Holly Anne Skole.'

That was enough for the judge. Particularly the Switzerland flight. As much as Joe Varlack and his well-heeled sidekick tried for the next twenty minutes to downplay the evidence as circumstantial and unreliable, and discredit Manny as biased, sloppy, lazy – and a zillion other disingenuous adjectives – there was no way that even liberal, let-'em-go, Slow Steyn was going to give Talbot Lunders a bond. Enough dots had been connected to keep him behind bars pending trial. And the truth be told, it was an election year. If Steyn did let Talbot Alastair Lunders of the Palm Beach Lunders buy his way out of the pokey with $150,000 in cold, hard cash, the press would start screaming favorable treatment for the rich and it would be difficult for anyone to argue otherwise come the August primaries.

Harmony called up the next case and a fresh set of attorneys approached the podiums, ready to do battle. The lurid transfixion that had held the audience captive during Talbot Lunders's Arthur finally broke, and the hushed conversations and illicit texting started up once again as courtroom life returned to normal. Case file in hand, Daria made her way past the rows of spectators to the majestic mahogany doors. With her palm on the handle, she turned to look back at the box. Joe Varlack and Anne-Claire Simmons were standing outside the jury box, at the side of their client, who was at the far end of the box. Although they were speaking in hushed voices and she was too far away to hear what was being said, it wasn't hard to read the body language – both attorneys were pissed and the client wasn't listening. More than not listening, handsome Talbot wasn't even *affected*. And that was what held her attention as she stood at the door. Accused of a brutal murder, remanded to a jail cell for the foreseeable future, facing imminent indictment by the grand jury, and, ultimately, a possible death sentence, and the guy seemed about as interested or *affected* as if the crowd around him were discussing the weather in Nepal. She'd seen cold-blooded gang members more worked up over a traffic ticket. He almost seemed amused.

Just as she was thinking that her defendant's reaction, or lack thereof, to what was happening was bizarre and disturbing, she saw his lips move. Then, with a smug smirk, he raised his shackled hands together and pointed straight at Daria across the room. Those in the courtroom who had been watching the exchange looked over at her, which, in turn, started a chain reaction of courtroom rubbernecking – everyone wanting to see what or who the accused sadist was pointing at with his jingling chains, like the Ghost of Christmas Past.

The blood rushed to her face. It was as if she'd been caught peeking in someone's bedroom window and now the whole neighborhood was up and out on the front lawn staring at her. The case file slipped from her hands, spilling papers and crime-scene photos all over the floor. She rushed to pick them up and dropped her purse. Makeup, pens, tampons, loose change, and an assortment of hoarded receipts shot everywhere. Court again came to a complete halt. Dixon, the correction officer who was manning the door, and Manny both stooped down to help her.

'Thank you,' she mumbled to both men as she hurriedly stuffed papers into her file and things into her purse. 'It must've slipped.'

After a few painful, all-too-quiet minutes, the judge finally broke the rubbernecking trance. 'Okay, back to work, everyone. Ms DeBianchi, you got it together there? You okay now?'

Daria waved a hand in the general direction of the bench. She wished she could disappear.

'Harmony, where's my file on Acevedo?' Slow Steyn barked. 'This is the wrong one, I think.' Court started up once more.

'Let's go now!' Corrections shouted. 'Take your seats. That means you, too, Lunders! Caused enough trouble now, didn't ya, pretty boy?'

'I think she's hot for him,' she heard one observer in the gallery remark with a chuckle.

'I got the door, Counselor,' Manny said as Daria stood to leave. 'Have a nice day, Judge,' he called with a wave as she scuttled past.

Once in the hallway, Daria took a breath and tried to shake off her embarrassment. She felt like a complete idiot, dropping her file all over the floor like an incompetent intern. Or worse, like a flustered schoolgirl who'd made eye contact with the school quarterback.

Why the hell had she gotten so rattled? Why had she lost her composure? It pissed her off, was what it did.

Maybe it was curiosity. Maybe it was defiance. Or maybe it was an attempt to reestablish her authority that had made her steal one final glance in the direction of the box as the mahogany doors began to close behind her with a hydraulic hiss. Whatever her intent, whatever the reasoning, she instantly wished she hadn't. Because in all her years prosecuting terrible men for the terrible things they'd done, she'd never before felt the icy-cold sensation of fear race through her veins when she looked at a defendant. She'd never before had to fight off an overwhelming urge to run as hard and as fast as she could away from a moment. And she had never before wished that she'd not been assigned a case.

But that day had come.

Her defendant had not moved. He had not sat down. He was still standing in the box, still pointing at her with his manacled hands, a knowing smile frozen on his face, as if he knew exactly what she was thinking. As if he knew she would try to look at him once again, try to break him. The Ghost of Christmas Future now, staring at her as though she had none. Watching her at the door she'd just walked through, those beautiful hazel eyes of his fixed on the small sliver of her person that remained visible before the door finally closed and the judge ordered him removed from the courtroom.

8

'Looks like somebody's got herself a secret admirer,' Manny said with a touch of sing-song in his voice that made him sound like a pesky little brother. 'I wouldn't get too excited, though. Your new friend reminds me too much of Michael Myers. You know, the psycho from *Halloween*. The guy who chased sexy Jamie Lee Curtis around for a night in that freaky mask while he whacked all her friends to pieces—'

'Yeah, I got it, Detective,' Daria replied, as she turned away from the courtroom and headed toward the bank of escalators, the hurried clicking of her pumps echoing like a jackhammer down the deserted hallway. She was still embarrassed about dropping her file. 'The guy is definitely creepy.'

'So's his lawyers. The big guy, anyway. What's with the pony?'

'Ha.'

'What guy gets a fucking manicure? Come on. Don't think I didn't spot those pudgy, girly hands, Counselor.

Never worked an honest day in his life, I bet. Wait a second, he's a lawyer. Of course he hasn't. They're all scumbags.'

'Remember who you're talking to, Detective. I have an Esq after my name, too.'

'Present company excluded, of course. I meant defense lawyers.'

'Uh-huh.'

'We worked the room in there, didn't we, Counselor?' Manny said with a grin, waving at a couple of cops down the hall, who waved back. 'Like Sonny and Cher, we were. What a team.'

'Hmmm. Sonny and Cher?'

'You know, I remember Varlack from that news show he used to do on Channel Ten. "Advice with Joey" or whatever. He was a big bag of wind back then, too. Damn, has Father Time been hard on that guy. Looks like he ate Father Time,' Manny remarked with a chuckle. 'Do you think he really believed his deranged client was gonna walk out of here today because Mom and Pop were waving a big, fat check at the system?'

Daria stepped on the escalator going down. 'Well, if you'd been a minute later, he probably would have,' she replied coolly.

'Uh-oh. You're mad,' Manny replied, following her.

'You're quick.'

'I wasn't late. I was here the whole time,' he said, taking the fat file from her arms. 'Let me get that for you. It's heavy and you look so tired. And cranky.'

'Hey there, Manny!' a defense attorney called from behind them. 'You going to the game tonight?'

'Not tonight. I got tickets for Saturday.'

'See ya there!' the lawyer replied before disappearing into a courtroom.

He turned his attention back to her. 'Like I said, you look drained. Give me that.'

The man knew everyone and everyone knew him. She handed her file over without a fight. 'Bullshit. I texted you a dozen times – no Manny.'

'There's your problem. I never text. Hate that thing. The world is going to shit, Counselor; no one talks to nobody no more. Everyone just sends cryptic messages. Can't even bother to spell out the fucking words – pardon the English. I'm old school – call me if you need me. That's not so hard.'

'I can't call you when court's in session.'

'You're not supposed to text, either.'

'You were so not out in the hall.'

'I was, too. Dixon came and got me.'

'You were drinking coffee downstairs in the cafeteria; I can still smell the espresso on your breath. Don't lie.'

Manny smiled again. 'You're good. Let me clarify: I was in the *building* the whole time. My buddy told me we were on page twenty-two. I've been before Slow Steyn enough damn times to know that means I had at least an hour. That guy is never on time.'

'Your source is unreliable. We got moved up.'

'And I was still there on time. No harm, no foul.'

Daria shook her head. 'Next time I'm gonna lie to you. Have you here two hours before kick-off. That'll teach you.'

'I've been doing this for a long while, Counselor; I know every trick in the book. And I always make it. Always. Ask anybody.'

She sighed. 'I can't live like that.'

He laughed. 'I like how you shot down the Palm Beachers. Now that was fun to watch. You got a set of *cojones* on you, Little Lady. That's a good thing to have in this building.'

She really wanted to stay mad at him, but unfortunately it wasn't sticking. 'Thank you,' she replied. 'I'm ignoring the short comment for now, though I want you to know I don't like jokes about my height. The hearing went pretty smooth, considering. But don't count out Yin and Yang just yet. They get paid a lot of money for a reason. Today was a fishing expedition, and they netted more than a few fish and a real good understanding of where we are with our case. Or, more telling, where we are not. I don't imagine they'll be making deals anytime soon. Which brings me to my biggest concern: Kuzak's going to the grand jury on this tomorrow. You know that, right?' Guy Kuzak was a seasoned prosecutor and the only ASA who presented cases to the grand jury.

'I've already met with Guy. Don't worry, Counselor, I'll be there at nine.'

'Yeah, well, I am worried. But if everything goes like it did today, and you testify the way you did on the stand, I'm confident the good people of Miami-Dade County will do the right thing and indict. Now I'm thinking ahead. If our defendant's not talking and he's not plea-bargaining, then for trial purposes, we're gonna need something tangible to tie him to the murder: blood, semen, hair, smoking gun. Any of the above would be nice. Anything on the boat?'

'We're running tests on shredded fibers that were found in the bathroom of the cabin and the driver's

80

side floorboard of the Mercedes. They were black viscose and spandex with a shiny silver poly weave that would seem to match the shirt Holly was wearing when she disappeared, but because the shirt was never found, we have nothing to compare it to. I'll try to track down where and when she might've bought it. If it was recent enough, then maybe I can get the same shirt and test it against the found fibers.'

'How many fibers do you have?'

'About twenty or thirty strands in the boat. Another half-dozen in the car and in the trunk. They were torn, you know? Shredded. Enough to figure that the shirt was ripped off the girl, possibly on the boat, and then he carried some on his person that fell off in the car.'

'That would be something,' Daria said as they both stepped on to the next floor's escalator. 'Better still, find me that ripped shirt stuffed inside one of Talbot's toys. If we can also find something that can tie him to the sulfuric acid, that would be big. Really big. Receipts, Internet surfing. Where the hell do you buy that shit anyway? We have his computer, right? What's on that?'

Manny shook his head. He hesitated before speaking. 'We have it, but it's wiped clean. It had a sensitive password protection on it. One try and then it activated a virus that wiped the hard-drive clean. Our tech guy had never seen that sort of security before, and he blew it.'

She stared at him. 'You're kidding, right? We can't retrieve any of it?'

'Nope. The whole thing's gone. Whatever he was trying to protect must have been pretty important.'

'What about his cell? Tell me that didn't self-destruct.'

'Pulled the records. He stayed in Miami the night Holly

disappeared, according to the cell towers. Made two calls between four and five-thirty a.m. – both to the same number, and that was a throwaway. No way to find who owns that phone.'

She tapped her hand impatiently on the escalator's handrail. 'Well, we need something. Since you made the arrest already, time is ticking and we have to deal with the cards we have. I'd sure as hell like a better hand.'

'Hey, hey,' Manny said, his face growing dark as they stepped off and went to get on the final set of escalators down. He moved in front of her, blocking her from getting on. 'Are you saying I shouldn't have arrested the guy? No, don't answer that, because, yeah, that's what you are saying. Listen, he was gonna run and you and I both know it. So let me ask ya, Ms Hard-ass, would you rather be standing here with me now and the scumbag tucked away safely in a jail cell trying to figure out how to make a good case better, or be sitting in your office with what looks like a better case but your fucking psycho playboy nowhere to be found? Or worse – living the high life up at the family chateau in Switzerland, thumbing his nose at us while we sit here and beg the Swiss to extradite his ass before he ups and kills some hot-looking yodler, knowing full well they won't? And oh, yeah, by the way – your boy's family does have a crib in Lucerne. I checked before I popped him. Dad's a Swiss national. Ooh la-fucking-la.'

Daria shrugged. 'What I'm saying is that now we have a potential speedy problem. And what we don't have is the luxury of waiting for shit to fall in our laps. I don't want to see an acquittal because while we had plenty of evidence to prove the guy took pretty Holly for a spin in

Mommy's new Benz, we didn't have enough evidence to actually prove him guilty of murder, 'cause then he can sit across the street from my office and thumb his nose at both of us for the rest of our sure-to-be-shortened-careers, and even if I find the bottle of sulfuric acid with his name on it that he used to melt her fucking feet off, or the rope he used to tie her wrists together, there will be nothing I can do about it since it will be too late. Pardon *my* English. So let's get past the blame game, shall we? And let's build a case that will send his sorry ass to death row.' She moved past him and on to the escalator.

Neither said anything until they were halfway down to the lobby. 'This is not the best way to start off a relationship,' he finally remarked.

'Nope. And neither was you showing up an hour late to my Arthur Hearing and giving me a fucking heart attack.'

'You gotta get over that.'

'Oh, and by the way, since we are being honest, you're going to need a new tie if we do go to trial or have a motion or even walk down the street together – preferably one that does not have miniature Miami Dolphin helmets on it. And you are definitely gonna need a new suit.'

Manny peered down at his jacket, his brow furrowed. 'What the fuck? Now I'm hurt.'

'You shouldn't be. You should be grateful for my candor. I sent a habitual offender away for twenty years who strong-armed the manager of a Men's Wearhouse on Biscayne. He said he gives discounts to law enforcement. Go see him. And the next prosecutor you get will thank me. I'll also warn her or him way in advance of your problem minding the clock. I will not sugar-coat it, as was done to me.'

Manny shook his head. 'Let me be honest now: Are you always this much of a bitch?'

She didn't blink. 'Yes. Particularly when I've almost been stood up and, unlike you, I haven't had my afternoon coffee. I didn't even have my morning coffee, since I was here at *seven*, busting my ass to help my new C get the morning calendar ready.'

'I'm gonna buy you a cup. We need to get you some caffeine and get past this – you know, discuss a game plan, focus our anger on the bad guy, because I need to like you again. I really do.' He looked down at her legs and bit his knuckle. 'Okay, it's coming back to me now.'

'Very funny. Don't be a pig. That sort of flattery will get you nowhere.'

He sighed loudly. 'Because I'm trying to make amends here, I'll make sure Raul makes you a fresh pot, 'cause he won't after three, but he will for me. That's how much I'm trying. I'm pulling out connections. I'll even throw in a *pastelito*.' He rubbed his stomach. 'Yum.'

'Don't ask for favors on my behalf.' She finally smiled a little. 'It is the least you could do.'

He rolled his eyes. 'As long as you pull your fangs in.'

They stepped on to the main floor and headed to the courthouse cafeteria. Across the all-but deserted lobby, a well-dressed woman stood by herself at the bank of elevators. When she spotted Manny and Daria she began to walk toward them. She looked to be in her forties, with ash-blonde hair that was coiffed into a long, edgy, layered cut that could only have been professionally styled that morning. Daria's eyes fell on the Hermès Birkin bag and then on the baubles – as in plural – that rested comfortably on several digits of her slim, tan hands. Tennis hands, no doubt. Miami had its share of wealthy inhabitants, but there was a noticeable difference between flashy South Florida spenders and their understated sisters to the north. Another Palm Beacher had crossed the county line.

'Uh-oh. This is gonna get interesting,' Manny remarked.

Before Daria could ask why, the woman was upon them.

'Excuse me, Ms DeBianchi,' she said, extending her hand only to Daria. She nodded coolly at Manny. 'Detective Alvarez.'

Manny nodded back.

'Ms DeBianchi, my name is Abby Lunders. I was watching you in court this afternoon, listening to what you were saying, and I need to speak with you right away . . .'

9

The resemblance was uncanny. And given Daria's all-too recent experience with the woman's seemingly psychopathic offspring, a little unnerving. Mom had the same rich, polished skin tone, full lips, high cheekbones, and heart-shaped chin. Like Talbot, a preternaturally striking person. And the same intense, light hazel eyes. Eyes that didn't merely see – they studied. With a perfectly smooth forehead and almost flawless, wrinkle-free skin, Abby Lunders probably spent a considerable amount of time in the plastic surgeon's office. And with super-toned arms and a slim waist a teenager would envy, no doubt the gym, as well. In the right lighting, she could pass for her son's sister, which was obviously the look she was aiming for.

'It came in my inbox last week. Friday. I've no idea who sent it. I don't normally open up mail from people I don't know, but given its title and what's happened with Talbot, I did. I just can't believe what's on there. I don't even know what I'm looking at exactly, but after being in court this afternoon and hearing all the things that you said, Detective, about the body and how you found that girl. I . . .' She hesitated. 'There are simply too many similarities.'

The three of them were across the street at the State Attorney's Office, sitting in Daria's third-floor cramped cubby of an office that overlooked both the courthouse and the Dade County Jail. 'Can we use your computer, Counselor?' Manny asked, holding up the USB flash drive that Abby Lunders had given him.

'Let me make sure we have a copy,' Daria said, taking the flash from Manny. The security debacle that had happened on the laptop wasn't far from her memory. 'I'll get Investigations to scan it,' she said as she stepped out of the room.

'Mr Varlack didn't want me to say anything,' Abby began after Daria had left. 'He wants to use this at trial. But I . . . I don't want to wait that long. I mean, if it's so obvious Talbot didn't do this horrible thing and that someone else is responsible – then he shouldn't have to wait in jail for five more minutes. Not in that sewer pit,' she said with a disgusted shudder, nodding behind Manny at the imposing nine-storied mass of gray concrete outside the window that was the Dade County Jail. 'And Mr Varlack says it could be months, possibly a year before the case goes to trial. That's insane. Absolutely insane! How could it take that long?'

Manny nodded, but said nothing. He'd seen murder cases languish on a judge's docket a lot longer than a year before a jury was finally sworn.

'Talbot's a good man. I know you don't believe that, I know you don't want to believe that, but he is. I heard what you said in there. He's never been in any trouble. He's smart, hard-working. He would never do the things you're accusing him of because, well, frankly, he doesn't have to. He doesn't need to drug a girl to get her to go home with him or have sex with him. Just look at him. When he was eighteen, he modeled on runways in Milan and Paris. He does not want for beautiful girlfriends.' She nodded at the case folder marked *State v. Lunders* that sat on Daria's desk. 'And I mean *really* stunning girls. No offense to the dead.'

Manny resisted the urge to roll his eyes. 'Let's not get ahead of ourselves, Mrs Lunders. Rape's not a crime of passion, and the fact that your son can easily bed attractive women doesn't move me. Let's take a look at what was sent to you.'

Daria walked in right then, flash in hand.

'Did you view it?' Manny asked.

'Not yet.' She popped the flash into her laptop.

'It's the only thing on there,' Abby quietly noted. 'That's a brand-new flash drive. All I did was copy the email and download the attachment.'

Daria's F drive showed only one file. It was an email titled 'LOOK AT ME' with an .mp4 share file attached. She clicked on it, immediately launching a video.

A young woman hung from a low-beamed ceiling in a black room by her wrists, which were tethered with a black cord to a ring secured above her. She was dressed in only a thin, see-through bra and panties, but the bra had been cut or opened from the front and her breasts were exposed. She dangled in the air, twisting around, the toes of her bare feet barely touching the polished cement floor, sweeping back and forth, like a broom.

Her head was bowed and her honey-blonde hair, stringy with sweat, completely covered her face. Because of the hair and the stocky, athletic body type and what she'd been found wearing, Daria at first thought it was Holly Skole. Then a black-gloved hand came into the shot and tucked the hair behind the girl's ear, exposing half her face to the camera and she could see it wasn't Holly. A pair of pantyhose had been stuffed into the girl's mouth and the nude legs of the hose were wrapped several times around her head and knotted at the nape of her neck. Behind her on a metal table were syringes, gauze, several bottles of different colored liquids, a half-full refill bottle of window cleaner, a bottle of Drano and black electrical tape. The camera jiggled and moved. It was obviously hand-held.

The girl looked up and her scared blue eyes grew large. A muffled whimper came out of the computer. That's when Daria realized there was sound with the video. The girl shook her head violently at something off camera and her eyes bulged and darted about. Her body jolted in the air, twisting, as if she were running a marathon in place.

But she couldn't get away. There was nowhere for her to go. The hand returned, and in it was a shiny pair of kitchen shears.

The video stopped and the screen froze. The final frame captured the girl's frantic face as the nude, muscular back of a white male, scissors in one hand, a long-stemmed red rose in the other, entered the shot. The entire clip had lasted less than a minute. On the far-right bottom of the screen were tiny red numbers: 29:12:14, and 11/07/06.

'Jesus,' Daria said as she sat back in her seat. 'What the hell was that?'

Manny frowned. 'Is that it? Is there more?'

'No. Just that clip,' Abby answered. 'Like I said, I didn't know what it was at first. I don't know that girl and, while I can't see his face, I don't think I know that man. "Why would someone send this to me?" I thought. But after today, after what I heard, I think I understand now. *This* is what happened to the Skole girl. *This* is what you described in the courtroom today, Detective. The Skole girl had been tied up, and she had been injected with drugs and she had been raped. Just like what seems to be happening to this girl on the video. And someone sends it to me? Obviously because they know that Talbot didn't do this.'

'Maybe that's your son in the video, ma'am,' Manny said, nodding at the screen. 'It looks like the same build. Maybe someone wants you to know that your son has done this before.'

Abby's voice rose. 'First of all, that makes no sense. Because why would they send it to me? Why wouldn't they send it to *you*? So you'd at least have some evidence to support your twisted, sick allegations.'

Daria nodded. 'Could be an extortion attempt.'

Abby frowned. 'Extortion? There was no demand for money. Doesn't there have to be a demand for money?'

'We can't be sure this is anything,' Daria continued. 'This could very well be homemade porn. Sure, it's hard-core, but there's no law against making home videos as long as they star consenting adults.'

'Give me a break, Ms DeBianchi,' retorted Abby. 'This

is not some Paris Hilton sex tape that was leaked to the public by the help. You saw that girl's face. Does she look like she's enjoying this? She's terrified and you and I both know it.'

Daria's eyes narrowed. 'You'd be amazed what people do when the shades are drawn, Mrs Lunders. And what fantasies they get off playing out while their camcorders are rolling. All I'm saying is that we can't be sure what this is and I'm not ready to jump to conclusions. Not even close. We don't know why it was sent to you, or who sent it, for that matter.'

'Say what you're thinking, why don't you? Come on – spit it out,' Abby snapped. '"*If* someone even sent it to you," is what you meant to say. What do you think I did? Do you think I surfed porn sites in search of a bizarre S&M video that I could pawn off as a copycat victim in a far-fetched attempt to exonerate my son? Please, check my computer. Do it. I implore you. Check my email. Do whatever you're supposed to do as officers sworn to uphold the law and investigate crime. Because, while I'm no detective, this seems to me to show someone committing the exact same crime my son is accused of – and I am certain that that is *not* my son in the video.'

'How's that, Mrs Lunders?' Manny asked.

'Besides the fact that I am his mother and I know his body like I know my own, including the very prominent freckled brown birthmark in the shape of a waving flag he has between his shoulder blades, which is missing from that animal in the video, there's also the time/date stamp on the bottom of the screen to consider. And on November seventh, 2006, my son was a patient at Good

Samaritan Hospital in Palm Beach having his appendix removed. So, no, that is not my son in that video. But I believe it is *your* job to find out who it is, and why someone would want to send it to *me*.'

10

'That's one helluva coincidence,' Daria remarked after Abby Lunders and her ostentatious, mouthwatering, elephant-gray crocodile Birkin bag had finally up and left her office.

'What?' Manny asked.

'Not only did somebody else kill the girl who was last seen leaving a bar with your son, but that somebody else is now sending you video clips of the real murderer having freaky sex with another girl who looks like the girl your son murdered? Am I missing something, or does that sound a little out there?'

'When you put it like that, it does.'

She frowned. 'Well, how would you put it?'

'I don't know. This lady's son is accused of rape and murder. Claims he didn't do it.'

Daria shook her head. 'They all claim they didn't do it. When was the last time you had a killer take full responsibility for slitting someone's throat? Give me a break.'

'True. But you asked for the lady's perspective. Her son says he didn't do it. Her only kid, mind you. Claims he's a victim of circumstance. Then she gets an anonymous email right before his bond hearing showing a lookalike blonde being what sure looks to me like tortured, and in the background are an assortment of syringes and chemicals – all the fucked-up goodies her son is accused of using on his victim. Except the person in the video is not her son.'

'So she says. And the girl in the video is not dead.'

Manny shrugged. 'Not that we know of.'

'How the hell old was she when she popped out sonny-boy? Eighteen? All that Botox makes her look like his freaking sister. It's weird.'

'Careful, Counselor. You sound jealous.'

'I am. Of her bag, not her face. I'm only twenty-nine. The wrinkles you're giving me won't show for a few years.'

Manny laughed.

'And how old is Dad Freddy?' Daria asked. 'Isn't he, what, twenty-three or -four years her senior? She must've been a trophy bride.'

'It's actually Stepdad Freddy. He's about sixty-seven. Looks it, too. Abby is a trophy bride, but she wasn't a teenager when she and Fred got hitched. She was thirty. Freddy adopted young Talbot and let him in on the family name. I think he gave him the Alastair as an adoption present so he would blend in more with the Kennedys and Rockefellers,' Manny said with a chuckle. He pulled a pack of Marlboros from his jacket pocket. 'I, for one, thinks she looks pretty damn good for any age,' he replied, taking a cigarette from the box and tapping it on her desk. 'Not that that's influencing my opinion.'

Daria frowned again. 'Don't light that in here.'

'I'm getting ready for when I leave.'

'Hmmm. Well, I'm still not seeing anything but a bunch of smoke from the flash-bang she just dropped, and you're walking right into the room.'

'Listen, I'm no sucker, but I am a little puzzled,' Manny replied, sticking the cigarette behind his ear. 'Aren't you? I mean, what the hell is this video about? That's pretty fucked up, Counselor.'

Daria sighed. 'Her own attorney didn't want to bring it up today, Manny, because he's saving it for *trial*. Because he knew it wasn't anything but smoke and he'd rather sandbag us with some highly prejudicial, totally inflammatory video *after* I've sworn in a jury and jeopardy has attached. It's all bullshit – they're setting up a reasonable doubt argument. The more attention you pay to it, the more that's going to doom us when we get in front of a jury because it looks like we bought into the bullshit, too. It makes us look like we think there's some validity to this.'

Manny nodded thoughtfully. He jingled the flash drive in his hand and stood to leave. 'Probably. But I'm gonna see what else the lab can get from this clip. Maybe they can up the sound or enhance the video. And I'm gonna check out Trophy Mom's computer, see if we can trace who sent it to her, or, even better, where the video originated from. I'm not a computer geek, but I know there's a lot those geeks can do – I watch *CSI*,' he added with a wink.

'You're walking right into this. You're buying their

'one-armed man" defense hook, line and sinker,' she charged. 'Let the defense spend their own time and money checking out the bullshit, please. Save the taxpayers of Miami.'

'Like I said before, for such a pretty little thing, you have a tremendous set of steel balls on you. They must make it difficult to walk sometimes. Let me ask ya, just for my own clarification here: What do you do when you got a case that you can't prove maybe, but you believe the victim was wronged? How do you handle those?'

'Sometimes you have to walk away, Manny, and go after the ones you can solve. It's not easy. And I don't mean to sound callous, but sometimes you have no choice but to tell someone, "There's no justice for you today. Sorry, Charlie."'

'That's cold.'

She shrugged. 'That's life. Your job is to find the bad guy. My job is to prove he did it. If I can't prove it, then there's no case. It's not a matter of right and wrong. And I don't go looking for cases that might help the defense. I have a lot on my plate.'

'Listen, Counselor, I'm gonna find out more before I walk away. I have to. If it's nothing, then it's nothing and all I did was waste a little time. And if it's homemade porn, then maybe I'll get lucky and get to meet the actress live and in person. But I'm personally gonna have a hard time sleeping, wondering whose terrified kid that is on that clip.'

'How many children do you have?' Daria asked. 'No, no, scratch that – how many daughters?'

'None and none. No little Mannys or Emanuelas running around. At least, none that I know of.'

96

Daria rolled her eyes. 'I would've pegged you for the dad of a harem of teenage daughters with that last comment.'

'I may not have kids myself, Counselor, but it doesn't take much to imagine what it would feel like if my daughter was raped and whacked by a psycho with a camera and a thing for household cleaners. Maybe the dad of the girl in that video has no idea what happened to his kid. Maybe she went out one night and never came home and he has no idea what became of her. Maybe her family's hoping she had a car accident and bumped her melon and has amnesia, and they wait for the day she walks back through their door.'

'She's a little old to be calling a kid. I'm thinking late twenties.'

'Okay, so she's not a kid. Then maybe she's married and her hubby has been scouring every waterway within a ten-mile radius of their house thinking she had a car accident and that's why she didn't come home for supper. Or maybe she's not dead. Maybe she was raped and her assault was caught on camera and the bastard uploaded it to YouTube. Those are just a few of the scenarios that popped into my head. You and I have had to deal with the families of enough murder victims to understand that not knowing is the worst. I don't have to be a dad or a husband to feel for them.'

'What if she left home at sixteen to earn a living as an adult entertainer in LA and this shit she does with her boyfriend is mild compared to the other tricks she can perform with a rope? I just thought of *that* scenario off the top of *my* head.'

Manny shrugged and moved to the door. 'It's a

forty-nine second clip, Counselor. Just imagine what we didn't see, what footage might've ended up on the cutting-room floor.'

'That works both ways, you know. It could be ten minutes of foreplay and cigarette smoking.'

'Could be.'

'Ugh.' She spun her chair around to face the jail. 'I'm not heartless. I'm being practical, is all.'

'Okay,' he answered, but he didn't sound convinced. He pulled the cigarette from behind his ear. 'I'll call you tomorrow after the grand jury, although I'm sure you'll be on the horn with Guy to find out how I did way before that.'

Daria waited until the door closed before she sank her head into her hands. She wanted to scream. She heard everyone saying hello to Manny as he made his way down the hall and finally out of the unit.

Talbot Lunders definitely had headline potential. If she didn't see that before, she did now. The rape and murder of a pretty college coed by a privileged, former male model was intriguing enough to attract interest, and without adding yet more salacious detail, could prove a difficult story to control. But throw in a mysterious, lurid email, a homemade bondage sex tape, a secret family hideaway in Switzerland and the distraught, well-dressed, hot, young socialite momma of the defendant alleging lookalike blondes were being hunted and tortured by a real killer who the police weren't bothering to look for, and you had the potential makings of a national news sensation. A savvy publicist would pitch it to the morning talk shows as 'the perfect story'. Daria thought it more akin to the perfect storm.

After five years prosecuting everything and anything from shoplifting to homicide, Daria knew that Sex Batt was where she wanted to be. And she didn't want to settle for being a line prosecutor – she wanted to lead the charge. As the cliché went, she'd paid her dues. She'd spent years in the pits prosecuting crappy cases and winning them, and for the past two years she'd been Division Chief of one of the most congested trial units in the office, supervising three felony attorneys and responsible for a court docket of more than four hundred felonies. The average ASA lasted three years on the state payroll before heading out to greener pastures; anyone who went past five was considered a lifer. And on the lifer scale, there were those bodies that stayed on simply to earn a paycheck and keep the benefits, working their eight-hour shifts from the trenches of the Felony Screening Unit, taking witness testimony and filing cases all day long, or buried under mounds of paperwork, tucked safely away in some dull, specialized unit on the fifth floor, like Economic Crimes.

Then there were the lifers who made a run at bigger and better things.

Daria fell into the latter group. While she'd never consciously decided to spend her entire legal career as a prosecutor, besides the possibility of moving to the feds, she'd never really had the itch to circulate her résumé. Once you'd put a rapist behind bars for thirty years, a slip and fall at the grocery store just didn't seem all that exciting. Neither did bankruptcy law, corporate litigation, insurance defense, or helping sound the death knell on people's marriages as a divorce attorney. A rabid fan of all cop and lawyer shows and everything FBI since she was a kid, Daria figured being a prosecutor was simply what she was meant to be. Unlike her older brothers – a hospital administrator and an eighth-grade science teacher – she'd never dreaded going to work in the morning. And God knew she'd never spent a single second bored in her job. On occasion sad, and a lot of times pissed off, but never bored. That didn't mean she wanted to stay an overworked, underpaid division pit prosecutor for the rest of her career, though.

To prove to Vance Collier and the rest of Administration that she was a lifer with a future, in addition to trying cases that a lot of other ASAs would've pled out, she'd worked weekends, volunteered for on-call robbery duty even when it wasn't her rotation, and handled holiday bond hearings without complaint. Coming in early and leaving late every day, watching jealously at times and scornfully at others while the support staff headed en masse for the elevators at 4:30 and most of her colleagues followed by 5:30. Some a helluva lot sooner. She'd made the requisite sacrifices: no boyfriend, no hobbies, no life, outside babysitting her brother's ADHD triplets on her first long weekend off since Christmas.

If it was only a simple murder case that she needed to win in order to prove herself capable of heading up a unit full of specialized prosecutors, she'd have no real worries. The case against Talbot Lunders was circumstantial, yes, but the evidence, in the collective, damning. As a law school professor had once described it, making a circumstantial case was a lot like making a strudel: while a single sheet of paper-thin filo dough couldn't support the weight of ten apples, if you capably assembled sheet upon delicate sheet, eventually you had a pastry with enough layers to support a whole bushel of fruit. The key was in the dogged construction, and, of course, in the oven you ultimately loaded your dessert into, which had to be brought to the perfect temperature before actually introducing the food, and that temperature had to be maintained throughout the whole baking process. The oven in the analogy, of course, referred to the jury – already plenty hot and fired up by the time you opened the oven door, ready to bake anything to a crisp the second you closed it. Too cool and nothing would gel. Considering Florida was a death penalty state – and, until a few years ago, the state's preferred method of execution was a seat in Old Sparky – her professor's analogy of a jury baking anything to a crisp was completely intentional. In other words, you had to pick the perfect twelve people – none of whom watched *CSI* or *NCIS* – set the right tone of outrage and shock, and by the time you slid your assembled facts through the door of that deliberation room, the only thing you had to wait for was the timer to ding.

Daria could handle that. She had a way with juries, almost like a sixth sense when she was picking them. She wasn't sweating a conviction on Lunders, even with Manny Alvarez playing Wild West cop and making what was, arguably, a premature arrest. Because with the facts as she had them down at the Arthur, she could certainly set that perfect tone of grab-the-pitchforks indignation in the jury room, and she had enough circumstantial layers that when put together would be strong enough to hold together a death penalty request. The gruesome crime-scene photos would certainly help fuel the fire. The competition she faced, though well paid, was out of their element in Miami. Joe Varlack was a showman with a big voice who likely hadn't personally tried a criminal case in a long while. She could eat both him and his sidekick Simmons for breakfast, complete with Louboutins and fancy briefcases. She was also confident she could keep Talbot Lunders's pretty face off at least the front page of the paper and maintain the low profile the State Attorney was trying for. It was a fair assumption that if the cameras weren't in court this afternoon the matter wasn't on their radar.

Unlike other ASAs who saw certain cases as a means to make a name for themselves outside of the office, Daria was no media hound. If Lunders didn't end up pleading out – like 90 percent of cases that passed through the system – when it came down to trying him, she wasn't going to do it on live TV and in the court of public opinion, which could fuck up any verdict, as O.J. Simpson's prosecutors could attest. She reasoned that as long as she didn't go looking for press, the press wouldn't come looking for her. Or Talbot Lunders. There were too many other headlines to chase. Too much other gory bad news going on worldwide for the people to revel in their morning cups of joe.

Unless . . .

Unless someone led the reporters and their boom mikes straight to a story that had everything the public at large wanted to read about in super-sized portions – perverted sex, brutal murder, and Birkin bag money. And kept harping on it until someone with a press badge finally paid attention.

Daria saw the train-wreck coming up ahead if Manny followed this breadcrumb trail laid by the defendant's

102

sniffling, sexy mother. It had been a decade since the serial killer Cupid had stalked his comely victims from happening 'it' clubs on Miami Beach, and yet his crimes still defined Miami to the world – as much as celebrities, yachts, teal water, and Cuban refugees did. Then there was Picasso, another monster who had hunted and killed young runaways in South Florida, commanding headlines and craziness a couple of years ago. And of course, the high-profile murder of Gianni Versace by a serial killer a few steps from the white sands of South Beach in 1997. Versace's murder and the ensuing week-long hunt for Andrew Cunnanan had spawned an international feeding frenzy that had lasted for months on end. Three relatively recent, bloody blemishes on the suntanned reputation of a cosmopolitan city that drew an outrageous number of tourist dollars to its golden beaches, beautiful hotels and happening nightlife. It wouldn't be good PR if news got out that not only was there yet another sadistic killer in the city, but speculation existed within law enforcement that that killer was still at large, trolling for victims at the hot spots that the tourists and their money loved to frequent, making chilling videos of his conquests.

She nibbled on a thumbnail, staring all the while out the window at the jail where Talbot Lunders was being held. She had a terrible habit of imagining the worst-case scenario of any situation and then multiplying it exponentially until she imagined herself right out of a job and facing eviction from her apartment for nonpayment of rent.

The truth was, if this case did become a circus like Cupid or Versace, or worse, a completely bungled O.J. Simpson that she couldn't control, she knew she'd never get Collier's seal of approval. And while that might not force her butt out on the streets, it certainly wouldn't put her in the running for Chief of Sex Batt, or any other unit for that matter. She'd be a pit prosecutor for ever. A lifer stuck in neutral. Like a Hollywood actress that only got one shot at the box office, she knew she had only one chance to get this right. That meant she had to retain control over *her* case and make sure that whatever Manny Alvarez was doing to allay the fears his own conscience was conjuring up, it didn't become public knowledge and it didn't interfere with *her* prosecution.

She checked her watch: almost eight. The day was gone and she still had a ton of shit to do. The sun was starting to set over the Everglades, casting the jail in an ethereal, tangerine glow. If you hadn't noticed the razor wire and barred windows, and you didn't know there were violent, depraved rapists and murderers being housed inside, from a distance, in this light, one might think the normally dingy, unimpressive jail building looked inviting. Like Dracula's castle about twenty minutes before sundown.

She was reaching for the top file in her inbox when the time bomb Manny Alvarez planted in her brain suddenly went off. A barrage of unanswerable questions cut through her stream of consciousness like shrapnel: *What if it did turn out to be more than a distracting, consensual sex-slave video that Abby Lunders had thrown at them? What if there actually was something to this crazy 'other killer' theory Momma Lunders was alleging? What then?*

104

She pulled a hand through her hair and took a deep breath.

There was no way her tired brain could even begin to wrap itself around the exponential multiplication of *that* worst-case scenario . . .

11

The grand jury deliberated for thirty minutes before unanimously voting to indict Talbot Lunders for capital murder. While the indictment itself might not have come as a surprise, the speed with which it was delivered did; Manny hadn't even made it back to his office when Guy Kuzak called him. He could only hope the rest of this case would move as expeditiously through the system, yet still he couldn't seem to shake the 'calm before the storm' feeling in his gut. Holly's murder had been a chest-thumper from the second her body was fished from the dumpster – starting with the sad demise of Papi Munoz. And if yesterday's meeting with Mami Lunders was any indicator, he should probably be running to the pharmacy to stock up on antacids.

He sat at his desk now, twisting his mustache, studying the still photo of Jane Doe he'd pulled from the video, searching for tattoos, birthmarks, discolorations – anything at all that might make her more readily identifiable in a

ViCAP entry than, 'blonde-haired, green-eyed, white female, approximate height between 5'2" and 5'6"; approximate age between twenty and thirty years'.

He was probably clutching at straws, trying to determine who this girl was. The overwhelming fact of the matter was that she could be anyone. And she could be from anywhere. He wasn't sure if he should start his search for her in Florida, or halfway across the globe in Greenland . . .

The numbers on missing persons were mind-numbing. Nationwide, almost a million people each year were reported missing to police – most of these were teens or young adults, like Jane Doe. That averaged to around 2,300 people, each and every day. And that *wasn't* accounting for the throwaways – the poor souls who nobody gave enough of a shit about to report them missing when they didn't make it home. He was no expert, but Manny had heard estimates as high as another million or so throwaways that never made it into a police report. That sad fact alone made the prospect of combing through a haystack of missing person reports not just daunting, but probably useless. And if those were the US figures, Manny couldn't begin to imagine what the global number of missing persons might be. Which was probably why he was sitting at his desk, hours after the grand jury, still pulling on his mustache and still staring at the same nasty photo, trying to come up with a game plan to find a girl who may or may not be missing, and/or who may or may not be the victim of a sexual assault, and/or who may or may not be a homicide victim.

Mike Dickerson planted half a droopy butt cheek on

the edge of his desk. He was munching on a bag of Cheetos. 'Watcha doing, Bear?' he asked, in between crunches. The air smelled like fake cheese and Old Spice. 'Your face is all twisted up. You look constipated.'

Manny groaned and stretched. 'Arrgh . . . I got a puzzle to solve here, Pops. Problem is, I only got one piece and I ain't got no idea what the picture on the box even looks like.'

'That don't sound good.'

'Nope, it don't.'

'Okay, now stop talking in Chinese riddles and tell me what the fucking problem is. Is that it?' Mike asked, nodding at the photo. 'Is that your puzzle piece?'

'Yup.'

'Nice. Perky tits; they look natural. Now, is this a case you're working or is that a girlfriend you need advice with?'

'You're a hoot. It's a case. I think. Not sure, actually. But it definitely ain't a girlfriend, you sick geezer.'

'I was gonna say she's way too pretty to be one of yours.'

'I ain't responding to that.'

'Who is she?' Mike asked with another crunch.

'That's the million-dollar question. The case I'm working, the dumpster case—'

'Holly Skole.'

Manny cocked an eyebrow.

'Just 'cause I'm over sixty don't mean I have Alzheimer's. I listen when you talk,' Mike shot back.

Manny shrugged. 'Okay. Well, the mom of my defendant in that case claims that someone anonymously sent her a fucked-up video clip right before the Arthur

Hearing. She don't know who and she don't know why. But in the video that I made this picture from, *this* girl is being strung up from the ceiling by her wrists like a pig in a slaughterhouse, and she might or might not be being tortured by an unidentifiable white male. The clip's under a minute long, so it's hard to tell what's really going on. Could be real, could be fantasy role-play. So I'm not sure what I have, Mikey. Not sure what to do about it, either. But it's not sitting right with me and I want to see if I can get an ID on Jane Doe. Only I'm not sure where to start.'

'Most guys would walk away. Let the defense handle it. Sounds like it's their problem anyways.'

'Yup. Most guys would.'

'Have you run her through ViCAP?'

ViCAP – the Violent Crime Apprehension Program – was the FBI's largest investigative repository of major violent cases in the US. A computer database of missing persons, unsolved sexual assaults and homicides, and unidentified remains collected from police agencies around the country. In a perfect world, Manny could put in the information he had on Jane Doe and ViCAP would spit out a similar missing person or homicide victim in an unsolved case. But the world wasn't perfect. The system was only as comprehensive as the information put into it, and not every police agency was diligent providing cases for ViCAP. Most small agencies didn't have access and a lot of large agencies weren't assiduous about doing it.

'Yeah. I checked,' Manny replied. 'Didn't see anything that matched up, but I don't got much to go on here. I also looked at Broward County's Found and Forgotten website, but came up empty there, too. I'm trying to think of my next move.'

'Let me see that. You mind? And can I see the video?' Mike asked.

Manny nodded, handed him the picture, and got up from his seat. 'Help yourself. When did you figure out how to turn on a computer?'

Mike ignored the jab and moved into Manny's chair. He watched the entire clip through three times without saying a word, then ran it a fourth time and paused at forty-one seconds in, studying the screen. 'That window cleaner there . . . it's a knock-off.' He captured the shot and zoomed in on the far corner. 'I thought so,' he said, mumbling under his breath. 'I thought so. That there's the Shoprite logo. On the red part – doesn't that look like a grocery cart to you?'

'Could be,' Manny said, studying the screen. 'What's Shoprite?'

'Shoprite's a supermarket chain up north. New York, Jersey, Connecticut. I'm not sure it's around anymore, but that's where you need to focus, Alvarez. Have the boys in Tech see if they can enhance that picture – I'd bet my bottom dollar that's Shoprite. Been a while since I saw that brand. They used to have some crazy commercial about how Shoprite's got the can-can sale, with a bunch of French dancers singing about stocking up on peas.'

'I thought you were from the Midwest.'

'Ahhh,' Mike grumbled. 'I'm a native New Yorker, Alvarez. Born and raised in Elmhurst. That's in Queens, you know. I worked with the Minneapolis PD for eight years before coming down here for some sun.'

'Minnesota? Jesus, how the hell did you end up there? How does anyone end up there?'

Mike ignored the question. 'One day it will all become clear. Listen, sorry about the titty comment. I didn't realize she was a victim. That was bad of me.'

'Well, thanks for the tip,' Manny said with a nod.

'What I would do if I was you is put her in NCIC, and mark it special attention to the tri-state area – see if the boys up there got something for you. Send the picture, but let them know there's a video available.'

'That's a good idea.'

'Your long shot ain't so long now,' Mike continued smugly. 'And you got a date/time stamp on this, for whatever that's worth, assuming it's authentic. I'd put that on there, too. It'll help whoever is looking narrow down dates. I'd also send that video off to the Behavioral Analysis Unit at the FBI. Let the profilers take a peek. Could be they've seen the rest of your video. Or maybe they can tell you if it's for shits and giggles or if it's the real McCoy.'

'Okay, okay, I got it. Now it's your turn to speak English, Pops. What the hell is a "shit and giggle"? And what's a "real McCoy"?'

Mike rolled his eyes. 'Damn immigrants. Learn English.'

'I left Havana on a twenty-two-foot fishing boat that was missing an engine with twenty other people when I was five. Been speaking English from the second I stepped on the sand at Key Biscayne. You're yapping in old fart, not English. I'll send it to BAU. You're right. It can't hurt none.'

'Nope. It can't hurt,' Mike replied as he started across

111

the room to his desk. Then he stopped, turned abruptly, walked back. 'You know, I can work up that NCIC for ya. Maybe contact the cold case squads myself and see if I can shake some trees.'

'You're not busy with your own load?'

'Nah. I'm good. I got the time. And it looks like you need the help.'

Mike Dickerson wasn't the only one counting down days till his retirement party. Even though he still had about six months to go, Mike hadn't caught a new case in a long while, and he wasn't going to. He was in wind-down mode. The squad sergeant didn't want to hand out new cases to someone who'd have to be dragged out of retirement to be a witness for the next five years as those cases worked their way through the system. It was too much of a hassle. And if Mike was the lead on a case and he died – well, that would be terrible. And even more of a hassle. That was the danger of working cases when you were nearing seventy – your age became a liability and all that 'invaluable experience' that used to look so great on a résumé now added to the argument that your shelf life had expired. Until he officially called it quits, Mike was on 'light duty', which might seem like every government employee's dream, but Manny didn't think Mike saw it that way. The guy had been on the job for almost four decades, and he wore his pride the way he did his badge – right in the open for all to see. It might be hard to walk away, but Manny thought it was probably worse to stay and watch the world carry on without you.

Manny ran a hand over his smooth scalp. 'You think you can help me out?' he asked hesitantly. 'You know, this video is a fucking monkey wrench. I still have a shitload of crap to get done on Skole without this nipping at the back of my thoughts.'

'Sure, Bear, sure. I know some faces in the NYPD. It'll give me something to do.'

Manny nodded. Partnering up in Homicide was not done at the City. There weren't enough bodies or enough resources. And that was fine by him – he didn't like partners. And if he had to pick a partner, it never in a million years would've been ornery, stubborn, conventional, conservative Mike Dickerson. But Manny himself was only seven years away from collecting a check, which seemed like a lifetime . . . a lifetime ago. Now it wasn't so far off. Just seven more wild Miami-Dade PD Homicide Christmas parties. So he could feel for the old man; he didn't think he'd want to leave when the time came, either. Plus, being nice to a guy on his way out of the job and maybe even out the door seemed like the right thing to do. Of course it was exactly that sort of charitable thinking that had led him down the aisle three times. Manny had a feeling this partnership might not fare any better . . .

'I guess it's time for this young, handsome Jedi to learn from the master,' Manny said, handing his new partner the photo and the flash drive with a sigh. 'Go shake a tree. Damn, you know, you even look like Yoda. Same football-shaped head.'

'Oh you're a gag, is right. You're a fucking chuckle,' Mike groused as he returned to his desk. 'Shits and giggles we're gonna have together,' he called over his shoulder.

Manny sighed again. As a wise man whose name he did not know once said: no good deed ever goes unpunished . . .

12

'On for arraignment, page two: *State v. Talbot Lunders*,' announced the clerk.

It was half past nine on a Monday morning and Judge Virginia 'Ginny' Becker's small, sixth-floor courtroom was standing-room only. Thanks to a heat wave outside and temperamental courthouse air conditioning that wasn't quite broken but definitely wasn't working, the air was thick and stale and stunk and tasted of BO. People charged with felonies were already tense and sweaty, as were their lawyers, who ran from courtroom to courtroom handling multiple clients. The broken AC made the room feel like a rush-hour NYC subway train in July.

'Ms DeBianchi, is this one yours?' asked the judge impatiently, over the loud hum of the standing fan next to her bench.

'Yes, Your Honor,' Daria answered, as she made her way up to the podium.

'Joe Varlack for Talbot Lunders.' Justice Joe was back

at the podium, refreshed and determined. A little too determined. As if he'd spent the weekend reading West's Florida Criminal Procedure. Daria hadn't spoken to either attorney since last week's Arthur, but based on the cool looks he kept throwing her way, and the inability of his colleague to glance up from her file, she didn't think a cordial relationship was gonna develop between the three of them. Some defense attorneys were like that – they took the adversarial process too literally and too personally. That was okay with Daria. She didn't need any more friends. She checked out Anne-Claire Simmons's tootsies and bit a knuckle. The distinctive red soles were gone, but the nude, platform, suede peep-toes were to die for.

'I see Judge Steyn denied bond last week,' the judge remarked as she read through the indictment.

'We'll be revisiting that, Your Honor,' replied Varlack authoritatively.

'No we won't,' replied the judge without glancing up. 'Unless you have some new evidence that was not known to you last Tuesday and as such was not presented to Judge Steyn – and I do mean new – there is no need for another hearing. This is not the Swap Shop. Your client will remain remanded.'

Ginny Becker was a relative newcomer to the courthouse, having been appointed by the governor last year to fill a vacancy in circuit court. In her early forties, she was a spring chicken compared to some judges who haunted the bench until they died off. On paper, the woman was certainly qualified to be a criminal court judge – having worked as both a prosecutor up in her native New Jersey and a public defender in Tampa – but the jury was still out on whether she was actually a good judge. That was because no one liked her. Known as 'the Manicured Monster', in her nine months on the bench, Judge Becker had managed to alienate everyone, even her own support staff, and had earned a reputation on both sides of the courtroom for ruling with an iron fist and a sharp tongue.

'Mr Lunders,' the judge began in a nasally Jersey twang. She peered down at the defense table over red-rimmed specs that sat precariously on the end of her nose. 'You've been indicted by the grand jury on the charge of first-degree murder. How do you plead?'

'Not guilty,' bellowed Varlack. 'We'll be demanding discovery.'

'Naturally,' replied the judge, studying Lunders's defense attorney for a long moment. 'State, fifteen days.' She looked around her courtroom. 'You seem to be quite the popular one, Mr Lunders. Are these cameras here for your pretty face?'

Daria turned around so fast she almost got whiplash. Sure enough, two cameramen stood behind the gallery gate, each sporting shoulder-mount professional television cameras. One was for WSVN7 and the other was WTVJ, NBC6. An impressed murmur ran through the gallery. They hadn't been there when she'd first walked in.

'That seems to be the case, Judge,' Varlack replied a little too casually, which told Daria he was the one who had invited the vampires in for a pint.

'How far out are we talking on a trial date, State?' the judge asked.

'I'd say at least six months, Your Honor,' Daria replied.

'I hope the prosecutor's not serious, Judge,' scoffed

Varlack. He sounded completely flabbergasted, as if he was expecting a trial, say, next week. 'My client has been denied bond, which you're telling me won't be reviewed. Now State's saying it will take them at least six months to get around to trying him?'

'Well, the ball is in your court to some extent, Mr . . .' the judge hesitated for a moment, 'Varlack,' she finished, finally finding his name again on the court file. Obviously she had no idea who he was and, even if she did, she wouldn't have cared anyway. She must've been fighting traffic in Trenton when he was in every South Floridian's living room at six. 'You can file a speedy demand and Ms DeBianchi can give you the Jiffy Lube of trials this upcoming fall, if you want. You may find, however, that you need a little more time to prepare for a capital murder, sir. State, will you be seeking the death penalty?'

'It's under consideration, Your Honor,' replied Daria.

'Well, consider faster. Because I think that decision might just change opposing counsel's request to try this case before I dust off my Christmas decorations. Mr Lunders,' she began, looking straight at the defendant and speaking in a loud, slow voice, as if he were either deaf or mentally retarded. 'You have a right to a speedy trial. That means the state has to bring you to trial within one hundred and seventy-five days after your arrest. That is assuming you don't cause a delay yourself. Because once you ask for a continuance or announce that you're not ready to proceed or otherwise engage in activity that delays the state in presenting their case against you, the hundred and seventy-five days disappears like Cinderella's magic coach. Poof. Do you understand that, Mr Lunders?'

'Yes,' answered the defendant. Even his voice was handsome. Deep and throaty, like a sexy sports announcer. It was the first time Daria had heard him utter a word. He was dressed in that same bright orange jumpsuit, but he definitely looked better. His hair was brushed and pulled into a low pony that matched his attorney's and he was clean-shaven. He glanced in her direction and smiled. She felt the blood rush to her face.

'I have already explained his rights to him, Judge,' Varlack replied testily.

The judge sat back in her chair. 'Good. I'm really glad you have. And just so that you understand, Counsel, it is *my* business to make sure that the defendant knows his rights and understands them in *my* courtroom. Being a successful former defense attorney myself, I have found that sometimes either your clients don't hear you or they don't want to hear you on some very important matters. Since *you* raised a concern about trying this case quickly, it's good to get this all on the record now so that it does not become an issue later, say in a post-conviction motion for relief. Not that I am predicting a conviction, mind you, I'm simply making sure your client is informed. So, with all that in mind, Althea, get me a report date within the next two months so we can see how fast the case is progressing. If Mr Lunders is still on track for a holiday trial and wants to file a speedy demand, then we will give him an early Christmas present and everyone will be happy. Everyone except perhaps Ms DeBianchi, who will be far too busy to be happy.'

'Mmm . . .' the clerk murmured while fanning herself with a manila folder. 'We don't get many happy customers around here, Judge. August seventeenth for report.'

'Thank you for the unsolicited commentary, Althea. I'll see you all back here then, unless we need to handle matters sooner than that. Ms DeBianchi, if you do decide to seek the death penalty, file your notice post-haste. I am sensing timing issues and I don't want to sit here listening to either side boo-hoo to me later on a capital murder, because I won't have any pity for your plight and I won't be distracted by your tears. If Mr Lunders truly wants a speedy trial, we can and will accommodate him, and not with ten minutes left to spare on the clock.'

'Yes, Your Honor,' Daria replied quietly, swallowing the lump that had formed in her throat. The average murder took anywhere from thirteen to eighteen months to make it to trial. If she did decide to seek the death penalty, the judge was right, pushing this to go within the next few months meant that would be *all* she would be doing for the next few months. Ugh. No cruise to Mexico. There went the first summer vacation she'd booked in four years . . .

As Althea called up the next case, Daria gathered her file and stepped back to the state's table, watching as Justice Joe was followed out of the courtroom like the Pied Piper by the reporters and their cameramen. *Double damn.* It was obviously Varlack's firm who'd called in the press. So much for thinking the Palm Beach Lunders would want to keep Junior off the front page and out of the gossip columns. And while it was only local media showing an interest, you never knew how big a story could become. What might catch the public's fancy. With online news outlets, blogging, tweeting, YouTube,

Facebook – everyone was on the hunt for the next big crime story, wanting to comment on it, be involved somehow. And since you never knew what might ignite that passion or curiosity, Daria knew it could very well be *this* case. The case she'd promised Vance Collier she would keep out of the press.

She dabbed her upper lip with a crumpled tissue she'd found in her suit pocket. She was sweating now, but it wasn't the heat that was getting to her.

13

'I can't tell if he's bluffing, but it looks like Justice Joe will be demanding a speedy trial. And even if he doesn't file a demand, the Manicured Monster has a stick up her butt now and is making me prep like he is.' Daria ripped off the last bit of stubborn thumbnail cuticle with her teeth. She immediately wished she hadn't. Not only did it sting like a bitch, but bright-red blood began to seep from under the nail bed and run down her thumb in the general direction of her white silk blouse. She stuck the whole finger in the cold remains of yesterday's McCafe mocha latte that sat in her cup holder. 'I'm gonna have to eat the damn deposit on my cruise, I just know it. Your depo's a week from next Monday.'

Manny pulled the cell phone away from his ear, studied the number again and yawned. He sat up on his couch. 'Counselor? That you?' Rufus, his 90-pound Belgian Malinois, sat up at attention next to him, looked around and barked one, single, thundering, 'Woof!' before lying down again and going right back to sleep.

'Of course it's me,' Daria replied, looking quizzically at her dashboard, which had just barked at her. She sucked the latte from her thumb. 'Who else would it be?'

'Most people start a telephone conversation with "hello".'

She sighed. 'Hello. What was that sound?'

'That was Rufus. He's my dog and you woke him up.' Manny looked at the end of the couch, where Rufus had rolled over, all four paws in the air, eyes in the back of his head, sawing wood like a lumberjack. He knocked him playfully in the head, but the dog didn't budge. 'For a second there, anyways.'

'Great guard dog you got, Detective.'

'He's a former bomb squad K-9. He has narcolepsy, I think. Really enjoys his retirement here at the Daisy Hill Puppy Farm. Until my phone rings and wakes him from his slumber. Then he's mean as a bull.'

'I don't feel bad that I woke up your dog, Manny. Your depo is a week from freaking Monday. I just got notice.'

'You just got notice at . . .' He peered at the clock in the kitchen. 'Jesus, is it eleven-thirty? Are you still at the office?'

'I was. I'm almost home.'

He yawned again. 'What are you, OCD? Or maybe you really are a vampire. I thought I saw fangs . . .'

'Funny. Don't mess with me, Detective. I need you there at ten.'

'Here we go,' Manny said with a chuckle. 'You really mean twelve.'

'Aargh. No, I really mean ten. Tell me you have something more for me on this. Please.'

He turned down the volume on ESPN and tried not to watch the scores. 'You sound desperate. Didn't you just arraign the bastard?'

'Yes, and I repeat, your depo is in less than two weeks,' Daria replied with a frustrated sigh. 'Be forewarned: this is gonna go fast.'

'What were you saying about a cruise?'

'To Mexico,' she answered with a whimper. 'First vacation in four years and I'm not gonna be able to go. And I gotta eat the deposit, which really hurts. You do know how much I make, don't you? Or how much I don't make.'

'You don't wanna go to Mexico, Counselor. Don't you read the papers?'

'The cartels aren't killing off the cruise ship tourists. Just the locals. I would've been fine. Tan and relaxed. Drinking piña coladas poolside.'

'When's this cruise?'

'Last week in August.'

'Right in the middle of hurricane season,' Manny said with a laugh. 'Hope you got a hell of a deal, Counselor. Now don't start bawling; maybe Lunders won't file a speedy demand. Better yet, maybe this will all work out by then.'

'For that to happen, Manny, we need more evidence. More. Big. Something to smack him in the face with and get him to plea. Anything on the fibers?'

Manny stood up and walked to the fridge. He opened it up and started to poke through it. It was time for a sandwich. 'Well, it must be your lucky day. Or night. 'Cause I do have some interesting news for you. I've been doing some research and guess what I found?'

'I can't imagine. Talbot Lunders's sperm plastered all over the inside of that dumpster.'

'Twisted. No. But I repeat, I did find out something pretty interesting. Remember you asked where our boy might've gotten sulfuric acid from?'

She held her breath. 'Tell me you have a receipt.'

He grabbed the mayo, bread, ham and cheese and carried them to the counter. 'Guess what's an ingredient in detergent?'

'Nuh-uh.'

'Sulfuric acid,' he said smugly, as he began to assemble his sub. 'Who would've thunk it? And guess what company has a lab in the Acreage in West Palm that is testing a new line of laundry detergents?'

'Flower & Honey?' she asked excitedly.

'Yes. Actually it's a subsidiary company of Flower & Honey, because laundry detergent is far from all natural ingredients like flowers and honey. In fact, detergent is synthetic soap made with crude oil, believe it or not. Think about that the next time you snuggle up in a freshly laundered sweater. The name of the subsidiary is PowerX. And it is overseen by none other than our boy, Talbot, who signed off on the shipments of sulfuric acid himself.'

'Nice. Now why didn't you call me with this info, Detective?'

'Because, unlike you, I have a life outside of the office. I was gonna call you in the morning. At a normal hour,' Manny replied, sneaking a look at the TV while licking the extra mayo off his finger. He wished he hadn't. The Marlins had lost again.

'Great. Send me a copy of all the receipts with his

signature. Is there any way to chemically tell one bottle of sulfuric acid from another?' she asked hopefully.

'Nice try, Counselor, but no. We can't match up PowerX sulfuric acid with the shit that we took off Holly Skole's calluses.'

She sighed. 'Just a thought.'

He couldn't wait anymore. It looked too good. He took a big bite. 'I do have other news that you might find interesting,' he said as he chomped.

'I knew you were holding back. Are you eating right now?'

'Yep. It's about midnight, and time for a midnight snack.' He took another bite, swallowed hard and finished his thought. 'Well, you didn't seem so thrilled that I was sending in that video clip to the lab or that I was checking out Abby Lunders's computer.'

'Ugh. No,' Daria replied. 'Don't go waking sleeping dogs, Manny. No pun intended. You're only gonna make the defense's case for them.'

He took another bite. 'That's why I didn't call you.'

'All right. Don't sulk,' she said. 'Out with it. Now that you've gone and done it. Was there also a video on Mom's computer of Sonny Boy knocking boots with our victim before he killed her? Or better yet, was there a video on Mom's computer of Sonny Boy knocking *off* our victim? Swallow this time before you answer, please.'

He did. 'No and no. But that's what's so interesting, Counselor. The boys went over her computer with a fine-toothed comb, trying to figure out who sent her that fucked-up video, you know? And the really weird thing was they found nothing.'

'What do you mean?'

'I mean nothing,' Manny replied. 'As in it was the cleanest computer they'd ever seen. No connectivity history, no old files, no old emails. It was like she'd just freaking purchased the computer and hadn't put anything on it yet, run any programs, gone to any websites. Either that or Hot Mami Lunders had wiped the hard drive clean with the equivalent of computer bleach before she gave it to us to examine. Now why would she have done that?'

'I never liked her. I want that on the record. Stop calling her hot mami, Manny; it's giving me an inferiority complex. I can't compete with that kind of cash.'

Manny finished off the rest of his sandwich. 'It's not her money that makes her hot.'

'Great. So she's a freak of motherly nature and has a squeaky-clean computer and an affection for her son that I find odd. Anything else, or can we move on from the amateur sex tape?'

'Not just yet, Counselor. There is something else about the video that we found. Are you sitting?'

'What kind of question is that? I'm driving.'

Time for dessert. He whapped the top of a fresh pack of Marlboros on the counter. 'The boys at the lab enhanced the video. There's a bottle of window cleaner in the background of the shot which we think may lead us to at least a region where the video was made.'

'Okay,' she said slowly.

He pulled out a cancer stick and lit it, stepping outside on to his front porch. 'When they enhanced the still of the window cleaner they found something pretty weird, Counselor. Something that got caught in the reflection of the blue liquid.'

126

'What? The face of the guy who tied her up? What would they call him in S&M terms?' she said with a slight chuckle. 'The master? The dominatrix? Do they have male dominatrices?'

'Not a face, Counselor. Faces.'

The hairs on the back of her neck rose. 'What?'

'Caught in the reflection was what looks like a set of TV monitors, all lined up next to each other. And I'm not talking the answer board on *Jeopardy*. The monitors, they each had faces in them. And it sure looks to me like they were watching what was happening to the poor girl . . .'

14

Manny threw back his coffee in one gulp, tossed the plastic shot cup into the trash and nodded at the Cubano on the other side of the walk-up window at Little Havana's landmark Versailles restaurant. Next to him a cluster of old Cuban men heatedly prattled on in Spanish about the politics of an island they hadn't been on in decades, while a couple of obvious tourists hesitantly approached the window, looking at the menu quizzically, hoping to see something that remotely resembled a Starbucks frappuccino. His cell phone buzzed to life in his pocket. 'Alvarez,' he answered, wiping his chin as he started across the parking lot. He could already feel the double shot of caffeine coursing through his system and it finally put a smile on his face. He'd responded to a domestic murder-suicide last night and had been up and out since 3:15.

'Detective Alvarez, this is Detective Wayne Schrader of the Nassau County Police Department. I work Special

Investigations. I've got your NCIC alert here in front of me.'

Manny stopped walking. 'NCIC alert?'

'Yeah, on that Jane Doe in the picture you sent me.'

Jane Doe . . . The Holly Skole murder case. The switch flipped. 'Oh yeah, yeah. Sorry, I'm just working on something else,' Manny said, scratching at his head. 'Lost my brain for a sec. Detective Schrader, huh? You got something for me on that?'

'Yeah, I do. I think I have an ID on your Jane Doe. 'Cept she ain't missing – she's dead. I'm working a cold case homicide. No suspects, no witnesses. The body of a female – blonde, mid-to-late twenties – was found in November of '06 by some highschoolers skipping class to drink a six-pack out by a condominium dig in Westbury, right at the Garden City line. I don't know if you're familiar with Long Island at all.'

'Sorry, I'm not.'

'Well, it's about thirty minutes outside Manhattan by train. The place where this girl's body was recovered is where they used to have a big racing track. Now it's condos and a Home Depot. Back in '06, though, it was a construction zone. Detectives figured one of two things when they found her. Either, one, whoever killed her was hoping she'd be buried like Jimmy Hoffa under all that construction and debris, or, two, he wanted her to be found by the construction crews. Either way, she was only in the ditch for a few hours. Because of that, Homicide thought they'd be able to nab a suspect, but in the end, no one saw nothing.'

'Are you sure it's my girl?'

'Like I said, she was only dead a few hours and it was cold out – there was frost on the ground at the time – so she was in real good shape, considering what was done to her. She looks exactly like the picture you sent me.'

'Whatta ya mean what was done – wait . . . let's give her a name,' Manny said as he resumed walking. 'Does she have a name? Who was this girl?'

'Name's Gabriella Vechio. Also went by the nickname Gabby. She was last seen out with friends at a bar named Jezebels in the Village – that's Greenwich Village in Manhattan, in case you're not familiar with the city – five days before her body was found. She was a day or so shy of her twenty-ninth birthday when she disappeared.'

'And she was found on Long Island?' Manny knew New York City well enough to know that Long Island was a bit of a hoof from Manhattan.

'Normally she took the subway to work but that day she drove in. Had to drop off some shit for charity or something. Her car was found untouched in a lot in Midtown.'

'You said before, "considering what was done" – what happened to her?' Manny thought of the faces on the monitors caught in the blue window cleaner, watching.

'She was raped, maybe with objects. It was pretty nasty.'

'Cause of death?'

'Strangulation.'

Manny blew out a long breath. 'Let me ask ya, was there any evidence of torture?'

'Not sure what you mean. Hard to tell,' Detective

Schrader replied. 'She did have what could've been bind marks on her wrists. But without knowing the circumstances of how she got 'em, I can't say for sure she was tortured. I'd have to check with the ME on that, see if he's got an opinion. Hard to tell if the night started out with consensual, maybe rough, sex that went bad. People are into a lot of stuff nowadays. I try not to judge,' he added with a chuckle.

'Any chemicals?' Manny asked as he reached his Grand Prix. He leaned against the rear bumper. It was another scorcher today – 97, 98 degrees. Could reach 100, the weatherman had said last night. And the humidity was God-awful. Across the parking lot and next to the dumpster and kitchen entrance to Versailles, two boys about ten, twelve years old, were trying to fry an egg on a metal stool. Probably the kids of the workers inside. School had just let out this week for the summer and they were most likely bored out of their melons, doing stupid egg-frying experiments, magnifying bugs and setting off fireworks in bottles. Next summer they'd be smoking grass and feeling up their middle-school girlfriends behind that same dumpster. It reminded Manny of the endless summer days he'd squandered playing Little League ball and hanging at his uncle's garage in Hialeah, stashing away any worries for when he was all grown-up.

'You mean, was she using? Nah, she was an accountant,' Schrader replied. 'No evidence of that.'

'I mean in her blood. Was she doped up? Did the guy dope her? Shoot her with any weird household cleaners or anything?'

'Is that what you got going on down where you're

at?' the detective asked as he leafed through his case file. 'Not that I can see here. I don't think the ME looked, to be honest, because he won't look for some toxins unless we have a reason to go looking. I know he ain't looking for Clorox if no one tells him to.'

Manny lit a cigarette. In the humid air, the plume of smoke he exhaled hung around his head like a dust cloud. 'Can I get the crime-scene photos and the police reports sent down to me? Are your detectives who investigated still on the job?'

'Sure. I'll scan the photos and the reports and send 'em right now. If you need actual prints, I can do that, too. I'll also send the ME's report along. And yeah, Rick Narbi is still here, so you can talk to him if you need to. Now it's my turn to ask questions. First one is, can I get a copy of that video you referred to in the NCIC alert? Second, how'd you come to possess this video and this picture? Is this related to a case you're working? Do you have a suspect? 'Cause it would be great to close this one out up here.'

'It's related, but I'm not sure how. I got a defendant charged with murdering a college girl. His mom approached me with this video, claims someone anonymously emailed it to her. Initially, I wasn't sure what I was looking at—' Manny cut himself off. Now it was pretty clear what he'd been looking at over and over and over again. It was a clip – a trailer – of Gabriella Vechio's murder. A snuff video made just hours, maybe even minutes, before the girl got raped and whacked on camera. 'You gotta see it, that's all,' he finished, taking a final, long drag on his cigarette.

After exchanging emails, Manny hung up and got in

his car. He sat there for a few minutes, staring out the windshield on to busy 8th Street. Gray-haired, umbrella-toting *abuelas* making their way to their apartments, pushing metal handcarts from which hung grocery bags from the Presidente supermarket; hot *mamis* in tight pants and three-inch heels pushing babies in folding strollers; men in business suits scrambling back to their offices and cars after stopping off, like Manny had, for an afternoon pick-me-up. The two boys must have been successful in their attempt to make breakfast, because they were high-fiving each other as well as an old man who was standing there watching, puffing on a cigar and grinning with the one or two teeth he still had left in his head.

While he was happy to have gotten an ID on his Jane Doe and to have gotten it only a couple of weeks after putting Dickerson on the job, he was worried about what this other homicide was going to mean for the case he was trying to make against Talbot Lunders. Finally finding the answer to the question that'd bugged him ever since he'd watched that sick video had only spawned a half-dozen more questions: *Was the Vechio murder related to the Skole murder? If so, how? Could he possibly have the wrong person in custody? Or could there be another mope involved in Holly's murder? A partner, perhaps?*

He wasn't gonna get answers sitting in his car, digesting coffee and *croquetas* and reminiscing about sweltering after-noons gone by when catching baseballs and hanging with pals was the only thing he had to do all day long. He headed back to the office, his mind racing from the caffeine and the adrenaline rush. Detective Schrader's email was waiting for him in his inbox. He opened the attachment marked **Vechio Crime Scene, Raceway: 11/10/06** first. A thumbnail-sized photo montage popped up on the screen. Manny clicked through the gruesome pictures one by one. Something kept gnawing at him.

Then he clicked on the second attachment: **D. Vechio Autopsy: NC07-9876. 11/11/06.**

The thumbnail pictures of Gabriella Vechio's autopsy popped up on the screen.

Manny sat back in his chair, with his hand over his mouth. The puzzle pieces were coming together now. The terrifying picture was almost complete.

15

The body of what was once probably a pretty blonde woman lay crumpled on her side in a dirt pit. From the looks of it, someone had tossed some landfill on the body, but not enough to have done a good job hiding her – her pallid, white skin glowed under the sprinkle of earth like a night-light under a thin blanket. Maybe Gabby Vechio's killer had run out of time when he dumped her and hoped that the cranes and bulldozers would finish the job. Or perhaps, as Detective Schrader had suggested, whoever had strangled her was actually hoping someone would find the body when they showed up on site in the morning for work.

The crime-scene photographers had taken close-ups of all visible injuries while the body lay in its shallow grave: bruises on the wrists; choke marks on the throat; and, what appeared to be flogging lacerations on the buttocks and thighs. But it must not have been until the body was transported to the Nassau County ME that her other injuries were discovered.

In the series of autopsy photos, Gabby's nude body was positioned face down on a steel gurney with her long blonde hair pushed up atop her head, exposing the back of her neck for the camera. Right below the hairline in the shape of a circle was a raw, dark crimson burn – measuring 1¾ inches in diameter, per the ruler held up alongside it. Enclosed in the circle was a squiggly line that resembled the letter 'Z'.

Manny whipped out the autopsy photos of Holly Skole from his file. The physical resemblance between the two women was chilling. He wondered why he really hadn't seen that until now.

Sometimes people just don't see what they don't want to see.

He found the close-up photo of Holly's neck wound and held it up alongside the computer screen. To his eye, it was the same injury – a circle with a distorted zigzag through it, seared into the flesh of both girls' necks.

Both women had been branded.

In Gabby's instance, the skin was red and raw, but the flesh intact. It appeared that the branding had been done with a hot metal instrument pressed for a few seconds on the skin, causing a nasty third-degree burn. Had she lived, scar tissue would've formed and built up and the wound would've been raised into a three-dimensional scar, like a cattle brand. But with Holly, the metal was left long enough on the skin so that it had actually seared through flesh and muscle, almost to the bone, like a hot knife through butter, severely damaging all the surrounding tissue. When her body was placed in the dumpster, dinner was served for the zillion insects, rodents, and raccoons that liked to hang out in dark garbage bins. By the time

Holly was removed from the dumpster, blowfly maggots had already made a comfortable home in the gaping wound, along with God knows what other vermin that'd come to chow. It had been difficult at the time to see the injury for what it was.

But Manny saw it now. And there was no denying that the two murders were in fact related. The killer had left his unique signature on both women.

He sat back in his chair and stared off at the squad-room corkboard with its missing persons, wanted suspects, NCIC/FCIC alerts. Every day an analyst came in and tacked new information and new pictures up, right over the old. Being a cop in Miami sometimes felt like you were playing a bad video game – no matter how many zombies you took out, there were always more coming at you. Faster and faster. Meaner and hungrier.

On November 7, 2006, a then twenty-three-year-old Talbot Lunders was in the hospital mourning the loss of his appendix; Manny'd already confirmed that. If these two murders were committed by the same psycho, then who had killed Gabby Vechio? And who had held the shaking video camera while she was being assaulted and murdered? If there was a second killer out there somewhere, partnering up to kill Gabby, and then working with Talbot Lunders to kill Holly, then who the hell was he? And who had he partnered up with to kill Gabby? How many madmen were involved? And were there more victims to find?

Manny rubbed his eyes and reached for a cigarette. *How many fucking zombies were there out there?*

16

'We've gotta talk,' Manny began as he followed Daria into her office. He plopped down in a chair in front of her desk.

'I figured you had something on your mind since you've been lurking around the courthouse all morning,' she replied as she closed the door behind him with her foot, threw her purse on top of her file cabinet and kicked off her platform heels. They were an impulsive online purchase, and were pinching her toes something awful. She pulled a pair of ballet flats out of her desk drawer and slipped them on. 'What? Did you and Raul have a spat? You're no longer welcome in the cafeteria or something? I don't have connections there, sorry.'

He stared at her wide-eyed, as if she were buck-naked. 'Damn, girl, you are freaking short. Are you even five foot?'

She wagged a finger at him. 'I warned you already; no comments about my height. I don't call you a freak of nature for being seven-fucking-feet tall.'

'Six-five.'

'Same difference. It's nothing but hot air up there after six.'

'Let me ask ya something: can you reach the doorknob without help?'

She glared at him. 'Time for you to go, Detective,' she replied, sitting down at her desk and dismissing him with a wave of her hand.

'Not till we talk. That your dad?' he asked, pointing at a picture on her desk of Daria and her father together at her law school graduation. 'You don't look nothing like him.'

'Thanks, I guess. Yes, that's my dad.'

Manny glanced down under her desk. 'Does he have little feet, too?'

'Enough. Now I see how you get people to confess. You pick at them until they explode in anger.'

'I'm just joking with ya, Counselor. He's a good-looking man, your pops. He makes good-looking kids. Tell him I said that,' he added with a wink. 'It's always smart to get in good with an Italian father, I hear. Make a nice impression. Maybe he'll put in a good word for me when this case is over.'

She rolled her eyes. 'You're nothing if not an optimist. And you don't know Italian fathers. Forget about putting in a good word, you'll be lucky he doesn't kill you for insulting his little girl.'

'That your brother?' Manny asked, picking up another picture. 'He don't look like you, neither. He looks like your dad. Now don't tell me it's a boyfriend. That would be fucked up on a couple of levels. First of which was having a short boyfriend who looks like your dad . . .'

'What is this? Are you working on some genealogy project here? What is it that you've been waiting all morning to tell me, Manny?' She reached across the desk and pulled the frame from his hands and set it down on the desk. 'You're like a toddler.'

'Okay. Chit-chat's over. I found the girl in the Lunders video.'

Daria raised an eyebrow. 'Really?'

Manny sighed. 'She's dead.'

Daria sat back in her chair, folding her hands on her lap. Her face grew dark. 'That's unfortunate.'

He frowned. 'I know you want to know her name, Counselor. It was Gabriella Vechio. She was a twenty-nine-year-old accountant from New York City who turned up dead in a construction ditch on Long Island five years ago. Three days after that video was made, actually. She'd been raped, bound, whipped, tortured, and strangled to death,' Manny replied.

'Okay,' she answered slowly.

Her inflection made it sound as though what she really meant to say was, *And why should I care?* That pissed him off. He could feel his blood pressure begin to rise. This Vechio girl had died a horrible death and no one had been held accountable. And it sounded to him from his relatively short conversation with Detective Schrader that nobody had worked all that hard to develop a suspect up in NY – just shoved her into Cold Case after enough time had passed and moved on to the next dead body. Now Cold Case wanted a name and a Florida death penalty sentence so they could move her off their desks, too. It didn't happen with many victims, but for some reason Manny felt a connection to poor, pretty Gabby the accountant – an obligation to care.

'That video that Hot Mami Lunders gave us was a snuff video, Counselor,' he replied testily. 'Based on the date the video was taken and the date this Vechio girl's body was discovered, it was most likely shot right before she was killed. Probably finished with her being offed.'

'Okay again, Manny. That's terrible. And it also seems to be very valuable information that the police in New York would like to have. Why don't you forward them the video?'

'The two murders are related: Vechio and Skole. The same killer, most likely. Or killers.'

She shook her head. 'Wait a second. How'd you make that jump?'

'They were both branded, Counselor. Same mark. An elongated "Z" surrounded by a circle. Branded like a goddamn cow. Same spot – nape of the neck. I had Trauss enhance the pictures and take a look. He matched them up using a forensic overlay tool and confirmed that's what it is.' Manny slid the autopsy pictures of both women across the desk. 'It's a signature.'

'Branded, Jesus . . .' Daria said quietly. 'Is it a gang, maybe? Miami and New York both have branches of the same street gangs . . .'

Manny stared at her. 'Talbot Alastair Lunders running with the brothers in the Crips? Come on, Daria, be real. Gangs don't randomly target nice white accountants and they don't have privileged, male model heirs as their members. Neither girl had any known gang involvement. There were no illicit drugs involved that we know of. Both disappeared from popular nightclubs, willingly leaving with men. In Holly's case, it was Talbot Lunders. In Gabby's case, it was a tall white male with dark hair, which not only doesn't match Lunders, but I've already checked and Hot Mami Lunders was right – Talbot was in the hospital at the time Gabby was murdered. So it wasn't him. That's why I think there may be two killers working here. Maybe more.'

'Manny,' she protested again, 'to say it's the same killer or killers based on—'

'I've found others.'

She stared at him.

After last week's conversation with Nassau County PD, he and Dickerson had pored over ViCAP reports and online cold case files from multiple departments, searching for any and all homicides that had mutilation and/or disfigurement and, more particularly, burns or branding. They'd also searched for similar unsolved homicides with the same victim typology as Gabriella Vechio and Holly Skole: blonde, slim, attractive, aged 15–30, flagging disappearances from, or around, night-clubs or bars. Then Manny, who was no fan of the feds, swallowed his pride and called the Behavioral Analysis Unit of the FBI at Quantico to see if they were working something similar. No one was. And from the lackluster reaction of the Special Agent in Charge, it didn't sound like they wanted to.

It was a laborious process. He wished profiling and investigating crimes were as easy in real life as it looked on a *Criminal Minds* episode – one click and ditzy super-analyst Penelope had all the information her FBI agents ever needed, down to the name of Joe Bad Guy's second-grade school teacher and the nutritional content of the cereal he ate that morning. Shows like that gave police work a bad name, raising the already clueless public's expectations on crime-solving to completely unattainable heights. The general *CSI/NCIS*-watching public now assumed that, in addition to leaving their fingerprints plastered all over a scene, every bad guy also left his DNA behind, and damning test results from said DNA would be delivered to the police lab within a matter of hours, if not minutes, floating magically in front of some gorgeous crime-scene investigator on some invisible, hand-manipulated computer screen, created by, and found only in, a CGI room in Hollywood.

In the end, it had been old-fashioned, sand-pounding police work that'd led to the phone call Manny received yesterday from the St Petersburg PD, confirming the same grim news Dickerson had already gotten from two other police departments. There were more victims.

'I have two other homicides in Florida, both unsolved. One is over on the west coast in St Pete, one's down south in Homestead. Both are women, both have traumatic brandings, one on her neck in the shape of a zigzag enclosed in a circle. That was Cyndi DeGregorio, a twenty-one-year-old pole-dancer from Miami, who was found in a dumpster last July. The other one had it on her buttocks, but we don't have an ID on her. She was never claimed. She may be a prostitute. Jane Doe was discovered behind the baseball stadium at Progress Energy Park on opening day of the Devil Rays spring training in April of 2009. Much more troubling is that I also found a *male* in New Jersey who had the symbol carved into his right pec. He'd been gutted like a fish and disemboweled. Found him in a dumpster, too, in

Hoboken. Name was Kevin Flaunters. He was a twenty-two-year-old body builder and male escort; he was found in November of 2008. Three homicides in the past three years. That's only what I could find through ViCAP. There may be others who were never placed in the system. Maybe nobody recognized they had a branding. Maybe the bodies decomped before they were found and the brandings were not readily identifiable. Maybe they haven't been found yet. The point is, there are more, Counselor. There are more. And now we can't say we don't see it anymore.'

She sat there, dumbfounded. 'I'm not sure I get what you're saying, Manny . . .'

'I think we're dealing with a serial. Or serials.'

The word 'serial' always struck a note of fear in a detective's or prosecutor's mind. The enormity of who, or rather, *what*, you were dealing with in real life was overwhelming. It was the difference between reading about an earthquake and living through one – until you experienced the terror and devastation wrought by a living, breathing, human monster who randomly preyed on his fellow humans, you had no idea how wrong the books and movies got it, or how trivial they made serial murder sound. Fortunately, serial killings were actually pretty rare, accounting for less than one percent of all murders nationwide. Unfortunately, the identification and capture of a serial killer was very difficult, as Manny knew all too well.

'Several years ago I worked a case,' he began. 'Cops were being murdered here in Miami. It was back in '04.'

Daria had been in law school then, but she remembered the killings that had captured headlines all over Florida. 'That was the Black Jacket case, right?'

'Yes. In the course of that investigation, I had to interview a serial killer who claimed to have information about the case. His name was Bill Bantling.'

'Cupid,' Daria said slowly. Her heartbeat quickened. Certain names conjured up instant emotional responses in people. Bill Bantling was right up there with Ted Bundy, Jeffrey Dahmer and Charles Manson. The emotional response elicited was fear. The same unfamiliar, icy sensation she'd experienced at Talbot Lunders's Arthur Hearing raced down her spine and she shifted in her seat.

'Yes, Cupid. I worked that case too.'

'How many women did he kill?' Daria asked softly. She had been a hard-partying college student in Miami when Cupid was busy trolling nightclubs on South Beach. In fact, she was at Club Liquid the night one of Cupid's victims had disappeared without a trace from the very bar Daria was doing too many Kamikaze shots at. The eerie, potential close encounter had never left her. You never knew when your number might be up, when you might perhaps catch the eye of a serial killer.

'Eleven,' Manny replied with a drawn-out sigh. Eleven young women. All blonde, all strikingly beautiful. Their faces had covered the walls of the FDLE task force command center where he'd worked for two years. So had the pictures of their butchered bodies, posed in sexually provocative positions, their hearts cut from their chests while they were still alive. Manny saw those sweet, young faces sometimes in his nightmares, covered in dried blood, still begging him for help.

'Wasn't Bantling already in prison when the Black Jacket killings took place?' Daria asked.

Manny nodded. 'He was on death row. He'd been transferred to Miami for a hearing on his appeal and was about to be shipped back to Florida State Prison when his attorney tells me he wants to talk. Says Bantling's got information on Black Jacket and wants to cut a deal. So I go see him. And he starts telling me about this . . .' Manny paused for a long moment. 'This *club*.'

'Club?'

'Yeah. An underground club made up of crazies who like to watch people die. According to Bantling, this wasn't some bunch of obviously unstable sickos, but prominent citizens – Wall Street traders, politicians, doctors, corporate bigwigs, actors, even . . .' he paused before he said the next word, as if it tasted bitter: '. . . cops. And thanks to the Internet, we're talking world-wide, not just Miami. It cost a lot of money to get into the club – you gotta pay for the privilege of watching people die. And I don't mean of natural causes.'

'So they liked to watch snuff films?' Daria asked.

'They liked to *make* snuff films, Counselor. Now, none of this was ever substantiated – Bantling wouldn't give names and we wouldn't give him a deal, since we'd cracked Black Jacket by then.' Manny rubbed his smooth head and took a deep breath. 'FDLE was supposed to investigate the snuff allegations with Customs and Postal, but . . . Bantling's comments were dismissed as the ramblings of a man desperate to save his own ass. He was shipped back to death row and the rest of us just wanted to move on.'

He looked past her, towards the jail. 'But now . . . well, I keep going over that interview,' he said pensively.

'And I keep thinking about that video of Gabby Vechio's death and the faces on those TV monitors, watching. About the horrific scenes we didn't see, the torture and cruelty that were cut from that clip. And I can't help but hear what Bantling told me and wonder if that might be what we got here now, ya know? That maybe this is a snuff club we're dealing with, Counselor. And maybe we stopped looking, but it never stopped operating.'

17

'That's a mighty big leap, Detective.' Daria hoped she still looked reserved, but her heart had started to pound and her hands were sweating. *A snuff club. That was a dark twist she'd never heard before.* 'You're thinking snuff club because you have a snippet of a videotaped murder and a lying, locked-up serial killer from years gone by that once told you this secret club exists? And so this must be evidence of it?'

'Stop doing that,' Manny shot back.

'Doing what?'

'Making something sound stupid that made a lot of sense in my head. You twist shit with your lawyer thinking and your lawyer words. Stop and just hear me. Don't cross-examine, because I'm on *your* side here. And I'm not gonna make the same mistake I might've made seven years ago and walk away.'

He rubbed his head again. 'I have a gut feeling, Counselor. I knew when I first saw that Lunders video that there was something more to it than soft porn. I knew what I was looking at was bad. That's why I had to find the girl. I had to know. These killings, these girls, are like a page torn out of Cupid's book – pretty blondes disappearing from nightclubs, held for several days, or longer, tortured and then murdered.'

'Hold on,' Daria cut in. 'Holly and these other victims, they all had their hearts, didn't they?'

'Yeah, they did.'

'So what are you saying, Manny? That Bantling *wasn't* Cupid? That it was all the work of this snuff club and the real Cupid is actually alive and well and roaming the streets of Miami right now looking for fresh blood? That he changed his MO and is letting all the pretty girls keep their hearts this time around and branding them instead?'

'There you go, crossing me like some hostile witness.' Manny pounded both fists on the arms of his chair, so hard it sounded as if either the wood or his hands had cracked. He sat back in the chair and stared at the wall, trying hard to rein in his temper.

'I remember in his last round of appeals Bantling made the argument that he was a poor innocent. I also remember it didn't fly,' Daria finished, ignoring the temper tantrum. 'He's still on death row, isn't he?'

'For the moment. The man is like a cat – he's got nine lives, with a few still left to spare. He was supposed to get a new trial. Came real close. Too close.'

'What happened there?' she asked.

'His trial lawyer, Lourdes Rubio, had a change of heart some years after Bantling was convicted. Claimed in an affidavit that she'd fucked up Bantling's case on purpose and withheld evidence that would've exonerated him at trial. She was supposed to testify at the hearing for a new trial, only she gets killed in a robbery. The judge kept out her statements and sent Bantling back to Florida State Prison, but then the appellate courts said, nah, the trial judge should've admitted the affidavit. So the state appealed. Case went all the way up to the Florida Supremes. Ultimately, the Supremes tossed it back and said the appellate court was wrong in second-guessing the trial judge and reinstated the original verdict. Last I heard, Bantling was appealing *that* ruling through the federal courts, which'll probably take another five years. Then it'll be on to the next bullshit appeal, and the next.'

She cocked her head. 'The Cupid case had some other issues, didn't it? With the prosecutor?'

'Bill Bantling is a psychopath, Counselor,' Manny said dismissively. 'He creates chaos wherever he goes. It excites him.'

'Didn't he claim that he'd raped the prosecutor?'

'Like I said, he creates chaos. If you're old enough to remember the headlines, he conveniently made *that* claim *after* a jury had convicted him of capital murder. It was all he had left in the arsenal – a fucked-up accusation he was being railroaded on to death row by a vindictive prosecutor hell-bent on retribution. C.J. Townsend was her name. An amazing attorney, an even more amazing lady. The sad thing is that Bantling was smart enough to have dug up the fact that C.J. was raped when she was a law student in New York and that her rapist had never been caught. Found out her real name – 'cause she'd changed it, she was so scared the guy who raped her might find her one day – found out where she used to live, the car she used to drive.

150

All this he got from reading old police reports. There's no one more dangerous on this earth than a clever psychopath, I'll tell ya.

'How she managed to hold her head up after the things he said about her in open court, I don't know. It must have been like being raped all over again. Obviously, the judge saw through Bantling's bullshit theatrical performance and the jury sentenced him to death, but, in my opinion, C.J. was never the same after that. Not as a prosecutor, not as a woman. She was always more guarded, less happy. She was still effective, you know, but definitely anxious and uptight. She worked with the task force on the Black Jacket murders, but when that case closed, she up and left the office.'

'Where is she now?'

He shifted in his seat. 'No idea. Haven't seen her since.'

Daria nodded thoughtfully. She'd picked up on a slight, barely perceptible, change in the detective. Obviously, she'd hit a nerve. Perhaps he'd dated the woman. Or he'd wanted to. Or maybe there was more to her story than he wanted to get into. Daria remembered that, after Bantling was sent to death row, C.J. Townsend had been attacked by a Cupid copycat and almost killed. No wonder the woman had bowed out of the game early. If all that shit had happened to her, Daria would be making candles in some small, remote town in Iowa that had a zero percent crime rate – keeping a low profile and living a simple lifestyle.

'Listen, Counselor,' Manny continued, 'I'm not saying we have the wrong killer behind bars here. Talbot Lunders is guilty of Holly Skole's murder as sure as the day is long. I know it. And I'm not saying Bill

Bantling is not Cupid. What I am saying is that as far as *our* case is concerned, *we* have a problem that can't be ignored. There are scary similarities between these new murders and the Cupid murders. Maybe it's time we looked into Bantling's claim that he was part of this snuff club.'

'If it exists.'

'If it exists,' he conceded. 'And if he was in it, when and if it did exist. Maybe his fellow members get together to share tips or war stories or something, and somebody got an idea to relive the great ones. All I know for sure is that the murder of Gabby Vechio in New York is somehow related to Holly Skole's murder down here. The brandings prove it. And whether you like it or not, at the very least, you're gonna have to disclose that to the defense. It's Brady. And these new murders I just found – they're Brady, too.'

That got her attention. Brady referred to *Brady v. State of Maryland*, a US Supreme Court decision that required the state to disclose any evidence that was known to be favorable to a defendant's case and material to the issue of guilt and/or punishment that would tend to exculpate the defendant. Basically, anything that could prove the defendant wasn't guilty. Manny was no lawyer, but any detective worth his salt knew Brady, and knew the decision was pretty broad in its interpretation. To guess wrong and not comply could mean severe penalties, including, in extreme circumstances, the exclusion of evidence and even post-conviction reversal. There was little doubt in his mind that the existence of the murder video and identity of Gabriella Vechio, and now three more potential victims, would be considered Brady.

152

'The hell I do!' Daria cried. 'We don't *know* they're related. Only your gut knows.'

'Try out that twisted lawyer thinking on Judge Becker and see if she doesn't throw your cute ass in jail for willfully failing to disclose. Don't forget, Hot Mami Lunders came to *us* with this video.'

'Stop calling her that.'

'Joe Varlack supposedly knows of its existence,' Manny continued. 'It's not like you can hide it. The inevitable question the judge is eventually gonna be asking you is, "What did you discover about the video and the girl in it after Abby Lunders gave it to you?" I'm not gonna tell her, "nothing" when I know it's something. You have to disclose the Vechio murder. And the others, too.'

As much as she didn't want to agree, Manny had a point. At least as to Gabriella Vechio's murder. And she knew the detective would sell her out on the stand later if she didn't disclose. *Damn, damn, damn.* Things were starting to unravel at the seams after barely coming together at the Arthur, grand jury and arraignment. She bit her lip and swiveled toward the window so he couldn't watch her think.

Jesus Christ . . . a serial killer? Daria had never worked a serial murder before. And she wouldn't if Vance Collier and the administration found out that was the new direction *The State of Florida v. Talbot Lunders* was heading in. They would put a much more seasoned prosecutor on it, maybe even Collier himself. There went Chief of Sex Batt. There went an opportunity to prove herself and move out of neutral. To become a lifer with a future. *Fuck that.* She wasn't giving up that easy. She wasn't handing over the case of a career just because she didn't

153

have the experience. If Manny was right, and Holly Skole's murder was one of several serial murders that in some way related to Bill Bantling and an underground snuff club, then she would ready the case to the point that there would be no alternative but for her to try it. No one else would be qualified, especially seeing as there was likely going to be a speedy issue.

She swiveled around. 'I say we talk to Lunders. If he has a partner, or if he was recruited by a partner, maybe even a serial, or – and I'm not saying I buy into any of this yet – *if* he was a member of this club you're talking about, then we consider some kind of deal to get the other names. But let's not go looking for some psycho club membership with him just yet, Manny; Holly's murder could be the work of him and a demented unsub. I don't want to go planting ideas in his head. Or his lawyer's.'

Manny rubbed his temple. 'I don't think the kid's gonna talk, Counselor. He hasn't before. You saw him in court – he's about as fucked-up and unpredictable as Bantling. I think he actually enjoys the attention, in a warped way. This is his moment in the sun; his turn to create some chaos.'

'Well, give it the old college-try. I'm not releasing anything as Brady till I find out what the hell's going on.'

'After what happened with you and him at the Arthur, *I'll* handle talking to him and his attorney,' Manny replied, taking a pack of Marlboros out of his pocket. 'He might be less distracted. You, too.'

She nodded and reached for the cup of cold coffee so as to hide the rush of color that had flooded her cheeks. 'You can't smoke in here.'

'You've told me that before. But I can be ready the second I get downstairs,' he answered, sticking a cigarette behind his ear. 'Tomorrow's Wednesday, right? Damn, the week is flying by. I have an Arthur Thursday afternoon, so I think I'll arrange a visit with Pretty Boy that morning. Regardless, I'm gonna take a drive to Florida State next week to talk to Bantling,' he said, scooping up his file from her desk.

'I'm going,' she declared.

'Let me do the investigating here. You stick to prosecuting.'

'I'm still going. I never met a serial killer before.'

Manny frowned.

That sounded real dumb. 'I won't interfere,' she offered quickly. 'But I want to be there. I want to see him.'

'I'll take a picture.'

'Very funny. I want to hear what he has to say about this snuff club. You keep insisting that it's related to my case. I have a right.'

Manny sighed. Despite the smart part of his brain that was screaming 'Bad idea!' his mouth didn't get the message. 'Oh, the things you can get me to agree to when you're nice, Counselor. 'Cause I'm telling ya, I ain't driving five hours in the car with you if those fangs are bared.'

'I'll be nice. Promise. You know, I went to UF.'

Manny looked over at the framed law degree from the University of Florida that hung on the pale gray wall above the file cabinet. 'I see that.'

Her eyes followed his. 'They don't tell you on the admissions tour that your dorm room's gonna be located

155

within a thirty-mile radius of eight different correctional facilities – including two maximum-security prisons that house death-row inmates. My mom was so pissed,' Daria continued thoughtfully. 'She ripped my room apart 'cause she thought I hid that detail about the prisons from her. I came home that first Christmas to find what remained of my books, pictures, curtains and comforter carpeting my bedroom floor in two-inch strips.'

'That's extreme.'

'Yeah, well, she's extreme. She wanted me to stay home and go to UM so I could take care of her. The bunch of crap about how worried she was for me because of all those bad boys in the state pens next town over was just that – a bunch of crap. She was being vindictive, is all.'

'Did you?'

'Huh?'

'Did you lie to your momma about UF being located in the epicenter of Florida's prisons?'

'Hell, yeah. No way was I staying home another three years. I didn't have the healthiest home life, as you can imagine. Unlike the rest of my class, I couldn't wait to go to law school. I did it on student loans too, so don't think I'm ungrateful. Once Mommy Dearest got over her temper tantrum, she warmed to the idea that she could brag to all her friends that her daughter was gonna be some high-paid, hot-shot lawyer.'

Manny smiled. 'And out of all the legal careers to pick from, you chose to be a prosecutor – hanging with the bad boys all day long and bringing home shit for pay – knowing that would probably piss her off even more, huh?'

'We eke out a few sentences at Sunday dinners.'

'So you're passive-aggressive. I think I should remember that.'

There was a long and awkward pause. She'd said way, way too much. 'I've never been to death row before,' she offered. 'Anything I should know or be worried about?'

That sounded so green. But all she could think of was the creepy scene in *The Silence of the Lambs* when Clarice Starling is warned about Hannibal Lecter: *Don't get too close to the glass. Slide all papers through the drawer. Don't tell him anything about yourself.* It was only a movie, but still . . .

Manny stood up and headed for the door. He was already regretting his decision. 'Monday's the Fourth of July holiday, so I'm thinking Tuesday. I'm gonna get on the road by eight. I guess I'll pick you up here.'

'I'll be ready,' Daria said with a smile.

'I hope so,' he replied before he walked out the door. Based on the last question she'd asked, he already knew how wrong she was about that.

18

The corrections officer buzzed the door to the interview room at Dade County Jail and the steel door slid open. When Manny had cleared the doorway, it slid back in place with another loud clang, and a second steel door slid open. When he'd cleared that one, it, too, slid into place with a bang, locking him into the mint-green interrogation room that smelled of mildew and urine, even though it lacked both a toilet and a water source.

Anne-Claire Simmons and her client were already seated at a metal table that was bolted to the floor. The three metal chairs set around the table were chained to the table's legs. The one thing that was not chained or locked to anything was Talbot Lunders. No cuffs, no shackles, no restraints. The accused murderer was free to walk around the cabin. He might not be able to steal the furniture, but he *could* throttle his attorney with his bare hands if he really wanted to. Manny had interviewed scores of defendants in this very room, and he couldn't recall one other who hadn't been dressed up in at least cuffs. It irked him. The rules must be different for good-looking, privileged, white murderers.

'Good afternoon, Detective,' Anne-Claire began somberly. 'Is Ms DeBianchi joining us?'

'Nope. How about Mr Varlack?'

'Unfortunately, Joe had a prior commitment in Palm Beach. He knew this must be very important, so I'm here and Mr Lunders and I are both listening.'

Listening, but not authorized to actually do shit. Clever. Each team had sent their second string. Manny took a seat across from the two of them. He could spend a few minutes chitchatting about how Talbot was enjoying prison life, but life was too short and Manny didn't like to waste time on matters he truly didn't give a shit about. 'Let me get right to the point, Ms Simmons: I want to talk to your client about the night Holly Skole disappeared.'

'I've instructed Talbot not to say anything, Detective.'

'Bully for you, Ms Simmons. You're here and I'm sure, if he needs counsel, you can give it to him. And if he wants to give answers to some of my questions, he can.' He looked directly at Talbot. 'You were on the phone within minutes after you left Menace, Talbot. We have the records. We know the number: 305-697-9980. We also know it was a throw-away. What we don't know yet is who you were talking to. So, would you like to share?'

Anne-Claire looked at her client and shook her head. Talbot said nothing.

'Okay.' Manny pulled out his notepad. 'You made five phone calls to that same number between 4:12 and 5:30 in the morning. You made them while you were

159

in Miami and you transferred cell towers on the last two calls to the tower located in Turkey Point, indicating you were travelling southbound. Who were you talking to, Talbot? And why were you talking to them?'

Anne-Claire held her hand up, just in case Talbot was thinking of answering. 'You're the detective, you tell us.'

'Let's not play games, Ms Simmons. Please. I'll be honest here: I'm thinking Talbot had a partner, someone who might've participated in Holly's murder. I wanna know who that person is and what that role was.'

'You're making an offer?' Anne-Claire asked.

'I've spoken with the prosecutor. Depending upon the information you provide, a deal could definitely be worked out. A substantial deal, like maybe the death penalty goes off the table type of deal. But of course I need to know the information before I can tell you what it's selling for.'

Talbot leaned into the table. 'You don't have shit,' he whispered.

Manny frowned and leaned in himself. 'You're here, aren't you? Are you liking the accommodations, son?'

Talbot grinned. 'This case has gotten a lot of press. My attorney here tells me that Court TV is interested in broadcasting the trial. Live, this fall. Can you believe that shit? That's really exciting. Move over all you housewives! There's a new *Bachelor* in town!'

'What?' Manny asked, looking at Anne-Claire incredulously.

Anne-Claire stared down at her papers. 'I only mentioned to him that they'd called . . .'

'Live TV. Very exciting. Think about it, Detective. And *48 Hours*, too. She's even trying to fix up a *Dateline* special, my hard-working attorney,' Talbot continued. 'You gotta love an attorney with Hollywood connections. Maybe a made-for-TV movie, Mr Varlack tells me. How about a continuous series on FX? That one's my idea.'

'Talbot, please . . .' Anne-Claire said quietly. 'None of this was agreed—'

'Maybe they'll call it *Framed!* That's catchy, isn't it, Detective? We might have a role in it for you. Like on that old TV show my dad told me about, *The Fugitive*. You can play the hot-headed, bumbling detective who never gets his man. Week after week, he's always two steps behind the killer.'

'Is this what you're feeding him?' Manny snapped. 'That he's gonna be some reality-TV star? Are you joking me?' He turned to Talbot. 'Listen up, asshole. You're twenty-eight years old. You're a good-looking guy, no doubt. A former model and all. Loved to work that runway, I'm sure, with your pretty boy face and nice legs and cocky attitude. Yeah, I know all about your big-time aspirations that went south because you weren't quite good-looking enough. Or maybe you wouldn't put out for the boys. Whatever. You didn't make it in Milan, and you ain't scoring some fucked-up reality show here. You're just not that important.'

Talbot's face turned dark. 'You've been talking to my *mother*?'

Manny shrugged. 'The reality that will happen is that the boys are gonna tear you to shreds where you're going. This is not a game. And I am not a patient man who has time for games. I'm old and I'm grouchy.'

'What else did she tell you? I want to know.'

He'd hit a nerve. *Why?* 'What else is there to know?

161

Does Mommy know whose digits you're dialing in the wee hours of the morning? Maybe I should talk to her some more. Have a nice long talk with your pretty momma.'

'Leave my mother out of this. This is about *me*. It's about *me*.' He shook his head abruptly. 'No information. I'm not selling anything. I'll take my chances in court with all those cameras, because they're gonna love me. Oh yeah. Besides, I've seen who's trying to put me away, and I have to tell you, I'm not worried. But you should be.'

Manny thought about what he and Daria had discussed and had agreed not to discuss. *Don't feed him any ideas.* 'How do you know Bill Bantling?'

'I want to go,' Talbot replied flatly. He stood up.

'When did you first meet him?'

Nothing.

'I don't think this is the first time you've done this, Talbot. And I don't think this is the first girl. I think you have a mentor. And I think there are others,' Manny said, standing as well. 'Others who like to watch.'

Anne-Claire looked at her client. 'Talbot?'

Talbot banged on the door. 'I said I want to go now.'

'Would a deal cover other crimes?' Anne-Claire asked Manny anxiously.

'My attorney must be hard of fucking hearing!' Talbot yelled. 'I said I have no information to sell. And I have nothing to discuss with you, Detective. Officer!' He banged on the door again until it opened. 'I want to go,' he said calmly when the corrections officer finally opened the door.

Talbot had said nothing, and yet so much. Manny

now knew for sure that a club existed. 'I'll find the others,' he said to Anne-Claire as the officer slapped cuffs on Talbot's outstretched hands. 'And when I do, there will be no deal. Like I said before, I'm not a very patient man.'

'Wait a minute, I do have something to say,' Talbot said, turning to Manny. ''Cause now you got me all worried, Detective. I'm shaking here.'

'Talbot—' Anne-Claire held her hand up. 'Hold on, let me handle this.'

Her client ignored her.

'It's a real shame that hot little incompetent prosecutor of mine couldn't be here today,' Talbot continued, a smirk slowly leaking across his face. 'Please, please, please do me a favor and send her my love. And also a message from me, Detective . . .'

19

'"Little Lena needs to tend to that garden."'

'What?' Daria asked as she and Manny walked down the courthouse hallway on Friday morning. A string of defendants in cuffs shuffled past them on their way to DCJ. One of them whistled at her.

'That's what he said. That's all he said, basically. The interview was a waste of time, although I'm certain now that he knows Bantling. And I'm certain I'm right about this club. What the hell does that mean, though, that garden comment?' Bear asked.

Daria shrugged.

'Like I told ya, he's not gonna talk, Counselor. He's loving this. Wants to see himself in the spotlight. He also called you incompetent, although he did say you were hot—' He stopped short. 'Jesus! What the hell is wrong with you?'

Daria's face had gone ashen.

'Don't shake your head at me. You're as white as a ghost. Let's get you a seat.' He ushered her to a bench and sat beside her. 'Either you're sick or it was something I said. Please don't yak on my shoes. They're new. Also, I have an aversion to people puking. I can't handle it.'

'I'm okay,' she said. 'Just got a little dizzy. I didn't have breakfast.'

'Bullshit. For a lawyer, you're a shit liar. You gotta work on that. Are you upset he called you incompetent or that he called you hot?' Manny laughed. 'You shouldn't take it personal or nothing, Counselor. And what does, "Little Lena needs to tend her garden" mean? Is that from a book or something?'

She paused for a moment. 'Daria is my grandmother's name, Manny. I took her name after she died because I hated my birth name.'

'Which is?'

'Maddalena.'

'That's pretty.'

'Don't go there.'

'Let me guess, you were named after your mother?'

'You're a good detective.'

'And you really are passive-aggressive. You changed the name your momma gave you? Ouch.'

'I don't need a lecture.'

'And it was *her* name, too. Freud would have fun with you. So *you* are Little Lena. I'm guessing Lena is short for Maddalena.'

'Stop detectiving me.'

'I don't think that's a word.'

'He knows my birth name, Manny. How fucked up is that?'

''Cause you legally changed it, right? That's public record. There's no place to hide in cyberworld. *I* should've googled you, come to think of it. Put your own name into a search engine and see how much shit comes up that you didn't know about yourself. Could be Talbot's mommy looked you up. He didn't seem to like the thought of us talking to her. Doesn't want to share the spotlight with her, maybe?'

Daria glanced away, down the hall. She rubbed her hands together. 'But my nickname, Manny?'

'Not a quantum leap. I did it, right? Don't get all nervous on me. I like you better when you're mean and feisty. Now it just feels awkward. Listen, you can't let this two-bit punk kid get inside your head like that. You still up for Bantling next week? 'Cause if Pretty Boy Talbot Lunders can shake you up like this, just wait till you meet Cupid.'

She nodded. 'So what else did he say?'

'Nothing. He's looking forward to a trial on Court TV and a career on the big screen after he's discovered, and acquitted, of course. But I did notice something very interesting that I didn't see before. A tattoo on his right forearm. A dark red – get this – lightning bolt.'

'That's coincidental.'

'Isn't it? I don't like coincidences, Counselor. Usually I find there is no such thing.'

'I'm sure a zillion other skin-art fanatics in that hellhole have lightning bolts etched somewhere on their epidermises,' she said.

'But not all of them are suspects in our case.'

She stood up. 'So I guess we move on to Bantling now. Is that still on for Tuesday?'

'Not so quick, Counselor. What else is getting to you? And don't say "nothing", 'cause like I said, you're a shit liar. He knows your nickname. Okay. So what did he mean with that garden comment?'

She ran a hand through her thick hair. 'Maybe I'm taking it wrong. Maybe I'm just being paranoid . . .'

'What? What is it? Spit it out.'

'I . . . I live in a townhouse in Victoria Park. It's a nice, quiet neighborhood up in Fort Lauderdale and I have a garden in the back. A flower and herb garden. Not real big – a few roses, sunflowers, basil, simple stuff. I've tried everything, but I must have cinch bugs or something. In the last few weeks or so everything's been dying. Since the Arthur Hearing, actually, now that I think about it.'

'Okay. Horticulture ain't your thing. I'm betting you're not so hot at cooking, neither. You don't plug me as the domestic type.'

She shot him a look. 'Actually, my roses are usually really beautiful. Prize winners, I suppose, if I wanted to enter them in a contest. But not anymore. Someone would've had to have told him that, Manny. Someone who's *seen* that garden. Someone who's *been* to my house.'

Manny frowned. 'Okay. I see what you're thinking and why you might be a little paranoid, but—'

She wasn't done. 'And then this morning, I came downstairs, opened my kitchen blinds and they were all gone.'

'You mean dead?'

'No. I mean *gone*. Someone cut the tops off all my roses. Not the other flowers, just the roses, the ones that hadn't died. There's nothing left now but a garden of thorny stems.' She looked away. 'I thought it was a

167

disgruntled neighbor, you know. Maybe I parked in the wrong spot, or I hung my towels over my balcony railing without thinking. Who the hell knows what ticks people off? But now . . .' She looked at him. 'Jesus, Manny – what the hell am I supposed to think?'

20

Santa Barbara, California

As cold-blooded murderers went, Richard Kassner didn't look the part.

Dressed in a conservative charcoal suit, white shirt, and light blue tie, dark hair carefully parted on the side and combed into place, his chubby hands folded piously before him like an altar boy, the middle-aged, Fisher Price toy exec didn't *look* like someone who would intentionally try to blow up his house with his wife and disabled mother-in-law locked inside. Of course, Santa Barbara Assistant District Attorney Christina Towns knew better than anyone on this earth that not only could looks be deceiving in a courtroom, they could also prove to be quite the asset, if worked right. And Mr Kassner definitely knew how to work the baby face that God had given him. All day long he'd been exchanging smiles and understanding glances with several females on the jury – even through the gut-wrenching testimony given by his now ex-wife. For some reason the jury was loving him, and not the ex. To turn the *Titanic* around, Christina was going to have to step up her game. And the gut-wrenching.

But that would have to wait till next week.

'Will there be anything further, Ms Towns?' asked the judge, looking over at the People's table. The jurors all looked at her, too. It was past five on a Friday. Everyone was hoping for the same answer.

'No, Your Honor,' Christina replied. The last thing she needed was for her jury to hate her because they'd missed out on happy hour. 'We reserve the right to recall Jessica Kassner in rebuttal.'

'Fine, then,' said the judge. 'We'll resume Tuesday morning at nine.' He nodded at the bailiff to escort the jury out. 'We're in recess until that time. Have a nice, long weekend everybody. Happy Fourth of July.'

As the courtroom emptied around her, Christina finished up some paperwork and gathered her files, placing what she could in the leather mail satchel her mom had given her ages ago, and piling the rest in a cardboard box, which she loaded on a pull cart. From the corner of her eye she watched as the defendant, who was out on bond, dabbed a tear from his eye, hugged his new wife and tenderly kissed his new baby. Some of the elderly courtroom fixtures, who liked to hang around in court all day long, watched the gooey, PDA publicity stunt from the rear of the courtroom. She could feel them aaawwwing from thirty feet away. Fortunately, the jury was already gone. Led by Mr Kassner's expensive attorney, the new family began to walk from the courtroom, hand-in-hand. Then the droopy-eyed toy maker – who some jurors were having a hard time picturing as a violent, psychopathic sadist – turned and shot Christina a menacing glare over his shoulder, like the devil in a movie whose eyes flash red and teeth turn yellow when no one else is watching.

Her heartbeat quickened, but she stood her ground and watched him leave, making sure she did not break from his threatening stare until the door closed behind him and his trophy wife. The hell she was gonna let the bastard know that inside she was shaking: all he would see was stone. When the day came – and it would – that he was finally convicted of arson and murder, she'd ask the judge to put Richard Kassner behind bars for a good chunk of the rest of his life. He knew it and he hated her for it. She'd flash *him* a smug smile then – as he was led out of the courtroom in cuffs.

When the door closed behind them she sat back down at the People's table and finally exhaled. Underneath the table her hands were trembling. She wished it didn't bother her. She wished she could just blow off the threats and the dirty looks as part of the job – like she used to be able to do. She wished she were as tough on the inside as her reputation was.

She hung back for a long while, answering calls and returning texts until the bailiff finally came and told her it was time to lock up. There was no way she wanted to share an elevator ride with her psycho defendant. Nor did she want to run into him in the parking lot. Or, for that matter, the movie theater, grocery store, or post office, which meant that after she was done here tonight, she would be going home and laying low until Richard Kassner was officially a convicted felon and off the streets for good. Depending on how the case went, that might take several weeks. It was only then that she'd be able to actually sleep when she closed her eyes at night. Or so she told herself.

The eighty-five-year-old historic Spanish courthouse was deserted. The only souls left in the building beside her were a lone janitor, who was polishing the Mexican Saltillo tiles on the second-floor hall, and Joe, the night security guard stationed at the information booth on the first floor. Her case had been the only trial going in the normally sleepy courthouse and it was Friday night. Her colleagues at the DA's office across the street were most likely all gone as well, as was her boss. It was time for the holiday weekend to begin.

She waved goodnight over her shoulder to Joe as she stepped outside into the pristine courtyard. The evening air already smelled like night-blooming jasmine, even though the sun was not quite down yet. The Santa Ynez mountain range, tinged in fading hues of orange and plum, hovered over the red roofs and Santa Barbara foothills, like a scene captured on a picturesque postcard. Behind her, Joe moved to close and lock the courthouse's thirty-foot tall, hand-carved, wooden entrance gates. The screechy rattle of his keys working in the metal lock startled her. But she did not flinch or fly away. She willed herself not to look back, not to give in to her fears, lest they completely overpower her consciousness. Because then she would fall into full paranoia, and from there a darkness she might never escape from again. It was only old Joe, after all.

She took a deep breath and started down the walk. Her Explorer was parked in a lot a couple of blocks over. She'd get in, pick up Luna, her Akita, from doggy daycare, go home, call it a day. Take Luna for a long walk, maybe. Draw a bath. Make some exotic dinner for herself from a complicated recipe meant to feed a family of four.

She was so jumpy lately. So on edge. Always glancing over her shoulder, always preparing herself to meet someone sinister when she turned a corner. And the condition was worsening. It was both mentally and physically exhausting, always being on – like living in a video game. *The Prosecutor's Redemption*: a twisted labyrinth of dark alleys, basements, abandoned warehouses, vacant buildings, crack houses, sleazy massage parlors, rodent-infested crawl spaces. Every new level led her into a crime scene she'd once worked, where the bad guys and madmen lurked among the bodies of their victims, waiting for her return with their weapon of choice. It was a side-effect of the job, she reasoned, her escalating anxiety. Now the most dangerous defendant on her docket was, for some unfathomable reason, out on bond without so much as a bracelet to track where he was going. As far as her brain was concerned, that could very well be to her house. And she always had to be ready. She always had to be on when the doors opened on to the next level of the game.

Christina had made a lot of enemies over the years. Nasty enemies, like mass murderers and rapists and psychopaths. It was the frightening reality that came with a career prosecuting criminals. She'd reconciled herself to that truth some seventeen years ago, when she was first sworn in as a prosecutor in Miami. But what she didn't appreciate at the time was that the longer you lasted at the job, the more enemies you created, and the more dangerous those enemies became. It was one thing to be hated by a shoplifter who was pissed you'd sent him to the county jail for ten days; it was another to be loathed by a man convicted of attempted murder, who'd viciously beaten his wife into a coma and blamed the break-up of his family on the prosecutor who had asked for, and received, a twenty-year sentence. Focused on putting the bad guys behind bars, she hadn't thought much about what life would be like when the men who hated her re-entered society when their sentences were up. Free to do what they want, go where they wanted. Twenty years had seemed like a life sentence when she was twenty-eight. Not so much anymore. It wasn't a good feeling, knowing that there were a lot more people in this world that didn't want her in it than did. What was even more disturbing was that, over the course of a long and distinguished career, she had prosecuted hundreds of men and women, whose names she could barely recall and whose faces she would not recognize, but who surely remembered who she was and what she looked like. And who couldn't wait to meet her again when those prison doors opened.

'Goodnight, Christina,' Joe called after her as she headed down the walk, because that's what people called her here. It was going on a year and she still wasn't used to the name. She wondered if she ever would be. Or would she move on once again? Pick another moniker out of a hat, another place to call home when the pressure she was constantly living under threatened to break her once again? How many names would she collect before the ghosts of her very fucked-up past finally caught up with her and put her into an early grave? Would they all fit on her headstone? Or would she be forever remembered only by the last name that she'd used? Of course, by that point, no one was going to remember her, anyway. She would just be a name, not a person that anyone really knew.

It was ironic that she had an alias. Aliases, actually. As a prosecutor, you were programmed to think that anyone who had an a.k.a. – an 'also known as' in cop lingo – was up to no good. An alias was reserved for those who had something to hide. Or perhaps somebody to hide from. She waved at Joe and turned the corner on to Figueroa Street.

She definitely met the definition.

In most big cities, the criminal courthouse was located in a sketchy part of town, where every other storefront housed either a criminal defense attorney or a bail bondsman advertising twenty-four-hour assistance for all your legal needs in blinding neon lights. The county jail was next door, in order to hold and transport prisoners for hearings. The area would be seedy enough during the day, but when the sun went down and the judges and attorneys all went home and the supporting restaurants, print shops and process servers closed up, the neighborhood would become a deserted zombieland – with druggies and criminals lurking in dark corners, looking for a bondsman, or dope, or for their loved one to get sprung from jail.

But Santa Barbara was not a big city. In this beautiful metropolis by the sea, beloved by Oprah and other A-listers, and only ninety minutes north of LA, the historic courthouse was part of the town: movie screenings and get-togethers and dances happened regularly in the green-lawned part of the courtyard known as the Sunken Garden. Located a few blocks off State Street, the city's

175

main thoroughfare, in a quiet, residential neighborhood, the courthouse was removed from the hustle and bustle of the city's nightlife. When Christina had lived in Miami, she would never have thought of casually strolling the streets around the Dade County Jail at twelve in the afternoon, much less after dark. Things were different here. Which was why she was here.

It was by accident that Christina had picked Santa Barbara for the fresh start she'd convinced herself she needed. Not so much an accident, really, as an ill-thought-out, spur-of-the-moment decision. *Poor impulse control is a manifestation of PTSD* her therapist would have told her, back in the days when she was in therapy. *The overwhelming compulsion to run away from a moment because of fear often induces poor decision-making.* The ghosts from that very fucked-up past that had induced her post-traumatic stress disorder and subsequent poor decision-making had had her on the run for the past two decades, chasing her from New York to Miami to Chicago and now all the way to Santa Barbara. The latest marathon had gone like this: the California social worker who'd helped place Christina's Alzheimer's-stricken grandmother in a nursing home had called to say a bed was ready and could she come and help settle Nana's affairs? She was it as far as next of kin went – everyone else, including Christina's parents, was dead. So she'd said yes, hung up the phone, packed the car, taken the dog, locked the door and headed west on I290 out of Chicago. She'd told no one, including her husband, who was coincidentally out of town on business without her for the very first time in their marriage. A few days turned into weeks, turned into months, and by then . . . it was impossible to go back.

176

The damage was irreparable. He was still not over it. Neither was she.

In her defense, feeble as it was, when she'd left, her head was like a malfunctioning pressure cooker set on high. The nightmares that had tormented her for years – another manifestation of those nasty PTSD ghosts – were still causing her to wake in the middle of the night, dripping with sweat and screaming. It wasn't fair to blame Dominick for any of it, but every time she looked at her husband after one of the night terrors, every time he held her and soothed her and said everything was going to be okay, she knew he was thinking about all the terrible things that had been done to her to make her scream so loud. She knew when they made love and Dominick looked at her in the sliver of light that snuck in from a crack in the blinds, he was seeing . . . *him* – the man who had repeatedly raped her, tortured her and then left her to die in a pool of her own blood so many years ago. The man whose name neither of them ever mentioned. The man who had changed both their lives forever – entwining them in the web of a dark and deadly secret. Christina couldn't escape her past, but neither could Dominick. Maybe that was one reason she'd made such a bad decision.

The air was cool. She could smell the comforting aroma of sautéed garlic and grilled meat coming from the kitchens of all the al fresco restaurants that lined State Street, a couple of blocks over. Italian food, that's what she'd cook tonight. Maybe some pasta and sautéed shrimp. Pull a recipe from a Batali cookbook. She'd make a little extra for Luna because spaghetti was her favorite.

The garage on Canon Perdido was open until midnight,

but after six no one parked there and the place was deserted. It was mainly used from 8–5, for the downtown businesses and law firms, who all shut down when the courthouse closed. Normally she parked at a garage closer to her office, but court had started up late today and by the time she got in that lot was full. And the only spots available at the Lobero Garage on Canon Perdido were on the roof. The hairs on the back of her neck rose as, key in hand, lodged in her fingers like a weapon, she pushed the button for the elevator.

For years after the rape she couldn't venture outside. Couldn't walk down a street, eat at a restaurant, go to the gym. Couldn't do anything normal people did. Locked away like a prisoner inside her New York apartment with her blinds drawn and a gun in her lap, the lights on the alarm in her apartment always flashing red. The system was always armed – whether she was locked in or locked out. She'd had to fight her way free of that prison with intense therapy. Day in, day out, the doctors worked to get a.k.a. Christina back to normal, to the fun-loving, uninhibited, trusting girl she used to be. Unfortunately, they'd never quite succeeded.

She breathed a mini sigh of relief when the elevator doors opened to reveal it was empty. She got in and quickly hit the button for the roof, holding her breath until the doors closed and she was alone once more. She could have asked old Joe to walk with her, but that would have seemed silly to him. Nothing bad happened in Santa Barbara. This wasn't LA, or New York, or Miami. Then he might have started asking questions, and she might have been forced to tell him lies. It was best to keep relationships to a minimum, that way no one got hurt. She shifted her satchel on her shoulder. Besides the key locked in her fingers like a shank, in her left jacket pocket was a can of mace. Just in case.

She'd left prosecuting behind when she'd left Miami behind, but when the opportunity arose in Santa Barbara, like a junkie fresh out of rehab, she'd returned to the courtroom for her daily fix of adrenaline, knowing that it might kill her. The human monsters that frightened the hell out of her, that repulsed her, that she knew full well wanted to kill her, when and if they ever got the opportunity, were drawing her back in. She was compelled to do what she did. Ironically enough, being a prosecutor helped her sleep. Most nights, anyway.

The doors opened on the fourth floor. It was well past six and most of the cars were gone. In fact, there were only three left. Christina looked around blankly. None of the cars was an Explorer. She stood there for a long moment, one hand in her left pocket, fingering the cold aluminum can of pepper spray, her brain trying to make excuses.

Maybe I parked on a different level. Maybe it was towed. Maybe, maybe, maybe.

Then it hit her, as it inevitably does all victims: her car was gone. She started to shake.

C.J. Townsend had just entered the next level of the game.

21

'Okay, okay. *Andiamo!* Blow out the candles already, Frank,' Lena DeBianchi, Daria's mother, impatiently pressed her husband the moment everyone in the DeBianchi clan had sung the final off-key note of 'Happy Birthday'. 'The candles! Jesus, Mary and Joseph – they're melting all over the cake! And the cake is melting all over the table . . . An ice-cream cake. Whose idea was that?' she asked with a short, forced laugh. 'Don't tell me. I know who has all the crazy ideas . . .'

Daria's dad, a crooked smile planted on his face, thought for a long moment then motioned with his hand for Daria to come closer.

Daria knelt beside his wheelchair. 'Want some help, Daddy? You make a wish yet?'

Her dad nodded and squeezed her hand.

'Come on, boys, let's help Nonno blow out the candles,' Daria said to the triplets, who'd stopped running around the house like rabid squirrels for ten seconds only because there was birthday cake to be eaten. 'Then

180

we can all have some. Everybody get close to Nonno.' She could feel her mother begin to squirm uncomfortably across the table. 'Stand up, boys, so you can get a better look.'

'On my chairs? Really?' Lena said with another nervous laugh.

'They're covered in plastic, Ma. The boys can't hurt 'em. Sonny, stand next to me,' she said, grabbing a triplet who was lunging, open-fisted, at the cake. 'Michael, Fredo, wait for us. Okay, on the count of three . . .'

With one enormous show of force and the magic of triplet spit, everyone helped Nonno blow out the assorted mess of candles that Daria and her brother Marco had found in the kitchen junk drawer and piled on his Carvel cake, including the fat, red taper dinner candle from Christmas that Daria had stuck right in the center. There weren't sixty-six candles, but it was still an impressive enough display of firepower to worry about the smoke detector when they blew out. Of course, that worry was short-lived. Before everyone had managed to inhale again, Lena had whisked the cake away into the kitchen, all the while muttering both Italian and English expletives under her breath.

'Good job, Daddy,' Daria said as she gave him a kiss on his head. 'I know what you wished for. Me, too.'

'Thank you,' he whispered.

'Let's fatten you up, now. Nothing like Carvel to put meat on the bones.'

'Coffee.'

'Let me get you a cup.'

'Hey, D,' Marco said to Daria as she started for the kitchen. 'Any chance you can watch the boys Tuesday, at, like, six thirty? Our sitter's busy and CeCe has to work late and I'm meeting the Dean over at Nova for coffee.' Nova was Nova Southeastern University in Davie. 'It won't be for long, I promise.'

'The Dean of Nova? Why?' she asked.

'I'm trying to get an adjunct position. It's only a night class. It's like my final interview – coffee with the Dean. I think that means I probably got the job.'

'That's great, Marc, but I can't. Maybe Anthony can do it,' Daria said looking across the room at her other brother. 'I have plans. I don't think I'll be back in town till real late.'

Marco laughed. 'I wouldn't trust Anthony to watch the ferret, much less the boys.'

'That's okay,' answered Anthony. 'I decline the nomination. Watching the Corleone boys on their sugar rush right now is enough for me. And I'll only watch the rat if I can bring Ralphie. He hasn't eaten in two weeks. That'd be all natural entertainment for the kiddies, so even Granola would approve,' he finished, nodding at Marco's wife, CeCe. The family Bohemian.

'Ferrets are in the *weasel* family,' corrected CeCe, sharply, as she struggled to put a sneaker back on one of the boys she'd intercepted on a run around the table. 'Sit still, Sonny. And your boa constrictor is not welcome around the children. What guy your age has a seven-foot long snake for a pet? Compensating, Anthony?'

'Wait a minute,' Marco said. 'Back to Daria. Was that "back in town" I heard? Does that mean you're going out of town? And Monday's the Fourth, so you're going out of town for a long weekend? Ooh . . .'

Anthony sat up and slapped his thigh. 'She's red. It's

a guy! Going out of town for the weekend with a guy!'
He folded his hands in prayer. 'Thank God, Daria, 'cause
we were all wondering. Not me, personally, but Granola
sure was. She's dying to know if birthing rabbits runs
in the family.'

'You're so damn funny, Anthony,' CeCe answered
testily as Sonny wriggled free and ran off, *sans* his Nike.
She turned to Daria, red-faced. 'I never thought you
were a lesbian.'

Daria rolled her eyes. 'What the hell, Anthony? Who
said anything about a weekend? And it's like a thousand-
freaking-degrees in here. I'm not embarrassed – I'm hot.'
Their mom rarely used the air conditioner, and when she
did, she set it on eighty. Lena believed in screens and
breezes, which was all she'd had growing up in Brooklyn
sixty years ago. If their roof wasn't barrel tiled and sloped,
and there wasn't the worry their dad would roll off it, Lena
would probably have held the party up there, handing out
wet towels if the heat became too much. 'Notice how I'm
completely ignoring the lesbian comment, Anthony?'

'Hot date then?' teased Marco.

'Finally.' Her mother was back from the kitchen, jelly
jars in hand and two stuffed under each armpit. 'Finally,'
she repeated with a smug smile as she set out the jars
on the table and poured a shot of limoncello in each
one. 'It's been a long time, right? Right? How long since
you even *had* a boyfriend? You're gonna be thirty. I was
already married with not one but three babies when I
was thirty.'

Anthony laughed.

Daria's jaw set. Just one of the many reasons she
loathed family celebrations and dinners.

'I'm only saying that you're not so young,' her mother added with a disappointed shrug. 'It's time you took life seriously. Got a real job, started a family.'

'You're kidding, right?' Daria glared at her brother. 'Great, Anthony. See what you started? Why don't you pick on Anthony, Ma? He's thirty-six and not married.'

'He's a man. There's a difference,' answered Lena quietly.

Daria pushed the drink away. 'No, he's Anthony. That's the difference.'

'No one has a hot date on a Tuesday night, Marco,' CeCe interjected, trying to calm the seas. 'That would be defined as cold. Tepid at best. Excuse him, everyone. It's been a while since he's taken his wife on a date, much less a hot date.'

'What the hell was that floating vacation I just took you on?' Marco remarked as another one of his kids ran by screaming, this time with a butter knife in his hands.

'You slept the whole time,' CeCe returned. 'Every day. Then you gambled. Nothing hot about it.'

'I was *exhausted*. I *am* exhausted. And forgive me, but every day of the week is the same to me now: Monday, Tuesday, Friday. It's all one big blur. Who knows? Give me that, Fredo,' he said, exasperated, as he plucked the knife from his son's little fingers. 'Don't run with the goddamned, freaking knives!' he yelled.

'Marco!' scolded CeCe.

'Don't *play* with the goddamned, freaking knives is what Daddy meant to say,' Daria corrected. Another identical face crawled from under the table and disappeared into the kitchen. Followed by another. 'And don't chase your brother, Sonny.' She knew for sure the last one was Sonny, because he was still missing his shoe.

'Back once again to Daria,' a bemused Anthony started up again. 'You going out of town with a guy? What's that about? Who is he? I want all the juicy details. Spare nothing.'

'Don't get all big brother on me now, Anthony. Yes, it's a guy. No, it's not a date; he's a detective. We're going up to Starke to interview an inmate for the day. We're leaving early Tuesday, probably be back that night.'

Marco shook his head. 'Why the hell you going up there, D? Don't you have enough of those fucking animals down here to play with?'

'Hey, hey,' Daria's dad mouthed with a scratchy whisper. 'Language.'

'Sorry, Pop,' Anthony mouthed.

'This guy's on death row and they won't transfer him just for an interview. Too high a security risk. I'm interviewing Cupid,' she blurted out excitedly.

The room went completely quiet. Except for her nephew, Sonny, who hobbled by with another butter knife in hand.

'Cupid? The serial killer Cupid?' asked Anthony incredulously.

'Yes. Bill Bantling. I have to talk to him about this homicide I'm working. The dumpster girl.' She grabbed the butter knife from Sonny's fingers. 'Speaking of maniacal killers, Marc. There are early signs you should look for,' she teased, waving the knife at him.

'That's pretty damn cool,' Marco added. *'You're* gonna be interviewing Cupid. Wow. Holy shit. Will he be behind glass like Hannibal Lecter? Or fitted with, like, a bite mask or something?'

Daria shook her head. 'This isn't the movies, Marco.'

But the truth was, she had no idea what to expect herself on Tuesday. She'd never gotten up close and personal with any of the murderers she'd prosecuted – interviews were a detective's province. By the time a case crossed her desk, a defense lawyer was involved and the talking had stopped.

'You have the most interesting job, Daria,' added CeCe admiringly. 'You should write a book. Like Michael Connelly, ya know? Or John Grisham. I always like his books, and they're about legal stuff.'

'That's a plan. Become an international bestselling author when I get a chance. I like it.'

'This case could make you famous,' Marco added. 'Think Kim Kardashian, D.'

Anthony laughed and held his hands out in front of him as if he had tremendous breasts. 'I know Daria doesn't have *that* in her. No offense, sister.'

Out of the corner of her eye, Daria spotted her mom slip into the kitchen. The last thing Lena wanted to listen to was how her daughter might one day be famous. Or successful.

Daria rolled her eyes. 'I'd like her body, not her life, Marc. And thanks, Anthony.'

'What does Cupid have to do with the dumpster case?' Anthony asked.

'I can't talk about it yet.'

Her dad motioned her over again. The lopsided smile was gone. He was frowning.

'And Kim Kardashian just happened to be the first famous person that came to your mind? Huh, honey?' CeCe fired at Marco. 'What's with your obsession with her?'

Anthony smirked. 'Someone's in trouble.'

'You okay, Daddy?' Daria asked, bending over him and putting her face close to his while everyone else prattled on, ribbing her brother.

Her dad grasped her hand, harder than before. She knew that wasn't easy for him. 'Daddy?' she asked again, alarmed.

'Careful now,' he whispered harshly. 'I don't have . . . a good feeling.'

The hairs on the back of her neck stood up. The first thought that popped into her head was the creepy, cryptic message that Manny had delivered to her in the court-house that morning. She'd been trying not to think about it all day – to not let Talbot Lunders get inside her head, like Manny had warned – but every time she glanced at the clock she thought about returning to her empty apartment. To the dead garden outside her kitchen window. 'Okay, Pop,' she whispered in his ear. 'I'll be careful.'

'The man's an animal. Don't want you . . . involved. Bad things gonna happen, you'll see.'

'No worries, Daddy,' she said quickly standing up, and patting his hand.

'. . . I'd be scared to death to face a serial killer, even if he was behind bars. Just thinking about what he did to those women makes me want to throw up,' CeCe said with a shiver. 'Aren't you nervous, Daria?'

No one else had heard her exchange with her dad, although from her sister-in-law's last question Daria would've thought she'd read her mind. She shook her head. 'Let me get Daddy his coffee.'

'You'll never get that past mom,' Anthony called out.

'I tried to slip him a cappuccino last week and she almost bit me.'

Daria ignored him and walked into the kitchen.

'Hi there. Did you make coffee? Daddy wants some,' she said as she headed to the coffee pot.

'He's not allowed to have any.'

'Says who?'

'Says Matt Valitudo.'

'The dry cleaner?'

'He told me coffee makes the cancer worse.'

'The dry cleaner told you that? He doesn't have cancer, Ma. He has Parkinson's.'

'It's cancer, is what it is.'

There was no point in arguing. There never was. 'Fine. I'll make decaf,' she said, reaching for the vile container of Taster's Choice instant.

'He can't have coffee. And that's that,' her mother said sharply.

'It would be the caffeine he can't have, Ma, if anything.'

'He can't have coffee,' Lena repeated.

Daria put her hands up and sighed. 'You win. You need help?' Her mother had made a *panettone* in addition to the Carvel cake Daria had brought because her mother was the only person on the planet who actually hated ice-cream. She was also not gonna be outdone by her daughter, who'd brought the birthday cake. Not in her house.

Lena shook her head as she arranged the last slice of *panettone* on a silver platter. 'Lord, where did you get those shoes? They're so high.'

'You like 'em?' Daria asked. 'They're Donald Pliner's. And they're comfy, too.'

Her mom shook her head and pursed her lips. 'No. Uh-uh. Your style is a little . . . eclectic for me. I like something more classic. Something nice. You know that. As long as you can walk in them, I suppose,' she called over her shoulder as she stepped back into the dining room. 'Come on, *andiamo*! I'm putting out the cake.'

Daria stood in the kitchen for a long while, willing away angry tears. As Lena had pointed out, she'd be thirty years old soon. And for most of those thirty years she'd sought her mother's approval, even when she'd insisted that she was through with that. Now here she was yet again, standing in her fancy heels, licking her wounds.

One of these days she was going to have to face the fact that, no matter what she said, did, wore, married, how successful a career she had or how much money she made, she was never gonna get it. Her mother would still go on dangling that elusive approval over Daria's sad-eyed, eager little head. *What was Einstein's definition of insanity again? Doing the same thing over and over again and expecting a different result?* She and her brother Marco were like Pavlov's dogs – always showing up at the bowl with their tongues hanging out, hoping Lena might toss them a crumb of acknowledgement or at least a kind word. Marco did whatever was necessary for peace – he'd gotten married and made triplets and had a normal job. Daria had rebelled – a wild adolescence, no husband, and a job her mother detested. And Anthony, well, he had smartly opted out of the game years ago. He didn't give a shit if he was successful, if anyone else was happy, or if the world ended tomorrow. He smoked inordinate amounts of weed on the weekend, hang-glided, slept with lots of women, and drove without a seat belt all the time. He'd declared that he had no intention of getting married or having kids. And yet he was the only one in the family who their mother was not perpetually disappointed with. Anthony could do no wrong.

Why didn't she simply walk away? Make other plans? Send a birthday gift and a card instead of continually setting herself up for failure? Daria had asked herself that question a thousand times – usually after coming home from visiting her parents. Friends of hers had cut off relations with their relatives over a lot less. But she couldn't and that was that. Her mother was, after all, her mother. And her mother now stood directly in the path of her father.

Daria's relationship with her dad had always been different. He'd taught her how to ride a bike, fix a toilet, shoot a deer, make handmade mozzarella. Growing up, he didn't care if she wore 'boy' pants to her aunt's house or an ugly-ass dress that cost way too much anyway. On Sunday mornings, they'd slip out of the house before Lena was up, kayak into the ocean and meet the sunrise with a Thermos filled with orange juice spiked with Asti Spumante. He sat front row for her law school graduation and her first trial, both of which were missed by her mother, who'd conveniently developed a splitting migraine right before both events – the only two migraines she'd ever had in her life. Even when Daria had grown out of pigtails and princess dresses, she was still her daddy's baby. And throughout her childhood and super-rebellious teens, it was her father who had been her ally in that crazy, scream-infested house – always attempting to negotiate the dangerous, spike-covered fence that existed between his wife and his only daughter. When diplomacy failed and her mom's destructive comments and wooden spoon beatings and weird temper tantrums for which she should have been medicated became too much for Daria to take, with the pounding of his fist on a table her dad would command, 'Enough is enough, Lena! Let her be!' and that would temporarily end it. Her parents were Italian, after all, and her mother had been programmed by her own off-the-boat parents to listen to her husband. But he couldn't order his wife to not be jealous of their daughter. And he couldn't force Lena to go to the doctor or get help for her temper, not that he even tried – psychiatrists and the like were tantamount to witch doctors to a red-blooded Italian male from the old school.

Now, though, her father was trapped in a body that no longer worked the way it should, facing down a disease that had ravaged his muscles and put him in a wheelchair within two years of being diagnosed. It also put him at the complete mercy of her mother, who he was now physically and emotionally dependent on. The rules of the game had changed. He no longer demanded that Lena behave herself. He no longer demanded or ordered or commanded anything. He had a particularly aggressive type of Parkinson's, and the prognosis was very grim. It was only a short matter of time before he'd be in a nursing home, his mind functional and his body useless. When he was no longer able to breathe, they'd vent him and that would be the last time her dad would ever speak. It would be the last time Daria would hear his voice. It was a day she couldn't imagine, but one that would be here soon enough. Then she would be left with her mother.

She wiped her eyes and looked over at the kitchen counter. The slices of ice-cream cake were still sitting there, melting into shiny piles of white and brown goo.

Careful, now. I don't have . . . a good feeling . . .

Her dad's cryptic warning applied to so many facets of her life. Anger swelling inside her, she threw the cake plates on a metal cookie sheet and pushed open the swing door that led to the dining room. 'Not so fast, everyone! Who wants *ice- cream* cake?' she asked as she strode back inside and the dining room erupted into tiny, enthusiastic cheers of 'Me! Me! Me!'

22

Sometimes we don't see what it is we don't want to see. Always remember that, Manuel, and maybe you won't go completely blind . . .

Manny's uncle Cesar, a seasoned Miami-Dade homicide detective with twenty-nine years on the force before he died, had shared that slice of wisdom with him the day Manny was sworn in. Uncle Ces was like that – always throwing out these deep quotes that you never quite got right away, like he was the Dalai Lama or something. It wasn't until Manny was promoted to detective himself and cracking mysteries became his own life's work that he finally understood half the shit his uncle was trying to say. He was still waiting on the other half.

Manny sipped at his beer while he stared at one of the twenty-seven TVs in the crowded sports bar, a plate of spicy chicken wings in front of him. The Marlins were actually winning a game. Norman's Tavern was not an establishment he normally frequented, but it was close to home and the food was good. Plus, he wasn't much of a cook and the house was lonely. Though he didn't want to be alone, he didn't want company either. Tonight, all he wanted was to eat some wings and a burger, down a brew and think about all the deep shit his uncle had prophesized so many years ago . . .

It was a cold and rainy night in Miami on January 21, 1999 when the decomposed body of Cupid's first victim was discovered in an abandoned supermarket in southwest Miami-Dade County. Twenty-five-year-old Andrea Gallagher was Bill Bantling's first victim. No one knew at that time that the gaping hole in the center of her chest would soon come to be recognized around the world as the signature of a serial killer. Less than three months later, Manny himself would be called out to the homicide scene of Hannah Cordova, a twenty-two-year-old aspiring singer who'd disappeared weeks earlier from Penrods, a nightclub on Miami Beach. Her body was found in a shuttered-up crack den in Liberty City, a neighborhood within the City of Miami's jurisdiction. Her chest, too, had been cracked open, her heart removed, her body perversely staged. It didn't take long after that to realize that the two very brutal murders were related. And the identical traumatic injuries also made it clear that it was a serial. A third victim was discovered in a shack on Miami Beach six weeks after that. Three victims, three different police jurisdictions, three different police agencies investigating. Not a good scenario. A task force was formed, headed by Florida Department of Law Enforcement (FDLE) Special Agent Dominick Falconetti, and everyone moved across town to the new command center at FDLE headquarters.

For the next two years Manny would eat, sleep and breathe the Cupid case – ultimately reporting to the homicide scenes of eight more young, pretty blondes. As the body count continued to rise and the leads fizzled out, the case grew more and more frustrating. The man was a ghost – snatching beautiful girls from busy nightclubs, all under the watchful eyes of their friends, and surveillance cameras, and a thousand witnesses who never seemed to see a thing. There was no rhyme or reason as to why he selected his victims – other than their being blonde, young, and comely – or how it was he chose them. There was never any physical evidence left behind at staged crime scenes that were so horrific Manny had seen veteran detectives lose their cookies in front of everyone. Not a drop of semen. Not a single hair. Not a speck of blood that didn't belong to a victim. After a year and a half of chasing their tails, the body count was nine dead, two missing and the task force of elite detectives still without a bona fide description of Cupid. He was a phantom, walking among his prey, possibly brazen enough to mingle with his hunters, as many serials do. And Miami's Finest had not a clue where to find him or how to stop him.

Then a routine traffic stop had changed everything. A rookie cop named Victor Chavez ended Cupid's eighteen-month reign of terror when he pulled over furniture salesman William Rupert Bantling for speeding on the MacArthur Causeway. A subsequent search of the vehicle led to the discovery of gruesome evidence in the trunk – namely the body of model Anna Prado, one of the two missing girls. Over the next few months the task force pushed to ready the case for what the international press was already calling 'The Trial of the Century'.

The prosecution was headed by C.J. Townsend, one of the state's most accomplished attorneys. A Major Crimes prosecutor, C.J. had been assigned to the Cupid task force since its inception. Dogged and determined, she labored to put Bantling on death row for the murder of Anna Prado, all in front of the rolling cameras and the international press. It was only after Bantling was convicted that Manny had learned of the enormous emotional pressure that C.J. had been working under. Right after the jury had announced its verdict, but before the reporters had the chance to tell the world, Bantling had started screaming in open court that he had raped C.J., back when she was a law student in New York. Claiming C.J. knew he was not guilty of murder, charging she'd destroyed and covered up evidence in the Cupid case because a murder conviction was the only way she could make him pay for what he had done to her. It was the only way to get him sentenced to death.

Manny remembered the chaotic scene as if it were yesterday. C.J. had denied the allegation, but she'd then been forced to make a painful and personal admission in open court, and simultaneously to the whole world: she *had* been violently raped in law school by a stranger. Her rapist had never been caught. Her rapist was not Bill Bantling.

Manny had felt so bad for her, standing there, so small and pale and thin, telling everybody what some creep had done to her when he broke into her apartment. And then salacious details of her assault had run for days and days in the paper as reporters did exactly what

Bill Bantling had done and dug up the girl's past. In light of what she'd once been through and what she had put aside to prosecute Bantling, Manny was even more appreciative of all she'd done to put the son of a bitch behind bars. So were the rest of the boys on the task force. C.J. was one of Manny's favorite people in the world – down to earth, honest, hard-working and a ball-busting bitch when she needed to be. And if his buddy Dom hadn't been sweet on her, Manny might've tried a shot at the big leagues himself, instead of ending up with her insane secretary, which cost him a couple of years of his life, untold amounts of money, and almost another walk down the aisle.

Realizing justice, though, can be a long process. Especially when you're talking about a death sentence. Ten years had gone by and the case wasn't over. Bill Bantling was still breathing. And with the current state of his appeals, there was no end to his miserable life in sight.

Manny ordered another Corona and watched for a while as the Marlins inevitably screwed up their lead. But all the while his eyes were on the game he was hearing that warning from Uncle Ces: *Sometimes we don't see what it is we don't want to see*. When William Bantling told him about a snuff club, had he dismissed it because he couldn't face re-examining all the irritating details that didn't tie together and the strange coincidences that were too coincidental? Or was it something worse than laziness – a condition Manny had never been accused of in all his years on the force – that kept him from resolving the lingering questions that surrounded the Cupid case?

Had he kept his mouth shut and his eyes closed to save a friend?

The Cupid case was a lot more troubling than he'd let on to Daria. Shortly after Bantling was convicted, there had been a violent attempt on C.J.'s life by Dr Gregory Chambers, a state forensic psychologist – someone C.J. said she had considered a friend as well as a colleague. Turned out Chambers had also been Bantling's shrink. Listening to his client's sick fantasies must have flipped some switch, turned him into a wannabe Cupid, obsessed with C.J. If she hadn't managed to grab a pair of scissors and put a hole in his chest, he'd have cut one in hers. There was no question but that she'd killed him in self-defense, and there was no evidence to link him with any of the other murders so Manny had closed the case, and Bantling had been shipped off to death row, but . . .

In 2004, three of the cops who had worked Cupid were murdered, including Chavez, the traffic cop who pulled Bantling over for speeding. Since pretty much everyone in law enforcement had assisted in the Cupid manhunt in some capacity, it wasn't grounds for launching an investigation, but it was thought-provoking, nonetheless. Then the judge died in a car accident, and Bantling's old attorney, Lourdes Rubio, was found with her throat slit in her Colorado office, days before she was scheduled to fly home to Miami to testify in Bantling's appeal. It was then that Bantling told Manny he was part of a snuff club organized by none other than the deceased Dr Chambers. And with this information, Manny did . . .

Nothing. Absolutely nothing.

And now there were more murders happening with possible connections to Bantling. And Daria, the state's prosecutor in those murders, was being harassed, possibly stalked. He pushed his half-eaten plate away.

Sometimes we don't see what it is we don't want to see, Manuel.

Like a hologram turned just the right way, he was seeing it all now. Manny chugged the rest of his beer, almost wishing the alcohol would hit him hard enough to stop this forced self-revelation crap. If it was true that he'd turned his back on the facts a decade ago because it was inconvenient, or too mind-boggling to fathom, or because he was looking away in order to save a friendship that, sadly, was no more, anyway, or because Bantling was getting what he deserved even if it might not be for the exact crime he was convicted of, would that make him responsible for the deaths that followed? The Black Jacket cops, they were dirty, they could be reasoned away. But Holly Skole, Gabriella Vechio, Cyndi DeGregorio, Jane Doe, Kevin Flaunters – would they be alive today if Manny had acted on his gut when it told him there was more to the snuff-club story than just a desperate pack of lies?

He lined up the empty bottle of Corona next to the other three he'd finished off. The problem with alcohol was that it worked like a truth serum. He'd drunk too much tonight, and yet not enough to forget what he'd been thinking about. He'd discovered the hologram, and he would forever see the picture that he hadn't wanted to see all along. It was right there in front of him. Now it was impossible to miss.

Manny's only hope at this point was that he was

wrong. That when he got to see that manipulative psychopath Bantling on Tuesday, he'd ask a few questions that he should've asked long ago and finally be satisfied that Bantling's story of retribution and snuff clubs was just that – a story. A story that could not be corroborated and could never be proven because it simply wasn't true. It was a tall tale concocted to get Bantling's ass off death row. Then Manny could get back to building the case against Talbot Lunders – a budding psychopath himself, if ever Manny had seen one – track down his possible accomplice or accomplices and put Pretty Boy in a cell right next to Bantling.

He thought back to Talbot's odd reaction to the mention of Bantling's name.

Maybe they'd already met . . .

That was a chilling thought.

He dropped two twenties on the bar and waved goodnight to the cute bartender. Hopefully, he thought, as he shrugged off the shudder that had run down his spine and headed for the door, he could pack away this bad penny once and for all. Hopefully, come this time Tuesday night, he would be able to forever dismiss the disturbing thoughts that had been nibbling at his brain for far, far too long.

23

Quaint brick homes, their front lawns sprinkled with laurel oaks and swing sets, their backyards crisscrossed with clotheslines, dotted State Road 16. Kids skateboarded down long driveways, and horses grazed in green fields. Tractors could be heard working their way through neighboring citrus groves. The smell of freshly cut grass filled the summer air. All that was missing from the live Rockwell snapshot of a small American town was a silver-haired granny doling out glasses of lemonade and slices of apple pie on her rickety front porch. As Daria had commented to Manny when they'd first made the turn on to SR16 from Highway 301 – if you didn't know you were driving straight into Inmate Central, you'd have no idea you were driving straight into Inmate Central. The only indication that things had changed, and not necessarily for the better, were the rather unassuming signs that sprouted up alongside the road, warning drivers not to pick up hitchhikers. These were followed a mile or two later by neon orange road diamonds that advised **STATE PRISONERS WORKING**. Put two and two together and it wasn't hard to figure out Dorothy wasn't in Kansas anymore. And if you weren't good in math, the tiered mile-marker signpost at the turnoff eliminated any guesswork:

**LAWTEY CORRECTIONAL INSTITUTION,
6 miles;
UNION CORRECTIONAL INSTITUTION,
18 miles;
NEW RIVER CORRECTIONAL, 11 miles;
FLORIDA STATE PRISON, 11 miles;
RECEPTION AND MEDICAL CENTER
(RMC), 5 miles;
RECEPTION AND MEDICAL CENTER (RMC)
WEST UNIT, 4 miles.**

The five-hour drive up to Starke had been pretty easy; it was only the first half-hour or so that had felt strangely awkward; more akin to a first date, Daria thought, than a sobering business trip to interview a serial murderer. She and Manny had politely chatted about the weather and how horrible Miami traffic was, all the while sipping their giant cups of Starbucks jet fuel. Maybe it was the prospect of spending so much time one-on-one together in a car and outside of a courthouse, coupled with the fear that they'd eventually run out of things to say – or worse, have too much to say about the wrong thing, spurring a fight – that had initially made the situation feel so weird. But by the time they'd made the Palm Beach line, the idle, restrained chatter had slipped into conversation that bounced from corrupt South Florida politicians to the latest episode of *Chopped*, to roses and gardening, and of course, bad guys.

As they drew closer to the prison, the easy conversation dropped off, as did the Rockwell homes and picturesque countryside. The landscape within a mile of the facility had been leveled to flat, brown wasteland to thwart escape attempts. In the event an inmate did make it out of the sprawling maximum-security prison, past the armed guards in the watch towers, and over the double razor-wire fencing, there would be no place for him to hide on the other side. Not so much as a single skinny palm tree.

'It's bigger than I remembered,' Daria commented as Manny turned the car into the complex. They passed underneath an iron arch announcing *Florida State Prison*. The sign made her think of the infamous ironwork twisted above the gates of German concentration camps: *Arbeit Macht Frei* – 'Work Will Set You Free'. Except here, there was no such false promise. Most of the fourteen hundred men housed inside those prison walls would never see freedom again. Nor should they – they weren't tragic innocents caught up in genocide. Florida State Prison housed the most violent offenders in the entire state of Florida – murderers, rapists, pedophiles, armed robbers, kidnappers. Many were serving life sentences, or sentences that numbered in the hundreds of years. And for forty-five of those murderers, the ultimate fate awaited them on death row.

The visitor's lot was empty. 'You've been here?' Bear asked as he pulled into a spot. 'I thought you said you hadn't.'

'Not *in* here. My friends and I drove out one night when I was in my second year of law school, just to see

203

what the place looked like. You hear so many stories about what goes on here. I'd never actually seen a prison before then.'

'What'd you think when you saw it?'

'We got as far as the welcome arch. We were so clueless, Manny. Unbeknown to us – or at least to me – there was an execution scheduled the next day. Glen Ocha was the name. I'll never forget it, because there were like thirty people waving anti-death penalty signs at us with his face on it, holding up candles and handing out bibles. It gave me nightmares. Sometimes, when I dream of bad guys – you know, like I'm being chased or robbed or something in my dream? Well, it's Glen Ocha's face I see.'

'That's weird.'

'Considering the scum I've put away, I should see someone else coming to get me,' she added, stepping out of the car.

Manny followed. 'You might just get your wish after today.'

Abutting the prison was an interconnected maze of chain-link cages. Hundreds of them. Inside the individual cages, inmates paced back and forth like stressed tigers. Some jumped rope or worked out. Others sat around and did nothing. Uniformed Department of Corrections guards patrolled the walkways.

'What are those?' Daria asked as they walked up to the prison entrance. A loud buzz sounded and a green uniformed CO pushed open the steel-meshed glass door.

'Those are the runs,' Manny answered as he stepped inside. Some of the inmates had stopped what they were doing to stare in their direction.

'Dawg runs,' said the CO, whose badge read SGT TRU

204

ZEFFERS, in a thick-as-molasses Southern drawl. He checked their credentials and frowned. In his late forties, Sgt Zeffers had a mop of unnaturally thick and unnaturally still jet-black hair that was brushed into a swirl atop his head, like a gigantic soft-serve cone. 'That's where the boys git their exercise. Have to be separated at all times, else they'll kill each other. Like bad dawgs,' he finished, letting the 's' drag on. He studied Daria for a moment, then turned and motioned with the hook of his finger for them to follow.

'Twenty-four/seven they have to be kept apart,' Zeffers continued, leaning against the security booth after Manny went to check his Glock into a gun locker.

No weapons were allowed to be brought inside the prison. The COs themselves were unarmed. Manny had explained that if a riot broke out, or the prison went under siege, there were guns and ammunition the staff could use, but it was all locked away so that the inmates could not gain access. She wished she didn't know that.

'They eat 'lone, shower 'lone, exercise 'lone,' Zeffers continued. 'They're cuffed when they leave their cells, and they only leave those to go to the runs or take a shower. Place don' need 'nother turn like what happened in the seventies. Took hostages that time, 'fore they set everything on fire.'

Daria frowned. 'That doesn't sound good.'

'No, darlin', it don't.' Zeffers looked down at her shoes and smiled. 'I'm thinking maybe you didn't see the recommended list of dress attire? It's gonna be awful hard to run in those, sugar, if you need to. And a skirt, too. You know, in a worst-case scenario, which I hope won't never happen, I'd have to make special plans to come rescue you. Plus, I think them heels are jus' high enough and pointy enough to be considered weapons.' He wiped a hand on his pant leg and it left a stain.

'Don't worry about the Counselor and her fancy kicks, Sarge,' Manny said, moving Daria through the metal detectors. 'I'll pick her up and run with her if we get into trouble. We're kinda late, Sarge, and here comes the tour guide, I think. So we'll catch you on the way out, okay?'

Zeffers glanced at his watch. He shook his head dismissively at the approaching CO. 'I've decided to play escort, Detective Alvarez. Bill Bantling is a very special inmate here. One who we take extra precautions with.' He put his hand on Daria's shoulder. He stank of cologne and old cigarette smoke. 'Don't go running off on me now, ma'am,' he said playfully. ''Specially not in those shoes. Ma'am's so formal. Can I call you—'

'Counselor?' Daria answered quickly. 'That's Detective Alvarez's moniker for me. DeBianchi is what the judges in Miami—'

'—Dairy-uh?' Zeffers finished, totally ignoring what she'd just said. 'Now am I sayin' that right? 'Cause that's a real nice name. Real different.'

'Thank you.' She held back both the annoyed sigh and the impulse to cringe. She'd promised Manny that she would sit and listen. Like wallpaper. 'Close enough on the pronunciation, unless you can master an Italian accent. It's a family name.'

'I-talian, huh? Don't get many of those here in Starke. They seem to like Miami better. Ya know, Tru isn't short for Truman, in case you were wondering. It's jus' Tru. You can call me that, if you like.'

206

Manny rolled his eyes.

Twenty minutes later, after a lot of testosterone-fueled prison anecdotes from Jus' Tru, the three of them finally reached the security station for the death-row housing block. In the event of one of those worst-case scenarios, assuming her new friend wasn't as big and brave as he was trying to pretend to be, Daria realized that even if she could find someone to open all those six-inch-thick steel security doors they'd passed through to get to where they were, she wouldn't remember the damn way out anyhow. The place was a concrete and steel maze. Like a carnival haunted house, shrieks and catcalls came from every direction, whackos and murderers lurked behind every corner. She'd put enough men in here that the very real, very uncomfortable fact was she might actually run into one of them today. *What would happen then*, she thought with a chill, and hung a little closer to Manny. If all hell did break loose, she was putting her money on her supersized detective. Like he said, he really could put her under his arm like a football and run her out the door.

The death-row cell block, for obvious reasons, was different than all other security levels they'd passed through. Zeffers had to place a key into his side of the door with his counterpart doing the same on the other side, and both men had to turn their keys simultaneously in order to open the locking mechanism. It seemed antiquated, but Jus' Tru explained that, in the event someone gained access to the prison's online security system and overran the rest of the prison, they still would not be able to gain access into, or out of, the death-row block without an actual key and assistance on the other side.

Devoid of windows, the small command station was painted a dull gray and lit by long fluorescent tubes that clung to the ceiling, caged in wire mesh to prevent them from ever being broken or used as a weapon. The brains at the Department of Corrections had thought of everything. A CO sat working at a desk doing paperwork. In front of him was a multi-screened TV monitor that captured every conceivable angle of death row, as well as the general population and the prison at large. A chalkboard listing each inmate's name, the crime he was convicted of and the cell he was in hung next to another desk, where the CO who'd opened the door now sat. Daria could see the inmates on the closed-circuit monitors, moving in time-delayed, super-slow motion. From behind a cell door off to the right, she could hear the chatter from their televisions, the music from their radios, the flushing of a toilet somewhere, the shuffle of feet across a cement floor. When she'd asked to come here with Manny, she'd not realized she'd be this deep in the prison, standing a few feet from some of the most brutal murderers in the state. She'd imagined the interview would take place in an interrogation room in the main wing of the prison. To be this deep in the belly was definitely disturbing.

Zeffers pulled her aside, jerked his head in the direction of the barred cell door off to the right. The one where the noises were coming from. 'If you want, you can walk the row, Dairy-uh,' he said, his voice little more than a whisper. 'None of 'em's gonna say nuthin' to you. I can promise you that.' He jingled the keys on his belt.

'Is that where the interview room is?' she asked.

'The interrogation cell's on the other side of Row B, but I was thinking, since you took the trip up and all, you'd want to walk it – the Row. There's not many people I make that offer to, 'cause this is the Row, after all. But none of the boys are gonna say nuthin' to you. I promise you that. Even in those heels,' he added with a wheeze.

She frowned. 'Now why would I want to do that, Sergeant? Walk the Row?'

Zeffers shrugged. 'Show 'em who's boss. Show 'em who has the power. They're in there and you're out here. Might help you in your interview with Bantling. He's a difficult one. But no one's gonna say nuthin'. See, I'm the staff sergeant tonight. They say anythin' to you – anythin' perverted-like, anythin' at all – they know I will make their lives miserable. There are some pretty badass people in here that don't respect nuthin', but they respect *that*. They respect *me*.'

It took a different type of person to babysit murderers and rapists all day long with only their wits as a weapon. In that regard, some COs were better equipped than others. There was a long-standing in-joke at the State Attorney's Office, that unfortunately wasn't far enough from the truth to be funny: 'the only difference between Corrections and the defendants is Corrections passed the test'.

It didn't take a rocket scientist to figure out the ulterior motive behind Jus' Tru's proposition. He wanted to capture ASA Dairy-uh on surveillance video, strutting in front of the convicted rapists and murderers, getting them all hot and bothered in her high heels and power suit. Jus' Tru would then surely make a bootleg copy of his *Prosecutors Gone Wild* footage, so that every night from the comfort of his worn recliner he could rub his potbelly, play with his thick hair, and relive his wicked fantasies with the shades drawn.

'Not today,' she answered coolly and went to join Manny on the other side of the room.

Zeffers turned red and the smile disappeared. 'We decided not to transport Bantling till ya'all got here,' he announced. 'He don't know you're coming, just in case that news was gonna upset him. It's a tough job to get an inmate out of a death cell when he don' wanna go. Gotta call in an extraction team, take the necessary pre-cautions. It gets messy and a whole lot dangerous, 'cause they got nothing left to lose.'

'How long's it gonna take to get him into the room?' Manny asked.

'Depends on if Mr Bantling wants to cooperate or not.'

'I'd like to interview him today, Sergeant. Not when he feels like it.'

'Any of these yours?' Zeffers asked Daria, motioning to the chalkboard with the defendants' names on it.

She shook her head.

'You know, you should pay a visit to hell before you send a man down into it.' Then Jus' Tru turned and headed down a corridor that ran parallel to Row B, motioning with another hook of his finger for them to follow. He stopped outside a solid-steel cell door, gestured up at a camera and the door buzzed. Inside, more caged fluorescents lit the gray cinderblock. Three chairs had been set up around a metal table. Iron restraints hung from thick bolts in the wall. The room smelled dank, like the muddy crawl space of an old house that vagrants had continuously pissed in.

'Let's hope he wants to cooperate,' Zeffers said as he walked out. 'Use the buzzer if you need something, or just shout. One of us'll be here in the hallway.'

'What the hell happened back there?' Manny asked with a bemused smirk when the door slammed shut. 'What'd you do to that guy? You pissed him off, didn't you?'

'Yuck.'

'Nothing like letting 'em down easy, Counselor.'

'I didn't want to walk death row is all.'

'Not in those heels you don't. You'd be the star in a bunch of fantasies come tonight.'

'Yuck.'

'You wanted to come.'

'Yuck again.'

Manny nodded at the steel door. 'You do know what this guy did to eleven women, right? He may harbor a few fantasies of you himself tonight. If you can't handle it, you can wait outside with your new friend. I'm sure he won't mind. Maybe give you a private tour of his office.'

'Very funny. I'll take my chances with the serial killer. You can protect me in here.'

'I'll do my best, but don't piss Bantling off. I gotta get inside this guy's head. You may be the distraction I need to do that, 'cause I don't think he's gonna be too happy to see me. We didn't part on good terms.'

She stared at him. 'Great. Now you tell me I'm bait?'

'There's always Tru, Counselor. He's outside that door, waiting for you to call his name. Oh, Tru!' he cooed in a high-pitched voice. 'Tru, you handsome thing, you! Come save me! Let me run my fingers through your fabulous hair!'

She rolled her eyes. 'Fine, fine. Stop. I'll be bait. You owe me.'

'You may want to lose a few buttons on that blouse. For the sake of my interview, of course.'

She stared at him again. 'What?'

Manny laughed. 'Just kidding, Counselor. Relax.'

Down the hall, chains jingled and jangled, mixed with the heavy-soled thud of shoes lifting and dragging on cement. Daria recognized that sound. She'd heard it before in the halls of the courthouse many times. It was the sound of an inmate being transported.

'I don't like the idea of my being in debt to you, though,' Manny said, with a sigh and a shake of his head.

Closer.

She could actually feel the fear down in her belly, crawling like an alien, trying to escape up into her throat. She shivered, though the room wasn't cold.

'You know what they say about that,' she answered softly.

The footfalls had stopped. The jangling had stopped. Right outside the door.

'What's that?' asked Manny.

'Payback's a bitch,' she whispered, as the lock buzzed and the steel cell door swung open.

24

'You got company. Move it out.'

Bill Bantling looked up from his book. A black-suited, helmeted, three-man extraction team stood outside his cell.

Sergeant Zeffers banged his baton against the cell bars, like the ring master at the circus, trying to get the tigers up and moving. 'Let's go,' he barked. 'Don't make this difficult, now, Billy.'

Such drama. And delivered with a grating Southern twang.

Bill put his book aside and sat up on the edge of his cot. At moments like this, when the anger began to swell inside him, he was comforted knowing that the little men who worked in this damned place did so not for the pittance they were paid or the state benefits, or because they wanted to keep society safe from mass murderers and other villains. Or any other such selfless bullshit. He knew the *real* reason misfits like Zeffers put on their ugly green uniforms every day was because they fed on power and lived for some drama – any drama – in their sad, empty lives. The excitement that was generated simply by punching a clock at a supermax prison was enough to power more than a few conversations with the whores and barflies congregating down at the local watering hole come quittin' time. Add a little more drama, like a confrontation, and they would score big. Of course Bill knew, as did every other inmate, that on most workdays, those same, small, self-important men were nothing more than waiters delivering room service to the inmates, escorting killers to the showers and occasionally sticking their fingers way up a prisoner's asshole to find out if he was hiding something special in his bowels. Not much drama in that. So they had to make some up whenever they could. It was clear from the baton-waving and barked commands that Sergeant Tru Zeffers was trying to impress someone.

Bill just stared at the three blobs in body armor. One started to scratch at his head under his clear face-mask. Another kept shifting his weight from one foot to the other. The third wiped a thick band of sweat from his lip with the back of his hand. Take away the power hose, body armor, and deflection shields, and Bill knew that none of the drama-seekers standing before him would voluntarily go three minutes in the ring with either him or any one of his neighbors on the block. And that included the not-so-big, not-so-bad, and not-so-brave-when-no-one-is-looking Tru Zeffers. Everybody else knew it, too, save for those desperate women and thirsty drunks waiting on someone in a green jacket to come tell them a good story . . .

Bill slowly rose to his feet and made his way calmly

to the cell bars. There was a horizontal slit in the center of the door, so that inmates could stick their hands out and get cuffed before an officer opened it. He put his hands into the slit. 'Company?'

'No questions. Step back,' Zeffers barked after the cuffs were snapped on. 'Now get face-down on the cot.' Bill complied, the officers entered the cell, and a set of leg irons was slapped on his ankles.

As they wrapped him in chains, he let his mind drift. It had been a long time since he'd had a visitor. Even his latest attorney just phoned in when he needed to deliver news. He had no family and he had no friends, so that eliminated social calls. He did have lonely, and unfortunately usually homely, women from all over the world, who sent him love notes and pictures, hoping for a marriage proposal, but they would never get a visit without being on a list of individuals pre-approved by the warden, which meant they would never get a visit.

There was an off, off chance that it could be a media visit, but seeing as the warden didn't allow those either, at least not for him, Bill doubted that was it. He was already a celebrity, a once-upon-a-time household name. And no one in Prison Administration wanted to see that name resurrected on Internet trending boards or appearing on *Dateline* investigative specials. Society wanted to bury Bill Bantling in supermax, far away from the cameras and the microphones, hoping that – unlike the infamous, crazy Charles Manson, who continued to make press whenever he came up for parole – Billy would one day fade into the cinderblock and finally be forgotten by the outside world, and the name Cupid would once again only be thought of as belonging to a fat, naked angel with a bow and arrow and incredible aim.

'Dead man walking!' Zeffers barked loudly as they paraded him down the row. A dog-and-pony show meant to impress someone. Probably the head of prisons, or some other useless figurehead. More drama. Unless you were taking someone off the row and moving them to the basement on Death Watch status – which was the period after a death warrant was signed but before it was executed, when the machines were tested to make sure they were in working order for the big day – nobody on the block gave a shit if their neighbor was taking a walk or taking a leak.

Zeffers turned a corner that led to Row B. They headed down another corridor, before stopping in front of a solid steel door with a small slit resembling a mail slot halfway down the door. It was the interrogation room. He'd met his attorney there once.

That was when he smelled it.

The unmistakable scent of Chanel No. 5. It hung in the air – just a hint, the memory of a fragrance that had been sprayed hours before, and now only lingered on clothes and hair.

He stared at the door.

There was a woman inside that room.

His heart began to pound. His pulse quickened. He inhaled deeply.

Perhaps not just *any* woman . . .

Zeffers motioned at the camera. 'Open up!' he shouted. The door buzzed. 'Don't get stupid on us, now, boy. Play nice, and so will we,' Zeffers said, pushing Bantling from

216

behind into the room. 'Use the foot restraints to lock him,' he commanded the team.

Bill shuffled into the room, his arms extended before him, attached by a steel bar to the leg irons on his ankles. Standing behind a table, facing away from him, he saw her shapely figure, the curves her black suit could not hide. Long, dark red hair, that spilled down her back. The pale, nude flesh of her sculpted calves. Her slender fingers, resting on the edge of the table, their nails painted a light pink.

'Hi there, Bill,' said a familiar voice, complete with a slight Cuban accent. To the woman's left, her companion rose like a mountain at her side, a notepad and folder in hand that he'd pulled from a briefcase on the floor.

And then the woman in black turned around. He was instantly disappointed.

This was not the 'she' he'd hoped to see. Nonetheless, she was pretty. Very pretty. Light blue eyes watched him carefully, like a bird might watch an approaching cat. She was obviously frightened of him, although she was struggling not to show it. Any sudden movement, and she would surely fly away, hide behind the grizzly beside her for protection. Her smooth skin was the color of talcum powder; her full lips, painted a deep, matte red, were drawn. The sight of him had drained the color from her already pale face.

A vile, delicious thought popped into his head. *Oh, the things he could do to that luscious red mouth . . .*

Detective Manny Alvarez had come to pay him a visit. And he'd brought along a beautiful woman in a business suit. Not the woman he wished the detective had brought with him, but a woman nonetheless – something Bill hadn't seen in a long, long time. Too long. But the equipment down south still worked – he was growing hard as a rock.

The incredible anger that had coursed through his veins earlier was gone. *It was going to be a great day, after all,* he thought, the wheels turning in his head. He sniffed at the air again.

A really great day.

25

'Open up!' yelled a voice on the other side of the door.

Daria stood at the table and swallowed the thick lump that had formed suddenly in her throat. She turned away to face the wall and compose herself, to make sure her expression did not betray the fear that had gripped her insides. She could hear the jangle of chains and shuffle of bodies on the concrete floor on the other side of the door, a few steps away. Like a scene written for a horror movie, the cell door opened slowly, with a long, screechy creak.

He's just a man, she told herself. *This is not Hannibal Lecter. This is* not *a movie. Don't lose yourself in the drama. You've handled bad cases before. You've gone up against terrible men. You've kept it together. You're only wallpaper. Don't let him get inside your head.*

She bit the inside of her cheek and turned around slowly.

And there he was, standing in the doorway in his orange shirt and blue pants, his body backlit by the bright fluorescents that lit the corridor behind him – Cupid.

Arguably, the most infamous living serial killer in the world. Right up there with Jack the Ripper, the Boston Strangler, the Original Night Stalker, the Green River Killer, the Zodiac Killer. She watched as Corrections moved him into the room and sat him down before her, no more than two feet from where she stood, her arms folded across her chest, trying her best to look like an unemotional hard-ass. Only the metal table separated their bodies. Two COs locked his leg irons into a long chain that reached the wall and attached his wrist cuffs to the chair arms at his side. All the while he never took his eyes off her.

'Hi there, Bill,' Manny said.

Bantling did not blink. But he did smile. At her.

As much as she'd tried to tell herself over the past week that Bill Bantling was just another defendant, that this was just another interview, she knew now she'd been fooling herself. Her knees had never before shaken when a subject simply entered the room. Her heart had never pounded so hard in her chest, her skin gone clammy. Maybe it was his reputation that chilled the air – knowing what those chained hands had done to his victims before they'd finally, mercifully, died – but the creepy feeling that raised the hairs on the back of her neck was almost supernatural. She was surely in the presence of evil.

'Normally we unlock them if they're gonna be meeting with their attorneys, but considering who this guy is, we don't ever take off the restraints outside his cell, 'cept for the shower, of course,' Tru Zeffers announced, looking purposely over at Daria when he did. 'Call me when you're done. Or sooner, if ya need to.'

'Detective Alvarez,' Bantling began pleasantly enough after the cell door had shut. 'It's been a real long time.' Although he was addressing Manny, his eyes had not yet left Daria.

'Yes, it has. I'm over here, Bill,' Manny answered, waving a paw in Bantling's direction.

'Who's your new friend?' Bantling asked.

'My name is Daria DeBianchi. I'm a prosecutor with the Miami-Dade State Attorney's Office.'

Bantling's blue eyes crackled to life. 'DeBianchi, hmmm? I don't think I've heard your name before. But then again, you're so . . . young.'

'Let me tell you why we're here,' Manny started.

'Please do. As you can see, I'm glued to my seat, waiting on your every word, Detective Alvarez. Nowhere to go, so don't be boring.'

'Do you remember the last time we spoke?'

'It's been some time.'

'It has. Several years. You told me about a club you were once a member of. A snuff club, you called it. Do you remember that conversation, Bill?'

'Perhaps.'

'I want to talk to you about that club.'

'Really?'

'Yes.'

'Well, I guess you can talk to me about anything you want, Detective Alvarez. But that doesn't mean I'll tell you anything. As for club memberships, I will say that I'm not much of a joiner nowadays. I don't get out too often. About once a year I take a mini-vacation down

221

to the basement of this facility for a week or so. They call that Death Watch, Detective. It's a larger cell, better food. The view . . .' Bantling shook his head. 'Not so good. Then my attorneys pull off what they like to call another miracle and I move back upstairs. "Dodged another bullet, Bill," those attorneys always say. "More like a needle," I always reply.'

'You said this club was headed up, or run by, Gregory Chambers.'

'Ooh . . . a name I really don't like to hear. Hope he's finding hell hot enough.'

'What was your relationship with Dr Chambers, Bill?'

'Initially? Therapeutic. He was supposed to cure me of my nasty thoughts. Instead, he gave me some great ideas.'

'How long were you a patient of his?'

'Long enough to figure out he was sicker than me.'

'When did the relationship change? When did Dr Chambers bring this club he was a member of to your attention?'

Bantling didn't respond.

'How did he tell you about it? How did it operate? Did you ever see the other members?'

'That's a million-dollar question.' His eyes were still glued on Daria. His chained hands were in his lap. She saw that they were moving. She shifted in her seat and looked away.

'I need to know if it's still operating,' Manny asked.

'You mean is it still up and running without the real Cupid there to hold down the fort? Now that Greg Chambers is among the not-so-dearly departed, did the group he loved to show off his illustrious talents to

222

disband? There is a point to your questions, right? You know, you had an opportunity a few years ago to find out all you wanted to know, but you chose not to listen. You chose to walk away. And I haven't heard from you since. Not a note, not a visit. Nothing. What's it been, Detective? Five years? Six? No, I'll tell you, it's been *seven* years. *Seven* years. That's how long ago I was shipped back to this hellhole to die for crimes I did not commit. You walked out on me because you didn't want to hear it. Because it was *inconvenient* for you to know such things, because then you'd have no choice but to see the ugly truths about your special agent friend Falconetti and his not-so lovely bride, Chloe. Or is it C.J.? What alias is the little minx using nowadays? Or should I say, hiding behind? I hear that she's no longer with the office. No longer putting innocent men on death row. That's a relief.'

'No matter what you tell me today, innocent is not a word that is any way associated with the likes of you, Bill. You want to put your hands back on the table for me, please?'

Bantling smiled and complied. The chains landed on the metal with a loud bang. 'I thought perhaps you'd brought Chloe by today for a visit. Nothing against the company you're keeping, Detective Alvarez,' he said nodding at Daria. 'See, if you'd listened to me back then, you'd have seen the scheme the two of them, Agent Falconetti and his bride, concocted to pump me full of poison and put me in the ground. And of course, then you'd have *known* that they were both guilty of multiple felonies. Felonies that would've sent the pair of them to prison for the rest of their lives. But you knew you'd

223

have to slap the cuffs on your very own pals if you asked all the right questions, so you didn't. You didn't ask any. Not back then.'

Manny tapped a finger on the table. 'Two juries convicted you on two separate occasions. Both voted unanimously for death. The appellate courts have listened to your arguments, and still, here you sit on death row.'

'Well, there's an interesting twist to that, too, Detective. But the years have flown by and now, here you are with your very pretty companion as a distraction, asking me for information while I stare at her lovely face and get lost in those beautiful eyes, thinking of all the things I would love to do to her if only someone would take these chains off of me and put them on her.'

Daria looked away again.

'I'm a smart man, Detective,' Bantling continued. 'Using those smarts that I've been genetically blessed with, I'll venture a guess and say that you and your lovely, distracting assistant are here on *another* case. One that you fear may be related to what I told you a long time ago.'

There was no sense lying. Manny nodded. 'We are investigating another murder. Murders, actually. They all look connected, but the perpetrators may be different.'

Bantling slapped his palms on the chair arms. 'Hot damn! I knew it!'

'Now I am listening, Bill. If you have information you'd like to share. No matter what that information is or who it might implicate.'

Bantling put a finger to his lips. 'You know in here there's a saying, Detective. "Everything for a price."

Cigarettes, dope, sex, favors . . . That applies to this situation as well.'

'What are you proposing? What do you want?' Daria interjected.

Manny looked over at her.

'She speaks,' Bantling said, grinning. 'I've been unjustly entombed in this concrete and steel coffin for the past decade, biding my time, waiting to be lowered into the ground, Miss Prosecutor; I'm in no mood to be charitable. So be prepared to take out the prosecutorial checkbook. I know what you want, Detective Alvarez. I'm also aware that you would not be coming to me, groveling for information, if you had any other source. I am the absolute last resort. And *that* tells me that you two really, really need to know what it is I know. It tells me you're desperate. It tells me that there are more than a couple of murders. So, go check out your nasty crime-scene photos and look at all those dead, pretty faces snuffed out years before their time, and think what it is *you're* willing to do for *me*. Then come back and we'll talk. But don't bother if you're not going to make me a really good offer. I want out. In exchange for that, I'll give you names. Lots and lots of names. Enough names to keep both your offices busy for years to come.'

'Out?' Manny scoffed. 'Never happening.'

'So it exists, this club. Still?' Daria asked excitedly.

Bantling smiled and motioned his hand across his lips, as if zipping them shut.

Like Talbot Lunders, Bantling was a good-looking man, even in middle age – chiseled face, strong jaw, defined cheekbones. He still had all his hair, although

225

the blond had mostly turned to gray. His smooth skin was sallow from being indoors for so many years, deprived of sunlight, and he was definitely thinner than how she remembered him from TV coverage of the trial, but he was still in great shape. His bulging fore-arms, thick neck, and tapered waist were not hidden by his prison-issue garb. Daria found his good looks, his tight body, his charming grin, frightening – just as she had with Talbot Lunders. Probably because, in and of itself, good looks were disarming. Both men had used their comeliness as an efficient, deadly weapon, luring women to their side, right out of busy clubs and bars, right into their cars and lairs without a backward glance. It wasn't that Daria thought good-looking people couldn't commit crimes, it was more the fact that not one but *two* better-than-averagely handsome men had been charged with atypically brutal, misogynistic crimes that was troubling. It went against her own ultra-suspicious instincts. Either man could have almost any woman he wanted. Both men had money in the bank. If either of them had tried to pick her up in a bar or a library she'd have gone willingly, too. In addition to frightening the shit out of her, that fact totally pissed her off.

'Don't think, Mr Bantling, that I'm going to walk in here next week with the keys to your cage simply because a convicted serial murderer tells me to trust him. You may think I'm stupid because I'm a woman, but let me assure you, I'm not. Tell me how it works, this club, or we're not coming back at all. And then you can tell all the nasty stories you want about your former fellow clubbies to your neighbors on the block. Maybe they'll give a shit. Maybe they'll be smart enough to give me a call so I can work with them on their own sentences.'

Bantling's eyes narrowed. 'Feisty. Detective Alvarez, do you let her speak to you this way?'

'You heard me,' she said.

'They're the fun ones.'

'Not in the mood to chat?' She reached for her briefcase and stood up, hoping he would not see her knees shake when she did. She had to get out of this place. 'I'm not going to stand here while you size me up for lunch. I know who you are and I know exactly what you're capable of.'

Bantling's pallid face turned beet red. 'You have no idea what I am fucking capable of, lady,' he hissed. 'Not a clue.' He pulled at his cuffs as he leaned toward her in the chair. 'Or else you'd know that I've been railroaded into this hell by a manipulative, pretty little bitch just like yourself. Another woman who thought she was so damn smart. That she could play me and this system you call justice. But I'm still here, aren't I, Detective Alvarez? Alive and kicking.' He pulled at his leg irons and they jangled menacingly. 'I'm not going away, either.'

Daria backed up and stumbled over her chair. It fell to the concrete floor with a hair-raising screech.

Manny stood up and moved to help her.

'In your seat, Bantling!' squawked Tru Zeffers over the intercom. His scratchy, drawl filled the small space. He was obviously monitoring the room via one of the surveillance cameras.

Bantling leaned back in his chair. 'Karma's a bitch, Ms Prosecutor. It takes a while to come around sometimes, but personally I've found that it always does. Always. So you better watch yourself.'

Daria brushed Manny's offer of help away and picked up the chair. She waved at the camera in the corner to indicate she was okay.

'Let's not beat around the bush,' Manny barked. 'Answer the questions and we'll be gone. Maybe get you some more channels on your TV if you play nice. Maybe more if you have some decent information. What I want to know is how does this snuff club work? How do the members get in touch with one another? How do they find victims? Are the victims consenting in some way?'

'Subtlety was never your style, Detective Alvarez,' Bantling answered, shaking his head. 'It's all just a game.'

'Game? This is a *game*?'

'Every game needs players,' Bantling continued, cryptically. 'Einstein once said, "First you have to learn the rules of the game. Then you have to play better than anyone else." He was such a smart man, that Einstein. Split the atom, right? Helped develop the first nuclear bomb, right? The mother-bomb that brought about peace by killing hundreds of thousands of people. But a game is nothing if no one wants to watch it, right? The coliseum was built because thousands of Romans wanted to see the lions gut those Christians. And you don't fill stadium seats with scabs. It's the Derek Jeters and Michael Jordans that people want to spend their hard-earned money to come watch. Of course, finding talent worthy of competing with the Jeters and Jordans is very hard to find. Sometime scouts have to search through literally hundreds of faces to find that one perfect face.' He turned to Daria. 'Here's your bone, Miss DeBianchi, to show you that I am, indeed, someone you can trust. The word of the day is Lepidus.'

'Lepidus?' Manny repeated. 'What's that?'

'Lepidus?' Daria echoed. 'I know that name from somewhere.'

Bantling nodded. 'You should.'

'Wait – Lepidus. Reinaldo Lepidus? Is that who you're talking about?' she asked.

Bantling smiled. 'Quick.'

'The Florida Supreme Court judge?' Daria asked.

'He likes to watch.'

'What?' she asked.

Bantling smiled again.

She slung her briefcase over her shoulder. 'Convenient. Judge Lepidus is dead. Maybe you should pick another name. Someone who can defend himself.'

Bantling shrugged. 'That's tough luck. I bet poor Pat Graber would've liked to hear that.'

Manny looked at Daria.

'I don't know that name,' she said softly.

'Remember how smart you just insisted you were?' Bantling leaned his body into the table again. His muscular forearms tensed. On his left wrist was an ugly, raised, jagged scar, about an inch and a half long. 'Or should I say, how stupid you weren't? Well, I'm sure that feisty brain of yours will figure it all out. Detective Alvarez here can help with any missing details – if he wants to, that is. Then you'll come back to me and we'll talk again. A nice long chat. But remember to bring that checkbook, or we won't have much to say.'

He sniffed at the air as he relaxed in his chair. 'Love your perfume, by the way. Chanel No. 5. So very . . . haunting. Just like the woman who wears it.'

26

'The lightning bolt is a symbol in satanic worship,' Daria said, reading from her iPhone as they drove down University Avenue in Gainesville, past college bar after college bar, in between which was jammed every fast-food restaurant imaginable. The staples of an American college kid's diet all within a short, neon-lit, twenty-yard walk: beer, Big Macs, Whoppers, chalupas, and more beer. 'Apparently it's worn so as to have power over another person or object. It's called a "Satanic S". Zeus used a lightning bolt as his weapon of choice, the SS wore it on their jackets in Nazi Germany. And it's supposed satanic meaning comes from the Bible. Luke 10:18: "And he said unto them, I beheld Satan as lightning fall from heaven."'

'What if it's enclosed in a circle?' Manny asked.

'If used within a pentagram, it symbolizes Satan's life force going into matter. But I don't see anything about a plain circle. I don't think it's the same thing.'

Manny shook his head. 'You saw his wrist in there, right? I forgot he had that.'

'I don't know, Manny,' Daria replied skeptically. 'That scar could have come from a mishap with a serrated knife or jagged can. Not sure I see a lightning bolt.'

'Ain't no such thing as coincidence, Counselor. Remember I said that? Every victim has this lightning bolt/zigzag either burned on their skin or tattooed on their body, as do both our bad guys, and what you just read to me is that it symbolizes power. I see a connection, is what I see.'

'Okay, Miss Cleo. Listen, I wouldn't put too much faith into my impromptu Google search. According to this, Lady Gaga is a Satan worshipper because she face-painted a lightning bolt over her eye. Wait . . . same goes for Kiss, AC/DC, the Rolling Stones, and Harry Potter . . . wow. I never knew.' She scrolled down. 'Hold on – the Power Rangers and the US seal are also evil symbols.'

'All that's on your phone? Damn . . .'

'You really need to come into the twenty-first century, Detective. I bet you don't TiVo, either.'

'What's that?'

She sighed. 'Are we there, yet? I need a drink.'

'Mother's Pub,' he said, pulling into a parking lot. 'Looks good to me. Pub means food *and* drink; I still gotta get us back to Miami tonight. This place your old stomping grounds?'

'Those three years were a blur, Manny. I was either locked inside a building somewhere studying or I was out drinking with wild abandon. Can't remember where. Can't remember much.'

He pulled into a spot and raised an eyebrow. 'I can't imagine you doing anything with wild abandon. You're way too calculated.'

'Thanks a lot. You'd be surprised. Cut me off after two.'

'Hell, no!' he replied with a laugh as they headed across the lot. He studied the menu posted outside the door and rubbed his stomach. 'Check out these burgers, Counselor. I don't know about you, but I'm starved. I just remembered we didn't have no lunch.'

'I saw what they were serving the inmates; we didn't miss anything.' She looked at her watch. 'Damn. It's almost seven. Where'd the day go?' At this rate, she probably wouldn't be home till four in the morning. Ugh. She had court at nine.

'Well, I'm buying, Counselor. And get anything you want on that burger of yours: cheddar, bacon, jalapenos – the works. For you, sky's the limit.'

'You sure know how to treat a girl. I'm glad we're just friends.'

'If you want something more than that, I'm up for steak and lobster.'

She laughed. 'You're funny.'

'They even have a burger soaked in Guinness, in case you got some mick mixed in with that guinea blood of yours. That would account for that red hair. Oh, and just so you know,' he said as he held the door open for her and she started inside, 'we're not negotiating with him.'

Daria stopped. 'That sounds final.'

'It is. He's a rapist and a murderer. A serial murderer.'

She pushed the door closed with her hand. 'Not according to him. I was gonna ask you – what's with the railroading argument? And who's Chloe? He said C.J. was her other name. Did he mean the prosecutor on his case, C.J. Townsend? Is that who he's talking about? Did she really marry the lead detective? I never heard that. Were they involved during the trial? Wouldn't that be considered a conflict of interest?'

'Slow down, Lois Lane,' Manny warned. 'He's a condemned man. Like you reminded me only a few days ago, he's desperate. And what happened to our agreement that you would be wallpaper back there?'

'Well, you didn't tell me that he was gonna start screaming he'd been railroaded on to death row by the lead detective and his prosecutor bride. That changes things up a bit. What kind of felonies was he talking about that they'd be guilty of? Don't you want to know?'

They moved aside to let another couple enter the restaurant.

'You're surprised that a convicted killer might make shit like that up?' he said when they were alone again.

'No, it doesn't surprise me. He did sound pretty upset, though. Like he knew things. Like *you* knew things. Or, as he put it, there were things maybe you didn't *want* to know.'

'Don't get me mad. Desperate people say desperate things. We're not cutting him loose, Counselor, no matter what names he purports to know. I'm telling you that right now, so don't start thinking you're Monty Hall and this is *Let's Make a Deal*. Because the truth is, you've no idea who you're dealing with.'

'*Let's Make a Deal*? Monty Hall? How old are you anyway?'

'How young are you? It's in syndication. I think.'

'Judge Lepidus, huh? You think Bantling's BS-ing

about him? Maybe he's the twist that Bantling was talking about.'

'That'll be easy enough to find out. We gotta see what the connection is between the judge and that other name he gave us. I already got a call in, before you start making noise. But we gotta be real quiet, 'cause that's something that will get the media calling – linking a Supreme Court judge to a snuff club.'

'Lepidus only sat on the Supremes for a couple of years, if I remember right. Less than a full term. I think he filled the spot after Justice Kramer suddenly retired.' Unlike US Supreme Court justices, who were appointed for life, justices on the Florida Supreme Court were appointed by the governor for six-year terms. At the end of each term, the public voted in a general election to retain them on the bench or not. She couldn't remember whether Lepidus had stepped down or was not asked back. 'If Bantling knows names like Supreme Court justices, we have to listen to him, Manny,' she said as she reached to open the door again.

He placed his hand on hers, pushing it closed once more. 'We are not letting this guy out, Counselor. I repeat. I don't care if he tells me Barack Obama is a player in this. A new cell, maybe. A new prison, maybe. A room with a view. Maybe we consider commuting his death sentence to life as a reward if he coughs up really important info, but he ain't ever getting out. The man is a human monster. Trust me on this. I've seen what he is capable of.'

She shrugged, moved her body under his arm, so that it dropped to his side and she opened the door. 'I get it. But he said be prepared to deal. So if he is being honest

I think we need to have something better to offer him than ESPN and a view of the trees.'

'You're new at this, so I'm gonna cut you slack. I'm telling ya, he won't show you his till you show him yours, and by then it'll be too late to see you've been BS'd,' he answered, following her inside. 'It was probably a mistake to bring you up here . . .'

'You're gonna need to be straight up with me, Manny.' She turned to him, her blue eyes narrowed to slits. 'I know you're holding back. I don't know what and I can't figure out why. But I will.'

'Don't get all Matlock on me, now, Counselor,' he returned, signaling to the approaching waitress they needed a two-top.

'*Matlock*? Is that in syndication too?'

Then the waitress was upon them with menus, escorting them through the busy restaurant to a table, and the uncomfortable subject of Bill Bantling was lost somewhere in the noisy crowd.

Three hours later, they were still at Mother's, although they'd moved to the bar. After the burgers, they'd had a couple more beers, then the band had taken the stage and they'd decided to stick around and listen, and since they – Briggs Ditch Revolution – were actually pretty good, Manny suggested they stay for a few songs. One more beer had led to two had led to a hell of a lot more. The crowd had gotten thicker, the air hotter, the distance between their bar stools and bodies narrower. The music had gotten so loud, that talking into each other's ears was the only way to hear anything. Daria couldn't remember who'd leaned in first. Who'd said that first seriously flirty thing that had led not to a rebuke but to the first seriously flirty response. She remembered his hand on her knee, and then her hand on his. She remembered looking at biceps the size of her thighs that she could make out even through the rolled-up sleeves of his dress shirt, and thinking something stupid like how she was really happy he'd been so big and strong back in that creepy prison, and how she knew he would have protected her in a worst-case scenario event and how incredibly sexy that was. And then his lips were on hers. Or maybe hers were on his, but that was how it all began. That was why she always stopped at two.

But not tonight. Tonight she drank with wild abandon, and left tomorrow to deal with all the regrets that were sure to follow.

27

'Anything on your car, Christina?'

C.J. glanced up from the mess of paperwork on her desk. Santa Barbara Chief Deputy DA Jason Mucci was standing in the doorway of her office. She shook her head. 'Nope. Special Investigations is working it, but I'm not expecting much. The insurance company's gonna write me a check.'

'It sucks, having your car stolen, especially at work. What kind was it?'

'A forest-green 2007 Ford Explorer,' she replied with a sigh. 'Affectionately known as the Green Giant.'

He laughed. 'You named your car?'

'Green Giant was the first brand-new car I ever bought. Don't ask me why I picked green, it just called to me from across the lot. I thought I'd have it forever.'

'May the Jolly Green Giant rest in peace, then,' Jason proclaimed. 'Or, as is more likely, in pieces. You do realize your first brand-new car has probably been chopped into a few dozen small parts and scattered about the county by now.'

'Sounds like a few victims I've known.'

He laughed again. 'Well, now you can relate to what your victims go through. You're officially a victim yourself.'

C.J. already had him there, but said nothing. She just nodded.

'What're you driving now?'

'A rental. A red Saturn something.'

'Not so affectionately called the Red Ass?'

It was her turn to laugh.

'Time to move up in the world. How about a Bentley?'

'How about a raise?'

He smiled. 'The forfeitures are going to auction next month in Ventura. You should pick yourself up a Ferrari. Something zippy. I think you'd look real cute in a convertible. Shades on, long brown hair blowing in the breeze.'

'No, thanks, Jason. I don't need some convicted criminal, pissed off their car was seized by the government, coming to reclaim it from my garage in the middle of the night. I have enough troubles. I'm thinking maybe a Jeep Rubicon. Something rugged.'

'Very California. Is that where you're from?'

'Originally,' she replied softly. 'I guess I'll have to go car shopping this weekend, although I think I prefer root canal to dealing with car salesmen.'

He glanced around and then stepped into her office. 'Want some company?' he asked quietly. 'We could grab some dinner afterwards, maybe hit a wine bar.'

'I'm married, Jason,' she replied quickly. 'Separated,

actually.' She fiddled with the ring finger on her left hand. It was bare. 'But still married,' she said softly.

'Oh. Didn't know that.' There was a long and awkward silence as everything changed. He backed into the doorway again, red-faced. 'How's your trial going?' he tried.

'We're in a holding pattern. One of the jurors has a medical issue, so the judge has given everyone a couple of days off.'

'I saw your defendant, Kassner, with his attorney, down at Brophy's having lunch today.'

'Lucky you.'

He scratched his head. 'I can't believe that guy's out.'

She shrugged. 'Before my time. I get to put him back in, though.'

'Funny, he was driving a 2007 forest-green Explorer.'

Her stomach suddenly flip-flopped. 'What?' she asked anxiously.

'Only kidding,' Jason said with a laugh, happy, she was sure, that he'd panicked her for a split-second. It probably made him feel better about being turned down. 'Good luck with your trial. And car shopping. See ya, Christina.'

She listened as he walked off down the hall, his heavy footsteps finally fading as he rounded a corner. She blew out a breath. Where had that all come from? She never told anyone anything about herself. But suddenly she'd given away half her personal life in a few short sentences.

Originally from California. I'm married. Separated, actually.

Actually, Jason, I don't know what I am, where I'm from, or what the fuck I'm doing here. And by the way, my name is not Christina. So I guess I also don't know who I am.

She fingered the validated parking ticket on her desk. The one stamped Friday, July 1, 2011, 9:32 a.m. from the Lobero Garage. She swallowed the lump in her throat.

And I'm hoping no one else knows that information either . . .

While she couldn't remember the exact time she'd parked and she couldn't be one hundred percent positive it was the same ticket, it sure *looked* a lot like the ticket she'd had stamped when she pulled into the lot on Friday morning. She'd left it in the car, tucked up in the Green Giant's visor. And of course, her car was missing when she got back that night.

She took off her glasses and rubbed her tired eyes.

This morning when she went to court on Kassner, there it was, the ticket, sitting on the People's table, neatly placed between the water pitcher and a box of tissues. No one had taken credit for finding it or for putting it there. It was simply there, waiting for her.

Maybe she'd put it in her purse, after all, not the car. Maybe it had fallen out on Friday night and the janitor had placed it on the table for her to see on Tuesday. Or maybe it belonged to someone else's car, and it was all a big coincidence. Maybe, maybe, maybe . . .

Like the other night, the excuses kept coming, hard and fast. Because she was not ready to face the possibility of a different reality: whoever had taken her car had left the ticket right where he knew she'd find it come Tuesday morning. Thoughts of who chilled her to the core.

A disgruntled defendant? Richard Kassner, sending her a message?

Or worse?

241

There was a reason C.J. had left Miami behind seven years ago. Reasons, actually. Frightening reasons. They were the same reasons she had changed her name yet again when she picked up her life and moved it from Chicago to Santa Barbara. They were the reasons she guarded her identity like it was the Holy Grail. Why she was mad at herself for giving away a snippet of real information about who she was and where she was from.

Now you can relate to what your victims go through. You're officially a victim yourself.

She put her head in her hands and sucked in a deep breath.

It was July, 1988. A dark, horribly stormy night. She'd just gotten home from a date with her boyfriend. She'd turned on the air conditioner and gone to bed. She never heard him push up the living-room window, or creep down the hall of her apartment, or open the door to her bedroom. She awoke, wide-eyed and terrified, to a monster in a clown mask shoving panties down her throat with latex-gloved hands and tying her to her own bed.

There was no point looking through a book of perverts' mug shots – he wore a mask. He left her in a pool of her own blood, yet left nothing of himself behind: no hairs, no fibers, no evidence. *Sorry, Chloe*, the NYC detectives had said. *No justice for you today.*

Chloe Joanna Larson. That had been her name a long, long time ago. The name her parents had given her. The name she had throughout her childhood and high school and college, the name she took with her when she left northern California, where she was originally from, for

242

law school in big, bad New York City – an overcrowded melting pot full of burglars, robbers, murderers and rapists, according to her mother.

Turned out her mother was right.

When the man who had raped her over and over and over again, the man who had promised her he would be back one day for round two, the man who had sworn to her that he would always find her, no matter where she went, started calling her at work, she went, well . . . crazy. Doctors-hospitals-therapists-medicine-kind of crazy.

For a while.

Then something snapped inside and she realized that was what he wanted. This man who had ruined what, at one time, was a promising life with a bright future, wanted control. He wanted her to lock herself behind alarms, refusing to leave her apartment or make friends or be with another man. He wanted her to cry uncontrollably and quiver with fear when she looked at the scars that he'd left behind with his ugly knife. Chloe Joanna Larson's life was going to be spent waiting for the man who had raped her to make good on his threats, and it drove her insane. And that was what the monster in the clown mask wanted.

So she'd left NY. In the middle of the night, telling no one. Simply packed up and left. Moved down to Florida, changed her name, changed her occupation from prospective medical malpractice attorney to prosecutor and decided to make it her life's work to put monsters behind bars. But she carried on looking over her shoulder, carried on living behind locks and alarms, never letting anyone in. She dyed her natural blonde hair a drab brown. She wore glasses instead of contacts. She rarely wore makeup. Where other women spent a fortune on their appearance, hoping to get noticed, the Miami-Dade Assistant State Attorney then known as C.J. Townsend tried to make herself as unassuming and plain as possible. Forgettable. Because she never knew where he was. And she never knew who he was.

Until the day William Rupert Bantling ended up in her courtroom charged with murder.

Fate was a twisted, funny character. When Bantling had been standing before the judge at his First Appearance hearing, yelling at his attorney, it had all come flashing back to her. It had been twelve years. Twelve years since that terrible night, a night that, even now, she still relived in her nightmares. A night she could still taste and smell and hear when she closed her eyes. In those twelve years, she could have been anywhere on this earth, doing anything other than prosecuting, assigned to any other case but the Cupid serial killings, yet there she was, in a courtroom full of cameras and cops when the man who had raped her stood up to plead not guilty to the crime of murder.

It wasn't his face she'd recognized. It was his voice. Instantly, the world had changed once again. And C.J. Townsend had to make a decision: should she prosecute the man who had raped her?

From that one critical decision, others had followed in quick succession. Until finally, so many decisions had been made and put into play that, like the domino effect, it was impossible to stop the outcome. The bones toppled one after the other until, after twelve long years, justice had finally been served.

Or so she had honestly thought at the time. But fate was a funny, twisted character.

She reached for her cell phone, her fingers playing with the buttons.

I'm married, Jason. Separated, actually, but still married . . .

That status was about to change. According to the process server, Dominick had received the papers last week. He hadn't sent them back. Not yet.

She wanted to call him so badly. But what would she say? *Sorry?* Sorry would never be enough. *Sorry I walked away. Sorry I gave up on us. Sorry I couldn't handle the terrible secret that the two of us had promised to share until death do us part.* Even if he forgave her for leaving, she could not guarantee it wouldn't happen again. And the truth was that when they were together, he was a constant reminder of her past, of all that she was running from.

Oh, I know what it's like to be a victim, Jason. I can relate in ways you could never begin to imagine . . .

She shook the memories from her head and put the cell down. Then she picked up the parking ticket and placed it in the top drawer of her desk.

The bones were still falling, with no end in sight, set in motion by decisions made long ago.

28

When Daria opened her eyes, everything hurt. A tiny slice of sunlight had squeaked through the blinds and landed precisely on the nightstand clock that she stared at, blurring the red numbers beyond distinction. Next to it was a bottle of Tylenol, a half-filled bottle of Patron, her bra, and a paper cup with the *Days Inn* logo printed on it.

Then she remembered what had happened.

She turned and saw Manny was next to her in bed, sleeping. Presumably naked under the white sheets he was tangled up in.

Oh dear God. What have I done? She sat up much too quickly and put her throbbing head in her hands. Should she get up and leave? Take a taxi to the closest Enterprise Rent-a-Car and go home? Maybe leave a note on the pillow?

Damn. This was like being back in college. She was such an easy drunk. Why didn't she just stop at two? How many more past two had she had? She looked over at the bottle of Patron. *Tequila? Really, Daria? What the hell were you thinking?*

How was she going to be able to drive home five hours in a car with him? What was she going to say? What was he going to say? What would he think of her now? Her eyes darted around the room like a trapped animal who realizes the cage door is slightly ajar. She should go before he woke up. Get a rental car and deal with it tomorrow, over the phone. She could put off actually seeing him on the Lunders case. There was no reason for them to physically get together until the next hearing. That could be weeks, months even. She could let him handle Bantling from here on, which is what she remembered him saying to her last night. Telling her to back off and let him handle it.

Okay, okay, okay. Don't panic. It might not be so hard to ignore him once she got out of this cheap motel room . . .

She dry-swallowed two Tylenol and rubbed her aching head, trying to collect herself. Her panties were across the room on a chair, as was her blouse, and her skirt was nowhere to be seen. Manny Alvarez was *so* not her type. Big. Burly. Hairy. Bald. She'd never had a thing for cops, like other prosecutors did. The man-in-uniform-on-a-perpetual-power-trip crap was never her weakness. And he was so much older – she was guessing he had to be in his mid-forties at least. Maybe older.

She looked at him, sleeping on his side, facing where she'd been sleeping, eyes closed, his mouth lost somewhere under that oversized mustache. At least he wasn't snoring. And he hadn't given her his back, which she hated. It was a sign of disrespect when men slept on their side with their backs to you. Fuck the, 'But I was sleeping!'

247

argument her past exes had tried. Her thought process was, if you do it when you're unconscious, it's only a matter of time before you turn your back in the daylight, too. *Manny the Bear.* There was a reason for that nickname. He was big, burly, hairy. Menacingly bald. But he was sweet, too. Like a ginormous teddy bear, with an oversized smile and even bigger laugh. And she felt safe around him. That was what it was. That was her problem, she rationalized. It was being in the prison. He had protected her and she felt safe around him. It was the same thing as had happened with Matt Terrance, the soft-spoken guy in eleventh grade who'd actually punched out a football player on her behalf because he'd called her a bitch. Matt wasn't hot or anything, but she'd dated him anyway. Lost her virginity to him, too. After a couple shots of Jose Cuervo, come to think of it.

Somewhere in the room, a cell phone began to ring. It was the theme music to *Psycho*. It was hers and it was the office.

Please don't wake up. Please don't wake up. Please don't wake up.

She scrambled out of bed and found her purse, under his pants in a corner. *Damn. What time was it?* She checked her watch as she answered the phone. Nine thirty. *Jesus Christ! She was supposed to be in court at nine . . .*

Thanks to her hangover, she answered the phone in a voice that matched how she felt. 'Hello, Gretch.'

'You sound like shit,' said her secretary. 'What is it?'

'The flu. I was up all night and I . . . I overslept. I'm really sorry.'

'I'll have Artigas cover and reset everything. You don't have anything big on today anyway. No worries.'

'I should talk to him about—'

'Go back to bed. You have sick days for a reason. I'll call later to see if you're coming in tomorrow, which I'm telling you right now, I hope you don't, 'cause I'm having my daughter's birthday party on Saturday and I don't need the damn flu.'

'That was convincing,' a gruff voice said behind her when she'd hung up. She cringed. So much for a sneaky exit and dealing with the fallout in six months or so . . .

'Good morning,' Manny said with a yawn. 'What time is it anyway?'

'Nine thirty.'

'Whoops.'

'Do you have to work?' she asked.

'Nah, I'm okay. I'll make a couple of phone calls.'

She gathered her purse and blouse and turned to face him. 'Well, I have to get back, so I thought that maybe—' She sighed. 'I was gonna rent a car.'

He sat up in bed and leaned against the headboard, a crooked smile on his face. 'Rent a car? What? Why?'

'Because of this.'

'This?'

'Yeah, what happened. What *shouldn't* have happened.'

'Says who?'

'Says me. It was the alcohol, Manny.'

He rubbed his head and smiled full-on. 'I don't know about that. You seemed pretty happy. I never heard a scream like that before.'

She turned bright red, picked up her panties and headed toward the bathroom. 'It was a mistake.'

He grabbed his cell phone from the nightstand. 'Damn.

249

Seven new texts. Hasn't everyone figured out I don't do texts? Shit . . . and this looks important, too.'

She walked over to his side and picked the cell out of his hands. 'It's simple. Hit this button and read them. Don't be so damn old. When you want to reply, hit the reply button, type a message and hit send. It's not rocket science.'

'Thanks,' he said when she headed back to the bathroom. 'I just wanted to watch you walk over to me wearing nothing but my shirt. I know how to text. I don't do it, is all. My fingers are too big and those damn buttons are too small.'

She stared at him.

'Listen, I think mistakes happen for a reason, Counselor. I like you. I think you like me. Why don't we just see where this goes? Stop trying to control everything, including what you should or shouldn't be feeling, and relax.'

'Don't tell me what I should or shouldn't try to control,' she snapped in a hoarse voice. 'You don't know what I'm thinking here.'

'I can see the wheels spinning in your pretty, red head. "He's not my type. He's my lead on this. He's older than me. I'm so short and he's so handsome. We argue a lot." Driving next to me for three hundred miles in your own rental car seems a little extreme, though. I don't bite.'

He was right. Now that he was awake and talking to her, running away in front of him sounded stupid.

'You do, though,' he continued with a sly smile. His hand touched his throat. 'I think I have a hickey.'

Her face lit up once again and she turned away. 'I'm so embarrassed.'

'I've seen your body. There is absolutely nothing to be embarrassed about. If I had a body like yours, I'd walk around naked all the time.'

'Now I'm even more embarrassed. This is not me, Manny. I would never do something like this.'

'Okay. It's not you. You're a good girl, if it makes you feel any better to hear that. You were a virgin until a couple of hours ago, if that's what you're saying. Whatever. But you have today off and I have today off and we're both sober now. Hungover, maybe, but sober. And I still like you. A lot. A real lot. I have since I met you. Even when you're mean and grumpy, I still like you. And we're in a hotel room, coincidentally. And you're practically naked . . .'

She looked around the room. 'Absolutely not. This isn't going to work between us, Manny. Jesus, I have to get back. I have to. I have court to prepare for, cases that need my attention. Attorneys I'm supposed to be supervising. I can't be having sex in a cheap motel room with my lead detective! What the hell is fucking wrong with me?' she yelled.

He held his hands up. 'Okay, okay. Don't flip out on me, Counselor. I'll drive you home and that'll be that. I won't see you different and we'll pretend this didn't happen and you don't have to worry about how to ditch me in the courthouse when you see me coming. Is that what you want?'

She said nothing and stared at a spot on the floor.

'Let me get dressed. We'll hit a Mickey D's for coffee and be on our merry, or not-so-merry, way.' He sighed heavily. 'I guess I'll be needing my shirt back. That just sucks.'

251

She closed her eyes. *What was happening to her? Who was this girl?* She slipped the shirt off her shoulders and stood before him.

'That's mean . . . doing that to me,' he said softly.

She dropped the shirt on the floor and opened her eyes. He was staring at her. She grabbed the Days Inn cup off the nightstand and took a swig of tequila.

'I don't know what I'm doing or why I'm doing it,' she said. 'I don't know anything this morning. But, well, if you want your shirt back, you're going to have to come here and get it, Detective. And you better hurry up before I change my mind . . .'

29

Life is what happens when you're
busy making other plans.

Quasi-religious bumper stickers covered the back of the
beat-up mini-van in front of Daria. She was tailgating
to read them all.

Jesus is coming. Look busy.
WTFWJD?
I plan, God laughs.

The last one got her thinking. Wasn't that the truth?
For the past however many years she'd been dating,
searching for her Mr Right, or at least her Mr Okay, I
Can Probably Fix You – and nothing. Internet dating,
real-life dating, social clubs, nightclubs, bars, coffee
shops, friend fix-ups, work hook-ups. Weekend after
weekend, happy hour after happy hour, blind date
after blind date, she'd put herself out there only to be

continuously disappointed. Ever since college it was as if a drought had hit the dating pool. With each passing year the water level continued to fall. The good fish had long been caught and tagged. The only thing she was catching lately were the throwbacks – the bottom feeders and slimy eels nobody wanted to begin with. The computer tech with the wandering eye who still lived with his mother. The former ballplayer with not one but two 'crazy' baby mamas. The swim coach who consistently forgot his wallet when they went out to dinner. She could only hope that down there, somewhere in the blackness, were left one or two good catches. Maybe even a throwback who didn't measure up for someone else's dinner plate, but would work out fine on hers. That romantic sort of nonsensical thinking was what kept her casting her rod. But at almost thirty it'd gotten to the point that the only relationship Daria *wanted* to be in was the one she had with work. If she had to choose between staying late on a Friday and happy hour, she always picked the office. Because with that relationship she knew that, if she put the time in, it would eventually pay off.

Daria didn't think she was being difficult in her demands for a soul mate. In fact, she always thought she knew exactly what she wanted in a guy and what would make her happy – down to what he would do for a living, what he'd look like, and what he'd sound like. Mr Right was made easier to envision when she checked off the boxes on her eHarmony application. As she got older, more self-assured, and less patient, she'd narrowed her tastes down further, not wanting to waste precious time on someone who was obviously – even without all the bullshit that people put on their online descriptions – not her type. She wasn't being picky; she was being honest. She deserved someone who could make her happy. And she, of all people, knew what made her happy and what didn't.

It turned out, maybe not so much.

It turned out maybe being alone all this time was her own stupid fault. That perhaps *she'd* gotten it wrong. That her list was flawed because she'd checked off all the wrong boxes. *Blond? Yes. European? Yes. Financier? Yes. Doctor? Yes. Cop? Never. Snorer? No way! Divorced? Next, please.* Manny Alvarez would never have made it on her list – even his zip code didn't fit. He was too tall, too bald, too hairy, too loud, too funny, too old, too ethnic. Not only did he work in law enforcement – a general no-no with limited exceptions – he was a homicide detective, a notoriously dark and twisted breed, complete with a warped sense of humor and a distorted perception of reality. He'd been married several times before, which meant he was a throwback who other women found difficult to deal with, and he was always late. If it hadn't been for a bottle of Patron and a great Irish rock band, this relationship she found herself in would never have come to be.

But weeks later, that was what they were still in – a relationship. Neither had declared it. Neither had denied it. It just was. They no longer bothered to preface the first few minutes of their conversations with work-speak. They had dinner together most nights – pizza, burgers,

Thai. Steak and lobster. She knew about his crazy Cuban family; he knew about her whacked, abusive mother, overprotective brothers and sick dad. She called him and he, on occasion, texted back. She was surprised that they never ran out of things to say. And the sex . . . well, that was mind-blowing. Daria had been with men before who were younger, better-looking. Sculpted, confident, well-endowed guys who had to fight off the women. Forget that dating someone with those kind of looks could make even the most self-assured woman insecure and jealous – the raw truth was, none of them compared with her Cuban teddy bear in the sack. How crazy was that?

Daria knew she was falling for him, which bothered her. A lot. One of the things she should be able to control in this world was having romantic feelings for someone who, on paper at least, she should be completely incompatible with. Yet here she was, heading home after a crazy day at the office, disappointed he hadn't called before she left, anxious to know the reason why, wondering like a teenager when she was going to see him again. It was completely bizarre. Her workaholic self didn't want to work so late at night anymore, or on the weekends. She was betraying *that* relationship. Weaning herself off it to be with him.

So here she was, sitting in traffic behind a mini-van owned by a religious nut with a sense of humor playing junior psychiatrist and trying to analyze herself.

Maybe it was the taboo of dating Manny that excited her – dating against type, a clandestine work relationship that no one could know about. Oooh . . . that was the plot of many a bad bodice-ripper she'd read over

256

the years. Maybe she was craving some drama herself, a pre-middle age crisis. A say-goodbye-to-my-free-loving-twenties-'cause-oh-shit-now-I'm-thirty-and-everything-matters-and-my-mother-keeps-reminding-me-my-clock-is-ticking crisis. So far she'd successfully managed to keep their affair under wraps. She'd sworn Manny to secrecy, and even Lizette – who was first to know everything in the office – hadn't quizzed her about why she was spending so much time with her lead. Maybe it was clandestine because no one would ever suspect her and Manny as a couple. Of course one day, if it kept up, people *would* eventually find out. That was equally troubling. What then? Would the drama be gone? She liked to think she didn't give a shit about what people thought, but what *would* people think? Would their incompatibility be as glaringly obvious to others as their height difference? And why did that possibly bother her? Would she be proud to be with him? Or was her anxiety an omen?

She pulled a hand through her hair and blew out a measured breath. And of course there was Talbot Lunders to consider. While relationships between prosecutors and cops weren't forbidden by office policy or even necessarily by ethical constraints – theirs would certainly raise eyebrows. It would appear improper. The irony wasn't lost on her that she herself had questioned the relationship between C. J. Townsend and Dominick Falconetti, C.J.'s lead detective on the Cupid case. It was even more ironic that it had been *that* very same night that she'd ended up in bed with Manny.

She looked at the cute guy in the convertible next to her, smoking a cigarette and chatting on his cell. He smiled at her. She looked away.

On the seat beside her, her purse buzzed to life. Al Pacino, a.k.a. Tony Montana, started yelling *Scarface* lines at her in a thick Cuban accent.

It was him. The Cuban Teddy Bear. She exhaled.

'Where you at?' he asked when she picked up. 'I'm downstairs looking for your car, and you're nowhere to be found. What do ya think, you work for the government, you can just go home at, what? Seven at night? Jesus, is it really seven?'

She smiled. 'Stalker. I'm on I95 heading home. When you didn't pick up I figured you were working or something.' Or something. She wasn't about to get into all the 'or somethings' her mind had wondered he was doing. The prickle of anxiety she'd felt thinking about them had made her mad at herself. The BS dating rules and mind games were now in full force. The switch had been flipped. The control freak in her was to the fore. Think three steps ahead. *Don't you dare let him think you're jealous. Or that you care. This is a stupid, dumb fling, that's all this is, right? It makes no sense. You're acting out, Daria, that's all.*

'I was. Damn dead bodies,' Manny said. 'They have no respect for anyone's schedule. I got called out at four this morning. Gangbang in Liberty City. It's been a day, I'll tell ya,' he finished with a yawn.

'You sound tired.'

'Not so much.'

'We can talk tomorrow. No big deal.'

'You called before?' he asked. 'I never got it. I was locked in a warehouse. A/C wasn't working, neither. Damn, they stunk.'

'They?'

'It was a triple. No matter. Each of 'em had a record the length of my arm. Nobody but their mommas will be missing none of 'em tonight. Maybe not even their mommas. So you called?'

'Only to tell you Lunders is on for report tomorrow afternoon. No big deal,' she repeated. *Remain aloof. Detached. Don't let him in.*

'Do I need to be there?'

'No, it's nothing but a status conference to see if he's bluffing about wanting a trial in the fall.'

'Is he?'

'I'll find out tomorrow.'

'Are you hungry?' he asked.

'You're tired.'

'Not so much.'

'You probably smell like dead body.'

'I got a fresh shirt in the trunk. And some Vicks, if you need it,' he said with a laugh. Vicks VapoRub was an old cop trick. Rub a little under your nose and you couldn't smell decomposing flesh. Homicide detectives and MEs used it all the time at smelly crime scenes and autopsies.

'I'm almost home,' she replied.

'Turn around. There's a new rib joint just opened in North Beach.'

She was quiet for a minute. 'Ribs, huh?'

'I can take you for steak and lobster, if you want. That's always fun. The cleaning lady came today, so my house is respectable. And Rufus misses you. He says he's sorry about that flashy red pair of Stuart Weitzman's. They were delicious. I'll have to take you shoe shopping and make it up to you.'

259

She smiled. 'You sound exhausted.'

'I want to see you, Counselor,' he said quietly. 'I do. I need to. Turn the car around.'

'Okay,' she answered.

It's a stupid, dumb fling. You're acting out.

You miss him today, but tomorrow is another day . . .

She shook her head at that last thought. *You miss him today. A lot. You miss him every day. There's no reason why. There's no planning around it. There's no getting out of it, Daria. It is what it is.*

Although she was already at Hollywood Boulevard, a few miles from her own exit, she got off and turned around.

Just as he had asked.

30

The second she saw Justice Joe's face at the defense table,
Daria knew something was up. Then his head turned red
and he opened his large mouth and started bitching on
high volume and she knew she was screwed.

'This woman looks almost identical to Holly Skole,
down to her hair color, body type. Jesus, even their
underwear matches, Judge!' he barked. Once again, the
well-heeled Anne-Claire Simmons sat quietly beside him
at the defense table. 'And there are others. There's no
doubt the state's holding back on us; this is Brady material
and a clear discovery violation and Ms DeBianchi damn
well knows it!'

Daria stared at the wood grain that ran through the
state's podium, biting the inside of her cheeks to keep
her mouth from popping open like a broken trunk. So
much for a routine status report. She'd been blindsided.
Joe Varlack knew about the video and apparently so
much more.

'And the method of torture inflicted on the female in

the video is almost identical to how the state describes Holly Skole as being brutalized: household cleaners, bondage, S&M. Coincidence? I don't think so. And neither does the state, which is why they've spent a lot of time investigating the murder of this other woman and developing suspects in that case. In every way these two victims match, down to the manner of their deaths.'

'You seem to know an awful lot about a video you supposedly didn't know anything about, Mr Varlack,' Judge Becker remarked, frowning. 'State?'

'Judge, I thought this was on for report and to set a possible trial date.' Daria tried to collect herself. 'This is the first I am hearing from Mr Varlack of a Brady violation, so I'm not really prepared to respond. I think Counsel should file a written motion—'

'Nonsense. We're all here,' interrupted the judge with a shake of her head.

'State knows exactly what video I'm talking about. And she knows what other suspects I'm talking about, too. We also believe the state has identified additional victims of this same murderer. That changes the game quite a bit, Judge. And considering the case against Talbot is purely circumstantial, it casts even more doubt on his guilt. The defense is entitled to a copy of the video, the names of the victims who have been identified, and the names of any suspects. I find it absolutely incredible that all this time the state has been sitting on information that could very well exculpate Talbot. Incredible, unethical, outrageous! All while Talbot languishes in a jail cell, denied bond!'

'State? Is there such a video?' asked Judge Becker.

Daria blew out a low breath. Uh-oh. 'Yes, Your Honor.

However, as this video was given to me by the defendant's mother, Abigail Lunders, I assumed that she'd also given it to her son's lawyer. I'm not sure what kind of games the defense is playing. They've known about the video's existence as long as the state has.'

The judge shook her head again. She was mad. 'Have you identified the victim on that video, State?'

'Her name is Gabriella Vechio. It's a murder out of New York that happened five years ago.'

'Still unsolved, I assume?'

'Correct.'

'Hmmm . . . a five-year-old homicide out of New York doesn't sound related to Ms Skole's murder, on the face of it. Let me ask you, Ms DeBianchi: is Gabriella Vechio's murder investigation related to the murder of Holly Skole?'

'Mr Lunders is not a suspect in Ms Vechio's murder,' Daria answered. That much was true. She prayed the judge would stop with her questions – she was walking a fine line of semantics. Rephrase the same exact question, ask it again and the judge would hold her in contempt for lying. Or, rather, for not telling the whole truth.

Judge Becker sighed like she was tired of talking to toddlers. 'Are the two cases related – scratch that. Let me see for myself. Where's this video? And I want the police reports regarding this Vechio girl's death. Ms DeBianchi, you acknowledge being in possession of the video. I want to see it.' The judge stood up. 'I'm going back into chambers. Bring it to me along with the reports and I'll take a look and decide right now if this is Brady material. The rest of my calendar can wait till we sort this out.'

'There's more, Judge.' Varlack walked across the aisle and handed Daria a thick packet. 'I'm filing a motion to suppress the search of Abby Lunders's vehicle.'

'What?' Daria replied with disbelief. 'That search was conducted pursuant to a warrant.'

'A warrant that was based on the statements of a witness who is now unavailable,' he said. 'Your Honor, Marie Modic provided information to Detective Alvarez that led him to obtain a search warrant. Without her statements, law enforcement would never have located the vehicle and hence my client would never have been arrested. We can't find her, Your Honor. I've been trying to depose her, but she's gone AWOL. No one knows where she is. Without her, the warrant fails.'

And if the warrant was out, everything inside the Benz was out, too. No lipstick, no DNA, no hair, no fingerprints, no fibers. And that meant Daria wouldn't be able to prove Holly Skole had ever been in the car, which meant she could ultimately never prove she'd left the club with Lunders. No car meant no conviction. The day could not get any shittier.

'Okay, so make a Motion to Compel her appearance, but the remedy is not suppression of the warrant,' Daria shot back. 'Your Honor, Ms Modic only served a limited purpose in Detective Alvarez's obtaining the warrant. And I am not conceding she's unavailable.' Although the Investigations Unit at the State Attorney's had been looking for her for a couple of weeks, there was no reason to think she'd completely skipped town. Witnesses had lives that went on independent of a criminal case – sometimes all you had to do was look harder.

'Okay, everyone: I'm not hearing that motion today.

The state will need time to respond, and in the meantime, hopefully produce this witness. Althea, give them a date on that. Your motion to suppress, or compel, or whatever, is the least of the state's problems at this moment, Mr Varlack,' the judge announced as she stepped off the bench and headed toward the door that led to the hallway and her chambers. 'Right now, I want to see that video.'

31

The blue flash drive dangled from the neck cord the judge held in her manicured fist. With her elbows resting on the bench, she slowly swung it back and forth in front of her face, like a pendulum.

'I don't know what kind of game you think you're playing, State. The fact that *this* video was anonymously sent to the defendant's mother on the eve of her son's bond hearing raises eyebrows right out of the gate. At least for me it does. If it hadn't caused the same reaction for you, Ms DeBianchi, I guess that would be one thing. If you'd shrugged your shoulders and moved on to the next matter on your desk, I guess I'd be sitting here questioning your indifference. You are, I suppose, under no obligation to investigate the source of the video, or find out who the girl was or what became of her.' The judge paused for a long moment. 'But you did. And you discovered that she, too, was not a consensual partner in an S&M tape, but rather the victim of a brutal murder that had occurred under circumstances alarmingly similar to your own case, albeit in a different jurisdiction.

'I don't know if a jury's ever going to get to see this video. I don't know what kind of a defense Mr Varlack will be raising, although I'm pretty sure I see it coming. But at the very least, Mr Varlack had a right to be informed of the video's existence, had a right to see the video, and had a right to know the name of the victim so identified in it. As the crimes do appear similar, he also has the right to know the names of any suspects the police have identified in Ms Vechio's murder, including those developed by the authorities in New York, as well as any possible victims from other jurisdictions that have been identified, as this may lead him to develop another theory of his case. If it turns out that someone *other* than Mr Lunders committed those murders – murders that do appear, as I just said, alarmingly identical to Ms Skole's murder – *that* is information that might very well exculpate the defendant. What is the most disappointing factor in all this is that you are a smart woman, Ms DeBianchi, and you knew you had to turn it over, but you didn't.'

'Judge—' Daria started.

'You didn't. That being said, Mr Varlack, you can't just sit on something that you had in your possession till the last minute so you can scream you've been done wrong, hoping to engage my ire. Your client's mother had the video. She has a copy in her possession, I'm sure. You've obviously seen the video; according to Ms DeBianchi, Abigail Lunders said she'd shown it to you the morning of the Arthur Hearing. So yes, you are entitled to the information that the state has derived from investigating the video, but you are culpably negligent. The state, remiss as it is, is not legally obligated to hand you your defense. I suggest you put some of those well-paid investigators of yours to work and engage in some defense work yourself.

'Give him the names, Ms DeBianchi,' the judge finished with a sigh. 'Give him the police reports. Give him the video. And I don't want to hear so much as a whisper of a rumor that you are withholding evidence, or I'll be the first to file a bar complaint. No conviction is ever worth your character.'

Varlack smelled opportunity. 'Your Honor, I'd like to revisit bond. You said that was possible if there was new evidence that came to light. I think this surely qualifies.'

'Yes, Mr Varlack, I did say that,' the judge replied.

'Mr Lunders needs to be able to assist in his defense. He doesn't have a criminal history, not even a traffic ticket. He'd be willing to surrender his passport, commit to an ankle bracelet. And, of course, post a substantial bond.'

'Of course,' replied Becker, nodding.

'Your Honor, Judge Steyn heard all this—' Daria protested.

But the judge waved her off with a fire-red claw. 'Perhaps this will prove as incentive for you to be completely forthcoming with the court and opposing counsel in the future. You're lucky this isn't happening during trial or post-conviction, because you'd be sitting in a jail cell. Bond is hereby granted in the amount of one hundred thousand dollars. In the event the defendant posts bond, he'll commit to a bracelet and be placed under house arrest pending trial. We're done for now.'

The judge swooped off the bench before anyone could utter another word, her black robe billowing in a puff behind her as she quickly strode out the door to her chambers. It slammed shut.

Daria stood at the state's table, completely stunned. Bond was in the discretion of the trial judge, so there was nothing to appeal. She just had to deal with it.

Talbot Lunders was now out of custody. A free man.

And it was all her fault.

32

'Patricia Susanna Graber was a victim on one of Reinaldo Lepidus's cases back when he was a defense attorney in '97,' Mike Dickerson was saying, peering at Manny over his thick glasses from his favorite perch on Manny's desk: one butt cheek on, one off.

Manny leaned forward in his chair. 'Go on.'

'The crime was a home invasion. The defendants were two career criminals from Miami, a Lazaro Nefaris and a Ricky Reeder. According to court documents, they were supposed to hit the house next door and rob it – the one with the meth lab in the kitchen – but they accidentally went to the neighbor's instead. The home of Joel and Emily Nachwalter.

'Unfortunately for Ms Graber, she picked that very night to pay her aunt and uncle a visit. Talk about wrong place, wrong time. Everyone in the house was tied up and pistol-whipped, and twenty-three-year-old Patty was fondled while the two Neanderthals trashed the house looking for the drug money that was being counted next door. Nefaris, the Neanderthal with a conscience, apparently realized they were racking up the felonies and pulled Reeder out before it got any uglier. Prints led BSO detectives to Nefaris, and Patty Graber's subsequent ID on both of them put the nails in their coffins. Nefaris flipped and got twenty; Reeder went to trial. Patty testified against him, and the judge gave him life.'

'Where are they now?'

'Nefaris got out in 2009, and died of AIDS four months later. Reeder's still in Union Correctional.'

'And Patty Graber?'

'Her body was found in a dumpster behind a construction site in Parkland in '99. She'd been raped and strangled.' Mike tossed a crime-scene picture across the desk. 'No arrests ever made. No suspects identified. They did check to see if there was any connection to Reeder or Nefaris, but nothing. Both boys were still in jail.'

'Mikey, I take back everything I ever thought about you that wasn't nice. How'd you find this shit?' Manny asked.

'A records check and manual review, since cases are not linked by computer to victim or witness names, only to defendants. I also ran both a newspaper search and a Google search with the name Pat Graber, but that wasn't so helpful, as you can imagine. I got, like, ninety-five thousand hits on my first search. It wasn't easy, which is why it took me a few weeks. Good thing this was one of Lepidus's cases from his early years in practice, or I'd still be sitting in the clerk's office going through shit, where I've been eight hours a day for the past month. My wife thinks I'm having an affair.'

'Trust me, she's happy you're out of her hair,' Bear said.

'Lepidus was appointed to the bench by Governor Bush in 2000. He handled hundreds of cases as a defense lawyer and virtually thousands of cases as a circuit court judge and then as an appellate judge with the Fourth DCA and the Supremes, where he lasted two years before he croaked. It would have taken me for ever to find that connection, if I ever did.'

Manny nodded thoughtfully.

'It gets better. Or worse, depending how you look at it. In my diligent research of the Honorable, or turns out, the not-so-Honorable Judge Lepidus, I came across something else which may or may not be anything—'

'Spit it out, old man.'

Mike smiled a crooked smile. 'Did you know that Judge Reinaldo Lepidus was on the Florida Supreme Court when William Rupert Bantling's appeal was heard? As votes go, his was the one that broke the tie. Sorry, no new trial after all, Bill. Judge Lepidus actually wrote the damn opinion. He said the appellate court overstepped its authority when it overturned the trial judge's denial of a new trial. Said the trial judge did not abuse his discretion when he denied Bantling's demand for a new trial on ineffective assistance of counsel grounds and newly discovered evidence, and so the Third District Court of Appeals should never have granted Bantling a new trial. Lepidus was the one who ordered the original verdict reinstated – ultimately sending Cupid back to death row in 2006 and quashing his state appeals.'

'Are you shitting me?' Manny asked, wide-eyed.

'I ain't no lawyer, sonny boy, so I can't explain all the legal mumbo-jumbo to ya, but I'm sure your cute girlfriend can. She seems pretty smart.'

Manny stared at him. Mike grinned knowingly.

'Insightful,' Manny replied. 'For an old man who's supposed to be at the age he's forgetting shit.'

'I've been called worse. I knew she had nice legs from Day One when you was rushing to see her for the Arthur on the Skole girl. Remember I told you that? I didn't even have to see her, I just knew.'

'You're slick.'

'You remind me a lot of myself in my younger days, Bear. Back when I was taller and had a lot more hair.' Mike rubbed his head. 'Although maybe we have more in common along those lines, now. I played baseball, too, ya know.'

'Yeah?'

'Little League, but I could've gone much further if I hadn't been drafted. 'Nam called.'

'A million excuses.'

'I always went for the legs. Gam Man, the boys called me,' Mike went on. 'Saw you two at the courthouse the other day. Hope you wear a better poker face when you interview street scum, Sonny. You looked like a fucking puppy, following Legs around. But she is definitely cute. Nice ass, too. Don't know what she sees in you, though.'

'Me neither, Pops,' Manny answered with a smile. 'I'm just glad she sees me. Course the same could be said about your wife. What you married now? Thirty?'

'Don't go there. My Etta never looked like your prosecutor, although she did have nice legs before the veins started popping.' He whistled. 'I'm jealous of you, Bear,

273

but I can't do nothing about it without taking a pill anyway, so what's the point in fantasizing?'

Manny shook his head and picked up a crime-scene photo from his desk. 'Good detective work there, Watson.' He frowned. 'I'm gonna need to blow these pictures up, if possible, Mikey. I need to see if there are any marks—'

'Done,' Mike said, slipping another crime-scene photo across the desk.

'Jesus . . .' Manny said, looking up at Mike, wide-eyed.

'Jesus is right,' replied Mike. 'I knew this one would get you.'

The blonde-haired, brown-eyed Patricia Susanna Graber lay naked in a dumpster, her crumpled legs folded beneath her. But Mike had enlarged the photo, and what Manny immediately noticed was not the strangulation marks across the girl's pale throat, or the bruises on her thighs, or the vacant stare in her lifeless, open eyes.

It was the small, jagged black thunderbolt, seared into the flesh right over the girl's heart that immediately got his attention.

33

Daria had debated heading straight to Vance Collier's office on the fourth floor and telling him what happened before he saw it for himself tonight on the news, or read about it in the morning. Face up and take the medicine. But when she hit the elevator, she just couldn't do it. Not yet. She headed to her office to regroup her thoughts over a cup of coffee. Perhaps she should call Collier instead . . .

She looked out the window at the jail. In a few hours Lunders would be back on the street. Back in the mansion with his odd, hot mom. An out-of-custody defendant meant headaches on several scales. If he was entertaining a plea in that warped pretty head of his, extracting it would be a much more difficult task now. Jailbirds, once they'd tasted freedom, didn't ever want to go back in the cage. Especially if they were facing a long sentence. If Lunders was involved in a snuff club, being out of custody also meant he could contact witnesses, potentially destroy evidence, and alert possible co-conspirators – his fellow murderers.

Of course the snuff-club theory was nothing but a theory – it had been weeks since she and Manny had been to see Bantling and they still had not found any connection between Judge Lepidus and 'Pat Graber'. Other than the word of a convicted serial killer, they'd found nothing to corroborate the club's existence. Although Manny was actively working the other murders out of St Pete and south Miami, and following up leads, nothing so far had led to either Talbot Lunders or Bill Bantling. For his part, Bantling was in prison at the time of both Florida murders; Lunders was in the Bahamas with his mother when Cyndi DeGregorio, the stripper from Florida City, had disappeared. Although Jane Doe, the unidentified victim from Tampa, was seen leaving the bar in the Don Cesar Hotel last April with a man who matched the description of Talbot Lunders, one year later the hotel employee who'd offered the initial description was unable to pick Talbot's picture out of a photo line-up.

Maybe it was pure coincidence that the victims had these similar tattoos/brandings on their persons. Maybe she and Manny had opened up a big bag of worms and handed the defense their defense. Or maybe, just maybe, Daria's gut had been right from the beginning – Abby Lunders had led them down this weird trail for a reason. Behind the concerned mom demeanor, there was something not to be trusted about the woman. Daria recalled the intimate embrace she'd witnessed in the courthouse between Abby and Talbot. It brought to mind the murdering mother–son grifters, Sante and Kenny Kimes, who'd shared a hell of a lot more than psychopathic genes. Yuck. Nothing much surprised her in this job anymore.

The phone rang at her desk and she jumped a little in her seat. It was probably Vance calling to scream at her because he had watched the news. She couldn't avoid his wrath forever. 'State Attorney's. DeBianchi.'

'I like that you're sitting at your desk, waiting for me to call,' Manny said with a chuckle when Daria picked up. 'Not even one full ring. Now tell me, what are you wearing?'

She was relieved it wasn't Collier, but she also dreaded telling Manny how her morning had gone. She was no good at eating crow. 'Funny,' she answered. 'I was about to head upstairs to see Vance.'

'Too bad for you. I don't like that guy.'

'Really?'

'Really. I've heard things about his "hands-on" approach. Watch yourself.'

'It's cute you're jealous, but he's old enough to be my dad. Technically, at least.'

Manny cleared his throat.

'I forgot – you are, too, I guess,' she added. 'You have nothing to worry about.'

'He's a limelight bather, Counselor. I'm not so much worried about him stealing my girl as I am him stealing your case.'

She bit her lip and swallowed hard. 'We have to talk,' she said, twisting the phone cord in her fingers.

'Yep. Something's happened,' he answered.

'Where'd you hear it? On the news?'

'Hear what? What's on the news?'

She swallowed again. 'You first.'

'Well, we found the connection between Reinaldo Lepidus and Pat Graber. Patricia Susanna Graber was a victim in a home invasion Lepidus handled as a defense attorney. She's dead now. They found her in a dumpster in Broward County in 1999, about two years after Lepidus's client went off to prison on a life sentence. All this happened before he took the bench. The murder's still unsolved.'

'What? You're kidding!'

'She had a lightning brand over her heart, Counselor.'

'Jesus . . .'

'What did I tell you about coincidences, huh? There ain't no such thing. Oh, and another thing that ain't so much a coincidence, now that I'm thinking about it. Judge Lepidus was on the Florida Supreme Court when Bantling was shipped back to death row. He cast the deciding vote and wrote the fucking opinion.'

'No shit . . .' she sank into her chair, flabbergasted.

'No shit. You'll have to read all the reasons why and then explain them to me. I love it when you talk to me in legalese. It's sexy.'

'I'll have to read the opinion, but I'm guessing here that you're thinking Lepidus steered his cronies on the state's highest court to throw out Bantling's appeal, thereby effectively sending him back to death row? That's pretty steep.'

'Something like that. All I know is that it was done. And nothing surprises me anymore, Counselor. Ponzi schemes are old hat, some cops are murderers, all lawyers – present company excluded, of course – are scum, and judges have flipped out before. Think of those knuckle-headed judges in Pennsylvania who sent kids to juvenile lock-up for cash kickbacks a year or so back. Nobody would've believed *that* until it happened. And remember that guy Wachtler? Wasn't he the big cheese on New York's highest court when he started stalking his ex-girlfriend and racking up the felonies?'

Daria stared at her votive candleholder filled with paperclips. Manny was right. No one – not even a judge – was above reproach.

'Okay. I just might buy that,' she said. 'But if this club has that sort of reach, Manny . . .' Daria didn't finish her thought. 'So why didn't you find this Pat Graber when you found Cyndi DeGregorio and the Jane Doe from Tampa?'

'Graber's dead going on twelve years. We didn't look that far back. She might not be in ViCAP or the lightning brand might not have been entered in distinguishing marks. There're a number of reasons. Makes you wonder how many more we might be missing, Counselor. How big this thing might be.'

'Okay,' she said slowly, trying to think like a defense attorney, three steps ahead. If Manny was right, this was probably the biggest scandal Miami would ever see. A snuff club of voyeur killers operating around the nation, possibly the world, with a Florida State Supreme Court judge as one of its members, officially sending another snuff-club member to death row to keep him quiet. *Who else might be a member of this club? How high would it go?*

'But we have to have something other than, "she was the victim in a criminal case he handled as a defense attorney" to implicate Lepidus in her murder, Manny.'

'Like a video, you think?'

Daria sucked in a breath. 'No way.'

'The judge's widow was wife number two. Before he

died in a boating accident last year, the happy couple hit an unhappy patch, that at one point looked like it might lead to divorce. The prudent little woman made and kept a copy of his risqué video collection, apparently as an insurance policy he wouldn't fuck her in a divorce settlement. Claims she never watched them all. Her attorney has them now – they're stuck in probate. He's not sure what's on them, or so he claims, but I got a feeling, Counselor. One of 'em's labeled *The Snitch*, according to the lawyer. Even though the judge is dead, his wife's attorney wants a warrant.'

'Okay. I'll get it started,' she replied. 'Right away.'

'So what happened?' he asked.

'Huh?'

'What's on the news that I missed?'

She took a deep breath. Time to get it over with. 'Judge Becker granted Lunders a bond. A hundred grand. He's gonna get out, probably this afternoon.'

'Shit. On what grounds?'

She sighed. 'Varlack wants everything: Vechio's video, the police reports. The other victims. The judge is really pissed off. I can't believe she let him out.'

'He screamed Brady, didn't he?' Manny asked smugly. 'Come on, tell me.'

'Shut up.'

'I knew it. *I* should've gone to law school. Do you want to say it with me, or should I say it all by myself?'

'Get it over with,' she replied.

'Told you so, Counselor. Now go redeem yourself and get me that fucking warrant.'

34

Vance Collier tapped his pen on his desk. Behind him, the tops of palm trees swayed angrily under menacing black skies, skies that ten minutes before had been beach-worthy blue. A volatile summer thunderstorm had suddenly appeared, as if conjured up by the Chief Assistant to fit his mood. 'That's one helluva story,' he said to Daria, his brow furrowed. 'What other connection do you have to Judge Lepidus and this girl? There has to be some physical evidence, something more than the assurances of a convicted serial killer. A serial killer who, coincidentally, is calling the same judge who sent him back to death row a murderer.'

Daria nodded. 'Lepidus died in a boating accident. His estate is still in probate. Second wife is battling it out for her fair share. Apparently there were certain videotapes her attorney was holding on to because of a possible divorce action. More like holding hostage. We got a warrant and took a look. They're all pretty extreme, Vance – bondage, S&M, animals, latex, weird fetishes. Really hard core. Some look homemade, maybe borrowed or downloaded from a homegrown site. Lepidus features in a couple of them, but those seem to be consensual. We'll have to track down the girls to make sure, I suppose. Spliced into one of the homemade tapes was Patty Graber. It's her murder, Vance. It's just like the Gabriella Vechio video clip – bondage, S&M, black silk ropes. Only this one goes all the way to the finish line. The male in the video, who is definitely not Lepidus, strangles her with his bare hands while he's screwing her from behind and she's tethered to the ceiling.' She placed a flash drive on his desk. 'It seems you really can trust a serial killer – Bantling was telling the truth.'

'Holy shit . . .'

She nodded.

'I'm gonna guess it's not Talbot Lunders committing the murder. I assume that would have been the first thing you told me. Although I'm still waiting for the courtesy call to inform me that he's back on the street.'

She decided not to respond to that. Focus on the positive. 'Correct. We don't know who it is. He's young, buff and has a tattoo across his back of an archangel throwing lightning bolts. He's also wearing a mask. Lepidus is too old for it to be him, plus in the videos the judge is featured in, you can tell he's tattoo-free. Manny is checking tattoos with those documented on inmates, but that's a daunting task. Law enforcement only recently started to keep records and photos for that purpose, and this video was made twelve years ago.'

Vance picked up the flash and fingered it. 'You shouldn't have held out on me. From the very beginning, Daria, this is something the State Attorney and I should have been in on.'

'I wasn't sure at first what I was looking at, Vance,' she explained. 'The video clip that Abby Lunders gave me could have been a homemade S&M tape Momma was trying to lob as a distraction. I wasn't gonna come to you with that until I investigated. It wasn't until the connection between Gabriella Vechio and Holly Skole became apparent – after the similar brandings were identified through crime-scene and autopsy photos – that Detective Alvarez first suggested a possible connection to Cupid. But he couldn't be sure if it was anything more than a hunch based on something the guy had said years before. So, like I said, I wasn't really sure what we had, or didn't have, until we met with Bantling. When he dropped Lepidus's name I thought he was probably BS-ing, because, as you already pointed out, convicted killers don't make the most reliable witnesses. It's only now that the connection between Judge Lepidus and Patty Graber's been exposed, I felt I had something for you. Because now I know it's for real, Vance. Now I know it's big.'

The Chief Assistant said nothing for a long moment. 'You weren't around when Cupid was tried in 2001. I was. It was a zoo. I've never seen a case – a defendant, actually – transfix the public the way that case did, except maybe O.J. Simpson.' He tapped the pen again on the desk and scowled. 'Jesus, you've never tried a serial before,' he added, almost like a note to self.

'A rapist. Corey Lightsey. Seven consecutive life sentences.'

'There's a big difference between a rapist and a serial

killer. This whole thing is so complicated now. Much more so than when I gave you the case. Then it was a single homicide with a little bit of local publicity to worry about containing. Now you're talking potentially a criminal enterprise with multiple defendants, and we're looking at a maelstrom of publicity, the center of which might very well be a notorious serial killer.'

Daria felt her stomach drop. *There was no way she could lose this case. Not now. Not after all the work she'd done . . .*

'So what is Lunders's role in all this? Is Holly Skole's murder a snuff-club killing?' he asked. 'Is it related to this club that Cupid claims to know so much about? Did he tell you that?'

'Bantling told me this was a game,' she answered. 'He gave some cryptic analogy to baseball players and scouts and stadiums. He said Lepidus liked to watch. So I have a theory. Based on Talbot Lunders's good looks, the surveillance video of Holly Skole getting in his Benz willingly, and then the cell phone records the night she disappeared from Menace, I'm thinking Talbot's role in this club was to *supply* victims for the game – a game of murder that Lepidus and others like him would pay to watch, most likely on some sort of Internet connection like Skype, only heavily encrypted. Manny Alvarez said that when he first interviewed Bantling years ago, he mentioned this club having international connections. If that statement's true, then it would have to be via the Internet. That would be the easiest way, the most discreet way, to assemble the watchers. Postal and Customs have nailed dozens of worldwide Internet kiddie-porn clubs that way, as well as money-laundering outfits, sex traffickers, and terrorist organizations. I believe Talbot

Lunders was a hunter – a "scout" was the euphemism Bantling used – trolling bars and charming women, probably drugging them. That supposition is based on Marie Modic's statement describing how she felt and why she believed Lunders had spiked her drink.

'When you think about it, Vance, the crime has a lot of similarities to Cupid's MO. As for Patty Graber's murder, that happened during the Cupid rampage but because she wasn't missing her heart no one made a connection. It's possible some of Bantling's murders were captured on video. He might have had a whole following of watchers himself – although I can't for the life of me figure out why Bantling wouldn't have pulled this snuff-club card out during his trial to try and save himself or shave a few years off his sentence. Why didn't he cough up names then? Or maybe he did, but the prosecutor didn't believe it. C.J. Townsend's long gone, and no one seems to know where, so I guess I can't ask for her input in the thought process.'

'C.J. left the office years ago,' Vance answered. 'She moved out of state, as far as I know. Cupid sucked the life out of her. I liked her, but mentally she was a mess when she left. A wreck.' He jotted down something on his legal pad. 'So what you're saying now is you *don't* think Talbot Lunders actually committed or participated in Holly's murder?'

'I don't think he actually killed her, but I believe he transported her to her death. He picked her out like he was shopping for meat at a supermarket, which makes him guilty of felony murder. And I can still get the death penalty on felony murder.'

'Maybe. But if he didn't know he was whisking her

285

away to a slaughterhouse, it presents as a much more difficult case. Now we have to prove he knew or should have known he was leading her to her death.'

'Regardless of what he knew, he still participated in the felony.'

'What's the underlying felony?'

'Kidnapping.'

'You said she went willingly.'

'I also said I think he drugged her. That's not willingly.'

'Supposition. You can prove there were drugs in her system when you *found* her – six days after she disappeared. You can't prove she was drugged the night she went missing. In fact, the surveillance tapes show otherwise. They show her walking out of her own accord and getting into that Benz with a big smile when he held the door open.'

'We can connect him to purchases of sulfuric acid. That's what was used to melt her feet.'

'Interesting. Can you tie the sulfuric acid he purchased to the acid that she was burned with?'

'No.'

'So it's interesting and circumstantial, but it's not direct evidence of his involvement in her murder.'

She stared at him, embarrassed that she hadn't thought it out this far before entering his office. 'Well, this is frustrating.'

'You see the problems we have now? Because now we *know* there's a third party. If Lunders claims he was just taking Holly to party with some boys, then he left and that's the last he heard of it, you don't have much of a case.'

Daria bit her lip.

'That's the problem with circumstantial cases – they're circumstantial. And since we don't get to depose Talbot, we don't know what he's gonna say or what his theory of the case will be until his trial. So we're gonna need to find a witness who can explain what Lunders's role was in Holly's murder. And we don't have much time, seeing as the speedy clock is ticking. So if you really think he didn't kill her, then let's have him give up who did. If it is a snuff-club operation he's involved in, like Bantling has detailed, we're gonna deal him if he hands us the other players and tells how this club works.'

'He won't talk. Manny Alvarez tried.' She didn't mention the creepy message he'd forwarded to her through Manny. If Vance thought she was spooked, it might give him the excuse he needed to pull the whole case from her. 'He's pretty smug.'

'He has reason to be. If his role in this is defined by the rules of the sick game you describe, then he's done this before. And he's learned from someone. Dig deeper, Daria. Phone records, exes, current girlfriends. Like Lepidus, he must have been into kinky shit that somebody can tell us about. See if he can be linked to any of the other dead women. No matter how slight the connection. We need to scare the shit out of him and let him know we're not playing. He's gonna pay for Holly's death if he doesn't give us someone who will.'

She nodded.

Vance grew pensive. 'The bigger fish in this, though, is Cupid. He gave us Lepidus as an appetizer. He wouldn't have given us the biggest name *before* working some sort of deal, which means he knows a lot more names. It's possible he can give us Lunders. The kid might not be a newbie, he might have been involved in this club from before Bantling went away. What did Bantling say when you confronted him that Lepidus wrote the opinion on his overturned appeal?'

'I wasn't aware of that at the time I interviewed him,' she answered sheepishly. She felt embarrassed, as if she somehow hadn't done her homework on Bantling before going up to Starke to interview him, although there was no way she would've known about Lepidus's remote connection to Bantling when he first mentioned the judge's name. Who the hell would have memorized all the appellate judges' names that touched a defendant's case before questioning him? She looked at Vance's frowning face and then down at her fingers. Maybe she was in the office of the one person who would have.

'I want to know who else has been watching these murders go down all these years,' he continued. 'Who might be a player or a scout. I want to know how many other killers are out there living amongst us, how many might be sitting beside me in a courtroom or joining me at a midnight crime scene or presiding over one of my cases, for Christ's sake. That's much more disturbing – wondering who might be more influential than a Supreme Court judge on Cupid's list. A snuff club operating right here in Miami . . . That's gonna make headlines, all right. Especially if the star witness turns out to be none other than Cupid himself.'

It was funny how quickly the pronouns had changed. Vance no longer said 'hers' or 'yours', instead it was 'us', 'we' and 'ours'.

She had to ask. 'Is this still mine?'

'What does Bantling want?' Vance asked, ignoring her question.

'I'm not sure what he'll settle for, but he said he wants out for the information he has. And he said that a couple of times. Of course, that's out of the question, I—'

'Depends on what other names he has. If they're as big as Lepidus, we deal him.'

She said nothing for a minute. She remembered what Manny had said to her after they'd interviewed Bantling at Florida State Prison. 'I didn't think that was an option, considering what he's done, all those women.'

'Ray Lepidus sat on the Florida Supreme Court. If he was the appetizer, think of what the names on the main course must be. Hell, you could be talking CEOs, politicians, priests, rabbis, international fucking figureheads. If Lunders won't talk, then we work with those who will. Cupid can give us the names of the other participants and how the operation works, we deal. They're murderers, too, whether they watched, scouted, or stuck the damn knife in. They need to be brought to justice. And we need to find out who they are. It's unfortunate, and it sounds sordid, I know, but deals are cut all the time, Daria. It's how the system works. Murderers are flipped against one another, sentences are reduced because we need to find the body. Because a family needs closure. And sometimes we have to negotiate with monsters. Governments swap terrorists. It sounds counterproductive to steadfastly refuse to pursue these murderers because the information we want is going to potentially come at a tremendous cost.'

She nodded.

'"Better that ten guilty men escape punishment than

that one innocent suffer." You've heard that saying before, I assume?'

She nodded. 'Of course.' English jurist William Blackstone's formulation was a basic principle of American criminal law.

'It would seem to follow that in this case it is also better to let one guilty man go free so that we can rid the streets of ten more scumbags.' Vance looked at the disturbing autopsy photo of Patty Graber. 'Maybe a hell of a lot more than ten. It's a last resort, of course, freedom. There are other options to consider.'

'Is it still mine?' Daria asked again, though she already knew the answer.

'It's *ours*. I'll be trying this case with you. We'll work it together from now on. And the first thing we're gonna do is pay another visit to our friend in Starke.'

35

'Now what can we expect if this storm hits as a Cat 5?' the perky anchor on the television asked the weatherman.

'Well, that depends on where it hits, Jennifer,' the weatherman replied with a smile. 'With sustained winds over one hundred and fifty-five miles per hour, Category 5 storms are monsters. There will be extensive damage wherever it makes landfall, if it makes landfall as a five. With sustained winds right now of one hundred and sixty-two miles an hour, Artemis is a whopper of a storm, but it's still seven to eight days out. That's a long time in the life of a hurricane forecaster. The computer models are literally all over the board on this thing, from a southeasterly turn over Cuba to a march across northern Florida, to a dead hit on Miami like Andrew in '92. We have a system of high pressure that is moving in from the Canadian Rockies, which could change the whole game. So we don't know what to expect at this stage. What everyone in the state of Florida should be doing right now is going over their hurricane preparedness checklist . . .'

'It's a sign,' Tru Zeffers said as he walked up to join Daria in front of the small portable TV that sat on the CO's desktop next to the security station in death row. 'All them tornadoes, earthquakes, tsunamis, floods – it's all a sign. World's ending in 2012, just like them Mayans predicted,' he added with a chuckle. 'Might as well have some fun 'fore we go, don't ya think? Glad to see you back up here, Dairy-uh, though I'm sure missing them heels.'

Daria offered him a half-smile. 'I took your advice, Sergeant. Found the flattest pair in the closet. Don't remember even buying them.'

'Tha's a damn shame. It's a crime to hide them-there legs of yours in pants, too,' he said, biting his knuckle. 'Forgive me for being honest. Where's Detective Alvarez? Thought your bodyguard would be up here with you today.'

She felt her face flush with guilt. Manny had no idea she and Collier were back at Florida State Prison. She figured she'd cross that bridge and have that conversation after they got the names out of Bantling. Manny was definitely gonna be angry, but he'd also have some more bad guys to go catch. A lot more. This was a case that could ultimately define his career. 'No,' she replied softly. 'He couldn't make it.' She peered down the hallway and glanced at her watch. She'd been sitting there like a dolt for almost an hour. 'Do you know if Mr Collier is ready for me, Sergeant?'

'Yep. He sent me to rustle you up. He's an ornery fellow, that DA boss of yours. Sure-footed, too? You'd think he was the one running things.' Obviously, Jus' Tru didn't care much for Vance Collier.

Zeffers walked her to the room on Row B, the same one she and Manny had interviewed Bantling in weeks before. Zeffers motioned to the cameras and the door opened with a buzz.

It was immediately obvious the party was over. The deed was done.

Vance glanced up from his notepad and nodded for her to sit next to him. 'Names, Mr Bantling,' he continued, without missing a beat. 'Now it's time for names.'

Bantling kept his eyes on Vance's legal pad. 'We were just talking about you, Ms DeBianchi. I hear your partner, Detective Alvarez, won't be joining us today. I'm assuming he doesn't approve of Mr Collier's deal with me? Maybe you don't either, since you were not here to broker it yourself.'

Vance tapped the pad with his pen. 'Don't worry yourself over who approves and who doesn't, Bill, because, frankly, *I'm* the only one who matters in that department. You should be worrying about giving me those names, or there'll be no deal. You can carry on enjoying the view from here.'

Bantling glared at Vance. 'I'm not stupid enough to give you anything without an agreement in place, so don't try to bully me, Mr Collier. And that agreement will be authorized and signed off by a judge in front of my very eyes. Forgive me, but I don't trust my attorney and I don't trust the government and I especially don't trust your office, Mr Collier.' He turned to the slightly disheveled man in a jacket and tie who sat beside him.

'Sorry if I offended you, Henry. I'm sure you understand, since that we just met an hour ago.'

The man nodded and extended his hand across the table. 'Henry Davies, Office of the Capitol Collateral Representative.' CCR, as it was known, was the state-funded office of appellate attorneys who represented indigent death-row inmates in their appeals. Underpaid and overworked, his talents likely stretched thin dealing with dozens of clients, Bantling was probably not exaggerating when he said he'd met the man for the first time today.

'Daria DeBianchi, State Attorney's Office.'

'You're lucky I'm sitting here, Mr Bantling,' Vance cautioned with a dark look. 'Perhaps you don't know who I am. I don't make deals I can't make good on.'

'No deal, no names – until I see it in writing, stand in front of a judge and hear it from his lips,' Bantling insisted. 'Then I'll tell you what you want to know. All about the pretty new kiddies on the block, too. The scouts. That should help you climb the ladder, Ms DeBianchi.'

Vance stood up. 'We'll bring you back home, Bill, but the deal will be contingent on all the information, and I do mean every last bit, panning out. It is also contingent on the value of the names provided. I'm expecting to eat filet mignon, here, not chop meat. Do I make myself clear? And if I bring you down to Miami and you fuck with me – you don't tell me what I want to hear, what your attorney is suggesting that I'm going to hear – you will rue the day you were born. Understood? You will also be required to testify in any and all proceedings that we need to secure convictions against the individuals you identify, so don't expect to be sunbathing on South Beach, Mr Bantling. If you keep your end of the bargain, if you satisfy all the conditions I set forth, then you will get what you want. I'll draw up the agreement and send you a copy, Mr Davies.'

The CCR attorney nodded. Daria thought he looked more than a little uncomfortable when she and Vance were buzzed out and the cell doors closed behind them, leaving him all alone with his new client.

They said nothing to each other as Zeffers escorted them through the steel maze to the main entrance. Jus' Tru made a couple of attempts at small talk with her along the way, but he seemed generally demoralized and intimidated by Vance, who glowered at the sergeant every time he opened his mouth. Especially after the Chief Assistant, who was a former Marine, picked up not only a Glock .40 from the gun locker, which he always carried under his tailored suit, but also the Sig he toted in an ankle holster. Maybe Tru had felt a fellow-cop camaraderie with Manny that let him loosen up, whereas today he was both outgunned and mentally outmanned. He skulked away without even saying goodbye to Daria.

'Okay. Our flight's at eight and we have an hour's drive to Jacksonville airport,' Vance said, sliding on sunglasses and checking his watch as they walked through the parking lot. 'Damn, it's hot, isn't it? Like an oven up here in the boonies. No sea breeze. Not that Miami is much cooler, I guess.'

'Dragonflies,' she remarked softly, looking at the ugly monster insects that flew around them like drunk drivers. 'It's gonna storm.'

He looked up at the sky. 'Speaking of which, you hear anything about that hurricane?'

'It's still too far out to say, but I'm worried,' she replied. 'I'm hoping it turns north; I don't have renter's insurance.'

Vance laughed. 'Sweetheart, if that thing hits Miami at a hundred and sixty miles an hour, we're all fucked. All the insurance companies will go broke, along with the state, so it won't matter whether you have insurance.'

When they'd reached the car, Daria turned to look at the prison. Dark tiny figures, silhouetted by the setting sun, walked the outer-ringed deck of the watchtowers. A line of chained inmates was being brought back from the runs and into the facility for the night. Even though she was clear of the prison walls and out in the sunshine and fresh air, she still felt dirty, like she'd taken a bath with the devil. Instead of being clean, his slime was now all over her. 'Jesus, Vance,' she said quietly, 'I hope we're doing the right thing here.'

'Oh, he's never getting out,' her boss replied. He knew exactly what she was talking about.

'How is that possible?'

'You heard me in there. I said *if* he keeps his end of the bargain. And that won't happen. He'll be testifying till I say he's done. And he'll never be done. This is the best offer he's ever gonna get – the only offer. He no longer faces the death penalty and he has a sliver of hope to one day walk the streets again. It's a great plea. Henry Davies could've insisted on specific language in the agreement, something more definite, more pro-Bantling, but he didn't. Why? Because he probably has a wife and daughter of his own. See? The man's own attorney doesn't want him ever roaming the streets again. He's representing the devil and he knows it.'

He opened the car door. 'Now let's get going. I need to grab something to eat and I don't think there's another flight out tonight. The last place I want to be stuck when the sun goes down is in this bumfuck town,' he said, nodding in the direction of the watchtowers as he got in. 'It's like Salem's Lot.'

Better to let one guilty man go free so that they could put ten more guilty men behind bars, she told herself as she, too, got in the car. It made sense. It was for the greater good.

Yet she couldn't shake the corrosive feeling in the pit of her stomach. The one that she'd woken up with. The one that'd gotten progressively worse throughout the day. Like a scared animal who senses the devastating earthquake that is to come days before its arrival.

He was only one man. Just one guilty man. And he would never actually get 'out'.

But even as they drove under the twisted iron sign and away from the prison, the feeling did not subside. That was when Daria realized that she couldn't outrun what she had done any more than she could justify it.

36

Bill Bantling looked around the six-by-nine-foot cell that had been his home off and on for most of the last ten years. A cot, a TV, a plastic mattress, a pillow, a toilet and a sink. A collection of books. Some magazines. His drawings. The mental inventory was complete: he didn't have shit.

With his back to the surveillance camera that constantly watched him, he lay down on the cot. With a jagged thumbnail, he carefully opened the three-quarter-inch slit where the seams met in the mattress's corner. Using his little finger, one by one he slowly pulled out the drawings he'd stashed away inside. Over the years, different administrations had come and taken his drawings away from him, some while he was still creating them, calling them gross or inappropriate or, his favorite – menacing. The pictures that he had finished, the ones he absolutely couldn't stand to part with, he'd stuffed into his hiding spot, which, surprisingly, no one had ever found. It was his own little photo album from the past, created solely from memory.

He peeked at each one until he found the one he was looking for. He unfolded it and placed it next to his face on the pillow. His fingers moved over the crumpled paper. No matter how many times he gazed at it, it still stirred him. In his head he could actually feel the curve of her face, her heart-shaped chin, the ripples in her trachea. With colored pencils, he'd shaded in her green eyes, her silky, long blonde hair, her pouty red lips. He could smell her in his mind. He could still taste her in the back of his throat.

Chloe . . . My not-so-sweet Chloe Joanna . . .

And now he was one step closer to out. A fantasy that had played in his mind so many times might at last become reality. He might actually see her again – an encounter he fantasized about more than the prospect of freedom itself.

He was obsessed. She was all he thought about. He could understand now how that happened to someone – how all they dreamt of, thought of, imagined was that one face. That one person. He understood why someone would give everything in their lives up – their jobs, their marriage, their children, their parents, their freedom – and risk it all for the object of their fixation. He also understood why someone would want to snuff out the very life he lived for. How love and obsession could easily jump the line into pure, unadulterated hatred.

She had used her legal degree to railroad him into a death sentence. How much of his persecution had been coincidence and how much had been the calculated maneuvering of others, he might never know. Was it pure happenstance that it was *her* courtroom he'd ended up in after an unlawful traffic stop had netted the police their big break? Someone had put the body of Anna Prado in the trunk of his car that night for the police to find. Someone had called in an anonymous tip to the police that there was something of interest in that trunk. Was Chloe behind that, too? How far back did her plans to murder him originate?

Yet here he was, ten years later, alive and kicking. And thanks to the ambitious efforts of another pretty prosecutor, he might soon be a free man.

The moment he got out, Bill was going to pay a visit to the woman who'd been his addiction for almost two decades. And he was going to hold her once more in his arms and tell her just how much he both loved her . . . and despised her. Then those arms would close around her and crush the life breath out of her once shapely body. When those pouty red lips turned fat and blue he would be the last man on this earth to kiss them goodbye.

Boy, was she going to be surprised to see him. *That* moment was going to be priceless. It would be worth the risk. He was going to take his time with her, even more so than their first night together. This go-round he'd make sure that the moment lasted, in what would, for her, surely feel like a lifetime of pure agony. She would be begging for him to finally end her.

He smiled at his picture and kissed her on her cheek. He had drawn her how he remembered her when they'd met years ago, which was, sadly, probably not the way she looked now. He wondered if she still dyed her fabulous blonde hair that drab brown, or was she completely gray now? Did she still dress like a school-marm, with conservative, dark suits and clunky heels, hoping to melt into the background? Would she have rivers of wrinkles cutting through her once flawless, creamy, sun-kissed skin? Would she hide her emerald eyes with unremarkable brown contacts? Or wear a pair of thick Granny glasses so no one could read the fear in them when she was up close and personal? He knew *that* was still there, no doubt. It was a gift he'd given her, that she always carried with her – fear. And she always would, no matter where she lived. Because Chloe Joanna, of all persons in this world, knew that until a needle was shoved in his veins and a doctor actually pronounced him dead, Bill might well come for her again, as he had promised. Metal bars and steel doors could not offer 100 percent assurance that she'd be safe. She could run again and again and again, but he'd always find her – eventually. The mafia found stoolies in the Federal Government's Witness Protection Program – eventually. Nowadays it was even easier to resurrect the dead and the AWOL – thanks to the Internet and, sometimes a few, small, despicable favors to people who had access to the Internet. So no matter how clever or thorough Chloe thought she was at hiding her tracks and starting anew, she wasn't. She could change her name to C.J. or Christina, or whatever other new alias she wanted, because it was only a name. People always left a piece of themselves behind; you couldn't erase a life completely. Someone like Chloe couldn't simply walk away from the people she loved.

Over the river and through the woods to grandmother's house we go . . .

He looked at her long flowing hair, curling in gentle spirals as it cascaded over her shoulders. Those defined cheekbones, her mouth. Hopefully she'd gone back to a bit of her old self. He imagined her slender, curvaceous body outfitted in tight gym clothes, her perky tits bouncing about braless in a tight, white T-shirt as she hummed and sang show tunes in her kitchen – like the good old days. And high heels. Oh, yeah. Those pretty high heels she used to love to wear. Stilettos and pumps and straps. In shiny black patent leather or fire-red leather. Perhaps he would bring her a present and make her wear a pair of those for him again. And her hair – it would be long and honey blonde and wavy, the way he remembered it. Smelling of Herbal Essence shampoo and Aquanet. It would be long enough for him to lose his fingers in it. Long enough for him to wrap it around her throat and tie it in a nice tight knot . . .

His tongue wandered into her waiting mouth, which he had drawn open. His fingers stroked her exposed breasts. His other hand slid into his prison pants and moved south to relieve the pressure. He couldn't wait till he made her do it for him.

Just like the good old days.

When he was done, he wiped the sweat from his lip and folded his very best work into a neat square before tucking it into the mattress. It was the only possession he had in the world worth taking with him when they came to tell him it was time to go home to Miami.

Like a boomerang, karma was coming around. Like he had told that pretty redheaded prosecutor, it always did. Sometimes it took a while. Sometimes it took a lifetime, but it always came in the end.

He nibbled off a sliver of fingernail and smiled to himself.

This time around, retribution would be his.

37

She couldn't wake up.

Her mouth tasted . . . chalky. Her tongue was pressed down and it hurt. There was something in her mouth and she couldn't talk. She struggled to move her hands, to take the thing out of her mouth that was preventing her from calling for help, but her hands wouldn't move. They were tied up.

In this nightmare her brain kept insisting she was having, her hands were strapped above her head to the bedpost. Soft, amber light flickered in the room. Shadows moved across the ceiling above her like ghosts.

Her feet. She couldn't move her feet, either. She tried to kick out, but all that happened was her body jolted up and down. Her legs were spread and her feet were tied down, too, one to each rung of the foot post.

Her brain was so foggy, the thoughts thick, tripping over one another. This must be a nightmare. It had to be. So how could she make herself wake up and get out of it? She couldn't talk, or move her arms or kick herself awake . . .

Dear God, how could she wake up and stop what she knew was about to happen?

The shadows moved again. He was next to her now. She heard him breathing, hard and fast. He was excited. She felt his eyes roll over her body. Oh God, she was naked. She was tied down and naked, her pajama top cut open, exposing all of her. She smelled his coffee breath and the stench of old cream. It filled the room now, along with the sickening, sweet scent of coconut. She wanted to vomit, but there was something in her mouth and she couldn't move.

Panic filled her, making her shake and cry. She had to wake up. She had to get out of this nightmare. She turned her head and there he was.

The clown stood over her, his bulbous nose and blood-red grin lit by the flickering coconut-scented candle on her nightstand. Tufts of red polyester hair stuck out from the side of his head. His face was bright white. In his hand he held a long, jagged knife. Through the cut-outs in the mask she could see his blue eyes dance.

She started to scream but no sound came out. Not even a whimper.

'Hey there, Chloe, my girl,' the clown whispered as he leaned in. 'I'm back. Wanna have some fun?'

C.J. sat up on the couch with a start. The TV was on. There was an Infomercial on for a special face cream guaranteed to take years off your skin. There were no candles burning. As she looked around the empty house, her hands went to her mouth, finding only the drool of saliva that was running down her chin. She studied her hands. There was nothing around them, no rope, no handcuffs, no plastic ties. She stood up and walked about the room on feet that were not bound.

She sat down again, shaking.

It was a nightmare. It wasn't real.

C.J. looked at the clock: 5:20 a.m. She'd slept for four hours tops. Luna was sitting at her feet, whining. The dog knew instinctively something was wrong, even though she couldn't see the intruder that had gotten past her and inside her owner's head. C.J. stood up again, turned off the TV, and headed into the kitchen to make a pot of coffee.

Sleep would not come again tonight. She would not let it.

The fog was thick and the morning air chilly. Although it was still summer, the cloud cover kept temperatures down and the sunshine out until late morning. C.J. pulled on her UCSB sweatshirt, turned on her iPod and put on her Oakley's, though it wasn't bright enough to be needing sunglasses yet. It was 6:30 in the morning and 51 degrees. From the porch landing of the one-story ranch that had been her grandmother's home, she surveyed the sleepy Goleta neighborhood. There was no one around. She took a deep breath and disappeared into the soupy fog.

'Conquer the fear by facing the fear,' her therapist in New York told her. 'Rape victims have scars that the rest of the world can't see. If you let the scar tissue build up, Chloe, eventually those scars will define the walls of your prison. You may think you're safer shutting yourself off so that no one can ever get to you again, but you're not. Because even from a distance, without

306

laying a finger on you, your rapist is exercising the power over you that he craved when he physically assaulted you. By letting him imprison you in that cage of scar tissue, you'll be giving him the very thing he most wanted – control.'

'So what should I do when I can't move? When it gets hard to breathe?' Chloe whispered.

'Conquer the fear by facing the fear. Reclaim the power. Don't let yourself be locked in that cage. Get out and prove to yourself that he will not win. He will not win. Just keep saying it till you believe it. "He will not win."'

'He will not win,' C.J. said to herself as she ran. Past quiet houses and shuttered stores, down towards the oceanfront. Running was cathartic. It empowered her. All she needed was a pair of sneakers to distance herself from the rest of the world, leaving everything and everyone way behind her.

People who didn't know what it was to live through rape often made the assumption that it was something you could get over in time. Just as the physical wounds healed, so should the emotional ones. *It was only an act of sex after all, something that the average adult human enjoys two or three times a week. More if they're lucky. Ha, ha.* For a while, she'd been driven into virtual isolation by that kind of thinking. The expectation that she should be all better now. That it somehow wasn't that bad anymore. Then she became a prosecutor, and worked with other rape victims and heard their stories, and she realized how common that ignorance was. It might not always be expressed, but it was always there, nonetheless. She could feel it.

More than anything, she mourned the loss of

innocence. Until she was attacked, Chloe Larson had never *seen* evil before. She knew bad things happened, she heard about them on the news, but these were things that happened to other people, and they happened for a reason – the victims lived in bad neighborhoods, or associated with bad characters, or they did drugs or drank alcohol.

And then it happened to her. And there was no reason.

The man who had raped and almost killed her had known everything about her before he'd laid a hand on her – her favorite perfume, what she ate for dinner the night before, her nickname, where she'd vacationed, where her boyfriend lived, her grades. And he'd relished telling her all the things he knew about her while he was raping her. He knew so much that the detectives told her the assault had not been some random, opportunistic attack – she had been hunted. And the most devastating realization was that she'd had no idea. She must have met him somewhere, yet she'd never singled someone out as weird or creepy. Or gotten a 'bad vibe' about a guy she'd met. Or noticed that someone might be following her. It wasn't until after her rape that she'd realized her assailant had probably been in her apartment many times before the night he attacked her. He'd rummaged through her drawers and touched her underwear. Read her mail, memorized her diary, eaten from her fridge, listened to her answering machine. Sitting with detectives who were so hardened they seemed bored she'd survived, she looked – at her own insistence – through mug shots for any scars or markings that she might recognize. That was when it hit her: the man who had raped her could be any one of those faces. And any of those faces could be sitting on the bus ride home from the police station, or serving her coffee at Dunkin' Donuts.

Everyone was suspect, every situation a threat. There was no way of telling who the evil ones were, who got their kicks inflicting pain and creating fear, who fed off the misery and torment of others. Psychopaths mingled with the crowd, unnoticed by the prey they stalked, biding their time until they were ready to strike. *Who was real? Who was a threat?*

The scar tissue was building up, just as the therapist had warned. Incapable of trusting anyone, she became imprisoned inside her own mind.

'So what makes you want to be a prosecutor, Ms Townsend?' asked the Miami-Dade Assistant State Attorney at her interview. 'I see from your résumé that you have experience in civil litigation and medical malpractice. Why the turnaround?'

'Someone close to me was the victim of a violent crime. I want to use my skills as a litigator to do some good. I want to put away monsters,' C.J. replied.

The ASA nodded. 'I'm sorry about your . . .' His voice trailed off, waiting for her to fill in the blank.

'Sister,' she lied.

'What happened to her, if you don't mind my asking?'

'She was raped. The perpetrator was never caught. It changed my perspective on the direction of my career.'

'Do you think this experience has jaded you with regard to the criminal justice system? Can you still be fair in your assessment of cases?'

C. J. nodded. '*I was taught in law school to seek justice. I can do that. Whatever justice turns out to be.*'

Chloe had never once considered practicing criminal law when she was in law school. After graduating top of her class, she was supposed to start a brilliant career as a medical malpractice attorney. But that never happened. She was supposed to get married to a lawyer from another big-name law firm. But that never happened either. In the end, she was far better as a prosecutor than she ever would have been as a med mal attorney. And it was a blessing in disguise that her lawyer boyfriend dumped her after the rape, just when she needed him the most. She got to see the man's true colors when it truly mattered.

Ironic as it seemed at the time, she decided that the only way to regain control of her life was to put on a suit and go to court and stare the psychopaths in the eye while she did everything in her power to put them behind bars. It was an unconventional, in-your-face therapy. A working therapy, so to speak. And the added bonus was she got paid for it.

Then came the Cupid investigation – and it had been anything but therapeutic. Assigned to assist the task force hunting Miami's most infamous killer, she'd attended crime scenes and autopsies, and she'd seen for herself what that sadistic son of a bitch did to his victims. When news came through of William Rupert Bantling's arrest, the name meant nothing to her. She had no idea he was the man who'd raped her until that first day in court, when she heard his voice and saw the scar on his hand. She should have excused herself at that point, let someone else step in, but with a case of such complexity that would mean a huge setback for the prosecution. She knew the case inside out, she was the best prosecutor the office had, and she owed it to those eleven women he'd butchered – and to the women who'd be in danger if he wasn't stopped – to see to it that he was convicted. It wasn't about retribution for what he did to her, she told herself; it was about justice. The statute of limitations on her rape had run out; there was no way to prosecute him for that. But she was prepared to endure hearing his voice and seeing him in court for the duration of the trial if it meant his other victims would be avenged. It was for their sake that she wanted him to fry in the electric chair. And for her own sake she wanted to be the one to put him there.

The case against him began to unravel almost before it got under way. Under C.J.'s questioning, Officer Chavez admitted that he had been acting on an anonymous tip when he stopped and searched the vehicle. In the eyes of the law, the search was therefore illegal, and any evidence found in the course of that search would be inadmissible – and that included the dead body in the trunk. That did not make Anna Prado any less dead, though. Or the man any less guilty. To secure the conviction of a serial killer, C.J. and the three police officers who'd conducted the search had agreed to an alternative version of the events that had led to Bantling's vehicle being stopped. The tip never happened. Officers Victor Chavez, Sonny Lindeman, Lou Ribero all agreed with her that, for the greater good, personal integrity must be sacrificed. A dark coven was formed. A pact was made with the devil – and there would be no turning back.

It was only after Bill Bantling had been sentenced that she discovered he was telling the truth about being set up. Cupid was still out there. And she was to be his next victim.

Dominick looked exhausted, as if he'd been keeping vigil by her bed all night. It took him a moment to register that she was awake and watching him. 'For a while there, I thought I'd lost you,' he said. 'You're lucky to be alive.'

C.J. nodded. Thanks to a punctured lung and broken ribs, it was hard to breathe, much less speak. Lucky was an interesting word, she had found. For the second time in her life a psychopath had hunted her down, held her captive, tried to kill her.

'Chambers . . . ?' she asked.

'Dead. Manny's over there now. He says it's like a house of horrors, but there's no dead bodies, no sign of the heart you think you saw, no evidence whatsoever that Greg Chambers had anything to do the Cupid murders. It looks as though it was all some sick game he was playing with you, trying to make you believe you sent an innocent man to death row.'

A tear rolled down her cheek. For seven years she had considered Gregory Chambers her friend as well as her therapist. She recalled that easy grin, the salty hair and those pale blue eyes. She used to think they were the kindest eyes she had ever seen. She had let him in on secrets no one else knew. Secrets that no one could ever know. She had trusted him. And all the while he had been manipulating her, just as he had manipulated Bantling. The rape victim and her rapist, prosecutor and prosecuted, a case study for the sick doctor's entertainment.

Dominick rubbed her hand. The one that had not been sliced to ribbons with a scalpel. 'He was just trying to mess with your mind, C.J., there's no truth in what he said. Bantling murdered those women. You proved it. A jury convicted him. A judge sentenced him.'

She nodded. She could not bring herself to tell him what Chambers had said to her before he died. That he had orchestrated the whole thing as an experiment, a case study in what would happen if a rape victim was given the opportunity to prosecute her rapist for murders he did not commit. How far would she go in the name of retribution?

Dominick leaned over and kissed her gently on the cheek. His face lingered there for a long time. 'You did the right thing, baby,' he whispered in her ear.

In the course of the Cupid investigation, C.J. had discovered that rapes with an MO identical to hers had occurred in each of the cities where Bantling had lived, in each country he had visited. Like her the victims had been tortured, cut, scarred. If he ever got out of prison, she had no doubt that more women would be raped, and given the level of brutality there was every possibility he would escalate to homicide. She had no regrets about putting him behind bars; so long as he remained there, the world was a safer place.

But then Bantling filed a motion for a new trial, claiming he'd been set up, and suddenly the bones started to fall again. Officer Victor Chavez was brutally murdered and his tongue cut out. Sonny Lindeman's corpse was found with the ears sliced off. Lou Ribero's eyes had been gouged out. The Black Jacket task force discovered evidence that all three were dirty and concluded that their deaths were gangland executions. Only C.J. knew that they had died because they had conspired with her over the anonymous 911 call that had led to Bantling's arrest.

Bantling's former defense attorney was the next to die. After filing an affidavit in which she claimed to have a tape of the 911 call, Lourdes Rubio was killed in a robbery. The tape was never found.

It was then C.J. realized that Dr Greg Chambers had left behind a following. Bill Bantling wasn't the only psychopath he'd singled out for his special brand of mentoring. There were others who had shared his depraved fantasies and been encouraged to act upon them. The sick game Chambers started had not ended with his death. It was still in play.

She should have checked the back seat. But she didn't.

'Greg had a friend. A close friend, C.J.,' hissed the man who had been hiding in her back seat. 'A friend who understood his fantasies and shared them. In fact, Greg had several close friends.'

FDLE Agent Chris Masterson had served under Dominick's command for years. C.J. had worked alongside him on the Cupid task force. And the Black Jacket investigation. Another colleague she'd placed her trust in, never suspecting the sick mind that lurked behind the boyish face. And now he was holding a knife to her throat, pinning her head against the headrest as she tried to escape the feel of the jagged teeth pulling at her skin.

'It was a tragedy that he was taken from us just as he was realizing his dream of transforming his fantasies into reality.

314

And making it possible for the rest of us to enjoy them. His work was so . . . fascinating. Now I'm going to finish what he started. We're all very, very excited to have you back.'

C.J. had long since left the Santa Barbara campus behind her and was pounding along the cliffs that ran beside the Pacific. Usually by this point she would have outrun the memories, but today they were keeping up with her, flashing through her mind like a montage from a horror movie: the Jeep slamming into the overpass, then sirens and flashing lights and Dominick yelling at Masterson to get the fuck out of the car, Masterson taunting them, gloating about how he would cheat the system, suddenly reaching behind him . . . then the sound of Dom's gun going off.

The investigation into Masterson's death had taken almost a year, but at the end of it Dominick was exonerated. That very same day, he drove her out to the marina, led her aboard a 26-foot Sea Ray Sundancer and suggested that they sail away and leave it all behind. What he'd really meant was run.

The plan had worked for a while. Until both of them realized they were far too young and life was far too complicated to spend the rest of their lives doing nothing. Within two years they'd settled in Chicago and Dominick was hunting criminals again as a detective with the Chicago PD, while C.J. tried to step away from the bad guys and the violence by volunteering at hospitals and working with troubled kids. But it wasn't enough. She dipped her toe back in the water as a victim advocate with Cook County and said yes when they offered her a position as a prosecutor. She supposed she was drawn to the bad guys as much as they were to her. And Chicago certainly had their share.

It was almost noon by the time she got back to her grandmother's house. The sun was shining, the cloud cover had lifted. Apart from the blob of black storm clouds that lingered over the mountains, far, far away, it was a beautiful day. She checked her watch. She'd run twenty-four miles in a little over five hours.

Dominick would be proud of her: this was the farthest she'd ever run. She was only a couple of miles from completing a marathon, something he knew she'd always wanted to accomplish. He'd promised her he'd be on the other side of Manhattan waiting for her at the finish line, no matter how long it took her to cross it. She pictured his face across the kitchen table, his brown hair messy from sleep, a grin on his bronzed, handsome face as he told her she could do anything she put her mind to. He still had not sent back the papers. She thought again of calling him. Then she remembered that sorry would never be enough . . .

Even with the extra miles she had run, for some reason the run had not worked its magic today. The Clown, Bantling, Cupid, Chambers, Black Jacket, Masterson, the Others . . . The demons from her past were still hot on her trail. A feeling of foreboding hovered over her, like the storm clouds hovering over the distant mountains, a persistent sixth sense that something ominous was closing in on her. And it would keep closing in, slowly, steadily, until one day she would turn around and it would be on top of her. And she would never see it coming.

She shook off the unsettling thoughts, picked up the Sunday paper, waved at a neighbor and headed up the walk. Her case against Richard Kassner was wrapping up. Closing arguments could come as early as next week and she was going to spend the rest of the day preparing.

It was time to clear another level of the game.

PART THREE

38

The panic had begun to spread days earlier, starting with the old people. They had run out – or more appropriately, walkered and wheeled and hobbled out – to get their prescriptions filled and to stockpile more bread and milk than they could possibly consume in a month. It took a couple of days after that before the panic caught on with the general population. That was when water, formula, canned and packaged foods began to disappear from store shelves. Lines at gas stations and Home Depot were longer, and sales of flashlights, batteries, canned foods and candles were up. There was a nervous, excited, polite camaraderie that existed between people as they chatted while waiting on lines that were longer than usual.

By this morning that had all changed.

Overnight, the National Hurricane Center (NHC) had officially placed Miami under a Hurricane Warning: tropical storm force winds were expected within the next thirty-six hours. By the time Manny woke up at seven, store shelves were empty, gas stations were rationing or closed altogether, Home Depot and Loews were out of plywood, generators, water, batteries, chain saws, and, of course, flashlights. No one was nice to anyone anymore. Tempers were short. The entire county sounded like a construction zone. Power saws buzzed, drills whizzed, and constant loud banging filled the air.

As the hours wound down, and the rain bands edged closer to shore and the reporters and their cameramen in their shiny yellow slickers set out for their strongholds on the beach to preach about last-minute storm preparation and prattle on *ad nauseam* about the devastation that was coming, anyone who hadn't already left town was scrambling to board up what they could and get as far inland as they could.

Manny was one of those anyones.

He sat down on the stoop of his two-bedroom bungalow in Miami Shores to catch his breath and suck down a bottle of water with a beer chaser. It was a thousand degrees out. If you didn't know there was a monster storm heading this way, you'd grab a six-pack and head for the beach, because the sky was as blue as a Crayola crayon. He'd been putting up his damn hurricane shutters since ten in the morning and had so far punctured his thumb and put a nice gash in his right thigh. Manny had forgotten how heavy and cumbersome the metal planks were. And how many of them there were. That's why he'd waited – along with his fellow citizens who were similarly in denial – till the last possible second to get ready for a storm he'd been watching slowly cross the Atlantic for the past eight days. Because there was nothing more frustrating than sitting in a pitch-black house nursing a bad back and waiting for a hurricane to come and justify the three months of rehab you were now going to need, only to discover it was yet another false alarm.

This time, however, Manny would have preferred to be complaining about an achy back and bitching about another hurricane no-show. With only a few hours left before the first rain bands were expected to start swirling through and bending his palms to the sidewalk, it looked as though Miami was going to be hit. And hard. Manny had lived through Andrew back in '92, and the only thing he could hope for now was that the storm would shift a degree or so north or south. Better that it levelled Homestead again, or even Palm Beach, than a direct hit slamming Miami.

He sucked the blood off the tip of his thumb. It was still sunny, but not for much longer. The sun had begun its descent into the Everglades – melting into a citrus-colored sky – while over to the east, gray clouds were looming over the Atlantic. The wind had already picked up. Manny watched as a blustery tropical gust sent a rogue garbage can from the foreclosed house two doors down rolling out of control along the block. Sturdy thirty-foot tall Royal Palms shed their fronds like a stripper, sending heavy six-foot branches tumbling down from the sky into his front yard. It was a little taste of what was to come – the trailer to a disaster movie in the making. In twelve hours the city would be under siege. The full force of Artemis would strike under the cover of darkness, in the middle of the night. *Fucking great*, thought Manny.

His thumb was gushing now; he'd caught the damn thing with the drill and almost taken off his nail. He sucked down the rest of his beer and stood up to get himself a Band-Aid before he bled out all over the last of the shutters. One more window and he'd be done. Then it would be a matter of hoping it all held together. If his cute, handyman-special house would be there in the morning when he returned. If anything would be left, not just of his house, but of his cute neighborhood. It was one thing to be the least expensive house on the block; it was another to be the only house left on the block.

Rufus greeted him at the door with an intense bark, but it took a few seconds for the wag to kick in. Even Rufus knew all was not right with the world. The pooch had been acting wiggy for two days, hiding toys all over the house and pacing back and forth like an expectant father. Manny was planning to take him over to his OCD step-sister's house in Miami Lakes tonight and he didn't need the dog flipping Carolina out any more than she already was. Rufus needed to be as low-key and inconspicuous as a ninety-pound bomb-sniffing pooch with a nervous condition could be. Carolina and Rufus didn't see eye-to-eye at the best of times, by virtue of Rufus being a dog and Carolina having been almost eaten by a pit bull when she was five. It didn't matter much that she'd brought it on herself by yanking the dog's tail until it turned and tried to rip her face off. With the rest of Manny's family camped out on the couch – including their elderly mother, who got nervous when the doorbell rang and she wasn't expecting it – Carolina was sure to be running short in the patience department. Almost as if he'd read his master's mind, Rufus jumped up and barked full-on in Manny's face.

Maybe he'd slip the pooch some Benadryl; Carolina could be a cold-hearted bitch when she wanted to, and if she got pissed-off enough, she'd put both Rufus and Manny out on the front stoop with an umbrella to fend for themselves. Her house wasn't his first choice of evacuation accommodation, but, like him, Daria resided on the wrong side of the Federal Highway in an evacuation zone, and Carolina was the only family member who didn't live in a trailer. Plus, his mother had asked him to.

Manny was grabbing a treat for Rufus with his good hand and a dish towel for his bad when his cell rang. It was a number he didn't recognize off the bat, and one he normally wouldn't answer, but nothing was normal today. His phone had been buzzing all morning, with a lot of calls coming from his department.

'Alvarez.'

'Detective Alvarez, this is Sergeant Jose Castano down at Miami-Dade County Corrections. I hate to have to call you, sir, particularly with, you know, a storm bearing down on us and all. I know you're probably very busy . . .' He sounded young. And nervous.

'It's a little crazy round here. I'm sure it's the same where you are. What seems to be the problem?' Manny's chest tightened. It sounded as though the man was going to tell him his momma had died. Except, of course, Corrections wouldn't be the department calling to tell him that. They had on occasion called him when one of his defendants offed themselves or got into a fight. And they had called when one of 'em was ratted out by another. But this call didn't have that intimation. And with the clock ticking down to Doomsday, chances were nobody would be calling him about either of those situations right now.

'Well, there's been a misunderstanding. A mistake, actually, Detective, to be honest. It's being investigated as we speak, so you know.' The sergeant cleared his throat. 'But we felt it was only right for you to know and for you to perhaps initiate the proper security protocol that might be involved on your end. You know, sound the alarm, so to speak. Notify the feds, maybe. And we are doing all we can at this time internally to locate the defendant, so you know.'

'What the hell are you talking about, Sergeant? And who the hell are you talking about? Let's go, spit it out.'

'The inmate that you had transferred down here to DCJ was, well, it looks like he was released by accident. He was placed on the wrong evacuation bus and, well – we can't locate him, sir. It's been complete chaos, here, sir. Not that that's an excuse, but it has, what with the evacuations and all. I've never seen it—'

Manny cut him off. 'What inmate? I didn't have no one transferred down here. Not recently, anyhow. I do have a couple of murder suspects sitting in DCJ and Metro-West. Let's see – Herrera, Hoslem, Wilfredo Lemar. Who you talking about?'

'None of those names, sir. I'm calling about the inmate from Florida State Prison that arrived here several days ago.'

Manny sat down at his kitchen counter. His fist was clenched so hard, blood from his injured thumb oozed through the fingers and down his wrist, dripping into a small puddle on to the white stone. 'Again, I didn't transfer nobody. You must have the wrong detective.'

'Well, it had your name, sir, as the arresting officer on the intake sheet. You and an Agent Falconetti with FDLE as original arresting officers. I just assumed you'd authorized the transfer. Maybe the judge ordered it, but you should still be notified if it's your prisoner, I would think. Maybe I'm wrong, sir.'

Manny stared out the kitchen window. On the windowsill was a framed picture of him and Daria on South Beach. Across the street, his neighbor was teetering precariously on the top rung of a ladder while drilling a plywood sheet across his second-story window. Any minute he was going to come crashing down, and, ironically enough, it wasn't going to be the damn monster hurricane he was preparing for that did him in. It would be his own stupidity. His own misplaced trust. The ladder rocked. Like Manny, the guy only had a few seconds left before his world changed for ever. He closed his eyes.

'Who was it that was released, Sergeant?' Manny asked, although he already knew the answer.

He opened his eyes.

The ladder tipped. His neighbor flailed his arms, trying to keep his footing on a ladder that was no longer there. His body seemed suspended in mid-air, like a cartoon character who has just walked off a cliff.

'Um . . .' the young man swallowed hard, as if he himself did not want to hear the name. 'William R. Bantling, sir.'

And with those words, Manny's world came crashing down, just like his neighbor's.

39

When Hurricane Andrew devastated Miami, Daria was eleven and living in the same modest three-bedroom house in Cooper City that her parents still lived in today. She didn't remember much about the days leading up to Andrew, except watching the news – which was on every single channel without commercial break in the twenty-four hours before the storm made landfall. And no matter who was talking, in the bottom-right corner of the screen on continuous replay was the time-elapsed picture of the white swirling blob with the small hole in the center that was slowly but surely making its way across the Atlantic to Florida. While Marco and Anthony had helped their dad nail heavy, cumbersome sheets of plywood over the windows, Daria's job had been to make sure that every room in the house had a flashlight with fresh batteries. Their mother had completely panicked – screaming out longitudinal and latitudinal coordinates every five minutes like they made sense while she made vats of marinara sauce in the kitchen.

Daria could remember being both scared and excited as the storm approached on the TV map and the hours counted down to Doomsday. There was a secret part of her that wanted the hurricane to hit them dead on, like all the news channels were predicting. She wanted to see the devastation – flipped cars, torn-off roofs, downed trees and stop signs – from the safety and comfort of her bedroom, because of course nothing would happen to her house. When she suggested to her mother that a hurricane would be a lot of fun, Lena had smacked her in the back of her head with the wooden ladle she was using to taste her marinara. Hot red sauce went everywhere, splattering the floor and cabinets and white kitchen walls. In fact, when her dad heard her screaming and rushed inside, he took one look at the scalding red sauce running down her cheeks and neck and thought Daria had split her head open. When he found out what had happened, he blamed the incident on the tensions of the hurricane, which didn't explain away the other beatings he'd walked in on over the years, but it made both him and her still-shaking, screaming mother feel better for the moment. She remembered her brothers standing in the entrance to the kitchen as she explained what she'd said that had sent their mother over the edge, watching wide-eyed as their dad covered the parts of Daria's body that had been splashed with sauce in frozen pea packs. Neither of the boys said a word. Daria knew they, too, were wishing for Hurricane Andrew to pick up their house and fling it harmlessly into Miami, like in *The Wizard of Oz*, but after what had happened to Daria, neither dared mention their fantasy out loud. There were three pots of sauce still simmering on the stove.

Fast-forward nineteen years and the prospect of a major hurricane had Daria worrying about factors that hadn't occurred to her when she was eleven. Economic and environmental devastation. Days, maybe weeks without power in 95 degree heat. No AC, no refrigerator, no hot showers, no cooking. Probably no water or phone service either. Brutal traffic because streetlights and signs and trees would be down. No eating out at restaurants. Increased pain-in-the-ass crime, like looting and contractor fraud that would clog dockets. Domestic violence would go up too as the stress of the storm and its calamitous aftermath exerted its pressure on families. And then there was the worry about how her apartment would fare – if she would even have an apartment to return to. Everything she owned in the world besides her car was in that townhouse. The thought of it all blowing down Federal Highway was too awful to contemplate. She understood now why her mother had prayed over her spaghetti for Andrew to spare them.

Absently touching her cheek where the faded scar from the sauce incident still lingered, Daria stared out the window of the Miami-Dade Emergency Operations Center in western Miami-Dade County where she would be spending the next twenty hours, minimum. The center was built to withstand hurricane-force winds topping two hundred miles per hour and would operate as a central command station for multiple police agencies during the storm. Downstairs, a contingent of emergency responders, dispatchers, cops, technical personnel were waiting out the wrath of Artemis. Daria and two other prosecutors from the State Attorney's Office would be assisting the cops and judges, and dispensing legal advice for all the post-hurricane crimes that would be sure to ravage a crippled metropolitan city. Most of the assembled crew – at least the legal team – were not so much dedicated as they were homeless. Daria herself had nowhere to go besides her parents' house – where Anthony was camped out in his old bedroom, since he lived on the beach in Pompano – or Marco's three-bedroom insane asylum in Coral Springs, neither of which was an option.

Because Daria herself lived east of US1 – the north–south coastal thoroughfare that ran the length of the state of Florida – she was in an evacuation zone and was supposed to go to a shelter, the closest of which was Arthur Ashe Middle School in Fort Lauderdale. Double ugh. A thousand scared people jammed into a gym eating peanut butter sandwiches and lying on sleeping bags. *That* was also most definitely not an option. Manny had asked her to stay with him, but he, too, lived in an evacuation zone in North Beach, and was only blocks from the beach. The idea was cozy and romantic enough, but with a storm surge of twenty-three feet or higher possible, not only would the hotels and homes directly on the beach exist no more, neither would anything a mile or so inland – at least that's what the cheery meteorologist on Channel 6 was saying. There was also the very real chance Manny would either be called out by the City, or go off and volunteer himself to some entity, task force or in-need friends, leaving her with not only the storm surge to worry about but Rufus too, his shoe-loving pooch who got nervous when the door on the dishwasher slammed shut. Images of the catastrophic March tsunami wiping out coastal Japan filled her head. *No, thanks*, she'd said.

Besides, if she volunteered her services and worked the phones at the EOC, she figured she'd at least get some goodwill points from the State Attorney and Vance Collier. And in the event of a complete catastrophe and the end of Miami society as everyone knew it, she'd also be surrounded by trained people who could help dig her body out of the rubble, instead of a bomb-squad drop-out who would swim for shore before he'd risk his furry neck to help his master's girlfriend. So she'd called her mom, Marco, and Manny and told them all: *Thanks, but no thanks*. And that afternoon, after the cops had given up driving through her neighborhood warning everyone to get the hell out, she'd said goodbye to her house, packed a suit-case with her one and only pair of strappy Manolos that she'd gotten on sale at the Neiman Marcus outlet, locked her doors, and driven off down her deserted street. Back into a city that, like a creepy, apocalyptic horror movie, everyone and anyone with a brain was scrambling to get the hell out of.

Driving sheets of water pounded the windows of the EOC as strong gusts bent palm trees in half. The outer bands of Artemis had begun to make landfall. It would only get worse from here on. She hadn't spoken to Manny since late that morning, and now she began to wonder what had become of Rufus, and whether Manny would risk taking him to his step-sister's. She probably could have brought him here. No one looked as though they cared too much. She took her cell phone out of her pocket and checked for new messages. Emergency service only. The towers might even be down already . . .

A tap on her shoulder made her jump. It was Nigel Peris, one of the Miami-Dade PD cops from downstairs.

'Jesus, Nigel. You gave me a heart attack. Why don't you just wait for some thunder to boom and the lights to flicker before you sneak up on a person?'

'Sorry, Daria,' Nigel replied. 'But you got a call on two. You can take it here at reception.'

'Who is it?' she asked, walking over to the reception desk.

'Alvarez from City. And as for them lights, don't worry. We have a generator,' he finished with a nod as he headed off downstairs. 'You can still see that storm coming – right until it rips the phone out of your hand.'

'Great,' she replied, then turned her attention to the phone. 'Hey. Where are you at? I've been—'

'What have you done?' Manny demanded. He sounded beyond angry.

'What?' She felt her stomach flip-flop and a wave of guilt of unknown origin washed over her. She didn't even know why he was mad.

'You dealt him, didn't you? Didn't you?' Manny yelled. 'Why else was he down here at DCJ?'

Daria closed her eyes. She was hoping not to have to deal with this until after Artemis passed and after she had the names of the snuff-club members in hand. They would definitely soften the blow. 'Manny, it was Vance's idea—' she began.

'Collier? Don't you go blaming this on him. You made the deal, didn't you? It was you. 'Cause I know he wasn't gonna talk till you actually brought him down to Miami. He's not stupid. I told you that. I freaking warned you, which is what really pisses me off.'

'Listen, listen, it will work out, okay? He's giving us names. A lot of names. A whole book, in fact. And they have to all pan out, or he goes back up to Starke. Collier has it covered.'

'What did he get? Tell me, what did you deal that scumbag?'

There was a long silence. 'Lifetime parole. With monitoring. He jaywalks and he goes back in. But he's never getting out, Manny,' she added quickly. 'Vance says the agreement's airtight. We are under no obligation to let him out until he fully cooperates, and that's not gonna happen. He said—'

'You're a fool, Daria,' he said flatly.

She stood up straight. 'Don't talk to me like that.'

'And I'm a fool for falling. Yup. For falling. For liking you. For . . .' he hesitated, as he struggled to hold back words. 'For thinking you were different from every other fame-seeking prosecutor that comes out of that goddamned office looking for their fifteen minutes or, better yet, a shot at a reality show. The truth is, you want the fucking limelight. And you think Cupid is your ticket to the show.'

She sighed angrily. 'Manny, don't be so damn melodramatic. These things happen every day. You make deals every day. Don't be self-righteous.'

'You have no idea what you've done. You have no idea who you let out.'

A strange shiver ran up her back, but she ignored it. 'You're not listening. He's not out, Manny. He still has to give us the—'

'He was put on the wrong fucking bus during the hurricane evacuation, Daria! He got sent to Metro West. Someone out there read the paperwork wrong and let him go. They released him, do you hear me?

334

There'll be an investigation, sure, but he's gone. G-o-n-e. Gone.'

She felt sick. So nauseous that she sank to the floor, her back against the desk. 'What? What do you mean he's gone?' she said quietly.

'He got on that bus and he disappeared! No one knows where he is. He hasn't been accounted for. It's been hours. And I can tell you, he won't be found.'

'Gone? That can't be possible . . . Get the County cops out there, Miami-Dade, the US Marshals. He can't be gone—' She was yelling now, but her voice still sounded small and weak.

'Have you looked out a fucking window? Have you heard the news? Hello? It's a *hurricane*, Daria. There's a one hundred-and-forty-five-mile-an-hour hurricane coming right at us. No one is going anywhere looking for anybody. Everyone and everything is battened down until this thing blows through. Then we all get to pick up the pieces of what's left of Miami.'

'Oh my God, Manny. Oh my God . . .'

'Oh my God, is right. He's gone. This is *your* doing. Yours. You let a damn serial killer out and no one knows where the fuck he is! It's on *your* fucking plate!'

She wasn't sure if he hung up on her or if the telephone lines crashed down, but that was the last thing she heard him say before the line went dead and the storm of the century barreled into Miami.

40

'Opelika. If you're going on to Atlanta, we'll be departing at nine.' The crackly overhead announcement sounded like a worn 45.

Bill looked out the bus window and yawned. Opelika, Alabama. That was a city he never thought he'd visit. A gas station, a Piggly Wiggly, a Soapy Suds, more than a couple bars and liquor stores, some local restaurants, and, of course, a sizeable Baptist church. That was downtown. A playground, baseball field, a school, horse farms, modest, dilapidated houses spaced a quarter-mile or more apart, and acres of crop fields made up the rest. Most of the places he'd ridden through today looked exactly like Opelika. Small, cracker towns filled with simple, tired-looking people who eyed you with suspicion if they didn't know you. Because in towns like Opelika, if they didn't know you or weren't somehow related to you, then you were a stranger, and it thus followed that you were not to be trusted.

Bill stretched and turned away from the window. *Good guess.*

In towns like Opelika, surly strangers stuck out. Bill smiled at the old lady in the aisle across from him as she stuffed her shopping bag full of all the knitting crap she'd been working on for the past three hundred miles. She didn't smile back.

'Let me help you with that,' he said, quickly rising from his seat as the old woman's granddaughter moved to grab her rucksack and other bags from the overhead rack. 'They look heavy.'

'Thank you,' Grandma said and nodded an okay at her grandchild, who Bill guessed was probably still in high school. Maybe college. Although her height made you think she was older. Thanks in part to short-shorts, her long, tan legs went on for ever.

'No problem,' replied Bill as he reached for the bag, brushing up against the young girl's back as he did so. Her hair smelled of strawberries. 'You remind me a lot of my daughter,' he said as he handed her her bags. 'Same age, I'm thinking. College, right? What are you, about twenty?'

The girl grinned and blushed.

'Not quite,' said the old lady. 'Don't go rushing her, now. You getting off yourself here?'

Interesting choice of words, Grandma. 'Atlanta,' Bill replied.

'Well then, Marcy and I have it. Her daddy's waiting right outside. Thank you 'gain, sir. Have a nice trip, now.'

Bill nodded and sat back in his seat. He pushed his glasses up on his nose and ran a hand over his now smooth scalp, watching as Marcy helped her grandma off the bus in her cutoffs and tight hoodie.

He wondered when they'd start to miss him back in Miami. If they had already. When that hurricane pulled out of town and the good people of Miami rebuilt themselves a courthouse and put all their inmates back into the right cages, and poor 'Bantling, Willie R.' was wrapped up tight in shackles and chains and sent off to court only to find out he was now facing the death penalty – well, the screaming would begin. Poor Willie R., who was probably guilty of not much more than a burglary or robbery or beating the shit out of his wife, was gonna pitch a fit. Then the prosecutors, the jailors, the judge – everyone would be looking around to see if this was some sort of a joke. 'Where is Bantling?' someone would shout. A grungy green uniform would nervously reply, '*This* is Bantling.' And then would come the panic. 'This is not Bantling. William Rupert Bantling? Date of birth January seventh, 1961. Who the hell is this guy?' Then everyone would collectively start screaming and the finger-pointing would begin. Heads would roll. The look on that chief prosecutor's face would be priceless. Hopefully someone in the courtroom would have a camera and take a shot so maybe he could catch it on the news, because it would, without a doubt, make the news. Cupid's escaped! Man the torpedoes! Batten the hatches! Save the women and children!

Then again, perhaps not. Bill had a feeling that sly prosecutor had a thing or two up his sleeve. Bill suspected Mr Chief Assistant Collier was gonna keep the deal he'd made with the devil on the down-low until it came time to call a big news conference to announce that his office had rounded up a dozen members of a snuff club. So maybe there wouldn't be anything on the news after all. Even better. Bill didn't need to see his name all over the papers.

Bill stuck his hand in his pocket and found his folded drawing. He gazed out the window as Marcy and her grandma slowly made their way through the station and over to a waiting car. An older man – presumably Daddy, in a wife-beater T-shirt and jeans – got out of the car and threw their suitcases in the trunk. He scratched his belly and kissed his momma. All the while, young Marcy leaned against the side of the car, one long, tanned leg tucked up behind her, and texted on her cell, oblivious to what was going on around her, her long white-blonde hair spilling over her shoulders. Bill pulled out the drawing and put it on his lap. He was hard. He had been since young Marcy had stood up in her short-shorts. He looked down at the pitiful, beautiful face laying atop his thighs, her scared eyes staring up at him. He moved his thumb over her. The pencil smudged.

Then he stood up, grabbed his bag from the overhead rack and hopped off the bus just as everyone who was heading to Atlanta was getting on.

41

'We left it exactly as we found it,' Tru Zeffers said as he walked Manny Alvarez and Mike Dickerson into Bill Bantling's old cell on death row. 'Didn't touch a thing. Before we even heard he was missing we was thinking you might be interested in what we found.'

Tru had been hopping mad when he heard the news that Bill Bantling was unaccounted for down in Miami. He still was. But he couldn't help smiling some now as the arrogant suits from Miami paraded past with egg all over their red faces – starting with that supersized Detective Manny Alvarez and his geezer partner. Tru had been hoping that State Attorney Collier would be with them, maybe dressed in his fine suit and polished shoes, carrying on with his smarty-ass, haughty attitude. Tru couldn't wait for that one to call him a redneck under his breath again. *Who's the loser now, Chief? Just wait till the public finds out what you let back into society . . .*

Inmates had tried shit on Tru before, but in his fifteen years on the row, not one of those scumbags had made it past him. Not one. Those homicide detectives and prosecutors might think Tru's security precautions with the inmates were over the top, or put on just for show, but as a CO on death row you had to remember who you was dealing with and never forget it. There was no room for giving breaks, neither. The bad boys in this prison had nothing left to lose – even their basic right to keep on breathing was at the discretion of some judge in Tallahassee or Atlanta or DC. Tru knew better than to underestimate scum like Bill Bantling. Oh, that one was slick, all right. Mr Handsome and smooth talker. Always on the lookout for an opportunity, for a way out. He'd soon slit your throat if an opportunity to slip through those bars presented itself. And he wouldn't feel bad about it, neither.

'Holy shit,' exclaimed Mike Dickerson as they stepped inside what for seven years had been Bill Bantling's cell.

'Holy shit is right,' Manny repeated. He immediately went over to the empty cot where Bantling had once slept. The plastic mattress was leaning up against the wall, beside the metal bed frame that was bolted into the wall. Laid out on top of the bed frame were pictures. Drawings. Sketches. Manny picked one up and looked at it. Then another. And another. The same woman in each picture, fifteen in all. In some of the drawings the woman was nude and bound, obviously being violently tortured. In one she was being raped. He turned to Tru Zeffers. 'You didn't think to call somebody and tell them about these when he was being moved? These drawings didn't set off some sort of alarm in you, Sergeant?'

Tru stopped smiling inside, startled that instead of being praised for alerting the detectives, he was being

341

called to account for his actions. 'Notifying you about anything wasn't my decision to make, Detective. Take that up with the warden. I found them drawings tucked into the mattress, all folded up into tiny little pieces of paper. The mattress was gonna be thrown out. If it wasn't for me looking, no one would have ever found those drawings.'

'And when did you discover them?'

''Bout a week after Bantling went missing, I suppose.'

Manny looked at Zeffers. He raised an eyebrow. 'Here? You took the mattress apart here?'

Zeffers shifted. 'That's what I said.'

'I'm thinking maybe you wanted to keep a little souvenir of Cupid for yourself after he left for Miami, something nasty you could auction off on eBay one day when you retired from working this hellhole. But then you heard he was missing and that the mattress you took home was not on a list of inventory scheduled to be destroyed, and you got either nervous or curious and started to examine your booty a little closer. Is that when you found the drawings, Sergeant? Is that when you got real worried that they were gonna be evidence in the investigation of his escape? And is that why it took you a goddamn week after a serial killer was reported missing to call and say you had evidence? Or were you hoping to sell these drawings on eBay as well?'

Zeffers turned red. 'They were gonna throw out the mattress, like I said. It would've been long gone. You wouldn't have ever known about them. You should be thanking me.'

'Forgive me if I don't. Are these all of them? Or are you holding back?'

Zeffers shook his head. 'I ain't holding nothing back.'

'He drew these?' Dickerson asked, picking up one of the pictures. 'Bantling?'

'He was always sketchin' something. We didn't let him draw no porno, or violent stuff, which is why he most likely hid those. He didn't want us to take them.'

'Obviously,' Manny shot back.

'It's the same woman in each picture,' Mike commented as he studied the sketches. 'If you move them around, she almost looks age-progressed, like he drew her throughout the years.' He turned to Manny. 'You worked Cupid. She looks familiar. How do I know her? Is this one of his victims?'

Manny nodded. The woman in the drawings was beautiful, sultry, innocent, frightened. A woman who was naturally stunning, no matter what she wore or what she did to disguise it. By the later drawings, her long, wavy blonde hair had been chopped into a dark bob that tried to hide her face. Crow's feet had aged her eyes, marionette lines her mouth. Circles lined her hypnotic, fearful green eyes. The drawings were like looking at photographs, they were that detailed, that perfect, that accurate.

'You know who she is?' Mike asked again.

Manny ran a hand through hair he no longer had, wishing he didn't have to make the phone call that he was about to make. As much as he didn't want to think it possible, as much as he didn't want to believe he knew the inner thoughts of a madman, he did.

More than a week had passed since Bantling had walked off a corrections bus and disappeared into a massive hurricane that had all but leveled South Florida, from Fort Lauderdale down to Miami Shores. Thankfully, Artemis had made landfall as a Cat 4, with sustained winds of 139 miles an hour, rather than the devastating Cat 5 that was feared. It also came in slightly north of its anticipated target of Miami Beach. Yes, it could have been so much worse, but as it was right now, it was bad enough. So far 203 people were dead and the death toll was still rising. Most of South Florida was struggling to recover basic necessities – homes and businesses were still without power in Miami and Fort Lauderdale. Palm Beach was almost all in the dark and the eastern shore-line was underwater. Power crews from fifteen different states were working to get the city of Miami back up. Most of the county, city and state police force were working twelve-hour shifts trying to control the looting and price-gouging, and deliver water, food and ice to the hardest hit areas.

Although Tru Zeffers and the good folks in the rest of the Sunshine State – and in the rest of the country, for that matter – couldn't really wrap their heads around the enormity of it all, Miami was in complete and utter chaos. There was no time to hunt for fugitives or follow up on leads or work cases. Nothing was normal anymore; every cop in every law enforcement agency south of Martin County was in survival mode. While this trip to Starke wasn't exactly unauthorized, it was Manny who had made it a priority, coming up here the first chance he had free. Tomorrow he and Mike would be back working the Liberty City area. Their lieutenant had advised Manny to just get an arrest warrant for Bantling's recapture, notify the feds and the US Marshals and let them use their resources, which were not bogged down in hurricane response. 'And for Christ's sake,' his lieutenant had added, 'keep it the hell out of the press that he's gone.'

He's gone. Cupid has left the building.

As for that last request, Manny was running out of time. The media had reached saturation point with survivor stories and were out to find other angles on the hurricane aftermath. It was only a matter of time before someone called the *Herald*. The only reason no one had done it already was most likely because no one wanted to take the blame for letting loose a serial killer – and there was blame enough to go around. First, to the Department of Corrections for the colossal fuck-up in letting him go, and then to the State Attorney's Office for cutting a deal with Cupid, and now to the City of Miami and every other agency that had left it too long to let anyone know Bantling was missing. As for the folks at Starke not blowing the whistle, Tru Zeffers didn't want anyone to find out he was the collector of macabre serial-killer paraphernalia that he would someday try to hock on the Internet for a hefty price. Manny wouldn't be surprised if in a few years more drawings mysteriously surfaced on eBay.

With every hour Bantling was gone, the trail grew that much colder. The man had no family. He had no friends. He had no accomplices, and as far as anyone knew he had no help. He was like a damn ghost. As far as money went, that was something Bantling once did have. Enough to afford private defense attorneys and a nice bachelor pad in Coconut Grove. And he'd likely stashed some of it away, hoping an opportunity like this would one day come.

The feds had helped out, and had so far tracked Bantling to a Greyhound bus station in Orlando that had taken him to Opelika, Alabama. But the trail from there had suddenly dead-ended. Bill Bantling could be anywhere in the world by now. He could look like a completely different man – different hair, different eye color, different skin tone. He could appear to be fat or uber skinny. And if he did have cash, he would have access to plastic surgery, passports, transportation out of the country. He could completely transform his appearance and be unrecognizable within weeks. With no friends or lovers or family it was impossible to find a starting point.

Most prison escapees were caught within the first forty-eight hours. Here it was Day Nine and counting. Manny stared at the creepy sketches of the scared woman he knew all too well. While he didn't know where William Rupert Bantling was headed, he had a pretty good idea who the man was hoping to find.

'Give me a second, Mikey,' Manny said. Then he stepped out of the cell, picked up his phone and flipped through it, finding a number he hadn't used in a long, long time. Too long, but that was not his choice.

'Dom. Long time, brother,' he began when the man who used to be his closest friend finally picked up the phone. 'It's Bear. I have a situation going on here in Miami, and, well, you and me, we gotta talk . . .'

42

'The story's gonna break,' Vance said when Daria stepped into his office. He was reading something on his computer screen and had yet to actually look at her. She sat down in front of his desk. His cryptic statement wasn't so cryptic. Her stomach flip-flopped.

'I just got off the phone with Corrections,' he continued, still staring at his computer. 'The *Herald*'s been asking questions about Bantling. They've made a bunch of public records requests. I don't know how long we have before this is front-page news. We're doing what we can to hold them off – at least until the feds can tell me they have a lead on where the prick went.' He ran a hand through his hair and finally faced her. 'This is a clusterfuck, Daria. Definitely something you don't wanna hear at four o'clock on a Friday. It's worse if a story like this breaks on a weekend.'

Daria sunk into her seat. 'It was a matter of time, Vance. To be honest, I'm surprised it took as long as it did.'

He sighed angrily. 'We gotta get a handle on this. The conspiracy theories, I'm sure, will be up and running that there was some sort of cover-up going on.'

There was, but she wasn't about to say that out loud. Bantling had been gone almost two weeks and no one had notified the press. There'd been no attempt to warn the public. Only the top brass at the need-to-know agencies had been informed he had escaped. After Artemis had passed, the first person Daria had gotten in touch with was Vance, and it was he who'd flat-out ordered her to keep the situation under wraps – under the pretense of 'avoiding a public panic'. That sure sounded like a cover-up to her.

'They're gonna want to know why he was brought down to Miami in the first place, Vance,' she replied slowly.

'If that question is asked, the answer is, "He was cooperating on another investigation." Period. End of statement.'

'Okay. Next question: "What investigation?"'

'Repeat after me: "That investigation is ongoing, and we are not at liberty to discuss open criminal investigations." Now walk away. Or hang up. Change the subject. Whatever. I don't want to hear anyone with a microphone and a camera talking about snuff clubs. *That* will cause a goddamn panic. And it will cause any such sick operation, if it indeed still exists, to bury itself even further underground. Speaking of which, has anyone contacted you yet, Daria? Anyone from the press?'

'Me? No.'

'That's good. That means the *Herald* doesn't have a clue what case it was Bantling might have been cooperating on. Right now, I'm thinking they're just trying to confirm he's missing. Somebody from Corrections probably blabbed.'

'What about our deal with him? Is that coming out?'

'Nothing's on paper,' Vance answered, as he relocated his stapler to another prime spot on the other side of his desk. 'As far as I'm concerned, he was cooperating in an ongoing criminal investigation. There was no deal, because we hadn't made one.'

'Listen, Vance, if his attorney talks to the press, that . . . *arrangement* is gonna make us look real bad.'

There was no way around it – the elephant was in the room and she was tired of it. That elephant had already cost her her relationship with Manny, personally and professionally. While they were both still working Lunders, he would not return her calls and communicated with her only via email or text, the bitter irony of which was not lost on her. She'd called him a dozen times since the hurricane, but he wouldn't pick up. She'd driven by his house, stopped by the office – nothing. She'd left messages, but unless it related to Lunders, he would not respond at all. At first she thought he'd get over it and things would go back to where they were, but he hadn't and it didn't look like he was going to bother trying. It was over. Now all that was left for her was to accept it.

I'm a fool . . . for thinking you were different from every other fame-seeking prosecutor that comes out of that goddamned office. The truth is, you want the fucking limelight. And you think Cupid is your ticket to the show . . .

She'd scoffed at the accusation at the time, but . . . *Was it true? Was Manny right?* She'd had a lot of alone time lately to examine and analyze her own behavior. She'd never thought of herself as a media hound, but maybe that was because she hadn't really had a newsworthy case before. Then along came Talbot Lunders, a case with the potential to make her not only the next Chief of Sex Bat, but possibly the next Linda Fairstein, Vincent Bugliosi, Kimberly Guilfoyle – prosecutors who had all made headlines with a sensational murder prosecution and then parlayed that fame into a career in media. Except it wasn't riding the coattails of Pretty Boy Talbot that would bring her the rare, coveted, international fame and recognition she insisted she didn't want. It was Cupid.

And the truth was, she'd jumped right on it.

She hadn't protested when Vance started making deals with a monster. She'd taken the ride back up to Florida State Prison. She'd gone right along, hoping that Bantling would hand up dozens of names. Hoping that the investigation would lead them to some well-known politicians or celebrities that would command the world's attention. Hoping her name might catapult into the next stratosphere of prosecutor. It was hard to deny that doors would open up for her if that happened. Just being the ASA on a snuff-club case would start the cameras rolling, but with Cupid as lead witness for the prosecution, that notoriety could land her a job as an analyst on *Good Morning America* or Court TV when the case was over. Or better yet, give her the exposure to launch her own TV show one day, *à la* Nancy Grace. She couldn't kid herself that those thoughts hadn't entered her mind. As shallow as it sounded, she'd practiced her commentary in the bathroom mirror on more than one occasion and she thought she sounded pretty damn good.

She'd compromised herself and her integrity and the best shot at a relationship that she'd ever had with a funny, nice guy who had really cared about her on a pipe dream of being a legal rock star. It was a terrible feeling. And now she'd have to live with what she'd done. That was what was so devastating. Manny was right – this was on her fucking plate. And if Bantling did anything while he was on the lam – robbed, stole, carjacked, raped . . . She swallowed the huge lump in her throat. *He was a serial killer.* Time to use the right verb. If he *murdered* again – *that* would be on her plate as well. She would be responsible. She wasn't sure she could live with that.

'Henry Davies won't say anything,' Vance replied coolly. 'He knows if he does, there will be no hope of this office cutting any deals with his clients or those of his fellow liberals at CCR.'

Daria was quiet for another long moment. Then she snapped out of it. 'We never should have made that deal, Vance. This mess we're in now – it's all bad karma.' She heard herself saying the words – confronting her boss, jumping off the career ledge without a chute – but it was almost as if they were coming from a different body.

Karma's a bitch, Ms Prosecutor; it takes a while to come around sometimes, but personally I've found that it always does. Always. So you better watch yourself.

She'd lost her lover, now she might just lose her job. But at least she would have stuck up for what was right. At least she would have said something.

'What the hell are you talking about?' Vance asked.

'We made a deal with the devil, Vance. Or we tried to. Let's be honest here. The press is gonna crucify us

351

when they find out about that deal, because they should. If Bantling hadn't escaped, we would have quietly put him back out on the streets ourselves a couple of months later, exchanging one bad guy for maybe a half-dozen others, if we were lucky. You say no, he would never have fulfilled the terms of that deal, but I say yes. I say you're either lying or fooling yourself. Cupid would have figured out a way to beat you at your own game. He would have figured out a way to walk. Bantling's not a stupid man. I should have appreciated that.'

She pointed at Vance's computer screen. 'There's a posse of law enforcement officers out looking for him, including US Marshals and the FBI, and nothing. His face is soon to be on every news channel in the world, but I don't think that will matter. I really don't. I think he's gone for good. That's what we didn't appreciate, what I didn't appreciate – who we were dealing with. But I do now. If Bill Bantling hadn't escaped at the first opportunity he got, he would have strung us along until that opportunity finally came around. Because he was never gonna give up those names, Vance, if he ever really knew them. He played us as much as we played him. And now it's karma. It's coming around, because it always does.'

Vance's face grew dark. 'That's a first. If I recall correctly, Daria, *you* came to *me* and said you thought we could get names from Bantling, but he wants a deal. *You* came to *me*. Now you want absolution? You want to hide your role in all this behind karma? Bullshit. This is not on my hands, sweetheart, it's on yours. It's *your* case and *your* paperwork. As far as I'm concerned, it was a rogue decision to deal with Bantling to begin with.'

She stood up. 'So that's it? Now that there is nothing for us to gain out of this – like the names of some sadistic cops or politicians to prosecute – now it was *my* rogue decision to make Bantling a deal? Nice. If he'd given up the telephone book, then you would have proudly stood behind *your* decision?'

Here comes the part, Daria, where you officially get kicked off Lunders and moved back into Felony Screening. Or worse, told your services are no longer necessary and you may want to check out opportunities with the Public Defender's Office.

Then a thought occurred to her.

But wait, no, you won't be going anywhere. Because if he moves you off Lunders now, and the deal with Bantling does come to light, along with the case it was connected to, then there would be no scapegoat. No one to take the fall beside himself.

The same thought must've occurred to Vance. 'When is the motion to suppress on Lunders?'

'Wednesday. It was moved back because of the hurricane.'

'Aren't you speaking at the SMART conference in Orlando?' SMART was the acronym for the Department of Justice's Office of Sex Offender Sentencing, Monitoring, Apprehension, Registering and Tracking.

'Yes. But that's Monday and Tuesday. I'll be back Tuesday night,' she responded.

'When are you leaving for Orlando?'

'I'll head up on Sunday.'

'Don't take any calls from the press.'

'I don't talk to the press on any of my cases.'

'Are you prepared for the motion?'

And just like that, the pronouns had changed once again.

She studied his face for a long moment. Here was her opportunity for absolution, at least professionally: win Lunders. 'I will be,' she answered. 'The search warrant for the Benz was valid, even without Marie Modic around to testify about it.'

Daria had still not been able to locate the nail tech. The hurricane had only complicated things, because the woman lived in Hallendale, which had been hit hard by Artemis. Many homes had suffered severe damage. Power was back up, but hundreds of houses and businesses had been abandoned, including the salon the girl had once worked in. Some people would never return. It might prove very difficult to locate Marie Modic. 'The judge signed off on the warrant,' she continued. 'Procedurally, it's sound. I don't need her to support the warrant.'

Vance nodded.

She stood up. 'Let me know if anything happens with the *Herald*.'

'I hope that's the position the judge takes . . .' the Chief Assistant replied as Daria's fingers reached the door handle.

She turned around. He was staring at his computer.

'. . . because I don't think Ms Modic will be able to make it to a deposition after all. Her body was found this morning in a dumpster outside a condemned hotel on Fort Lauderdale beach, buried under a few feet of hurricane muck.' He nodded at the screen. 'She's dead.'

43

'Bantling is out, Dom.'

Dominick Falconetti rubbed his eyes and looked out the window of the plane. Thick clouds obscured the sprawling metropolis of Los Angeles somewhere down below. Or maybe it was smog. The conversation he'd had with Manny Alvarez the day before still sounded surreal in his head.

'What do you mean "out"?'

'I mean missing. Gone. Escaped. On the lam. He's out, Dom.'

'How the hell does someone escape from death row?'

'They don't. Bantling wasn't on death row no more, Dom. He was back in Miami, being housed at DCJ.'

Dominick sucked down the rest of his beer as the flight attendant came by with her trash bag. It was incomprehensible. How could a convicted serial killer be confused for a burglar with a similar last name, put on the wrong bus and allowed to walk free during a hurricane? How could such a colossal fuck-up ever have happened?

355

'But he lost his appeal, Manny. I read the damn opinion myself. What the hell was he doing back in Miami?'

Then Dominick had listened as Manny told him the rest of the story. That the Miami-Dade State Attorney's Office – the very same office that C.J. had poured her heart and soul into for eleven years – had decided to make a deal with the monster she'd put away and let him walk free.

'Why isn't this on the news, Manny? Cupid's escaped? Snuff clubs that are responsible for multiple murders? Corrupt Florida Supreme Court judges who fix death-row cases and are snuff-club members themselves? Why has Bill Bantling been gone for almost two weeks and I'm only hearing about this now and I'm hearing it from you? Not Corrections or the feds? Why isn't this all over the airwaves?'

'You know how it works, Dommy. The suits want to find him before they have to admit to the public they fucked up and let him go in the first place. That will make swallowing the news easier for the good voting citizens. And the snuff-club shit is on the down-low; Bantling never gave up the list of names he promised to. As for you being kept in the loop, I hope you weren't expecting special treatment. You don't live here no more.'

'I worked Cupid, it was mine. C.J. was the fucking prosecutor, for Christ's sake.'

'You both walked away, remember?'

There was a long, awkward silence.

'Yeah, well, I'm sorry about that, Bear.'

Manny hadn't acknowledged his lame attempt at an apology and Dominick couldn't blame him. They'd worked side-by-side on Cupid for two years straight. More than a partner, Bear had been like a brother to

356

him. But when he and C.J. had picked up and left Miami, they'd decided it would be best to leave everyone behind. And that included brothers. Dominick had made many acquaintances in the years since, but he had yet to find a replacement for Bear.

'Problem is, they don't know where Bantling is, Dom. Ain't got a clue.'

'But you do.'

'I think he's headed your way. I saw the pictures he drew up in his cell. He's a man obsessed – obsessed with your wife.'

'We're not together anymore.'

There was another long silence.

'I don't know what to say, Dom.'

'She left, Manny. Picked up in the middle of the night and left. Took the dog and a suitcase and left me a note. A fucking note, can you believe that? After everything?'

'Wow, Dom. I'm sorry. I don't know what to say.'

'She was . . .'

Dominick had struggled to find the right words. It had been fifteen months and he was still not over her leaving. Even now he was stunned, remembering how he'd come home from a computer-crimes conference in Phoenix to find her gone. The closet empty, the car gone, the dog missing. Given what she'd been through in the past, his first thought was that something really bad had happened. The worst stuff imaginable – someone had taken her. That perhaps her past had caught up with her and stolen her from him once again. Only this time he'd been too late to save her. But then he'd read the note she left behind in the bedroom and realized that her leaving of her own volition was worse than the worst stuff imaginable. Forget the two scribbled paragraphs of 'it's not you, it's me' crap she'd written, it was the last lines before her signature that were still burned into his memory: 'I'll always love you, Dominick. And only you.' *If that were the case, you'd still be here,* he'd thought bitterly as he'd crushed the note in his fist. *Love was supposed to conquer everything, wasn't that how the fairy tales told it?* The divorce papers were in his briefcase, unsigned, next to her crumpled attempt at goodbye.

'*. . . everything. It's been rough, Manny. Real rough. She was living with a lot, I know. I get it. I realize it's hard for anyone to get over what she's been through, and I never expected her to. Maybe I wouldn't be able to put it out of my own mind for ten minutes, either, if I were her. But no matter what I did, no matter what I said, she wouldn't let me in. The walls kept going up.*'

The words had continued to tumble out. It had been years since the two of them had talked. And given how Dominick had left, Bear had every right to yawn and tell him to find someone who gave a shit. But he didn't. From twelve hundred miles away, he listened as Dominick filled him in on the last seven years over a telephone line and a few cold beers. At least on the phone, it felt, at one point, as if the conversation had slipped back into the old and familiar, like putting on comfortable slippers that you hadn't had on in ages:

'*Where is she, Dom?*'

'*She didn't leave an address. She doesn't want any of this, Bear.*'

'*No shit. But a psycho she put on death row is now AWOL, and I think she might appreciate a heads-up. The Fibbies and the Marshals might be too dumb to find her, but something tells me Bantling's smarter and more determined than your average fed.*'

'She doesn't trust anyone. And she doesn't trust cops.'

'With good reason, after what happened with Masterson. I don't look at my brothers in blue quite the same anymore. We have to find her. We have to let her know what's going on.'

'She's got a new ID. She's underground.'

'Let me repeat – that won't matter to him and you know it.'

'All these years, we only talked about it once. Her rape. Even then there were details she couldn't speak of. Things that bastard had done to her. I saw the scars, and I read the police reports myself, but . . . there was so much she kept to herself. She could never let go of the burden, of the blame she put on herself for not locking a stupid window one night . . .

'And she would never admit it was Bantling who had raped her, Manny. She kept on denying it because she didn't want to get me involved with what she had done to convict him. She shouldered that guilt all by herself, too. That's a lot of weight to be carrying.

'But whatever she had done to make sure he was put away, I was okay with it. I've seen first-hand what he did to her. It affects everything she does, every day: the people she befriends; the jobs she takes; the routes she travels. We couldn't have kids because of this guy, Manny. He took that from her, too, that night in New York. I wish the state had fried his ass years ago. I wish they had let me do the honors.' He took a deep breath.

The alcohol was making him loose-lipped. The alcohol and the pent-up bitterness.

'Dom . . .' Manny tried.

'Masterson knew, Manny. He told me a lot of things the night he died. And what he didn't specifically tell me, I've figured out myself over the years. He was a member, Bear. Chris Masterson was a member of this snuff club you're working now. So was Greg Chambers. And Bantling. No one's supposed *to know anybody's real identity in this club; they all had code names. But Masterson was afraid Bantling could ID him somehow, and that he'd trade in a name for a reduction in his sentence. Then Bantling's old attorney, Rubio, filed an affadavit claiming she had a 911 tape that was never admitted at trial.*

'Manny, the voice on the 911 tape was Masterson. He'd called in a tip to get Bantling's car pulled over that night. He knew that the moment Bantling heard that tape he would figure out it was Masterson who set him up. And that was corroborative information that he could trade with law enforcement. Bantling was on death row and impossible to hit, so Masterson went after everyone who knew about that 911 call. That's what the Black Jacket murders were about – not gangland reprisals but Masterson trying to keep Bantling walking straight into the death chamber.'

'Jesus Christ . . . Dom, I don't think you want to be telling me this shit.'

'I want you to understand, Manny. I owe that to you. Masterson said he was going to make sure that if he went down, C.J. would go down too. For attempted Murder One. She intentionally manipulated a case to send the guy who raped her to death row – they'd have sent her down for twenty-five years for that. Masterson would've cut a deal for giving up C.J., Bantling would've walked, and C.J. would've been the one sitting behind bars. So I—'

That was when Manny had cut him off. Right there – before he said too much, as though he hadn't already. Right there – before he stumbled into a dark gray area that was definitely outside the bounds of friendship.

Sometimes when the confession finally comes, every bad thing a subject has ever done in his life pours out along with it. Dominick knew Manny could hear it coming. The Big One. And he knew that Manny didn't want to hear it, because so long as he didn't hear it, he could go on pretending he never knew. He could keep right on pretending that he didn't know exactly how Special Agent Chris Masterson had ended up with a bullet in his forehead and his ice-cold sidearm wrapped in limp fingertips.

'Sometimes justice isn't done, Dom. Sometimes you gotta take things in your own hands – I get it. Sometimes you gotta make things right, because the system isn't gonna give you justice. And that's all I'm gonna say or hear about that.'

The conversation had ended. Dom had finished off the last beer in the fridge and then booked the first morning flight to LA. He was buzzed by the time he hung up the phone with Bear, but not drunk enough to forget all that he had said. And the possible consequences that might follow. The funny thing was, he felt relieved. It was the first time in seven years that Dom had spoken of the night he'd killed Chris Masterson in cold blood. Not a day went by that he didn't go over it in his mind, trying to rationalize with his own conscience what he could or should have done differently. But he'd never spoken of it to anyone. C.J. had been there, she had seen the whole thing, but they had never talked about it, any more than they talked about the rape and the Cupid trial. It was as if so long as they didn't talk about these things, they could still manipulate the facts inside their own heads.

Maybe Masterson really had moved for his weapon. Maybe Dom really did see his hand going for his gun. Maybe . . .

The reality was, though, they both knew what went down that night. And they had both heard every word

Chris Masterson had said. They had both been complicit holders of a dark secret, yet they had never spoken of it. She shouldered her guilt, he shouldered his. Maybe that was why she had left – her back had broken first.

The flight attendant came around to make sure everyone's tray tables were up and electronic devices off. Outside, Dom saw skyscrapers and in the distance what looked like the beach. He'd promised Manny before he hung up the phone that he would find C.J. and he would be the one to tell her about Bantling. Not the feds or the US Marshals. Not even Manny.

He knew where she was. He knew how to reach her. He could've called and avoided the pain of seeing her. But there was no way he could break that kind of news over the phone. The news that Bantling had escaped would send her into a panic. A spiral. And she was out in California by herself, surrounded by bad guys once again.

The past fifteen months without her had given him a lot of time to think about why she wasn't there anymore. Why he'd thought things were fine, when all the while she was packing a suitcase in the other room. How it was he could've gotten it all so wrong. And the more he thought, the more signs he saw. The nightmares that were getting worse, not better. The looking over her shoulder, like she was expecting someone to pop out of the bushes. The obsession with running: faster, longer, harder, more often. The self-imposed isolation. The drinking. Her guilt was consuming her from the inside out and he should have seen it and insisted that they work through it. Insisted that she share. Then again, maybe she was better off without him. Maybe he was a constant reminder to her of what she had done, just as she was a constant reminder of his own crime.

Explaining away why she might have left, though, didn't ease the intense pain of missing her. If his struggling conscience were given the opportunity at a do-over, he knew the outcome would still be the same: he would pull the trigger with no hesitation, because that was the only way he could save her.

So here he was, flying to LA, racing against the clock to find her and tell her that her worst fears had been realized. That, despite his repeated assurances that he would never let anyone hurt her ever again, she was no longer safe. Because the boogeyman from her nightmares was back out on the streets.

Dominick looked at his watch and then turned back to the window as the plane began its final descent into the city of angels. He just hoped he made it to her before she read about it in the paper.

Or worse.

Before William Rupert Bantling got to deliver the news to her himself.

Live and in person.

44

'Come on, Manny, pick up,' Daria said quietly into her cell.

Potted ten-foot tall palm trees, uplit in funky purple and blue hues, were scattered about the contemporary lobby of the Hilton Bonnet Creek near Walt Disney World. She sat next to one in the lobby's piano bar, staring at an army of ant engineers that had surrounded a buried half-eaten ice-cream some kid had stuck in the dirt. If she could read ant minds, she was pretty sure they were trying to figure out how best to excavate the cone and carry it off. Even if they did manage to cart away something that was ten thousand times their weight, she wondered where it was they would go – it was a lipped planter and a two-foot drop.

'You can't hate me; it's not right,' she continued softly. 'I'm sorry. I'm sorry. I need to talk to you, Manny. I need to talk this out. We need to talk this out. I made a mistake, I know, but I thought it was the right thing when I let Vance make that deal. That's no excuse, I realize that, but I . . . I'm sorry. I shouldn't have hid it from you. I want—'

A machine-generated voice broke in. 'You have fifteen seconds of recording time left.'

Damn. She hated voicemail. 'You can't avoid me forever. We're still working this case, you know,' she said before being cut off once again.

'Goodbye.'

She hung up and took a long sip of her cosmo. The bar was packed with people, most of whom were either laughing or smiling or engaged with their partner in heavy conversation. It was crazy for a Sunday night. Loser Night, her roommate in college used to call Sundays. And that was exactly what she felt like – a Loser out on Loser Night. She reached into the palm planter and pushed the ice-cream cone on its side. The excavation issue was resolved. Now the ant army just had to move the damn thing.

'Come on, come on,' she said softly. 'Don't be lazy. Don't give up. You can do it. Move that rubber tree plant.'

She dialed Manny again.

'You've reached Detective Manny Alvarez. Please leave a message.' *Beeeeep.*

'Just so you know, Vance never told me that the story was breaking today,' she started. 'You're probably pissed, but I didn't get a heads-up either.'

The Corrections fuck-up had indeed made the *Herald* this morning, and Vance Collier had not bothered to call her and tell her it was coming. Or that it was out, for that matter. She hadn't heard from him all day. By the afternoon, after every damn news outlet in the world had digested the news, every damn news outlet in the world was now talking about Cupid's escape, and Vance was right – the word 'cover-up' was being liberally tossed around. Thankfully, she was in the land of everything Mickey Mouse, where bad news didn't seem to reach. Of course, if the Lunders case should be named as the investigation Bantling was assisting law enforcement with and her name should come out as the one who had brokered Cupid a deal, then tomorrow would most definitely suck. Monday morning was the beginning of the SMART conference and, unlike the happy, news-free tourists, everyone attending would be watching CNN and would also know exactly who to point at across a crowded room when Piers Morgan announced her name in association with Bantling's escape. Miami-Dade Assistant State Attorney Daria DeBianchi was one of the listed speakers. But that was tomorrow. Right now all they were saying on the news was that Bantling was on the lam and no one had any idea where he was.

'Listen, I'm not giving up,' she continued into the phone. She closed her eyes. 'On us. I'm not giving up on us. I know you're getting my messages and so I'm gonna keep leaving them. I'm sorry. Again with the sorries. I'm trying to fix this, Manny, I am. But I . . . I can't. I made a damn mistake. Can't you just pick up the phone? I miss you. Please call me back and we can talk. I really miss you.' She sighed. 'I hate voicemail. Isn't that funny? Me? I now hate leaving messages. Because you don't want to pick up is why I hate it. We make a good team, Manny, we do. I know you think that, too. I'm at this conference, see, and it's a hotel and I thought of the first time we were ever together. That first night—'

'You have fifteen seconds of recording time left.'

Shit . . . 'I thought of that first time we slept together, the first night we were together and, and . . .' She stumbled, and then full-out tripped over her thoughts and the proclamation just shot out: 'I . . . I love you. There, I said it. Whew. Now you have to forgive me. You have to, right? Please, baby—'

'Goodbye.'

Damn. She put her head in her hands. Then it hit her and she sat up straight and looked around.

Had she just freaking said that? Did she just say, 'I love you'? Did she leave that *on a voicemail?*

She had to stop drinking. Of course she needed another drink or maybe ten to forget that she'd said 'I love you' for the very first time on a voicemail to a man who wanted nothing to do with her and who had never told her he loved her. *Jesus . . . How desperate was she?* They had only gotten as far as the 'I like you a lot' stage when she had screwed things up with Bantling. Ugh. Ugh. Ugh. Now she was drunk-calling him, begging for forgiveness and slobbering like a stalker that she *loved* him? She downed what was left of her third cosmo. It didn't seem like the night could get much worse, but damnit, she was sure as hell gonna push it . . .

The phone beeped in her hand. A new incoming message.

It was from Manny. He couldn't possibly have listened to her last message yet, although she wasn't quite sure if that was good or bad. And if he had, his big fingers took forever to text back. She held her breath and clicked it open.

> Wrkng Modic murder w/ FLPD. Will advise you or
> Collier of progress in report shortly. Rec'd subpoena.
> Will be at motion to testify on Wed.

Daria bit her lip, hoping the pain would stop the tears. All over the hotel were colleagues in law enforcement, here for the SMART conference. She had to give a speech in the morning on Florida's sexual predator registration and notification requirements to some chiefs and task force members. It was hard enough to be respected in law enforcement as a woman, and she was still sober enough to know that what she wanted was for those colleagues to remember her when they left this conference as the authority on sexual predator and offender law, not as the blubbering drunk from the lobby bar. Or worse – the blubbering drunk from the hotel bar who was responsible for letting the most notorious serial killer in US history walk out of jail and disappear without a trace. It was time to head upstairs to a bubble bath and room service and a good long cry.

The waitress walked up. 'You okay, honey?' she asked with a frown.

'I think I have something in my contact,' Daria said, reaching for a cocktail napkin. 'My eyes are driving me nuts. Allergies.'

'Oh. Yeah. My boyfriend has terrible allergies. I feel for you,' she said, as she placed a cosmopolitan down on the table in front of her.

'I didn't order another one,' Daria replied with her hand up. 'In fact, I was about to ask you for the check.'

'Oh, no, honey. This is from the gentleman at the bar. And trust me, you don't want to go up to your room just yet. At least not by yourself. He's cute.' She flipped her hair over her shoulder and looked back at the bar.

Daria took a long time to blink before she followed the waitress's gaze, hoping it would be Manny. Like a slow-motion scene from a movie, from *Sleepless in Seattle* or *Jerry McGuire* or something. That he would be standing there in one of the new suits they'd picked out together, raising a glass to her. He would have listened to her voicemail and he would mouth, 'I love you, too, Counselor,' across the room. Then he would come over and they'd talk and he'd forgive her and they would go upstairs and make love till the morning and everything would be okay. Just like in the movies.

But Manny was not there. Instead, a nice-looking dark-haired guy in a cobalt striped dress shirt, white pants, and loafers smiled at her and raised his beer. He looked to be in his early thirties. He had a tourist tan, raccoon eyes and the hint of a sunburned chest, but the color he'd gotten from probably playing golf in the sun made his teeth dazzlingly white, which was fine. He had a nice smile.

'He had me check before to see if you were wearing a ring,' the waitress, whose name-tag read AZALEA said. 'That's real cute. You don't see that, girl. Take it from a cocktail waitress – guys either don't care if you're engaged or married, or it actually turns them on, because it's a conquest and men like to be hunters. It's the caveman thing. And as a bonus, if you're committed to someone else then you won't come around asking them for a commitment. So this guy is nice, I'm thinking.'

Daria stared at her. Thanks to the three cosmos, it was taking a little longer than usual to process information.

'Oh look, he's coming over,' said the cocktail waitress named after a shrub. She giggled.

Before Daria could protest, Azalea picked up the empty drink glass and left. Ten seconds later, the tourist was standing in front of her.

'Hi there,' he said.

'Hi,' she replied. The silence that followed was definitely awkward.

She looked down at her phone. No new messages. No voicemail. Nothing. Enough time had passed. He was at the phone, obviously, 'cause he'd sent her that BS text. Enough time had passed since she'd left that last all-embarrassing, all-important voicemail, which meant he'd obviously gotten *that*. And obviously it did not affect him. He was never going to forgive her. She needed to deal with it, was all.

The tourist looked down at the potted palm, pushing aside a couple of the fronds. The ant army had not only moved the cone, they had gotten it all the way across the dirt and were now trying to get it over the lipped side somehow. 'That explains it,' he said with a laugh. 'I was watching you from back there and I couldn't figure out what you were doing with this palm tree. I thought maybe you were talking to it, which is fine. I've done that on occasion after a couple of drinks. But you seemed pretty upset. I thought maybe it was talking back to you.'

She rolled the cocktail napkin in her palm. 'No, I don't talk to plants – just insects. Only kidding. I was on the phone. A business call.'

'Are you alone?'

'Yes. Just me and my friend the palm tree.'

He laughed. 'Do you mind if I join you two?'

She looked down at the phone again before answering. Nothing. *Fuck Manny.* She'd put her heart out there like a damn fool, drunk or not. No reaction to her telling him she loved him was worse than a bad one. It meant he didn't care. At all. Not even enough to call her and tell her she was a fool to say what she'd said. Or argue with her that she didn't mean it. Or tell her that he didn't feel the same way. What it meant was he didn't care enough to make the damn call. She meant nothing to him – just a casual, opportunistic office fuck who'd pissed him off enough for him to call it quits a little earlier than he normally would have. That's what she was – a conquest. Nothing more.

'Why not?' she answered. She gestured to the lounge chair across from her and took a long sip of her fresh cosmo. Fuck all the colleagues she was trying to look so perfect for. Half of them were probably looped themselves. She'd never met a cop who couldn't close the damn bar. Tonight she was gonna have fun. She'd show Manny what he was missing. 'Thanks for the drink.'

'The pleasure's mine,' he said with a smile as he sat down. He really did have a nice smile. She glanced down at his left hand. No ring. And no ring tan-line. That didn't necessarily mean anything, but since he had bothered to check hers, there was a chance that the waitress was right – he wasn't a jerk. That maybe he was a nice guy. She didn't need a prince right now, but she couldn't stomach an asshole. Not tonight.

She wiped the tear that had started to fall and looked over at the potted palm. The ice-cream cone was gone. She looked at the floor. It was nowhere to be seen.

She turned off her phone and slipped it in her purse. *Fuck that.* Bully for the ants and the hidden message of hope in that dumb childhood song that was now repeating in her head, but she was out of the business of trying. And she didn't want to read any more BS texts from him that were gonna upset her. *No mas Manny Alvarez.*

'My name is Daria,' she replied. 'Let me ask you – are you here with the SMART convention?'

He shook his head. 'The what?' he asked quizzically.

Good. No more cops. No probation officers. No judges. No prosecutors. No lawyers. No criminals. She tried to think of her original list – what she once thought would make her happy at the end of the day. A financier would be nice. A rich guy who could whisk her away on a private plane at a moment's notice. Maybe that was asking a bit much. Maybe a doctor or a fireman. Or a golfer. 'So you're not a cop? Or a probation officer?'

He laughed again. 'A cop? No, no, no. No way. I'm a filmmaker. I'm down here from New York on a project. It's nice to meet you, Daria,' he said, extending his hand across the table. 'My name's Reid . . .'

45

Manny stared at the phone and rubbed his head. Now what the hell was he supposed to do with that?

I love you?

Daria was obviously polluted. Three sheets to the wind. Slurring, sighing – a melancholy, mushy drunk tonight.

But, *I love you?*

He looked at the other side of his bed, strewn with papers and reports from the Lunders case, and now reports from Fort Lauderdale PD and grisly crime-scene photos of Marie Modic's broken and discarded corpse. Even though Daria wasn't next to him in bed anymore, she was still next to him in bed.

I love you. Now you have to forgive me. Please, Manny . . .

Finally, she'd apologized. It had taken her long enough to say the word sorry. It probably hurt when she finally coughed it up. He picked up his cell phone and dialed her number. Let's see if it was the alcohol talking. Let's see if she's still all, 'Oh forgive me, please. I didn't mean it. I love you,' when she'd sobered up. And if she was? If she meant what she'd said when she was drunk, when she was seeing straight, what then?

He took in a deep breath, closed his eyes and leaned his head back against the headboard. Women. Soft, sweet-smelling and warm. Kissable, full lips and curvy, full bodies. That woman-scent they give off. Those pheromones. It got him every time. He did like the ladies. Always had.

But *she* was different. Right from the start, everything about Daria DeBianchi, Esq., was different. A little red firecracker, with an amazing, pint-sized body and a personality as fiery and dark and snappy as her hair. She was not his type – smart, educated, conservative, save for those heels she lusted over. Manny liked his women big and Latin and curvy and flashy, and it helped if they weren't so bright or quick with a retort. Of course, none of those had worked out for him before. He'd walked down the aisle three times, but no woman had ever made him feel the way Daria did. Happy. Sexy. Masculine. Mad. Funny. Vulnerable. Stupid. Smart.

Happy.

That was it. That was the first word that came to mind. She made him *happy* when he was with her. Usually. And, as he had recently learned, he was completely miserable when she wasn't around. Grumpy, edgy. Like he was missing something. It wasn't just the wild sex – although he did love what he did to the conservative, uptight part of her. Making her scream words he didn't think she even knew. But it wasn't all physical: they could talk for hours about criminals and homicide scenes without her threatening to leave because it grossed her out or bored her.

They could argue about things like baseball or politics and she wouldn't sulk 'cause he didn't agree with her. She was a huge Dolphin fan. She understood when he didn't want to talk about something he'd seen because she knew all too well what it was like to witness something horrible and not be able to do anything about it. He loved her small hands, which fit completely inside his, like a baby's would. He loved her eyes, even when she was pissed off and they practically glowed. He loved her ruby-red lips – especially when they were on his. He loved that she liked to make a statement. He loved her petiteness. He loved her smile, when she decided to flash it, that was.

He loved her.

He banged the back of his head against the headboard again. *What then?* What if she meant what she'd said? What if a smart, sophisticated, sometimes bitchy, beautiful woman really meant it when she said she loved him?

Then he'd say it back. Because it was true. He'd been in love and in lust enough times to know the difference. And his little red firecracker attorney was everything every other woman he'd loved before was not, so this time it must be true. It must be real. And he was ready to forgive her and move on. Yes, he was still beyond pissed, especially since Bantling's supposedly accidental release from custody was all over the fucking news. If he didn't care about her, he would have no problem calling up Nadine Kramer from the *Herald* and telling her all about Collier's cursed deal with a serial killer. But that would only destroy Daria's career. Not to mention that the snuff-club allegations would then have to come out, and he didn't want to turn the lights on on that macabre cache of secrets yet, lest all those cockroaches go into hiding. No, he'd manage to get past what she'd done and maybe they'd tackle Bantling together, like some crime-fighting duo. Manny would find him and bring him back to Miami, and since there was no deal actually struck for his cooperation, they would send his sorry ass back to Florida State Prison. Then he and Dickerson and Customs and the FBI and FDLE and any other agency that wanted to join in would find this snuff club and infiltrate it. There had to be another way in. There had to be another way to disrupt it besides putting a convicted serial killer on the payroll as a snitch. And everyone would live happily-ever-fucking-after.

Then he looked over at the box files on his dresser. Maybe not.

The State of Florida v. William Rupert Bantling was scribbled across the side of one. *Black Jacket* across another. He hadn't looked in either box yet. He wasn't sure if he would or if he should. He'd only gotten as far as taking them home and putting them on his dresser. The past few hours, as he worked on Lunders, he'd glanced over at those boxes every so often, wondering what secrets would be revealed when and if he decided to open them up. That was why he hadn't done anything yet – he wasn't sure he'd be able to put the lids back on once he decided to take them off. And like Pandora's Box, he wasn't sure what evil he might be releasing into the world if he did decide to flip the lid . . .

He tapped his fingers on the nightstand as Daria's phone started to ring. *How would the crazy thoughts that had just run through his head spill out when he heard her voice? What if she was still drunk or too hungover to think straight?* But the call went straight to voicemail. Her phone was either turned off, or she'd turned it off when she saw it was him calling.

'Listen, it's me,' Manny began softly enough at the sound of the tone. 'I got your message. That's pretty heavy. And that's a cheap fucking shot, you know, telling me that on the phone. What the hell am I supposed to say to that, Counselor? You tell me you fucking love me on a voicemail?' He sighed. 'I'm sitting here buried in crap with stuff on your case and . . .' He broke off and looked around the empty room, his eyes avoiding the dresser. 'Well, I have a lot to say to you, but I need to know if that was you talking. If it was, if you meant what you said, then call me back. If this is all just a mistake, if you drank too much, is all, then, well I'll see you Wednesday at the hearing and we'll handle this as . . . professionals. Although, I don't know how I'm gonna do that, but, whatever. So, well, let me know,' he finished.

He hit the 'end' button and stared at the phone, his heart beating so hard, he felt it all the way up in his mouth. He sat there for what felt like an hour, watching the stupid cordless phone that sat atop Marie Modic's autopsy report.

She never did call him back.

46

C.J. stared at the wriggly, white ball of pure fluff that had popped its head out of a gigantic wrapped box. The red bow around the puppy's neck was bigger than its whole head. 'This is supposed to eat people?' she said with a laugh as the pup licked her face. 'This is gonna be a ferocious guard dog?'

'Yes,' Dominick insisted with a smile. 'She's nine pounds now, but she's gonna grow into a fierce, one-hundred-pound beast. A force to be reckoned with. Merry Christmas.'

'If you say so.'

'Now name her something mean. Killer. Chops. Tank. Cujo. Beast.'

She looked at him with a raised eyebrow. 'Tank?'

'You're right – she is a girl. How about Tankini? Tank can be for short?'

'How about Luna?' C.J. asked. 'She's so white and fluffy, like a fat, full moon. Luna. I think it's exotic. A nod to your Italian heritage, Dominick.'

'I have to be honest here, honey. Luna doesn't sound very mean. Crazy, maybe, but not mean.'

'She doesn't have to sound mean, Dominick. She just has to be mean – and only when it counts.'

'True. Well, she's your baby, so you can name her anything you want as long as you let me train her to eat people.'

'She's perfect, Dominick. Absolutely perfect. I love her!' she exclaimed as Luna jumped out of the box, knocking it over. She nuzzled into C.J.'s arms and attacked her with kisses. 'Thank you!'

'Welcome to the family, Luna,' Dominick said with a perfect smile. 'Something tells me you're gonna like it here. You certainly lucked out in the crib department, fluffy.'

'I know you were only playing, girl, but you can't chase the little yappy dogs around the trees. Their little yappy owners don't like it,' C.J. admonished as she and Luna walked into the house. 'They get very upset.' Luna licked her hand.

She tossed the keys and newspaper on the kitchen table. So much for a leisurely Sunday-morning walk to the dog park – a dog park that Luna hadn't been kicked out of yet. By tonight there were sure to be wanted posters up with her dog's mug shot stapled to the very trees she'd chased a pair of Malti-poos around a few dozen times. She wasn't nine pounds of fluff anymore. Dominick had called it – she'd shed the puppy fuzz and grown into a lean, furry, pure white, hundred-pound, dog-park-clearing force to be reckoned with. And while he might have trained her to eat bad people, he had never managed to train her not to chase and eat those yummy little yappy dogs.

She poured Luna a big bowl of kibble, made a fresh pot of coffee and headed off into the shower. She was gonna have to start driving out of town to look for dog parks, the way a bank robber might scout out fresh targets.

The hot water was not working for some reason, so she took a tepid shower, making a mental note to call the plumber next week. After she got dressed, she turned on the TV in the living room and joined Luna in the kitchen for coffee and a quick plate of scrambled eggs and toast. She had a ton of work to get done. After weeks of delay, finally tomorrow was the day for closing arguments on Kassner.

She gathered a mixing bowl and whisk as her brain reworked thoughts and sentences.

Premeditation: Ladies and gentlemen, you saw the store video of Mr Kassner casually shopping for accelerants at the Snappy Pro hardware store four days before the fire. A hardware store that was twenty-six miles outside of town and not on his way to or from anything. Just out of the way, so that no one would recognize him. He spent twenty-eight dollars on plastic gasoline containers and—

Her thoughts stopped in mid-sentence.

The eggs were not on the second shelf of the refrigerator. They were on the third. The bread was on the second. That was supposed to be on the third.

She closed the refrigerator door and backed up in a sudden panic, knocking over a dinette chair. Luna was at her side now, barking. She knew something was wrong. C.J.'s eyes darted around the kitchen, at the knick-knacks and old family pictures that decorated her grandmother's walls. She took a breath. Everything else looked the same in the kitchen. She switched the whisk for a chef's knife, and hesitantly headed into the living room, her heart beating

380

crazily in her chest, Luna at her side. Everything looked okay, there, too. Her magazines were in the same order on her coffee table. The photos were all at the same angles. None were missing. The curtains were in the same position, the blinds pulled down. She did the same thing through the rest of her house. Everything *looked* okay. The windows were all locked. The doors, too. And the alarm had, of course, been set when she got home. She would never make the same mistake twice.

But this was how it had started twenty-three years ago. He had been in her house, eating from her fridge, rummaging through her mail and drawers. Taking a shower in her bathroom. Maybe using her toothbrush. She had missed the signs because she hadn't paid attention. Now she always paid attention.

Okay, okay, C.J. Let's think about this rationally: Bantling's on death row in Florida, some 2800 miles away. Chambers is dead and burning in hell, some 2800 miles down. The experiment is done. What are the odds that another former defendant of yours is going to come rearrange your fridge as a form of stalking? You mixed up the eggs and the bread, is all. It happens.

She took another deep breath and headed back into the kitchen. She could not wait until this case was over. After nine weeks of a trial that should have lasted three, she was burned out and stressed. Plus, since her car was stolen, she'd been jumpier than ever. The thought of some stranger rummaging through her glove compartment or console, looking at old receipts and notes and wrappers – things in the Green Giant that had once belonged to her – skeezed her out. It had churned up a violent sea of memories. Now she was seeing invisible hands going through her refrigerator. After Kassner she didn't have another case scheduled for weeks. She needed the break. A few days' vacation in the wine country or something. Great food at restaurants like the Los Olivos Café and Brothers, washed down with gallons of Pinot Noir. Nothing but vineyards and horses and farmers markets.

She walked past the hall console table, where assorted pictures from her life before Santa Barbara were bumped up against each other in a hodge-podge collection of frames. Dominick was in every picture. Her wedding photo taken on a beach in the Keys. Boating in the Caribbean. Playing with Luna on Lake Michigan, sipping coffee in her rain jacket at Pike's Market in Seattle. Eating beignets at Café du Monde in New Orleans. In each picture she was smiling and he was right there beside her. In every picture.

Back in the kitchen, she sat down on one of her grandmother's vinyl dinette chairs and put her head in her hands.

What was she doing out here? Why did she keep running? Why had she let herself ruin the one constant, good thing in her life? Why was she hell-bent on self-destruction? Was that how she was going to make her penance?

She felt herself unraveling the way she had before, so many years ago in New York. That breakdown had ultimately led to a psych ward and, at one point, suicide watch at the age of twenty-five. Now the walls were slowly closing in again, an inch at a time. So slowly, months had passed before she'd taken notice that they were almost upon her now. She should resume therapy, she should talk to someone, she knew that, but . . . she could never again trust another therapist after what she'd been through. And even if she could, she could never be honest about why she was unraveling, about the horrible things she had done in her life. She was stuck with herself and only herself.

She reached for her cell in her sweater pocket and for the umpteenth time pulled up Dominick's number. Her finger poised above the 'send' button, like a runaway teen in a strange city who has found a pay phone and a quarter. She wanted to make that call so bad.

Sorry would never be enough.

A despondent parent would say, 'Come home!' wouldn't they? All that parent would want would be for that child to come home, no matter what it was she had done, no matter the reasons she'd left. If C.J. had babies she would be that way. *If only she could have had babies* . . . She wiped the tears away with the back of her hand. No questions asked. Just come home to me.

But she wasn't a kid. She was a grown woman. And she had left without telling him why. She put the cell back in her pocket.

From the next room over she heard the TV, like a small voice growing louder and louder as she focused in on the words.

'. . . In a shocking admission made earlier this morning, Chet Meyers, the head of Florida's Department of Corrections issued a statement confirming that the convicted serial killer had, in fact, gone missing as far back as the tenth of August. Denying a cover-up, Mr Meyer refused to elaborate on why the information was not made public earlier, only to say that there was an investigation pending.'

C.J. stood up and walked back into the living room.

Luna was sniffing furiously at the carpet, going round and round in circles. She ignored her, staring in disbelief at the reporter on the TV screen. A graphic showing the *Miami Herald*'s logo floated above the reporter's head.

Luna started to whine.

No, no, no, no . . . don't say it. Don't say it. Don't say it, or I will scream.

The graphic changed, replaced by a color picture of the man who held her hostage every night in her nightmares.

Luna stopped at the front door and started to bark.

'Bill Bantling was added to the FBI's most wanted list of fugitives this morning,' the reporter added somberly. 'The serial killer known as Cupid has debuted at number two.'

47

Luna was sitting at attention right in front of the door, barking, her teeth bared. Someone was out there. C.J. backed up slightly and hit the console. The picture of her and Dominick in Seattle at Pike's Place Market fell to the floor and broke.

Steps away in the living room, the TV kept spewing out information:

There is a national manhunt going on today for William Rupert Bantling, the vicious serial killer perhaps better known to the world as Cupid, who has reportedly escaped from death row . . .

His whereabouts remain unknown at this time . . .

. . . narrowly avoiding execution in 2004 . . .

According to sources, Bantling was in Miami to testify as a witness in a murder case . . .

The room began to spin. She bent down and absently started to pick up the pieces of broken glass, slicing her hand open. The same hand, coincidentally, that Gregory Chambers had severed a tendon in with his scalpel years before. Blood began to seep out of her palm, seemingly from her old wound.

How could he be out? How could this have happened?

Luna came over and licked her hand, then went back to the door, where she sat down and whined. Back to C.J. Back to the door. Back and forth, whining, barking. 'Luna, what is it? What's the matter, girl?' C.J. whispered, her voice shaking. Her whole body was shaking. She knew what the matter was. Someone was out there. Or had been.

The doorbell rang.

She fell against the wall. This couldn't be happening.

The doorbell rang again. Luna jumped up against the door, scratching. Barking furiously.

Crouched low in a corner or hiding in a closet wasn't going to tell her who was on the other side. It was a sunny Sunday afternoon. *Get a grip, C.J. Before you lose it forever. Get a grip and hold on to it. Hold it together and just check the door.* She stood up and tiptoed to the peephole, holding her breath. She looked out, quickly unlocked the deadbolt and opened the door.

'Hello' was all it took.

Dominick was standing on her doorstep, just steps away. Luna pushed past her and jumped on him, almost knocking him over. The ferocious-sounding barks were replaced with happy licks and a wagging tail. Dominick bent down to give Luna a hug and looked up at C.J. 'Hello,' was all he said, and she started to cry. She didn't want to, but the tears came anyway. And they wouldn't stop. They were a toxic mixture of fear, stress, anger, happiness, relief, guilt, sadness, love, grief. A zillion different emotions hit her all at once and she couldn't keep her composure. She just couldn't. She stood there sobbing in the doorway, blood dripping from her hand on to the carpet.

He took the two steps into the house and she literally fell into his arms, emotionally exhausted. Even though she'd given him a million reasons to let her go and watch her crash to the ground, he held her up and he held on to her. Neither of them said a word.

He led her to the couch in the living room and turned off the news with a flick of the remote. He examined her hand, ran into the kitchen and grabbed a dishtowel, carefully wrapping it around her palm. Sitting on the couch, her hand on his lap, he still held her, even though she couldn't fall anymore.

'Manny Alvarez called me,' he said finally. He moved a piece of her hair that was cemented to a cheek by her tears. 'I didn't want you to find out on the phone, so I came. I guess you saw the news.'

'How? How did this happen?'

'They cut him a deal, C.J. The State Attorney's Office. He was going to hand up names. Names of the snuff-club members.'

'Oh God.'

'He'd already given them a Florida Supreme Court judge who apparently was instrumental in sending Bantling back to the row. That was the bait. They brought Bantling down to Miami to hear the rest of the names and he disappeared in the hurricane. They're calling it a mistake. A Department of Corrections mistake, but I don't know what to believe.'

What was most telling was what Dominick was not saying. He was not saying, *Don't worry, he's long gone and out of the country.* He was not saying, *You're the last person he'd come find because he knows the feds would expect that.* He was not saying, *It will all be okay. He could never find you.* Because none of that was true and she knew it. She also knew he was holding back.

'What else did Manny tell you? There's more, isn't there?'

'They found drawings in Bantling's cell. They were of you. All of them. Manny thinks he's going to try and find you.' Dominick sighed. 'I think so, too.'

She nodded. There was nothing to say.

'I didn't tell him where you were, but trust me, you won't be that hard to find. You need to get someplace safe. I can call the feds. We can put you in witness protection till they find him.'

'You mean *if* they find him.'

'There is a chance he's left the country. We always knew he'd buried money somewhere. We just never found out where.'

C.J. shook her head. 'I won't live that way. When I left New York, I made the rules. I chose where to live, the career I wanted to have, the people I would associate with. Not the federal government. I don't want to be mopping floors in a Kmart in Little Rock in the hope he won't find me, Dominick.'

'This time it's different, C.J. This time he wants revenge. He's been dreaming of it for years. And we both know why.'

Dominick was right. There was no place she could hide, no place the feds could hide her where Bill Bantling wouldn't eventually find her. She looked around her apartment, thinking of the relocated eggs and the cold shower she took that morning. *Had he already found her?* Was paranoia breaking down her reasoning? Or were her hypersensitive instincts in tune? If she knew anything from too many years of being a prosecutor, it was that if someone wants to find you badly enough, he will. And if that someone wants to kill you badly enough, he will. When retribution becomes someone's mission – the purpose he wakes in the morning and the reason he dreams at night – nothing will stop him from looking. And eventually finding.

She was tired of running. Running from her past. Running from what she had done. Running from psychos. She'd spent most of her life running. Running and hiding. And she wasn't going to do it anymore. But there was only one way to accomplish that. To truly put an end to the hunt once and for all.

Dominick hadn't changed. Thinner, maybe. A little more gray in his brown hair. But he'd always had a great body and he still did. And a weathered, chiseled face with a tan complexion that belonged on a cowboy. The stress of the past year definitely showed in his brown eyes, though. Those looked tired, suspicious, angry, sad, distant. He studied her for a moment, as if inside his brain he was arguing with himself over his next words. 'Come home with me,' he finally said. 'At least in Chicago we know people.'

She ran a hand through her hair. 'They don't *know* us. No one *knows* us. You can't just lay our story on them, Dominick. It doesn't work that way. Besides, all the other heavy baggage you and I drag along, you can't just ask your friends for help and then spring on them that a serial killer may be hunting your wife.'

All the other heavy baggage.

'Let's talk about our baggage, C.J. We both know what it is. We both know what I did. We both know what you did.'

She pulled away from him. 'I can't do this.'

He took the divorce papers from his jacket pocket and dropped them on her lap. He stood up. 'Why? Why are you running? Why are you running from *me*? Tell me the truth. I don't care what it is, because I can't go on like this, C.J. I can't do it anymore. I'll still protect you. I'll still get you out of here, I'll find Bantling. I'll take him apart, but I can't go on. Tell me why you keep running from me. Why you keep running from us. I've done everything I can to keep you safe, to help you forget. To move forward. And I wish *I* could be the one that runs away. I wish *I* could move on. I wish *I* could . . . stop loving you and find someone else, but . . . that never happens. So tell me. Tell me you don't love me anymore and I'll sign.'

'I can't.'

'Can't what?'

'I can't tell you that. I'll never tell you that. Because I love you more than anything. I miss us, Dominick. I miss you every second of every single day. Most of those seconds are spent wishing that I never left. But my brain had no choice. It was exploding. I look at you and I see *him*. No – I see you looking at me and *you* see *him*. You see Bantling. You see the Clown. You see the police reports. You pity me. That's how you rationalize what I did. You pity me.'

'I do pity you. I know what that man did to you and I would kill him myself if I could. But I can't. I'm waiting for the system to do it for me, but it hasn't. I don't have to "rationalize" your putting the man who raped you on death row, C.J., because it *is* rational. It's the only rational act in a crazy, fucked-up system that has allowed him to keep breathing for a decade. I applaud you.'

She put her head in her hands. 'We hold this big secret, you and I. And I don't want it anymore. I feel like I'm always looking out the window at my past, just waiting for it to catch up. I try to break away, and surround myself with normal people who know nothing about anything. Who don't know me, who don't know my past – and that doesn't work either. I can't seem to get away anywhere. And now he's out. He's on the streets and . . .' Her voice tapered off.

'It's you, C.J.. You're the one who keeps rationalizing. You hate yourself. And you keep it all to yourself. Your conscience is eating you alive. It's consuming both of us. It makes you want to run from yourself and build a new life, but you can't do that. No matter how many miles you put between us, or Bantling, or your past, you can't run from yourself. You have to forgive yourself. You have to move on.'

'I can't.'

'There's no other alternative.' He looked around the small house, pointing at the locks on the door, the alarm system, the drawn blinds. 'Look at where you are. Are you happy? Did it work this time?'

She looked up at him. The tears were back. 'How did you know where I was?'

'I've always known. You keep on running, and I know you don't like to be chased. So I just waited for you to come home.'

She reached for his hand and saw that his wedding ring was still on. 'Don't sign those papers.'

He pulled her forcefully up from the couch. Her face was inches from his own. Her scent was like a perfume. It was hard to think when he was this close to her. He clenched a fistful of her hair behind her head and pulled her even closer. He wanted to hate her sometimes. He really did. 'Damn it, C.J.,' he said softly. 'I was never going to.'

48

'I need you to go back to Chicago,' she said as they lay together in her bed. Her head was on his chest, his hand buried in her hair. The early-morning light was slowly filling the room. Great sleep usually followed great make-up sex, but not last night. They had made love in the afternoon, gone for some dinner down on Hendry's Beach, then come back and, in a room filled with candles, made up again over another bottle of wine. Dominick had eventually dozed off, but C.J. had not slept well. She kept getting out of bed, checking the window, looking out into the black night and the thick woods that were her grandmother's backyard. Morning had come and the alcohol had worn off.

Dominick said nothing. He just exhaled.

'I'm coming home,' she whispered, her back to him as she sat on the edge of the bed. 'I promise. In a couple of days. I have to close things up here. I have to finish my trial.'

'I'll stay.'

'I'm not running anymore, Dominick. I want to work this out.'

'He's on the loose. What about that? How does that fit in with your plans?'

She said nothing for a long while. 'He may very well be looking for me, but I think I have enough time to finish up my trial and quit my job. I'm in closing argument. It's the end of a nine week trial. I can't just leave.'

'I'll stay,' he repeated.

'You have a trial yourself that starts on Wednesday.'

'If we leave tonight we can be in Chicago by Wednesday. Unless you want to fly.'

'I'm not putting Luna in cargo.'

'I'll get a continuance.'

'Good luck with that. You spent last night telling me what a bastard your judge was.'

'Here we go . . .' he said with an exasperated sigh. 'You're doing it again. You've got the wall up. Did last night mean nothing to you?'

'I'll leave when my trial is over,' she said again. 'I know you don't believe that, but I will.'

'Jesus, I don't even know if we should go back to Chicago, C.J.' He ran a hand through his hair. 'There's so much I have to think about. People I have to call. I'm kind of winging my thoughts, here, and you're not helping.'

'You're the lead on a murder case – you can't leave your prosecutor high and dry, any more than I can leave here this morning. That much is definite – finish your case and I'll finish mine.' She stared at the drawn blinds. 'It's not like he's out there right now.'

'We've no idea where he is. That should be enough

of a reason to have left last night.' He got out of bed and pulled on his pants.

'That can't happen. You told me to stop running.'

'I meant from me.'

'I know what you're thinking,' she said.

'Good for you,' Dominick replied, stopping to look at her. 'Because *I* don't even know what I'm thinking anymore. I'm thinking last night was—'

She moved across the bed and over to him on her knees. 'The way it should be. Don't treat it like it won't happen again. I meant what I said. I'm coming home. I'll get help. I'll never run from you again. But I am not going to race out of town because he might try and find me. All I need is a few days.'

He shook his head. 'You've made promises before, C.J. Promises like forever and always and death do us part. And that didn't stop you from walking out the damn door. I don't think I can do this anymore.'

'One week, Dominick. That's all I need,' she said as he turned from her and walked into the bathroom. 'Give me one week and I'll show you forever again.'

49

The room moved in and out of focus. *In and out. In and out.* Her eyelids felt like they had weights on them. Daria closed her eyes again. She was so incredibly tired . . .

Her mouth felt dry and pasty, her tongue thick, her throat parched. She imagined a big, cold Big Gulp cup of ice water being poured on her. Her mouth was open and she was lapping it up greedily as it splashed all over her, running down her neck and back. The cold water should take away her sore throat. It should make her wake up. Pull her out of this exhausted stupor.

Her eyelids fluttered open.

I must be dreaming, she thought as the unfamiliar room came into focus and then blurred again, like one might view the horizon on a bobbing ship. *Up and down. In and out.* She had to pull herself out of this dream. She had to. She was gonna be so tired for work today. She had to give a speech, right? That was today? No, she had court. She had a hearing, right?

Damnit! Try and wake up, girl! Concentrate!

Then she realized that her arms hurt. Her shoulders, in particular. Not just hurt – they throbbed. It was like someone was turning up the pain as they might adjust the volume for their favorite song on the radio. Her armpits burned, her back was all twisted. Her wrists – she couldn't feel them. Just pins and needles in her fingers.

She closed her eyes again and it started to rain. It felt good.

And then it didn't.

'Let's go. Stay with me now. Focus,' said a voice she didn't recognize.

She jolted about, trying to get out of the rain. Her arms would not move – they were tied to something. They were tied to the ceiling. Her feet were on the floor, though, her toes sweeping back and forth. They hurt, too. Everything hurt. Jesus, everything throbbed.

Her eyes opened and there was a shirtless guy she'd never seen before, standing in front of her, spraying water from a purple water bottle in her face. He slapped her on the cheek.

'Let's go, honey. Stay awake, now. How much shit did you give her?' he asked someone behind him. 'She's fucking useless this way.'

'I want her awake,' someone else said. Voice #2.

'What I always give,' another voice replied angrily. 'I know what I'm doing. She's here, isn't she?'

Daria looked to where the angry voice was coming from. It was the guy from the hotel bar. The tourist with the tan. What was his name? He made movies or something? He was standing across the room, next to a sink, looking at the shirtless man with the purple water bottle. Then he turned his back to look at something else.

'That's what I'm paying for.' Voice #2 spoke up again. 'I can watch you fuck a doll or a dead one anytime; I want her awake and alert. That's what I want.'

'Don't argue, please,' someone else said. 'Try some more water.'

'Ooh, a wet T-shirt contest,' cooed another.

'Use the prongs, now. That will wake her up.' And another.

How many people were in the room? Where were they all?

In and out. Up and down. It was impossible to see the horizon.

The shirtless man walked over to the guy from the hotel and pushed him out of the way. *Reid. Reid was his name.* She saw the tattoo then, the archangel wings etched across his back in an array of colors, the lightning bolt the angel held in his hand, ready to throw. It was the tattoo on the man who had killed Patricia Graber. She remembered it on the video seized from Judge Lepidus's house. When the killer flexed his back, the muscles made the wings look like they flapped. Her body began to shake uncontrollably. On the counter behind Reid was a laptop. The shirtless man reached over and hit something on the keyboard.

In and out. In and out. Please stay out. Don't come into focus. Stay unconscious. Go back to where you were, Daria . . .

'They're not supposed to tell me what to do. This is all *me*. They just get to watch, not direct, so mute them all. Got it? I don't need someone who can't get it up at home telling me what to do. You hear me?' the shirtless man snapped.

'It's getting late. Too late. Everyone has been waiting for you to do what they linked in to see, so stop with the excuses,' Reid replied. 'This feed is over at seven. Listen to the man – use the prongs if you have to. Think Roman, and just give the people what they want. They're paying enough for it.' He hit another button on the keypad.

Daria watched the two men argue. They were arguing over her. It felt like everything was moving in slow motion – their mouths, the hand gestures. Her eyes moved about the room, trying to take in what was happening. Trying to find a way out, to think her way out. But like everything else, her thoughts were moving so slow . . .

Then she saw the monitors.

Lined up against a wall, like a crazy, video line-up. On each monitor were faces. Faces of men. Above the monitors was a large multi-monitor TV screen. She counted them as her eyes moved down the line: *one, two, three, four, five, six—*

'Hello, my little Lena,' said monitor #6 when her eyes landed on his. It was the voice who had demanded she be awake. It was voice #2.

Only now the voice had a name.

'She looks terrible,' said Abby Lunders with a sigh as her face moved on to the screen. Sitting on the arm of a chair, she stroked her son's hair. 'All she's done so far is sleep. She was cuter in court. More feisty, too. This is a shame. I hate when they drug them down.'

'You do look tired,' a shirtless Talbot added and smiled. 'I am too. We've been up all night, waiting for you to come round, Lena. But we're running out of time, here. I gotta be in court in a few hours.'

'Maybe they can do it tonight,' Abby said. 'Hold it off till then. We can celebrate your getting out.'

Daria closed her eyes again and tried to play dead. She wished she already were, because she knew what was coming. Instead of seeing her life flash before her eyes, like they say in the movies, she saw her actual death before it happened. She thought about Manny's words in her office some months back:

It's a forty-second clip, Counselor. Just imagine what we didn't see. What footage ended up on the cutting-room floor.

There was no need to imagine any longer. Her murderers were making the movie. She was in the cutting room.

And then she saw the aftermath. Not the funeral and the eulogy and the flowers and crying friends and family members. No. Rather, she saw detectives and uniforms and ME techs gathered around her broken, naked body, stuffed under a pile of garbage, feasted on by rats and insects, a thin film growing over her open eyes. Surrounding her were the friendly, familiar faces of colleagues from the ME's office, the crime lab, the SAO. Detectives she'd worked with countless times, crime-scene techs she'd put on the stand, fellow prosecutors she'd had lunch with – all were now picking over her body and ogling the naked crime-scene photos, which would go on to live in perpetuity on some police department's computer and in their evidence room, maybe making their way up through the courts one day, too. And maybe on to the Internet.

Oh, please, she thought as tears began to run out of her eyes, *don't let it be Manny who responds. Don't let it be Manny who finds me in that dumpster . . .*

Manny. It was funny that the last thoughts she would ever have would be of him. How strange. She never would have thought *that* months ago, when he'd shown up in her office late for his pre-file. And he'd never know it, either. She wished they'd made up. She wished he'd forgiven her. She wished she could do over the last few months. She would never have taken this case. The one that was going to get her off the lifer list and rocket her to prosecutorial fame.

'*Remember this, honey,*' her dad had lectured her when she'd first moved up to felonies, after she'd missed a birthday dinner with the family. '*Have you ever seen a tombstone that had "Was a great worker" or "Beloved by all her employees" etched on it? No. Put life in perspective, is all I'm saying. Remember what's gonna matter when the lights go out.*'

All that she'd done for the past five years, all the late nights and wasted weekends and trials and motions and worry and stress – none of it was gonna matter a damn when the lights went out, would it? Criminals would be around long after they put her in the ground. She hadn't made a difference or changed the world. And when she was gone, all those badasses she'd sent away would eventually get out, anyway. They'd see the sunshine again and kiss their babies and hug their loved ones . . .

The shirtless man was coming back. She could tell even with her eyes closed. She could hear him walk towards her, his heels crunching on invisible grit on the concrete floor. She could smell his sweat. She could feel him watching her. Studying her. Calculating his next move.

Don't react, she thought. Play dead. Maybe they'll leave you alone, like an animal would. Maybe they'll skip all the horrible things in between now and death, because she was no fun to play with. Maybe they'll make it quick.

But then the shirtless man hit her with the prongs and the voices on the monitors went wild, like the adrenaline-fueled crowd at a boxing match, and she knew she would not be so lucky . . .

50

Judge Becker drummed her dark plum claws on the bench. The sound echoed in the mostly empty courtroom. She stared at Vance Collier. 'Is the state ready to proceed or not?'

'Your Honor, I have a problem,' replied Vance, his voice tinged with anxiety and anger.

'I see that. Or rather, I don't. Tell me, where is Ms DeBianchi?'

Joe Varlack checked his watch again and looked over at the state's table. He was going without co-counsel today. Beside him was his client, decked out in a grey Hugo Boss suit, his sandy, once shaggy, blond locks now cut to his ears and respectably combed back. Unlike his lawyer, his face was devoid of emotion. Seated behind Talbot was a smiling Abby Lunders.

'Your Honor, my office has been unable to reach Ms DeBianchi,' Vance stumbled. 'She, ah, was at a law enforcement conference in Orlando these past few days,

403

but she hasn't been in the office this morning. We're trying to locate her.'

'You do know that Mr Varlack has filed a speedy demand?' the judge replied. 'And that we've already lost considerable time due to the hurricane?'

'My office has been swamped trying to get back up to speed after Artemis. It's been very difficult.'

'Quite frankly, Mr Collier, that is not the defendant's problem. He's here. He's ready to proceed. Obviously, Ms DeBianchi is not doing hurricane relief work in Orlando. Perhaps she got lost at Disney World?'

'Just so the court knows,' announced Joe Varlack haughtily, 'Ms Simmons will not be attending the hearing today due to an unexpected illness. But *I* am still prepared and ready to go forward. Even if the plane loses an engine, it should still be able to fly.'

The courtroom doors swung open and George Schaible, the Chief of the SAO's Legal Unit walked in, accompanied by Daria's secretary. Gretchen looked real nervous. She stood at his side as he motioned for Vance to come over.

Manny had just walked in the courtroom himself, late as usual but only by about fifteen minutes, and dressed in the navy suit he and Daria had picked out on a rainy Sunday afternoon. He was surprised that the party was not in full swing. That Daria was not glaring at him with those fiery peepers of hers while she smiled in relief that he'd finally showed up. He figured he would mess with her head this morning. They still hadn't talked since she had drunk-dialed him. But now he watched as the frowning Chief of Legal shook his head at whatever Collier was saying and Daria's secretary kept shrugging.

Daria was nowhere to be found. A horrible feeling was building in his stomach.

He had started out the morning being both angry and anxious to see her again. Over the past couple of days he'd thought about the other night far too often and had come to the conclusion that she was either fucking with his head or she really did love him and she couldn't swallow that big fat Italian pride of hers to call and tell him it when she was sober. That made him even more mad. And really anxious. So he wasn't sure what he was gonna do after the hearing – scream at her or pull her into a hallway and kiss her. But the anger was gone. Now he was just scared. He made his way up to the threesome in the gallery, as Vance turned back to address the judge.

'Your Honor, we definitely have a problem and I am going to need a continuance till at least tomorrow,' Vance said.

'This is absolutely ridiculous . . .' Varlack grumbled loudly.

'Where is Ms DeBianchi?' the judge demanded.

'That's what we're trying to find out, Your Honor,' answered Collier.

'Is she hurt?'

'We don't know, Your Honor. We don't know where she is. She was supposed to speak at a law enforcement conference in Orlando on Tuesday, but I have just learned that she did not. No one knows where she is at this moment.'

Manny felt like he had been shot in the gut. He had the urge to run and do something, but he couldn't move. He was frozen in place.

'I would imagine that if she was in a car accident someone would have notified your office,' continued the judge skeptically.

'I'm not sure what we're dealing with yet, Your Honor.'

Judge Becker sighed. 'I don't mean to sound uncaring, but your office needs to get its act together. You have till two p.m. this afternoon, Mr Collier, to either find Ms DeBianchi, or handle this motion yourself. I'm not sure what stall tactics the state is trying, but I am out of patience, especially given Ms DeBianchi's previous disrespect of the court and defense counsel with that Brady violation.' She slapped the file closed on the bench and stood up.

'Your Honor, that only gives me three hours,' protested Vance.

'We're in recess till two,' replied the judge coldly.

Then she sailed off the bench.

51

'She checked in. She did not check out. Her suitcase is still in the room. But her cell, her car and her purse are gone,' the Chief of Legal said somberly. 'That's all we know right now.'

The four of them were standing in the hallway outside the courtroom: Gretchen, Vance, George and Manny. The door to the courtroom had been propped open slightly by Judge Becker's bailiff, who was transporting boxes to the clerk and didn't want it to lock automatically. Through the open sliver of doorway, Manny could see Lunders and his attorney joking and laughing with a couple of correction officers. Thank God the cameras had decided not to show up today. Even for blood-thirsty reporters, pre-trial motions were about as exciting as watching paint dry.

'Have you checked the hospitals?' asked Vance.

'We're on it now,' said George.

'Why are you only finding out about this now?' demanded Manny. 'What day did she check in? What hotel is it?'

Gretchen nibbled anxiously on a thumbnail. 'The Bonnet Creek Hilton in Buena Vista. She went up on Sunday.'

'That's three days ago. She was supposed to speak yesterday and never showed up? When was the last time anybody actually saw her?'

'Don't know that, either,' replied George.

'Didn't the damn maid figure out she hadn't slept in her bed for three damn nights?' asked Manny. His thoughts went to that voicemail she had left him Sunday.

I'm at this conference, see, and it's a hotel and I thought of the first time we were ever together . . .

She hadn't picked up when he'd finally called her back. And she hadn't texted him, either.

'There was a Do Not Disturb sign on her door,' Gretchen responded. 'The hotel just extended her room stay another night, since the SMART convention doesn't end till this afternoon, anyway. So no one actually checked the room until this morning, when we called. As for speakers not showing up, that happens. The organizers figured she'd gotten wrapped up in something, so they just covered her part with another speaker who was on the sexual predator panel.'

'I'm putting out a BOLO for her and her tag,' Manny said, reaching for his cell. A BOLO was police jargon for "be on the lookout for". 'I'll have Fort Lauderdale PD go out to her house in Victoria Park. Maybe she came home. Maybe something's happened with her family. I know her dad's been sick.'

'Was there a reason she would disappear? I know she's been stressed out about this, but, damn she's leaving us high and dry here,' Vance said with a heavy sigh. He looked more pissed off than concerned, and that was pissing off Manny.

Manny said nothing. All he could think about was that last phone call, how upset she sounded. How depressed. Alcohol and a broken heart don't mix. Jesus . . . A thousand bad scenarios were running through his head: Maybe she went out for a drive and was drunk and drove into a canal. Maybe she purposely drove into a canal. *No. No. Don't think like that.* Maybe she just got cold feet about the conference and the case and life in general and headed north on the Turnpike to see where it took her. Manny had thought about doing that a few times himself. Just up and walk out on everything, the way Dominick and C.J. had. And according to Dom, C.J. had gone and done it again.

But Daria hadn't answered her phone in three days. She hadn't texted him since Sunday. Right before they'd become lovers, she'd told him she'd never missed a day of work. Not one damn day. At the time he'd thought that was plain nuts – one more alarm he should be hearing that his firecracker prosecutor was a little OCD when it came to work.

'I'm putting a cell search out on her phone,' Manny added as he dialed his lieutenant. 'And I'm calling Orlando PD. I don't want no one touching that room till we get a crime-scene unit in there.' Something was wrong. Really wrong. He just knew it.

'Jesus Christ, Detective, let's not jump to conclusions now,' Vance protested. 'Especially crazy ones. We've had ASAs disappear before and the sky has not fallen in on them. All that's happened is that they had a personal

409

meltdown – some people can't help folding when they find themselves under pressure.'

'You mean like getting ready to take the heat for your bullshit decision to cut Bill Bantling a deal? Yeah, then she was under a lot of pressure.'

Vance's eyes became slits. 'I'm not going to get into a war with you, Detective. I'm not saying Daria ran away from the pressures she was under – which included, I'm sure, any personal damage she or her family might have suffered in the catastrophic hurricane that we all just went through. And any pressure she may have felt in trying a very important, very difficult, very circumstantial murder that has commanded the attention of the press. What I am saying is please hand all this investigating off to your lieutenant or someone else in your department or in Orlando or Fort Lauderdale, because you and I need to focus on the hearing that's going to be happening this afternoon.'

George looked around to make sure no one was listening. 'I have to ask this, Vance: was she on drugs?'

'No!' Manny erupted. 'What the fuck?'

George ignored the outburst. 'The question's going to be asked. Did she have a problem with drugs or alcohol?'

Vance sighed and shrugged, replying to the Chief of Legal as if Manny wasn't there. 'I don't know, George. I didn't know her very well outside the office. I hear she liked to party with the young ASAs, but does that mean she had a substance abuse problem? I don't know her well enough to say.'

'What are you two saying?' Manny slapped the wall behind him in frustration. 'Jesus Christ! I can tell you that Daria did not have a substance problem. She didn't

410

do drugs and . . .' He turned toward the door. 'She didn't even smoke. I'm not gonna sit around and let you smear her. I won't. I know her better than anyone else standing here. And she didn't just disappear to do lines or stretch her wings or get away from all of this shit and all of us. There is something wrong.'

'I agree,' Gretchen said quietly. 'I never saw or heard of Daria doing drugs or stuff. I do know she was under a lot of pressure from this case, though.'

This case.

Manny suddenly remembered the conversation he'd had with Lunders. He looked through the door into the courtroom, where Talbot was laughing with his attorneys as his smiling mommy in a low-cut blouse looked on.

It's a real shame that cute little prosecutor of mine couldn't be here . . . Little Lena needs to tend to that garden.

He remembered Daria's frightened reaction when he'd delivered Lunders's cryptic message to her, when she'd told him of the roses that had been massacred in her backyard, her once-colorful garden reduced to a graveyard of stems and thorns. Manny had dismissed it at the time, but now . . .

He looked back at Vance and his crony from Legal. He motioned to the courtroom. 'Where the hell has he been for the past three days?'

'Lunders? House arrest,' answered Vance, turning himself to look in the courtroom. 'You think he's involved?'

'Maybe . . . yes, I definitely think it's a possibility.'

'I'll check right now with Probation, but he's confined to his house on weekends and after-work hours, monitored twenty-four/seven with a GPS-equipped ankle bracelet that alerts his probation officer should he step one big toe off his family's compound. If that had happened, particularly on the eve of a court hearing, I would have had a phone call, and this morning I would've had a condition of release violation sitting on my desk, along with a request he be taken back into custody.' He reached for his cell and dialed. 'This is Chief Assistant Vance Collier with the Miami-Dade State Attorneys' Office,' he began, as he walked off down the hall.

Manny, Gretchen and George looked at each other for a long moment. It was Daria's secretary who finally said what everyone was now thinking. 'I hope she's okay, is all.'

Minutes later, Vance was back.

'I'm headed up to Fort Lauderdale—' Manny began.

'The hell you are. Didn't you hear Judge Becker?'

'Yeah. And I also heard your lead prosecutor is missing.'

Vance shook his head. 'As cold as this might sound, Detective, we have a hearing in three hours. A hearing that's happening whether we want it to or not. I'm not waiting for Daria to walk back in and save the day at one fifty-nine p.m. And I'm not going to lose this motion. If that happens, a murderer is going to go free, and I won't let that happen. So you and I need to get familiar with what it is you're going to testify to so we can at least get one scumbag back off the streets.'

Manny looked in the direction of the courtroom. 'Where was he?'

'He was home all night with his mother,' Vance replied quietly. 'It's just the two of them – his father's overseas

412

on a business trip. Your boy hasn't even been going into work. His probation officer did a fly-by on the house last night; he was home and everything looked okay. Said the most Talbot Lunders did was watch movies and surf the Internet.'

52

For the first time in a very long time, Chief Felony Assistant Vance Collier was sweating in a courtroom, even though the air conditioning was working just fine. The motion to suppress the search warrant of Abby Lunders's Mercedes was to have been handled by Daria. She'd never expressed a real concern with losing it. As a Division Chief, she'd handled her fair share of motions and knew the basic law when it came to challenging a warrant. But she was not here and, as Judge Becker had insisted, the show must go on. So Vance had done his best speed-read through Lunders's motion, Daria's response, the search warrant itself and Manny Alvarez's accompanying affidavit. And the first thing he'd noticed was the very fine, very particular, and very troubling problem that everyone had apparently missed, including defense counsel, because he hadn't raised it in his motion. For Vance, though, it was like looking at a misspelled word in the title of an otherwise perfect thesis. His brain kept returning to the mistake, again and again, wondering when everyone else was finally going to spot it, too.

Through dogged detective work, Manny Alvarez had identified Talbot Lunders as a suspect in Holly Skole's murder. Marie Modic – the witness who was now no longer going to be able to testify to anything because she was dead – had ID'd Talbot in the still-shot of the Menace surveillance video as the man she'd talked to the night Holly went missing. Marie Modic had given Manny the name 'T'. She'd ID'd the Mercedes key. And, most importantly, she had given Manny the name Automotive Experts on the Mercedes key ring, which was what led Manny to the car dealership and Abby Lunders's Benz. From there, Talbot Lunders was ID'd through his mother's insurance records and then his driver's license photo. Add in the video of Holly seen getting into the Benz, and there was more than enough probable cause to believe that the Mercedes might contain evidence of a crime, to wit: murder, and more than enough evidence to support the issuance of a warrant to search the car. Judge Paulus, the on-duty Circuit Court judge, had thought so, too, which is why he'd signed off on it. Perfect.

Except for one little, tiny, major fucking problem. Like the misspelling in the thesis title, it all came down to one word. *One cursed word* . . .

So that the whole system is not undermined because one judge's idea of probable cause differs from another's, a warrant that's been signed off on by a judge is presumed valid. End of story. The only legal way for a defense attorney to attack a warrant's probable cause – or lack thereof – would be to prove that the detective lied about

415

the facts or intentionally misled the judge in the affidavit. In other words – fraud. Talbot Lunders's misplaced argument was that since Marie Modic could not be questioned by defense counsel about what she had witnessed, any hearsay statements she gave Manny Alvarez were suspect and the warrant should therefore be tossed, along with any evidence that was found in the Benz. And since the evidence in the Benz was what led Manny to search Talbot's boat, the fibers found there would go, too. There was no way the circumstantial case against Talbot Lunders could survive if the warrant was tossed.

The warrant had to survive.

And Vance had to avoid calling attention to the one-word landmine that was waiting to be stepped on. The fact Justice Joe hadn't raised an obscure, hot-button issue that could get his client off didn't mean an experienced judge wouldn't see it.

'The law is clear,' Vance said, carefully choosing his words. 'In order to challenge the warrant by attacking the veracity of Marie Modic's statements, the defendant must show that the detective intentionally, or with reckless disregard for the truth, included a false statement in the affidavit. There's been no evidence presented here today to support that, or that Detective Alvarez in any way misled Judge Paulus into signing the warrant. None whatsoever, Your Honour. The defendant has not met his burden and the warrant must stand. The defense can attack the veracity of a witness's statements at deposition and at trial, but not through a motion to suppress.'

It was like affirming the sturdiness of the roof of a house that's got water damage in its basement. His argument was legally correct, and the roof was definitely sound, but there still lurked a major problem somewhere. If you started to rip apart the walls, you just might see the rotten plumbing.

Judge Becker stared at Vance, her head slightly cocked, as though she was waiting for him to say something more. She waved off Joe Varlack, who'd opened his mouth to respond. 'Of course, that can't happen in this case, Mr Collier,' she remarked coolly, 'because Ms Modic won't be giving a deposition or testifying at trial. She's dead.'

'She was murdered, Your Honor.'

'Sad, but for purposes of this hearing, irrelevant. So the defense is stuck with what they're stuck with?' the judge mused. 'You get what you get in Detective Alvarez's warrant and you don't get upset.' She leaned back in her chair and tapped her finger on her copy of the motion. 'Ms Modic is dead and the defense can't question her about what she saw or how she saw it. They have no idea whether she was a *reliable* witness because they've never met her. They cannot assess her *credibility*,' she finished, deliberately enunciating her words.

Shit. Vance looked down at his notes on the podium. A drop of sweat had fallen from his forehead on to the paper. He watched it roll down the motion, smearing ink and distorting words as it did. The house was still standing, but here came the city inspector, knocking on beams and probing dark corners, looking for the damage she knew existed inside.

The judge pointed her pen at Manny, who was seated at the state's table. 'Detective Alvarez, you're still under oath. I have a question or two. Why did you refer to Ms Modic in your affidavit as "an anonymous source"? Why was she not named?'

Bing. Vance closed his eyes. The judge had spotted the misspelling in the title, too. The building inspector was now inside the house and headed for the basement stairs.

The questions that Vance had feared were now flying rapid-fire across the room. And of course, all that activity woke up Justice Joe from the nap his brain had been taking. Vance could see him flipping through notes, writing things down, his thin, yellowed ponytail draped over his shoulder like an old cat's tail. He may not yet know exactly what the issue was, but he'd figured out there was one.

'Because she was terrified that the defendant might find her if she was identified through the warrant,' Manny explained. 'Given what'd happened to Holly, I can't say I blame her. If Marie Modic hadn't escaped through the back door of that club that night, it might well have been her murder I was investigating.' He looked over at Talbot Lunders, who was staring straight ahead, unmoved. 'And now look how things turned out for her.'

'Let's not go there, Detective.' The judge sighed and peered over her glasses at Vance. 'Therein lies the problem, and you know it, Mr Collier. Oh, you definitely know it.'

Vance turned red. One cursed word had changed absolutely everything in an otherwise airtight search warrant. A warrant that had yielded basically the only physical evidence in a circumstantial case. *Anonymous.* Out came the sledgehammers. The walls were coming down.

'A search warrant is a powerful instrument,' the judge continued, choosing her words just as carefully as Vance had, but he knew that was for the court reporter's benefit.

She was laying a record for the inevitable appeal. 'It allows the police to go into a person's home, business or vehicle and search for evidence of a crime. The affidavit that accompanies a search warrant must establish that probable cause exists to believe that, one, a crime has occurred and, two, certain evidence of that crime will be found in the location to be searched. Probable cause is established by facts. Those facts have to be set out in the detective's affidavit, so that the judge can assess if there is probable cause just by looking at the affidavit itself. So the detective doesn't have to drag before the judge every witness who provided him with information, the courts have established rules regarding the credibility of witnesses.

'The problem we have with Detective Alvarez's affidavit is that probable cause was established by the use of an anonymous source, namely Marie Modic. Ms Modic's identity was not made known in the affidavit. It therefore was not made known to Judge Paulus. The courts have recognized a distinction between *named* citizen informants and *confidential* informants or *anonymous* sources. Information provided by a *named* citizen informant is presumed to be reliable, but information from a *confidential* informant or *anonymous* source is not. It may be an order of semantics in the case at bar, but that's the law. The reliability of a confidential informant or anonymous source must be established independently and specifically set out in the affidavit. Particularly dubious is any information provided by an anonymous source, which is the legal equivalent of a tipster calling into the 911 line. There's no way to independently verify the tipster's credibility because you don't know who he or she is.

'In his affidavit, Detective Alvarez relied on the hearsay statements of an anonymous source – a source whose identity he actually did know, but was understandably trying to protect. Unfortunately, though, the reliability of this source was not established in the affidavit.'

'Your Honor,' Vance protested, 'I know where you're going with this and I have to interject before you get there. Even if Marie Modic was improperly named as an anonymous source by Detective Alvarez, it was an unintentional oversight. As you said, it's semantics. She was obviously a citizen informant, because he *knew* her identity. But even if the court wants to treat Ms Modic as an anonymous source, the information that she provided *was* independently verified by Detective Alvarez when he searched Automotive Experts records and ultimately discovered Talbot Lunders's identity.'

The judge shook her head. 'That's not enough independent corroboration for me.'

Manny felt his gut churn. The fast legal banter was like listening to two people argue in Russian – he wasn't getting all of it, but he'd quickly figured out things were bad. It was hard enough to be sitting in this witness chair helplessly listening to suits duke it out over legal semantics while precious seconds ticked away and the world fell apart a couple of hundred miles to the north, but to see his case unravel because of some obscure legal bullshit that he maybe should've thought of but didn't when he wrote up a damn warrant months ago was too much to take. All he saw was Daria's face, all he could hear was the message she left for him three nights ago. He had to find her. Everything else seemed trivial in comparison; it was time to make everyone understand that.

He stood at the state's table. 'Your Honor, Judge Paulus knew who Marie Modic was. He knew she was not just some tipster off the 911 line. I told him her name, all the information I had on her. He asked me why she was anonymous. And I told him what I just told you, about her being scared and all, and he nodded and said, "Smart." Then he signed the warrant.' Manny turned to Vance. 'I'm sure Judge Paulus would remember.'

Judge Becker shook her head again and picked up the affidavit, dangling it before her as if it smelled bad. 'The law only lets me look at the four corners of the warrant. Any conversation you had with the issuing judge is outside these four corners.'

Vance was shaking his head in resignation and Manny knew it was over. 'This is crazy,' Manny yelled. 'I've been a cop for twenty-three years. This is totally crazy. Are you kidding me, Collier?'

'This is the law. Take it or leave it, gentlemen. Or better yet learn it so that these problems won't lead to the downfall of your cases. Maybe Ms DeBianchi stayed up in Disney for a reason, because she didn't want to come back to the mess she'd left here.' The judge sighed. 'This court cannot overlook that the state has already committed serious Brady violations, including withholding evidence from the defense about similar murders. This court is deeply disturbed by the state's lack of candor, and that includes you, too, Mr Collier. I watched you dance around the issue of Ms Modic being an anonymous source because you thought you could get away with it. Since Mr Varlack didn't think to bring it up you weren't going to, either. Well, the court doesn't work that way. So if I toss this

421

warrant, tell me right now – what is the physical evidence you have against Mr Lunders?'

Vance rubbed the back of his head. He didn't want to go into what he had or didn't have in open court, but the judge was beyond pissed. 'We have torn fibers from the victim's shirt that were found in the defendant's boat, along with the defendant's attempt to flee the jurisdiction before his arrest.'

'That's it in the physical evidence department, then? You don't have a smoking gun out there, do you? Or a video of the defendant with Ms Skole's dead body? Or, given the state's previous conduct, a video of *someone else* with Ms Skole's dead body? As far as your fiber evidence goes, perhaps Ms Skole and Mr Lunders had a passionate interlude on that boat and neither wanted to take the time to open a button.'

'Judge, Ms Skole was raped and murdered. The court's comments are in poor taste.'

'Don't play pious with me, State. And don't think for a minute that that's not how the defense will be explaining it to a jury. There was no blood or bodily fluids or DNA evidence on those fibers, was there?'

'With all due respect, I would think the defense would come up with their own theory of the case, instead of the court assisting them.'

'I am telling you how I see your evidence so far,' the judge replied icily.

'Thank you. I'm quite sure Mr Varlack appreciates that.'

'So *this* is what I am going to hear at trial? *This* is your case?'

'I really didn't think I would be trying my whole case in front of you today, Judge. That's not why we're here.'

'Get over your shyness, Mr Collier. If you can't share the facts of your case with your judge, who can you share them with?'

'This was supposed to be argued by Ms DeBianchi, Your Honor.'

'Get over that, too. You're the quarterback now and you've just been handed the football. You're running out of time to make a final play. Give me your best Hail Mary.'

The walls began to crack, fanning out through the entire structure, toppling the floors, as the house with the sturdy roof imploded.

'The defendant signed off on shipments to his company of sulfuric acid. That was the chemical used to burn off Ms Skole's feet.'

'Interesting, but I think your average science teacher can buy sulfuric acid.'

'Your Honor,' Vance tried. 'Ms Modic told Detective Alvarez that she believed she was drugged by Talbot Lunders.'

'Another very interesting fact that is also hearsay, because unfortunately Ms Modic will not be around to tell us that at trial.'

'There's more to this case than—'

'Enough.' The judge waved her hand, as she might to stop a child from arguing with her. 'The warrant is out. And I'm going to save the state a lot of money and time here. I'm going to do something it does not have the guts to do. I'm going to pull the plug on this dying patient. Without the physical evidence from the Benz I just don't see how you are going to get past a JOA, Mr Collier.'

A JOA stood for Judgment of Acquittal. If, after the

state presented its case, the trial judge found there was insufficient evidence for a conviction, she could take the matter out of the jury's hands and acquit the defendant herself.

'Even with the warrant,' she continued, 'you have torn fibers from Holly Skole's shirt, evidence she was in the car with your defendant and evidence that she's dead, but that's about it. And you have at least four other people who were murdered and branded in the same way, and your defendant supposedly has an alibi for each of them. It sounds like you have a serial killer on your hands, Mr Collier – perhaps Detective Alvarez should be out there looking for *him*. And while I agree it would be nice of Mr Lunders to volunteer some information about where he and Ms Skole went after they left Club Menace and exactly what they did on that expensive boat of his, he's just not going to do that. And you can't make him. So as far as I've heard, you don't have anything that directly connects him with her murder.'

'There's no motion to dismiss before you!' Vance yelled, exasperated.

'I'll entertain a motion, *ore tenus*. Mr Varlack?' asked the judge.

Justice Joe jumped up. He might have gotten a late start, but he performed right on cue. 'I move the court for a dismissal of all charges against my client.'

Vance knew what was coming. It was seconds away from happening. And once the judge actually uttered the words 'case dismissed' there would be no going back – Talbot Lunders would walk free. 'Your Honor, there is something that needs to be brought to your attention before you dismiss this case. Can we go sidebar?'

'No,' replied Becker.

'There is something the court needs to know, but as it relates to a pending criminal investigation, I would rather not say in open court.'

'Does it concern Mr Lunders and this case?'

'Yes.'

The judge waved her pen in the air again. 'Then out with it. I warned you already to keep the court fully advised. You and Ms DeBianchi love to play games, don't you? You know the road I'm headed down, and I'm just about at the door. You have my attention, Mr Collier, so say what you have to say. But I'm warning you, this had better be good.'

53

Bill Bantling stared at the pretty courthouse, with its towering arched doorways and quaint clock tower. The manicured lawn and colorful flowerbeds. The carved wood doors, where tourists like himself wandered in and out, admiring the architecture. He took a deep breath and inhaled the fresh mountain and sea air.

She was a long way from South Florida. The criminal courthouse in Miami was a dump. A 1960s design catastrophe that could never be corrected or updated, no matter how much money the taxpayers threw at it. There were no visiting tourists taking pictures of the ugly escalators, no docent tours being offered by cute, helpful old people. It was a crowded, chaotic pit of criminals and immigrants, most of whom had never seen a can of deodorant, much less had their shots. From Bill's recent brief stay in the Dade County Jail, it was safe to say that nothing much had changed in the years since his last visit.

He picked his false teeth with a matchbook cover as his

tour mates oohed and aahed in the Mural Room, touted proudly by the guide as 'the jewel of the courthouse'. But instead of admiring the lovely mural that depicted scenes of California's past, Bill's mind was wandering to the courtroom right above his head.

She hadn't slept a wink last night – Chloe. Tossing and turning. Up every hour, checking the windows, then the doors, then the windows again. She must have seen the news about his escape. Peeking out from behind Grandma's yellowed lace curtains into the black night, wondering, he was sure, if the Big Bad Wolf was out there somewhere, waiting for her in the dark woods that were her backyard. Licking his chops and sharpening his nails, biding his time – waiting for the right moment to come and eat her up.

Sleepy Goleta, California, was no Queens, New York – the city that never sleeps. Or turns off its lights. In the California mountains, when nighttime came, people went to bed, everything went black and you could actually see the stars in the sky. He'd enjoyed that – lying in the dark watching the stars twinkle above him, his hand on his cock, thinking bad thoughts of her wrapped up in nothing but Grandma's lace curtains. He hadn't star-gazed before he was sent to prison, but when he was in that septic tank, it was something he'd often dreamed about doing, probably because he'd been told he'd never again be able to. Same as feeling sunlight on his skin. Naturally, the first thing he'd done when he got off the bus in LA was find a patch of beach and get a sunburn. After a few minutes in the dark woods though, with just himself and an old fantasy, he'd had enough. The star-gazing shit reminded him of yet another thing that the bitch had deprived him of for the past decade, and his hard-on had deflated. Anger had replaced the sweet memories.

She hadn't slept at all. But she hadn't picked up and left town. When the morning came, she'd put on a black suit, taken her fat briefcase and her mean-looking doggie and headed off to the courthouse to ruin some other poor schmuck's life, probably figuring that she was over-thinking it all. Worrying too much. Rationalizing that he would not be able to find her, all the way across the country in sleepy Goleta. Or that he wouldn't waste his precious freedom trying to track her down. Or that if he really wanted to, he would've found her already – seeing as the news was reporting he'd escaped weeks ago – so therefore he must not even be looking.

Whatever she had figured, she'd figured wrong.

The group moved up the main staircase, its walls detailed in Tunisian tiles. He ogled the decorative bench, the terra cotta steps, right along with the tourists. The lady next to him with the enormous ass and flowered polyester shirt smiled when he offered to hold her cane and help her up the stairs. He pulled on his thick gray whiskers and smiled back. Romance was in the air.

The tour guide stopped outside a closed courtroom door. 'Is that a criminal case that's being heard in there?' Bill asked.

'Yes. The courthouse handles both civil and criminal cases. Right now, Judge Cassidy is hearing the *People v. Richard Kassner*. It's an arson and murder case. The defendant is accused of setting fire to his former residence with his ex-wife and mother-in-law sleeping inside. The ex made it out, but the mother-in-law didn't.' The guide put a finger to his lips, opened the door and stuck his head in. He popped back out and shut the door. 'Sorry. They're in closing arguments right now so we can't go in.'

'Oh, I would've liked to have seen that,' Bill replied, making a sad face.

'Me, too,' said his new lady-friend. 'I just love *The People's Court*.'

Bill grinned. 'I'm a *Judge Judy* fan. And *Judge Alex*. You name it. Anything legal.'

She grinned sheepishly and the tour moved on.

He couldn't help himself. He let the group work its way down the hall before he cracked open Judge Cassidy's courtroom door and took a peek inside. His heart was beating quick, the adrenaline racing through his veins.

There she was, standing in front of a jury in her snappy suit and high heels, her back to him, asking twelve men and women to convict a man. To send yet another one off to the Big House for a few dozen years. Or maybe she was asking for a death sentence. He wasn't really listening to what she was saying and he didn't care. He was just focused on her. The jury was, too. They seemed to be lapping up her every word.

Chloe did have a way with people. She drew them to her, like a magnet draws another magnet. They were probably mesmerized by her. The women included. Her chestnut hair fell to her shoulders, surprisingly still full and thick and wavy. He was disappointed to see it wasn't blonde, though. He watched as her small, delicate hands gestured to the jury, watched as she moved about before them. He listened to her soft, slightly raspy, forceful voice. He couldn't see her face, but he knew it was still beautiful,

429

even if it was now buried in wrinkles and worry lines. She would always be beautiful. Perfect bone structure, she had. Great genes. High cheekbones, heart-shaped chin, perfectly arched eyebrows, porcelain complexion, fiery, emerald eyes. A beauty that would defy time, like a Greek goddess. That's why he'd chosen her in the first place. Chloe was not merely pretty – she was exceptional. Without so much as a smudge of makeup, she was perfect. A beauty like that could not be restrained or hidden with a drab hair color and plain clothes and glasses. It was funny she would ever have thought so. He stood there and watched her until the judge turned in his direction and, with a frown, waved him off. He popped back out into the hall just as the prosecutor turned around to see who her judge had gotten so irritated at.

'I've never seen a live trial,' he whispered to his lady-friend, who was waiting for him outside the door when he came out. 'Couldn't resist taking a peek.'

She laughed. 'Was it exciting?'

'Oh, yes,' he replied, his hand gently supporting her elbow as he escorted her down the hallway to where the rest of the group was waiting. 'Thrilling. I can't wait to hear how it all ends . . .'

54

Vance didn't want to pull this card, but he was out of choices. With the warrant overruled, the judge was right – the case was gone. But if she at least kept the case alive, then he could appeal her ruling on the warrant, which would stop the speedy clock. It would take at least a couple of months for an appellate court to hear the issue. He thought he could make at least a decent argument with respect to Manny Alvarez's independent corroboration of Marie Modic's identification to get past the whole anonymous source/reliability problem. A pending appeal might buy him enough time to get Bantling back in the cage and to build a case for the snuff-club murders against Lunders.

'Your Honor, Talbot Lunders *is* a possible suspect in other murders. In fact, it is believed he is a member of an international snuff club.'

The few spectators who were sitting in the gallery collectively gasped.

'A what?' the judge asked incredulously.

'A snuff club. An organization of individuals who participate in the hunt for, and ultimately the murder of, select human beings. The murders are recorded on a live video feed before an audience made up of other members of this club. Their victims include Ms Skole and Ms Vechio – the victim seen in the video – along with the other unsolved homicides that Your Honor referred to earlier which the City of Miami is now investigating, hence my telling the court that this is an open investigation. Mr Lunders's involvement in this organization, even if only peripheral, may ultimately result in several other murder indictments against him. Dismissing this case now and releasing the defendant from the controls of at least house arrest before those indictments are readied will endanger the community. The state believes that should the defendant get his passport back, he will flee the country.'

'This is ridiculous! This is the first we're hearing of any of this!' erupted Justice Joe.

'So you're asking me to hold the defendant on this murder case, Mr Collier, because the flimsy evidence I have heard so far may ultimately tie Mr Lunders into this snuff club you speak of and other murders?'

'Yes.'

'So you want me to *not* do my job while you stall for more time to do yours, all under the explicit threat that if *I* let the defendant go, any harm that may come to the community as a result thereof is my doing?'

'No, that is not what I am saying—'

'That is exactly what you're saying. How long have you known about this supposed snuff-club involvement, Mr Collier?'

'I'm not sure. Ms DeBianchi is actively working it.'

'Aah . . . Ms DeBianchi, who has earned the glorious reputation of holding back on the defense. I'm going to guess you've known for a while, then, hence the reason for the Brady violations. What evidence do you have to support this snuff-club accusation? Please tell me there are actual witnesses this time. Witnesses who are still capable of testifying.'

'Yes, Your Honor. We do have a witness,' replied Vance slowly. He was treading on really thin ice. If Bantling's name got out, this would be all over the press. Everywhere.

'Don't ask me to trust you,' chided the judge. 'We are beyond that.'

He'd said enough. He'd revealed too much. But he couldn't let Lunders go free. Now that Bantling was AWOL, and Judge Lepidus was dead, Lunders was the last remaining known connection to the snuff club. If he skipped town and went to join Daddy in Switzerland, there would be no way to investigate him.

'I don't want to reveal the name at this time, Your Honor. It's an open investigation. Many lives are potentially in danger.'

The judge nodded thoughtfully. 'Okay. I'll listen to the witness myself, in my chambers. If I feel then that the state is not stalling and that there is enough evidence to support either an amendment of the indictment and/or additional charges, I will not dismiss this matter. In fact, I may just remand Mr Lunders, given the seriousness of these charges. Let's do this ASAP: there's a speedy demand.'

'Your Honor,' Joe Varlack objected. 'My client's done nothing to violate the conditions of his release—'

'One fire at a time, Mr Varlack. I want to hear from this witness.'

'Judge, may I request a sidebar again?' Vance asked quietly.

The judge's eyes became slits. 'What is it this time, Mr Collier? What is the problem with producing this witness for me? Because there is a problem, isn't there?'

'The witness is unavailable at this moment. That will hopefully be resolved very, very shortly. If we could just go sidebar . . .'

The judge cocked an eyebrow as it all became clear to her. 'Is your witness unavailable because he has absconded from the jurisdiction?'

Vance looked down at the podium. 'The witness is unavailable, Your Honor.'

The judge sat back in her seat. 'Now I understand. I got it. Whoo. Two plus two is four. Your witness is William Bantling, isn't that right, state? I can't believe this – your witness is Cupid.'

55

There were no cameras in the courtroom, but that didn't mean that what the judge had just said and what Vance was about to confirm would not be national news.

'Yes, Your Honor. The witness the state is referring to is William Bantling.'

The judge shook her head. 'Your witness is not merely unavailable. Your witness is a convicted serial killer who is currently occupying the number two spot on the FBI's Most Wanted list. He's a fugitive. Wow.'

'There are extenuating circumstances, Your Honor.'

The judge shook her head. 'I know what you are trying to do. I understand it now, Mr Collier. Apparently Bill Bantling has made some sort of a statement implicating Mr Lunders in criminal activity, which is probably why he was shipped down here in the first place, and you want me to hold Mr Lunders in custody hoping your friends at the FBI find him before your time on *this* case runs out. I get it. You cut a deal with a serial killer. But Mr Bantling is not in custody. He's on the lam and no

435

one has a clue where he is. He could be gone for the next twenty years. The problem I have is the same one I had a half-hour ago: it's not *my* job to keep *your* defendant behind bars when you don't have the facts to support holding him. The possible involvement of Bill Bantling as a witness against Mr Lunders, while disturbing, does not change things. Therefore, I am in the same position I was in a half-hour ago.'

'Your Honor, I would like to move once again for the dismissal of all charges against Talbot Lunders,' piped up Varlack.

The judge sighed heavily. 'Granted, without prejudice for the state to re-file. So if you can find more evidence or you can find William Bantling, have at it, Mr Collier.'

'Objection!' Vance began to yell.

'Noted,' replied the judge, cutting him off.

Talbot gave his attorney a huge grin. Then he turned to his mother, who was sitting in the row immediately behind him, and pumped his fist in the air.

'I'll prepare the order myself,' Judge Becker finished, rising. She looked over at the defense table with a frown that was different from the annoyed one she'd held on to for the hearing. This time she seemed worried. 'Case dismissed. Mr Lunders, you are free to go.'

56

'The hotel room was clean, Detective Alvarez,' said Brian O'Dea, the Orlando PD homicide detective, over the phone. 'No prints, no messages, nothing. We've pulled surveillance on the parking lots. We think we have her on a video leaving the Hilton with a tall, dark-haired guy. He slipped on sunglasses right before the camera caught him, so we're figuring he knew the camera was watching and knew not to get caught on it. That makes us think this was planned out. That it could be an abduction. We're exploring that. We'll get you a still shot of the guy, Detective, but I'm warning you, it's not great.'

Manny stood in Daria's kitchen and stared out her sliding glass doors on to her ugly, dead garden. There were no flowers. Just a barren patch of thorny stems where her roses presumably once stood proud. Any floral life that had survived the rose massacre was killed off or carried off by the hurricane. In the corner of her small cement patio was a pile of broken roof tiles, ripped screening and a heap of palm fronds – trash from Artemis.

This was the first time Manny had been to her townhouse since the hurricane. He had had coffee in her garden one morning, not so long ago. He'd watched, as he sat at a wobbly, wrought-iron table for two that his ass had barely fit in, while she potted some baskets with all sorts of colorful flowers whose names he didn't know and couldn't pronounce. She'd used some herbs she'd grown to make him an omelet that day. Or rather, he'd made the omelet because she couldn't cook worth a damn.

'Any luck on her cell?' he asked, rubbing his eyes and turning away from the doors.

'No. It's still off. Hasn't been turned on since Sunday night. If it goes back on, we can track it.'

'I got a subpoena into AT&T to pull the records and texts. Maybe there's something on it,' Manny said softly. 'I should have those by the morning. Normally that takes a few days, but they're rushing it through.'

'Good,' the Orlando detective replied.

'And her car?'

'It was in the lot, parked in the back. From the surveillance videos, it looks like it hasn't moved since Sunday, either. We got Crime Scene going over it right now, but nothing so far. We got the waitress working with a sketch artist to get a composite of the guy who she said bought Daria a drink Sunday night. Maybe we'll get something off that. And we're running tags of the cars that left the parking lot around the same time as Daria and this dark-haired guy left the hotel. We're hoping the car was in a ticketed lot.'

'Did he pay with credit? Did he pay the waitress with credit?'

'Wouldn't that be nice? No. Cash.'

438

Back to the question of what then? What if she meant what she'd said? What if a smart, sophisticated, sometimes bitchy, beautiful woman really meant it when she said she loved him?

'Okay, keep me advised.'

'Where you at now?' O'Dea asked.

'Her house in Fort Lauderdale. We're sweeping it, but like you said, so far nothing. Got guys fanning out across the neighborhood to see if anyone noticed something – anything – out of the ordinary. A suspicious person around her house the last couple of weeks, maybe; anyone following her to the Internet coffee shop down the block in Victoria Park, where she liked to do work, or maybe to the supermarket, or the bagel store, or the cleaners. I don't know. I'm reaching here, but it's all I got.'

'We'll find something, Detective Alvarez. Hold on, now. She's a prosecutor, right? She knows how to handle herself, I'm sure.'

The Orlando detective's words weren't helping. Because she was a prosecutor, Daria was a bit paranoid. And always prepared. She knew what was out there. She knew all the tricks on how not to be a victim. She always locked her door. She always locked her car. She never walked down dark alleys or in dark parking lots. She carried mace in her purse and a Beretta Tomkat in her glove compartment. She gave speeches to local schools and community awareness meetings on protecting yourself from cyber predators and parking-lot stalkers. She knew enough to avoid the bad guys, so the fact that she was missing spoke volumes about just how much trouble she was in.

Daria's brother, Marco, walked into the kitchen, arms folded across his chest. He had circles under his eyes. Behind him was his wife, CeCe, who gently rubbed his shoulder. Today was the first time Manny had met the man that Daria loved to tell childhood stories about. The big brother who was her best friend while they were growing up. The triplets that she often babysat and bought Poprocks and Charleston Chews for whenever she passed a candy store, were at home, Marco had told him, being looked after by Daria's mother. Daria's father, unfortunately, was not doing well with the news of Daria's disappearance. He'd started having chest pains and was now in ICU over at Memorial West. It wasn't looking good. Marco mouthed the word, 'Anything?'

Manny shook his head. 'Keep me advised,' he told the sergeant as a glum Mike Dickerson walked into the kitchen. 'We'll keep digging down here. Maybe we'll find something,' he finished, turning away from Marco and Mike. But he doubted it. Like Holly Skole and Gabriella Vechio and Marie Modic and Jane Doe and Kevin Flaunders and Cyndi DeGregorio, and all eleven of Cupid's victims, Daria DeBianchi had gone to a bar, met someone, and simply vanished into the night.

The big detective willed back tears as he watched crime-scene techs in protective clothing comb through her dead garden. He hated himself at that moment. If he had only picked up the phone that night when she kept calling. If he had only spoken to her . . .

Then he'd say it back. Because it was true. He loved her.

But he hadn't. He'd been mad and stubborn and stupid. He remembered her face as she worked in the garden. The sweat that ran down her cheeks, cutting a path through the streak of potting soil on her skin. Her red hair was pulled up into a floppy pony, her hands were caked in dark dirt. Dressed in his shirt, she wore four-inch platform sandals even for gardening and they showed off her legs, which were in desperate need of a tan, but still beautiful.

Now she was gone. And there would be no more opportunities to tell her how he really felt about her, because deep down in his heart he already knew he'd never see her again.

At least not alive.

57

'As to the lesser included charge of Murder in the Second Degree in the death of Elizabeth Fabrizio, we the people of the County of Santa Barbara in the State of California do find the defendant, Richard Kassner, guilty. As to the charge of Arson in the First Degree in Count II of the Indictment, we the people of the County of Santa Barbara in and for the State of California do find the defendant Robert Kassner guilty, so say we all.'

The twelve members of the jury looked everywhere but at the defense table as the judge individually polled them, then thanked them for their service and discharged them. Richard Kassner sat in silence at the defense table. His trophy wife cried. His ex-wife cheered. C.J. thought back to that day in the courtroom when he had shot her that smug, menacing look. Now it was her turn. But she couldn't gloat in the end. She looked away as he was led out the side door in cuffs, tearing up as he said goodbye to his infant son.

It had been a long, drawn-out, almost ten-week fight

for justice, but C.J. did not feel victorious. She never did after a verdict. A woman was dead, a daughter lost her mother, a wife lost her husband, a baby would grow up without a father. Life was irrevocably transformed for so many people. That didn't change with a guilty verdict.

There was no longer a need to wait for the defendant to clear the courtroom before C.J. herself headed out. She packed up her files and shook hands with Jessica Kassner, assuring her that the People would seek the maximum sentence at her ex-husband's sentencing hearing, which the judge had set down for October. C.J. felt slightly guilty, knowing that Jessica was under the impression that it would be ADA Christina Towns physically standing at that podium arguing for a life sentence, when C.J. already knew she would be long gone from the office by then. She watched Jessica slowly walk out of the courtroom alone, dressed in a long-sleeved suit that covered the disfiguring burns on her arms. She was followed shortly thereafter by an inconsolable and dramatically aged Trophy Wife and her new baby. No, there were no winners here today. There was no cause for celebration.

It was only 2:30 in the afternoon. The streets around the courthouse and city hall were busy with workers still on their lunch hour, citizens paying light bills, tourists taking pictures. Dozens and dozens of strange faces all around her. Bill Bantling was a master of disguise. She knew he could be anywhere. He could be anyone. Just because she didn't see him didn't mean he wasn't there. Her heart beat hard in her chest. She fought back the beginnings of a panic attack and headed across the street to the office.

She briefed Jason Mucci – the Chief Deputy DA who had been clumsy around her ever since she'd turned down his offer to go car shopping – about the verdict. She told him what she was expecting at sentencing, which had been set down for the early part of October. And she told him she would be taking some time off, starting this afternoon. He just nodded, no questions asked. Of course, like Jessica Kassner, he thought she would be coming back. Then she made her way to her office to clear work off her desk. She hated leaving ends undone, particularly seeing as she had no plans to return. Criminal cases always had issues to worry about, so she spelled them out and pasted them on hot pink sticky notes to all of her files.

When she finally looked up at her window it was dark out. The streets were empty and quiet, the office deserted, apart from the cleaning crew. She took a final look around, packed up her briefcase and grabbed her purse.

She was going to make good on her promise to Dominick. He didn't believe it. He didn't trust her. But she knew she would make good. He had given her a second chance. She would make things right between them. She swallowed the lump in her throat.

First, however, she had things to do.

Then she flipped out the light and headed for home.

58

Manny wasn't quite sure if it was the six-pack he'd downed or the fact that he'd been up all night drinking it, but the front doors of the Palm Beach mansion were starting to blur. He put down his binoculars and rubbed his eyes. They hurt. Everything hurt. Nowhere was the pain as severe as his chest.

Five days. It had been five days since Daria had disappeared. Since she'd stepped out of the doors of the Hilton hotel and vanished. Every police department from Orlando to Miami was actively looking for her. Every police department around the country had been notified via teletype with her photo that she had gone missing under suspicious circumstances. BOLOs had been issued, a missing persons alert had been placed in FCIC/NCIC. But the problem was, no one knew where to look.

The most promising lead they had so far was also potentially the most disturbing. A surveillance camera had captured the tag numbers of all vehicles exiting the parking lot of the Hilton around the same time cameras had caught Daria leaving the hotel with a tall, dark-haired, sunglass-wearing stranger. A check of all those tags had been done. Most of the tags belonged to rental cars, and each renter had been tracked down and questioned. All but one had been found.

A black Ford Flex SUV was rented from Hertz out of Orlando airport the Sunday morning of Daria's disappearance to a Reid Smith from Uniondale, New York. It was returned the following day at the same location. Nothing remarkable there. But when Nassau County detectives tried to contact Reid Smith at the address on his DL, they found that he hadn't lived there in years. Even more troubling, though, was where that old address was located – right beneath a long closed and shuttered funeral home that had been the scene of a horrible crime back in 2007.

Kreller's Funeral Home had made news when the young daughter of its owner, John Kreller, told a preschool classmate some of the gruesome things she had seen in her daddy's basement involving bodies that might not have been dead yet. The four-year-old classmate understandably had terrible nightmares that caused him to wake in the middle of the night screaming. Eventually his concerned mommy took him to a child psychologist, who pried out of the little boy the terrible secret he had sworn to keep, and a criminal investigation was reluctantly opened. As the ME's office worked to identify the owners of the multiple body parts that were subsequently found stored in a plastic tub in the funeral home's basement, and assess how those owners might have died, John Kreller killed his wife and his four-year-old daughter, Eva, with a shotgun before putting a bullet in his own head. Two teenage prostitutes were identified among the tub victims. The remains of another two bodies were found, but never identified.

Reid Smith was the cousin of John Kreller. Although he was never implicated in the funeral home murders, he was wanted for questioning at one time by the Nassau County PD. He had never been found.

Although his eyes were hidden behind sunglasses on the surveillance tape, the picture on Reid Smith's driver's license looked a lot like the dark-haired stranger Daria was last seen leaving the Hilton with. The hotel cocktail waitress who had served the two of them that night agreed. And when Manny pulled out a map of Long Island, he found that Uniondale was only a hop skip and a jump away from Westbury, where Gabriella Vechio's body was found dumped in a construction ditch back in 2006. Reid Smith also matched the general description of the man last seen talking to Gabby Vechio the night she disappeared.

There was now a BOLO out for Reid Smith. A records search of the DL pulled up little information of value. The man had no criminal history, no military history, no medical history. No DL address prior to Uniondale, no forwarding address since. No surviving family members. His name had not appeared on the passenger lists of any flights out of Orlando. Like Daria, his picture had been sent via teletype to every police department in the country. In the BOLO, he was wanted by the Orlando Police Department simply as a 'person of interest' in connection with the disappearance of Miami-Dade County Assistant State Attorney Daria DeBianchi.

While everyone else in Orlando and Miami law

enforcement was getting all excited about finding the dark-haired stranger from New York, Manny continued to unofficially plant himself every night in front of Talbot Lunders's mansion, a pair of night-vision binoculars in his hand, and two six-packs on the seat next to him – one of Coronas and one of Red Bulls. He wanted to drink himself into a stupor, to forget everything his brain had been thinking about for the past 116 hours, but he needed to stay awake and keep watch. Because he knew the man was involved. Despite whatever BS some probation officer had told Vance Collier about Talbot and his hot *mami* innocently spending the night of Daria's disappearance in Daddy's big nine-bedroom mansion, Manny wasn't buying it. There was no such thing as coincidence. Not in his line of work.

Talk had been thrown around that it could be Cupid. That somehow Bantling had found out the conference Daria was going to be speaking at and where she was going to be that night, and he'd waited for her at the Hilton in the lounge. In a bar full of law-enforcement personnel in town for a conference on how to catch predators like himself, he had waited for her, perhaps dressed in disguise. It did, after all, match Cupid's MO. The cocktail waitress wasn't 100 percent sure the man who had chatted up Daria was the man pictured on Reid Smith's DL. She was more like 75 percent sure.

But Manny didn't think Bantling was involved in Daria's disappearance. At least, not in the way the talk was going. And that was what scared him the most. Twisted thoughts of a snuff club returned to his aching head. Images of Gabriella Vechio's vicious murder was what he saw when he closed his eyes, except it wasn't the pretty accountant's terrified face he saw, twisting about, her arms tethered to the ceiling. It was Daria's. Those were the thoughts he wanted to banish with alcohol. What if it was a worst-case scenario? What if Daria had been abducted by a snuff-club member? What if she'd been scouted, and then taken someplace, kept alive and tortured for days by predators that Bantling had called 'players'? What if she *wasn't* dead yet? What if every day she inched closer to death? What if that was what was happening to her right now while sick men called 'watchers' watched and he sat uselessly in his car downing beers and Red Bulls? Manny knew the stats. With every day that passed, every minute that ticked by, the odds decreased dramatically of finding Daria alive. If she had been taken by the snuff club that had done those terrible things to Holly Skole and Gabriella Vechio and others, he knew she would wish those days and hours and minutes passed by even quicker. She would welcome death. Yes, he had considered Bill Bantling's involvement. And he, no more than anyone else besides perhaps C.J. Townsend, wanted the psychopath found. Because aside from Talbot Lunders – who was never talking and no longer had any reason to – Bantling was the one person who could lead them to the snuff-club members. He was the one who supposedly knew the names. He potentially held the key to finding Daria alive. And no one knew where he was, either.

He closed his eyes. Now he would beg Vance Collier to make that deal.

He'd spoken with Dom and there was nothing new to report. He had talked to C.J. She had not been contacted by Bantling. There was no indication he was in her area, wherever that was. She was coming back to Chicago in a few days. He was in talks with the federal witness protection program. Dom was hoping that things would turn around for them now. *Good luck with that,* Manny had said.

How ironic. The rapist who had torn Dom's relationship with his wife apart might just be the one responsible for reuniting them. A happy ending of sorts. Manny wasn't sure how happy it would ever be though, given that Bantling was still out there. How happy can one be in witness protection?

The front door opened then. As his mother watched from the doorway, Talbot Lunders walked out, keys in hand, and got into the Benz. The same car that probably still had dust from where crime-scene techs had lifted Holly Skole's fingerprints off the interior door handle. The same car that had driven her to her death. Manny gripped the steering wheel hard. It took all his strength not to get out of the car and beat the information he knew was in that piece of shit's good-looking head while his weird mother watched. The mother who he suspected Daria was right about all along. The anonymously emailed video clip of Gabby Vechio's murder was a ruse. A diversion to get them to start looking in other directions at other possible suspects. A perfect set-up for a reasonable doubt argument if the case went to trial. The fact that it had led to a Brady violation and Talbot's release on bond was a bonus. There was just no way to prove it.

As the gates opened and the Benz slowly backed out of the long driveway, Manny started up his car and popped a Red Bull. He waited until Talbot had zipped off down the block and the front door had closed before heading out behind him, hoping, as he had for the past five sleepless nights, that the bastard might eventually lead him to Daria.

59

It must be an omen, Bill thought, looking up at the sky.

The stars were gone. The black night sky was just . . . black. Or more like smoky gray. The thick clouds had moved in early and had stolen all the light from the sky. Heaven, it seemed, had shut down early for business tonight.

How appropriate.

He crouched in his spot in her backyard, dressed in black and hidden by the thick shrubs and tall trees, a brand-new bag of tricks at his side. A brand-new smiley face to wear when they finally met once again, up close and personal.

He wondered if she'd found his present yet. A tuft of hair cut from the latex clown mask that he'd picked up at a Party City. He'd spread it out underneath her sheets, so that when she climbed into bed she'd know he'd been in it. She'd feel it, tickling her skin. Like in that fairytale, *The Princess and the Pea*, the pretty little princess with the golden hair just can't seem to get comfy because someone had hidden something in her bed. Or, maybe the scene would be more like one ripped from the *Godfather*, when the movie producer wakes up in horror to find himself awash in blood and his beloved horse's head under the covers with him. It was funny that, after all she'd been through, she sent her big, bad and mean doggie off to camp to play every day, leaving the castle without any defense except a useless alarm that a street-kid with a pair of pliers could outsmart. The dog was probably more like the kid she couldn't have than the guard dog it was intended to be. Maybe, Bill hoped, she'd get up to go to the bathroom and find her sexy legs covered in strands of flaming orange polyester hair when she flicked on the light. That would be something to see. While Bill would've loved to have left the ex's bloody head under her sheets as a token of his love for her, former Special Agent Falconetti had skipped town before he could get him alone. Chloe must have shooed him out of her life once again. The poor fellow must have signed those very public papers, papers she'd filed in that very public courthouse back in Chicago, asking for a divorce. Sad.

If she hadn't caught on yet that he was in town, finding the clown hair would surely send her over the edge. And that was exactly what he wanted to see – his old Chloe, walking that fine line between the rest of the world and sheer madness. Going crazy because she knew he was near. Because she knew that he had found her. His fingers went to the knife in his pocket and waited for a sign from Grandma's house. But the house stayed dark. Maybe she was sitting on the couch with a gun on her lap waiting for him to crawl through her window.

Maybe the stress had already gotten to her. Maybe she had used a bullet on herself.

When he worked at Sal's Pizzeria in Bayside, New York, so many years ago, he would watch her from the kitchen when she'd come in with her friends or her boyfriend. Flirty, giggly, sexy. And so, so pretty. He knew that she went to law school from the books she carried around and the sweatshirt she wore, and he knew that she must be smart, too. She was the whole package. Everyone wanted to be around her – even the waitresses wanted to wait on her. She was magnetic and Bill was drawn to her. Then one day he'd delivered a pie to an apartment on Rocky Hill Road and she'd opened the door. He was so taken by her, seeing her up close, that he couldn't speak. Couldn't even say thank you when she'd tipped him three dollars and flashed him a smile. He'd gone back to the car and jerked off with her tip money in his hand.

He'd often wondered if they would've gotten together the old-fashioned way if he'd ever summoned up the balls to ask her out. If he'd asked her to dinner, would she have said yes? Would they have dated? Would they still be together? Would they be married? Would his life be any different?

But he hadn't. So much for asking questions that could never be answered.

She was so pretty and nice and so perfect that she was unapproachable. No man could ask her out. No man would have the balls. And that was really what had pissed him off.

So he had taken her.

Then he'd watched as her life floundered and the fear

454

consumed her. She wasn't pretty anymore, or sexy, or flirty, or fun, or smart, or anything. She never went out, she didn't become a lawyer, the boyfriend dumped her. She broke apart. And that, Bill had realized with amusement, had been real fun to watch. Almost more fun than fucking her had been.

Then she up and disappeared one day. He went by her apartment and she was gone. Just gone. When he saw her again, twelve years later, she was a different woman. Brown hair and glasses, frumpy suits and a bitchy attitude. She was a hard-ass prosecutor and she was hellbent on revenge. She'd turned the tables on him, yes. But not for long.

He was out now.

And he was here.

He checked his watch. It was after one. He reached for his smiley face. Then the garage door quietly slid open. The light did not go on. If he hadn't been watching the house, he might have missed it.

But he hadn't.

He looked down in his bag where the small silver beeper had sprung to life, flashing red, like a ticking bomb, counting down the seconds and minutes until time ran out. Then he watched in the darkness as her car backed out of the driveway ever so slowly with its lights off and drove past him into the gray, starless night.

60

C.J. turned on to Cathedral Oaks Drive, heading toward State Road 154. The side streets were quiet, but SR154, also known as San Marcos Pass, was completely deserted. And pitch-black. A two-lane highway cutting through the Santa Ynez Mountains and the Los Padres National Forest, SR154 was a true mountain pass. There were no traffic signals or street lights to illuminate the roadway; no homes or businesses around for miles. The highway was a relatively narrow swath of asphalt that cut through a thick green forest and an intimidating mountain range. C.J. had driven that way many times – there were dozens of desolate trails she and Luna had hiked that sprouted off the back roads that snaked through Los Padres. It was also the scenic route that ran through the rural Santa Barbara wine country and into Los Olivos – home to Michael Jackson's Neverland ranch.

There was no one at all on the road. It wasn't crowded in the day. After ten at night, it was as desolate as the surrounding woods. She swallowed hard, rehearsing in her mind what it was she was about to do. God forbid she should hit a deer or a bear out here. That would be terrible any day; it would be catastrophic tonight. No, tonight, things had to go perfect. In fifty miles or so, after she passed through Los Olivos, SR154 would wind and catch up again with Highway 101, the main north–south coastal thoroughfare that ran up through San Francisco and ultimately to the Oregon/California border. She was heading north. At either Paso Robles or Salinas she could cut west and catch up with I5, a major interstate that would bring her into Nevada, or maybe up into Oregon and then Washington.

If she got that far.

'Oregon, Luna,' she said absently to her pooch, who was sleeping in the back seat. 'I think it rains too much in Oregon.'

She spotted the flicker of headlights in her rearview before she even hit Painted Cave Road, a paved two-lane road that led up to the preserved caves of the Chumash Indians. The headlights were a mile or so back. Possibly further. She felt her throat close.

Was it him? Or could it be some other guy out for a drive in the middle of the night, or headed home to Santa Ynez or one of the few remote homes that feathered off Painted Cave and San Marcos Pass?

Even before he flashed his brights at her with a wink, her gut already knew the answer: not many people took the scenic route at one a.m. – with the thick cloud cover, there was no way to make out so much as a mountain in the darkness. She gripped the steering wheel and sped up. The headlights went in and out of view behind her as the car made its twists and turns around the mountains. But the headlights faded further and further in her rearview as she pulled ahead. The driver was not trying to keep up.

She held her breath, her eyes practically glued on the rearview. Maybe it wasn't him. *Come on, disappear. Turn off. Let me be wrong. Let's move on to Plan B. Because I don't know if I have the stomach for Plan A . . .*

When she figured the car had finally reached the Painted Cave turnoff, the headlights disappeared completely. It was black behind her. She held her breath, waiting for them to come back on and continue their determined trek up the mountain. Nothing. Seconds felt like minutes. She let out a measured breath. She went on for a couple of miles. Then headlights lit up behind her once more in the far-off distance, the driver flashing his brights at her erratically, perhaps in some kind of code.

Her mouth went dry and she knew it was him. Just as she'd known it was him sitting out there in the darkness of her grandmother's woods, waiting for her. Just as she knew he had been in the house. Moving her bread, touching her pictures. She wasn't even shocked when she saw the clown hair in her bed. Terrified, but not shocked.

She would never lose him. She would never outrun him. On winding mountain roads or crowded New York streets. No matter where she went, she would always be looking in her rearview mirror, remembering the words he had whispered to her years ago as she lay on sheets drenched in her own blood. Promises that she knew he intended to keep.

I'll always be close by, Chloe. Watching. And waiting for you. Then we'll have another good time, you and me.

And if she were to call the feds? Tell them she thought he was behind her, flashing his lights at her in code? Assuming they could get here in the nick of time, assuming he could be caught once again and taken back to Miami before he made good on those terrifying promises of his, there were more appeals to be filed. More deals to be made. He had gotten out once. He had won a new trial before. And but for the corruption of a Florida Supreme Court judge, he would have had one. C.J. knew he could very well win round two. Plus, the information he had on a snuff club and its powerful members had been enough to buy him his freedom once. It would again, despite his escape. Her old colleagues at the SAO had sold out once. If it meant taking down an international snuff club, they would again. At the very least, Bantling's cooperation would mean a drastic reduction in his sentence. It would move him off death row forever, to a cell where he could count down the days until he was free again. And once he was out, he would hunt her down, like a programmed Terminator. He would not stop until she was dead.

A dozen scenarios ran through her crazed head. All of them led to the same conclusion. She would never be safe. She would never be normal.

She sped up and watched as his lights faded away again. A creepy thought came to her. What if he had put a tracker on the car? What if he could stay at the same speed, let her hit the gas into freaking Canada because he didn't *need* to follow her? All he had to do was sit back and follow the Yellow Bleep Road to the next place she laid down stakes? Maybe that was why the car behind her didn't need to speed up to follow her.

She turned off on to Kinevan, a remote single-lane paved road that ran into the dense Los Padres National Forest. Further along, Kinevan turned into West Camino Cielo, as it followed a ridge-top path through the Santa Ynez Mountains. After a mile or so, the asphalt ended and the road turned to gravel and dirt, then dirt and brush. She had run trails with Luna that spawned off Camino Cielo while hiking up to Brush Peak. There was never anything or anyone out there. It was a deserted no man's land. Given what she did for a living, C.J. had often wondered while she was hiking what secrets might be buried away under the thick, unforgiving brush, deep in the trees. She turned off the lights and pulled over.

It was time to stop running.

She got out of the car and quickly popped the hood. She ran a flashlight up and down the engine, but she had no way of telling. If he'd hard-wired it, it could look like a fuel pump for all she knew.

Fear pulsed through her veins. The cold mountain air was biting. She flipped on her cell. No service. She was all alone.

She walked around the car, pacing, looking out on to the darkness. *What the hell was she doing?* Miles from anyone and anything, standing on the ridge of a black mountain, waiting for a human predator to hunt her down like a wounded animal. Her brain flip-flopped again. She couldn't do this . . .

Get back in the car. Get to civilization. Call Dominick. Stay in a well-lit place till he comes to save you. Flee the scene. Get a new identity. Start life over. Wash. Rinse. Repeat.

Off in the brush, in the canyon below, she heard the wind howl and the unfamiliar sounds of wildlife: guttural chirps, the rustle of a lizard or a snake, the scamper of a raccoon or a skunk moving about somewhere. Or perhaps something much larger.

Don't panic, whatever you do, she told herself, shaking in the cold. She buried her hands in her jacket. *It's way too late for that. You're already committed. You're up here. He's been tracking you. To this exact spot. You need to throw him off his game. Think! Think!*

If he'd tracked her, he would pick something nice and easy. Something magnetized.

She stopped pacing. She was losing her mind up here. It was too dark. She still had time. She would see the headlights at least a mile or two before they made it up the mountain. No way could he negotiate that ridge in the dark.

She got down on her back and scooted underneath the Jeep.

61

She shone her flashlight on the tiny silver bump on the underbelly of her front bumper. A small red light gave it away. She was right – he'd stuck it on.

So she pulled it off – and smashed it into pieces with the butt of her flashlight.

As she started to pull herself out from underneath the car, the soft, seemingly far-off crunch of gravel stopped her dead, she switched off the flashlight as if by instinct, her body half-suspended as she clung to the bumper. Had she really heard that? Was it the wind in the trees? Was it an animal? She dropped back down softly on the floor and held her breath to listen. It was a repetitive crunch, very soft, but lumbering. Definitely footsteps. Something or someone was approaching and it wasn't a snake or a lizard. It was something that could walk. The question was, was it a deer or a wild boar, maybe? A bear or a mountain lion?

Or was it human?

Black bears were everywhere around Los Padres.

Freaking out a bear – or worse, a mountain lion – was not a good idea. She looked all around the underside of the car. It was too dark to see anything.

She held her breath, straining to listen. She could hear her heartbeat whooshing in her ears. Time stood still.

The crunch stopped.

She lay there under her car, eyes darting everywhere, not knowing what to do. This was not the position she wanted to be in. Even though she'd disabled the GPS, if he'd seen her pull off, he could be driving down the pass and up the ridge at this very moment. There were not many turnoffs on 154; it wouldn't be that hard to figure out where she might have turned. If that wasn't him out there already crunching his way toward her, he would be up here soon enough and she had to be on her feet when he got here. But if she stepped out and came face to face with a bear, that wasn't going to end pretty, either.

Think, damn it! You're smarter than him. He will not win. He will not win. You will, this time.

One hand held on to the underside of the bumper, and the other went to the inside pocket of her jacket. She felt the cold butt of the gun in her fingertips. She pulled it out with a shaking hand.

And she prayed for strength as the strange footfalls drew closer.

62

Every sense was on high alert. She strained to pinpoint exactly where the footsteps were coming from. The wind was blowing harder now, carrying off and mixing up sounds. Tricking her frazzled brain. Whistling at her. Howling. Shrieking. Closer. Farther away. To her left, to her right. All around her. Yet she couldn't see shit. It was completely black. Without a flashlight she couldn't tell if the foot that might be right in front of her face was furry or a sneaker. And she didn't dare turn her flashlight on.

This was all going wrong. So wrong. She'd finally summoned up the courage to do what had to be done, and it was spiraling out of control. Sweat rolled off her forehead and her neck, dripping down her back with a chill. *Could whatever was out there in the blackness smell her fear?* Her heart was thumping so loud, she could hear it. *Maybe he could, too. Maybe he could just follow the sounds of the telltale heart to where she was.* Her hands were wet with perspiration. They slipped off the bumper with a squeak that sounded as loud as a trombone.

She held her breath.

Then she spotted the beam of light as it swept across the blackness. The footfalls were definitely human. He was searching for her out there.

She was suddenly blinded by a bright light. He was crouched down looking under the car, searching with his flashlight.

'Gotcha!' he whispered when the light fell on her face.

His gloved hand reached under the car and took her by the hair. Pain ripped through her head. He began to drag her out.

That was when Luna suddenly sprang to life in the back seat, barking and scratching up against the closed window, as if she was rabid.

Startled, Bantling looked up and rocked back on his heels. And that was her opportunity. The one chance she was never going to get again.

She lined up the red laser sight and shot the son of a bitch right in the chest.

63

'They fall like a sad sack of potatoes when they taste the dart,'
a beat cop once told her. 'Never had one fail, unless they're doped
up. Then you gotta zap 'em a few times. You gotta be careful
that you don't shock 'em right into cardiac arrest. We've lost two
of them that way last year. Then come the lawsuits.'

The purple and white volt of electricity lit up the black
night, shooting out of the Taser like the bolt of lightning
that had brought Frankenstein's monster to life.

In this case, it had taken down a real-life monster. All
the way down, crashing with a thud on the dirt road.
Like a sad sack of potatoes. Fifty thousand volts of electricity had stopped Bill Bantling dead in his tracks,
jamming his sensory and motor functions and immobi-
lizing his muscles. He lay there, unable to move so much
as a pinky. All he could do was moan.

She scrambled from under the car and looked around.
No one. No cars. No bears. No mountain lions. Nothing.

The Taser website warned of a recovery time that
could be as little as thirty seconds for strong, aggressive

individuals. For civilians, that precious period of incapacitation was intended for them to escape their attacker.

C.J., however, had other plans.

He lay there on his back, dressed in a black track suit, a clown mask on his face. The two small probes containing inert, compressed nitrogen were buried deep in his skin. One had hit through his cotton sweat jacket and just under his neck, the other by his shoulder. The probes were designed to penetrate up to two inches of clothing. At his side she spotted the large silver knife that he must have dropped. She kicked it away with her foot. When he started to twitch, she hit the trigger again. Another brilliant zigzag of current traveled through the night. And down he stayed. Just like every cop who'd ever Tasered a subject and then testified about it in court for her had said he would.

The probes were attached to fifteen feet of insulated electrical wire, giving her room to walk around. She opened the car door, patted a snarling, still-barking Luna on the head and took out the backpack. 'It's okay, girl,' she said softly, her voice trembling, like her entire body. She wiped the sweat from her forehead with the sleeve of her jacket. Her back was drenched with perspiration, and the cold wind was giving her the shivers. She felt physically exhausted, as if she had just run a marathon. And it was about time to start another one. 'I'm okay, girl. I'm okay.' She closed the door before the Akita could jump out and rip the motionless clown to pieces.

She thought she saw his hand move and she hit the trigger. Down he stayed.

She ran her flashlight over the pathetic creature in his cheap rubber clown mask and track suit. It wasn't the same mask he'd worn when he'd raped her. She'd burned that one long ago when she found it in an evidence bin full of things taken from his house during the Cupid investigation. She remembered every detail of that face, which looked more like Bozo the Clown than the sadistic Pennywise in Stephen King's *It*. She saw it every night in her nightmares.

But the mask she stared down at now was meant to terrify. It was likely from a Halloween store, with sinister eyes and yellow fangs that dripped blood from its evil red grin. It was much scarier than the mask he had worn when he attacked her. It made her think of all the things he might have done to her tonight if he'd had the chance. Would his encore performance be even more terrifying? She grasped a patch of polyester orange hair and yanked hard. The rubber had stuck to his skin, and as she pulled it off, it made a small sound like a suction cup being peeled off a wet bathroom wall. It was almost a disappointment to meet the man behind it all. With shiny, saggy skin, a pallid complexion and a receding hair line, Bill Bantling would not look monstrous to anyone who did not know what he had done. Then again, neither did Dennis Rader, John Wayne Gacy, Gary Ridgway, or Ted Bundy. If everyone could spot the monsters coming, they would grab the torches and pitchforks before there was a body count.

As much as it repulsed her to touch him, with still-shaking hands, she grabbed his right leg and slapped leg irons on his right ankle. Then she followed suit with the left one. He couldn't control his muscles, but she could. She zapped him again before he started to move. She pulled out his arm from underneath his body and slapped a pair of Flexicuffs on his wrists, handcuffing him behind his back.

It would be much easier to control him from behind. She took the switchblade from her pocket and with one quick swipe, cut Bantling's sweat-jacket up the back, exposing his pale skin. Then she put a new cartridge into her Taser and shot him again, right between the shoulder blades. His face ground into the dirt. She pulled the probes out of his chest.

Exhausted, she leaned against the Jeep and took a deep breath. She checked the time on her cell: 1:21 a.m. She had only a couple of hours.

This time when he started to stir she didn't zap him. She let him come out of it. His muscles would be working, but they would be painful, stiff, exhausted. She only needed them to work for a little while longer.

She exhaled a deep breath. It had come to this. There was no other way out. No other way back to normal. After twenty-three years, the falling bones had almost reached the end of the effect – there were only a few pieces still left standing as they raced around the game's final blind curve. It was too late to stop them now.

'Okay, you bastard. On your feet,' she said, prodding him with the shovel she had grabbed from the trunk of her car. She shone her flashlight in front of her to where she knew the trail was. 'It's been a long time. I was hoping I would never have to see your face again, but you can't always get what you want. We have some unfinished business to work out, you and me. And this time, guess what? *I* brought along my own bag of tricks.'

'Whatta you gonna do?' Bantling sneered, his breath catching. 'Huh, bitch?' But he didn't sound half as cocky or menacing as she thought he would. He sounded nervous.

She smacked him hard in the back with the shovel. It felt good. 'Don't call me that. Mind your mouth and start walking,' she ordered, pushing him forward with the metal point of the shovel.

'Fuck you.'

She hit the Taser. He dropped to the ground.

'Now we could do this all night, or you could get on your feet and be a man and walk. The next place I aim the Taser is your balls.'

He got up.

'Stay, Luna,' she called out after her as she marched a shuffling Bantling down the trail and into the blackness. 'Momma will be back in just a little bit.'

64

Manny stared at the faded blue wallpaper in the reception area. He had walked through this building a hundred times, and never realized before that the walls were blue. He looked down at the stack of outdated magazines on the outdated coffee table, and wondered how many people had sat on the outdated sofa, waiting, perhaps, to be whisked off to the basement. He hated the Medical Examiner's office. Never more so than today.

The receptionist walked over to him. 'Detective Alvarez, would you like to see Dr Trauss?' she asked in a hushed voice, as if it was a church, or a library. Or a funeral home.

He couldn't bring himself to go downstairs. He couldn't bring himself to see her that way. He wanted to remember her the way he had at her house – planting herbs in his shirt with her hair in a pony and a smile on her face. 'No. I'm just here to pick up the autopsy report. I'm, I'm . . .' he stuttered, 'I am not working the actual case. I'm not the lead.'

She nodded and walked away as his phone rang. It was Dickerson. He didn't want to take it, but he couldn't put the calls off anymore. He closed his eyes and leaned his head on the couch. 'Yeah, Mike.'

'Hey, Bear. Where you at? Been trying to reach you for some time.'

'I'm working,' was all he replied.

'Nobody's seen that ugly mug of yours in a couple of days, Sonny Boy. The talk on the street is you're retiring, not me,' Mike said with a short laugh.

Manny didn't respond.

'Listen, I got something for you. I think you should come back to the office.'

'Tell me now, Mike. I've got an appointment.' Manny rubbed his eyes. They were so tired. And they stung all the time now. Nothing worked to fix that. Not drops, not sleep – when it came. Not even a good cry.

'There's been a development in the case,' Mike said.

The case. There was only one case that everyone in the entire City of Miami homicide squad now referred to as *the case*.

'I found the archangel in the Vechio murder video.'

'What?' Manny's eyes flew open and he sat up.

'Let me clarify. I found the guy who tattooed the archangel that's on the back of the bad guy in the Vechio murder video. A while back I sent out a bunch of teletypes and faxes to hospitals, jails, PDs, and tattoo parlors in the cities where we'd found snuff victims. I got a call yesterday from the feds. An owner up in the Bronx had recognized his own work in my fax and wanted to trade that info for a couple of months off an unrelated federal money-laundering charge he was facing. Name of our archangel is Gary "Nutso" Smythe. I did an NCIC/FCIC check and found Nutso through the prison system. He did time a while back in Jersey and Florida for some petty shit. Lives in Florida now, works for a video game company in Delray as a programmer. Problem is, the tattoo parlor guy must've tipped Smythe off we were looking for him. The feds pulled into the driveway and the house was in flames. The computers were torched. There was nothing left. The snuff site was probably taken down the second he typed the word "cop" in his computer.'

Manny was quiet for a long while. Long enough for Dickerson to ask if he was still on the line. 'Does Smythe know the names of the others? Is he talking?' he asked quietly.

'After he torched the house, he tried suicide by cop. Came out the front door with a gun in each hand. He's not dead yet, but there's nothing left upstairs, says the doc.' Mike sighed. He knew exactly what Manny was thinking. 'There's still that Smith character. Reid Smith. We're still looking for him.'

Manny nodded but said nothing. Nassau County PD had spent the last five years looking for the guy with no luck. 'Talbot Lunders left for Zurich yesterday. One-way ticket.'

'We'll get Interpol to keep an eye on him. If he jaywalks, we'll take him in.'

Again, Manny said nothing. There was nothing left to say.

'I'm sorry, Bear. I know this is rough.'

'It's a waste, Mike. Her death was all for nothing. It's gonna be one of those cases that you can't take anyone down for, and that sucks. Beyond sucks.'

'Could be we'll get something off the autopsy. They're still processing shit from the scene. We might get something from that. Blood, DNA . . .'

Manny nodded.

'We still have Bantling. When he resurfaces, we'll get him to talk, Bear. We just have to have some patience. We'll get those names. Customs works these Internet pedophile and kiddie-porn clubs all the time. Once you nab one of 'em, the rest will fall like dominoes, taking everyone in their path if it means saving their own ass. And there's likely a videotape,' Mike added quietly. 'You know, maybe we can find something off that – if one surfaces.'

Manny ignored the last comment on purpose. 'Yeah, well, it's going on two months since Bantling went AWOL and there's still no trace of the feds number two man.'

'Didn't you say you thought he was gonna go looking for his old prosecutor? The one in the drawings?'

'That didn't pan out. She's back in Chicago and there's been no sign of Cupid. Guy had a ton of money stashed somewhere, he's probably fled the country by now. I'm not holding out hope on Bill Bantling saving the day.'

There was nothing left to say. He hung up the phone and looked down at the ME's report with Daria's name on it that the secretary had just handed him. The paper was still hot from the printer. He wanted to look away, but he couldn't. His eyes were drawn to certain sections, like 'Final Pathological Diagnosis'. Certain buzzwords, like *rape, semen, contusions, abrasions, scarring, sulfuric acid, asphyxiation, diphenhydramine, branding*.

His friends had spared him the details the ME's report wouldn't.

He punched the faded blue wall as the tears fell. In his head, he could hear Daria saying the words he had once dismissed as the callous musings of a hardened prosecutor. Now he realized that she was actually foretelling her own future.

No justice for you today. Sorry, Charlie.

65

She had been different since she'd come home.

They had been different.

From where he stood next to the coffee pot, Dominick studied C.J. as she ate a bowl of Cocoa Puffs at their breakfast bar, sitting cross-legged on the bar stool in her old pajamas and robe. She had lightened her hair a little, and the sunlight streaming through the apartment's window made the blonde streaks even blonder. She looked a little younger, a little more carefree. Whatever – he liked it. But it wasn't only the hair.

He wouldn't call her relaxed, necessarily. Resigned would be a better word. Confident, but at the same time guarded. Less worried, maybe? More outgoing, and yet more reclusive. Colder. Warmer. He couldn't put his finger on it. She was like a walking antonym. It had only been a few weeks and they were still muddling through, trying to find their balance. He was trying to forget her leaving, constantly readying himself for when she up and walked out the door again.

'I got a call from Miami yesterday,' she said when he walked over to the breakfast bar, with two steaming mugs of coffee in hand.

'What? From who?' He was alarmed. No one was supposed to know where she was. Especially no one from Miami.

'Chuck Weekes is the State Attorney there now. Do you remember him? He was with Statewide in Miami when I worked for the office.'

'How the hell did he know how to reach you?'

'It's okay. I actually called him.'

Dominick was quiet for a moment. 'I don't understand.'

'He asked me to come back to the office. In Miami.'

'What?'

'Chuck and I worked a case years ago. He's a nice guy. He said that he'd lost a few prosecutors recently and he was hoping I'd come back as Senior Trial Counsel. Major Crimes is apparently no longer a division. Now my title would be Senior Trial Counsel.'

'Wait – you called him?'

'Yes.'

He shook his head. 'So I'm guessing that you *want* to do it, if you called him?'

'I wanted to see what would be available for me if I went back. One of the prosecutors that they lost was not through normal attrition. Apparently she was found murdered a few weeks ago. Buried in a dumpster in Miami Lakes with some sort of branding on her. It bears similarities to some other homicides that the City and County and your old pals at FDLE are investigating. And others across the state.'

Dominick nodded. 'Manny was working a case with her. They were close.'

'They think it's a serial. And Chuck wants me to assist the task force he's putting together. FDLE, the City of Miami, Miami-Dade, Tampa PD.'

'Because you worked Cupid?'

'And Black Jacket. There aren't many prosecutors who have worked two serial killer investigations.'

'And lived to tell the tale.'

She didn't reply.

'Are you actually considering it?' he asked incredulously.

'Yes, I am considering it.' It would be nice to be C.J. again. A woman with a past she was very familiar with – the good, the bad and the ugly.

He shook his head and stood up. 'What the fuck? You've been running from your past for years. We dug up our lives to put that past behind us, and now you *want* to go back? What the hell am I missing here?'

'I told you, I'm done running. You didn't believe me. You still don't trust me, but I'm done. I want my life back, Dominick.'

'And where do I fit into all this?'

'I was thinking you could get back with FDLE. You hate Chicago.'

'I may not like Chicago in the winter, but I wasn't so crazy about Miami when we left. Jesus, C.J., this is coming out of left field. I'm not getting it. Help me get it.'

'I'm not going without you, Dominick. I made that promise. I won't leave us again. So tell me we shouldn't go and we won't. I was just throwing it out there.'

'I'm still not understanding. Jesus . . . What about Bantling? He's still missing. He's still out there

478

somewhere. If you go back to Miami, he'll know where to look. How the hell will you ever feel safe again?'

She rubbed her temple. 'It's been months since he escaped, Dominick. I think he's long gone. I think Manny was wrong. Okay, he left some fucked-up pictures of me behind on death row, but that's where he left them – behind.'

'Maybe it would be best then to assume he doesn't know where we are and you should just stay put,' Dominick replied. 'I understand not wanting to uproot and go into witness protection, but to jump back into the fire is crazy.'

'I don't think it's so crazy. Have the feds got anything on him?' she asked, hoping her voice sounded casual, but not too casual. He would never understand what she had done. She would not drag him into another secret. This one was for her to carry all alone.

He shook his head. 'The trail went cold in Alabama. He was there for sure, two days after he got out of Miami, but that was it. Nothing since.'

'He probably made it over the border,' she said quietly. 'Canada, Mexico, Central America. Flew to South America from there, to one of those cities he used to visit all the time. He knows his way around, can get lost in a crowd, I'm sure.'

'I think Interpol has a flag on rapes and murders with his MO, so when he gets back on his game, there'll be people looking. We'll find him.'

'Maybe he's dead,' she said flatly.

'Huh?'

She pushed her cereal around in the bowl. 'Just saying that's a possibility. Think of the boys they never found who escaped from Alcatraz. The feds spent decades looking for them all, spinning great urban myth about how they're living on the lam under new identities, when the truth is, they tell you now on the prison tour that they all probably drowned and the current swept them out to sea.'

'If that's the case, we need to find a body. For your peace of mind. And mine. There would be nothing I'd like better than to watch them bury that guy six feet under.'

On that, she stood up and dumped her cereal into the disposal. She wasn't hungry anymore. 'I want my life back. I want to be me again,' she said quietly.

Me. She didn't even know who that person was. A person who had committed premeditated acts of violence that she, as a prosecutor, had once condemned. Acts that she had asked juries and judges to put defendants to death for. Who was this person? And why was she not conflicted about what she had done in the woods? Why was it not eating her up from the inside out? How was she able to close her eyes at night and, for the first time in years, sleep the whole night through without nightmares? What kind of a monster does what she did without feeling some remorse? In the end, it was easy. And that was what scared her most about the new C.J. It was easy.

He walked up behind her at the sink and rubbed her shoulders. 'Damn, C.J. How is it that I am always worrying about you?' His voice was choked with either anger or sadness or frustration. It was hard to tell. 'I gotta get dressed,' he said when she didn't say anything back. He walked off into the bathroom.

Her hand went to the small, folded-up piece of paper in the pocket of her robe. She pulled it out and opened it up.

It was surprising how fast Big, Bad, Nasty Bill Bantling had cracked. She thought it would be more like the movies – where the bad guy could take an interrogation with a garden tool without breaking, like a hard-boiled *Sopranos* character. She thought she would really have to get dirty, but no. Big Bad Bill was a bastard with a knife when he had a woman tied up and helpless, but when the tables were turned and the chains were on the other foot, he'd cried like a baby.

And begged. And pleaded.

And talked.

She looked at the thirteen names before her. An unlucky number, indeed. She didn't know any of them. Not yet, anyway. But she knew what had to be done.

'I left a lot of things unfinished in Miami, Dominick,' she said quietly, more to herself than aloud to him. 'Things I think I'm going to need to take care of now . . .'

Tempted.
Trapped.
Tortured.

Dozens of teenage girls are going missing in Miami. And for Special Agent Bobby Dees of Florida's Crimes Against Children squad their families' pain is all too real. So when thirteen-year-old Lainey Emerson doesn't return from her date with 'El Capitan', a mysterious figure she met online, he vows to do whatever he can to bring her back.

Then the girls start to reappear – as horribly mutilated corpses, complete with clues that there may be even more of them at risk than first thought. The killer is smart, the police always chasing, and Lainey's mother in increasing despair.

Bobby has sworn to save her – but how can he compete with a mind this warped?

Killer Reads.com

The one-stop shop for the best in crime and thriller fiction

Be the first to get your hands on the **latest releases**, **exclusive interviews** and **sneak previews** from your favourite authors.

Browse the site and sign up to the newsletter for our pick of the **hottest** articles as well as a chance to **win** our monthly competition!

Writing so good it's criminal